I0763349

TO DANCE AMONG THE STARS

To Dance Among The Stars

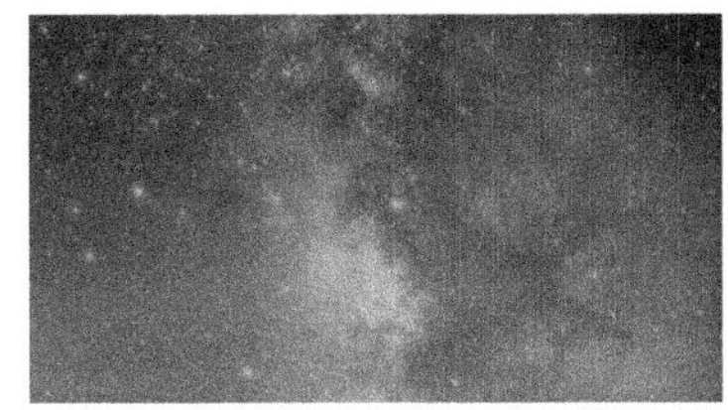

Immortality Ain't What It Used To Be

K. Adrian Zonneville

Mumford House Publishing

ISBN 978-1-7344332-1-0
ISBN 13-978-1-7344332-1-0

First Printing, 2020
Second Printing 2022

Dedication

This book is dedicated to those who believe there is a little magic in all spirituality and throughout the world. And that belief makes all things are possible. To my children for allowing me the life I have led. To my parents for gifting me the love of the written word. To David Spero for believing in me. To those who have supported my meager efforts in writing. But mostly to my wife who has supported my dreams, my endeavors, my love of writing, performing, and the road. Mostly she has been my inspiration and one true love.

Acknowledgments

It is with humility and appreciation I thank those without whom this book would not have been possible. To Marcus Roubideaux for instruction in Native American lore. To Paula Apynys for challenging me to write and rewrite this book. To Holly Gleason for inspiring me to write the song for the book. To those who took a chance on me and my books and writing such nice words to inspire me.

Cover art, design, and brilliance Janet Sipl

Edited by N. Mumford

It was a Wednesday, which has no bearing on this introduction. I was having lunch with Mr. Zonneville. It meant I had to be on top of my game. This was pre COVID, which also doesn't matter because the up-coming story preceded the lunch by a century and a few decades. We talked sports and music, friends and politics. Somewhere from the con-versation I told Mr. Z that it's like "dancing among the stars!"

Did that mean that people were dying, they were, or others were find-ing newfound success, also true, or was it just about life. A story, a tale, perhaps a day in a life, or a week, or even years. I've read everything that the prolific Zonneville has written, but he has surpassed all his prior works with this. Find out just what joy it is 'To Dance Among The Stars'. A well worthwhile trip.

David Spero 2020

Not For The Faint of Heart

∞

He was an immortal.

He had mentioned it casual to people over the past several millennia and especially over the last eight years, since, yeah, since. Usually to chuckles, knowing nods and a pat on the arm. It was a great conversion stopper. They didn't believe him. He didn't care. He didn't know why he tried. Yeah, he did, so they would leave him alone. He could prove his immortality if he had to, as he had a hundred, a thousand lifetimes before. He chose not to.

He'd thought, as humans had evolved, they would be more accepting of concepts beyond their limited understanding. Their minds would be open to possibilities previously thought impossible, but they were philistines! He would show them. It was simple. All he had to do was live forever. Or a reasonable facsimile thereof.

Though he didn't have to live forever, did he? Not anymore, not when everyday was an eternity. That was immortality, every single day without Her.

Shit, that's the way to wallow, you maudlin old fool. Of course, every day lasts forever when you won't let go of the past. How long you going to hang on to Her memory?

Forever.

The answer was always the same, he would think of Her forever because that was how long he would be here. Forever was the promise and the curse, especially with nothing to fill the hours, days, seconds except Her memory. Damn, if you ain't one lonely, depressing old dude!

Find something to fill the time, to distract the mind! He scolded hisself, take up a hobby, get drunk, beat-up bunnies, do something! Concentrate on life, forget about death. Take care of your responsibilities. Yeah, and make the world spin backwards on the head of a pin while you're at it. Infinity sucked. Things would get better, he told hisself. He told hisself a lot of things that wasn't true, but that was the big lie that kept him going. And then he remembered and smiled a little.

The youngest granddaughter would be coming over tomorrow. She would ride her bike over from her mom's, was only about a mile or so, like she did most Tuesdays, Thursdays, and Sundays—shit, she'd soon be driving over, the thought struck him. She loved coming over, especially Sundays, it was her way of avoiding church with her mom. Her mom, Helen, was balancing church with addiction, she was a constant emotional thunderstorm.

The granddaughter was a good girl, no drugs or alcohol—well, beyond teenage experimentation—but she was at the age, fifteen going on thirty-five, where she and her mom butted heads all the time.

He had butted heads with Helen when she was in her teens, guess it was a family tradition.

When his kids were just kids, 'fore the double digits kicked in anyway, they—Helen, the younger girl and the boy—used to love when he'd sit them on his knee and tell them stories from his past lives. He'd regale them with how he used to hunt the jungles of Africa and Asia Minor, he wrestled alligators and crocodiles, fought in wars, and traveled the world.

But the world had gotten smaller as the years went by and the people filled it with towns, cities, civilization. They took all the fun right out of exploring and discovering, running with his kin. They built great metropolis' and buried all the habitat. Chased all the First People up into the mountains and then followed them there. It made him sad when he thought too long on it, so he told them stories of when he was free.

Then, the teens hit them hard, and Helen, more so than the others, began to argue with him. She chastised him like her mother had done for years. She begged him to quit living in a fantasy world. She echoed her mother's disdain, demanding he stop saying he was immortal. What could he do, lie? The other two kids, by then, dismissed him out of hand. 'It was just the way dad was,' they'd contemptuously scorn. Yet, they loved the stories and saw no reason to make him quit. They never thought for one moment that he believed them himself, he just liked the fantasy of the telling.

Yeah, the youngest, Becky, Helen's sister, had enjoyed the time with him more so than the fiction. However, the boy had loved the stories, he could listen for hours, making Evan tell the same ones over and over. He especially loved the war stories. Even when the boy thought them silly learning fables concocted in his father's mind from books read and films watched. Still, he wanted every detail. He hung on every word of life in the trenches or standing nose to nose with an enemy, swords drawn or pikes at the ready. There was glory in facing death while eye to eye. More than possible with this cowardice of sending bombs or shells from miles away. Hell, you never knew who you killed anymore. Could be your worst enemy, some guy eating lunch or a little girl riding her bike to school, made no never mind. No, for thousands of years they faced each other, an arm's length away. You could smell their breath, their body odor, their fear. You could taste the blood of those who died by your hand.

The old man hoped they had brought his son some pleasure and comfort before he died in glorious battle. Hah, he spit in disgust, it was all bullshit. He had fought in too many wars to remember all the names of brothers in arms now dead and dust; he knew how horrible battle could be. It had not been his intention to send this only son off to his death. This was the guilt that had weighed on him like a boulder. He had made war glorious, exciting, an adventure of a lifetime. It had ended his son's life. He had not been an immortal. It wasn't genetic.

The boy was gone; the mourning had lasted longer than was healthy for either of them. Then the girls had grown up and left the house. Then it had been just him and Her, like it had been in the beginning. They had to learn how to be together alone again. They thought they had lost themselves in the kids and would never remember how to be themselves. How to be just a couple.

It had been easy, like falling off a bike. They fell right back in step, loving, sharing, spending every waking moment together. They loved the children, and soon the grandchildren, but they loved each other more. They had some damn good years until the goddamn cancer took Her. He missed Her. Missed her scent, the sound of her puttering around the house, the touch of her hand, everything. No, not everything, he didn't miss her doubt.

Now the granddaughter came on her days to help fill a few hours with love and companionship. They'd talk, put puzzles together and he'd take her out for ice cream and stories. Just an old man and his grand-daughter. She would tell him he wasn't old, not for an immortal. She was a good kid. He wasn't old when she was around, only when he was lonely. She loved to hear his tall tales, every story, even the ones she knew by heart. They delighted her, though her favorites were the ones about when he and grandma first fell in love.

She had picked up where his kids had walked away. Where once he had delighted all the kids when they were small, spinning yarns of all the things he'd done in his forever life, now, she was his only audience. So, she sailed with him around the lakes and rivers of North American, caught salmon in Alaska with his brethren, hunted with the big cats and ran the plains with Bison and Elk. In her mind they stood atop some of the tallest peaks on the world. Then she would stare as his picture, his constellation, lit the heavens at night. He missed having them all sit around him as he would regale them, and the children would laugh and scream in pleasure and terror. Good days.

Even when She told him to stop. Stop the stories, the tall tales, they would catch up to him. The kids would know he was fabricating them, and they would turn on him. They would never believe another thing he said. All because She didn't, because She didn't want to. Sometimes he thought She wanted him to quit the telling as She was feared they might be true. Sometimes he wanted to tell Her. Sometimes he wished things were different.

They had all believed, the kids, the grandkids, all of them, every word, until their Peter Pan year hit. It was when they stopped believing in his stories, his lives, him. He had lost his immortality for a while back then. Wandered a man alone throughout life, normal as the next guy. Fearing death and old age, his own mortality. Yeah, he'd forgot all about his immortality, until he'd found it again.

He smiled at the memory.

Now, here he was sitting alone at the corner bar, meandering through the past in his head while he meandered through life in the present. It was a joint he'd been in a few times, not a regular, just the only bar he frequented, just not frequently. No one knew his name or much about. Just a guy whose wife had died. No one knew him well enough to broach the subject. They left him to his beers, two, and then home.

Until today, the kid bumped him, spilled his drink down the old man's back and started to apologize so profusely the old man had to stop him with a kindly laugh, a shake of his head and offer to buy him a fresh drink. The kid was kind of slow, not retarded or such, just not quite right, up here. But he had a good heart, innocent as morning dew, just a sweet kid. It didn't matter that the kid had bumped him, he didn't want the young fella to feel bad about it, so he took the blame.

He bought the kid a beer and had the kid sit down next to him. He wasn't a 'kid' kid, he was old enough to drink, probably mid-twenties, and helped around the bar, washing dishes, stacking cases, and wiping down tables, just young for his age. If somebody needed help on a site or moving, nothing that involved precision or higher math skills, they'd put him to work for a few days. He was a hard worker, didn't slack off or back talk, right there was worth his weight. The old man didn't want the kid feeling guilty. So, he talked to him.

Quiet, like a dad or grandpa would, reassuring, calming. And he just kind of slipped into a story about one of the battles he'd fought back in the war. He knew boys liked war stories, but he'd learned his lesson with his son. He would not glorify nor make war alluring in any way ever again.

He spoke quiet, just for the two of them, sharing a beer and a story, though there weren't much more than a half dozen others sitting in their own silence. The rowdies would come in later, turning up the juke, telling lewd jokes, and talking stupid. The old man would be sitting on his porch by then. But for now, he was content to just tell a story to an attentive crowd of one.

He told the boy of the hardship of marching from D.C. twenty-five miles to Manassas, Virginia. There was damn near twenty thousand, if he recalled correct, and disorganized as any army ever had been in the history of war. He'd fought in a bunch of wars throughout the ages, and he knew. This was not going to be good. Nobody seemed to know nothing about fighting wars, not the generals on down to the guy slogging through the mud. Which was kind of funny, in its way since there'd been a war in this country 'bout every damn year since its' inception.

But they'd dithered and tried to organize disorganization and all it did was let the enemy get organized—though truth be told, they wasn't much better off than we was—and bring up more men! You can't give the other guy time for reinforcements.

"Wow, I never knew nobody who'd actually fought in a war before," the kid was all in.

"We attacked; it weren't pretty. Just a bunch of guys all dressed alike running across a field and getting shot at and shot. They were dug in pretty good on the other side, we didn't stand much of a chance, but we gave it all we had." His voice got quiet with remembering. "We thought we could surprise them on their left flank, it was going pretty OK at the start. We all thought we was going to be drinking whiskey and dancing with pretty girls by the weeks end." He coughed a laugh and slapped his hand on the bar with a crack. Then turned to apologize to the others for being loud.

"Yeah, we got caught up in winning just long enough for them to bring up those reinforcements. Then things got real ugly real quick. Damn." Quiet filled the space as he sipped his beer. "You want another?" He offered the kid, thinking three would be his own limit today.

"Wait a minute," came from the bowed head down the bar. Bloodshot but keen eyes darted at the two a couple stools up, "Are you trying to bullshit this kid that you was at the Battle of Bull Run?"

"The only bull involved was the name of the battle, and yeah, I was there," he held his ground better than the yanks did that day.

"But that was a hundred fifty years ago," the fella wanted to scoff but audacity bought some respect in a joint like this.

"Bout that," the old man agreed, "I was a lot younger then, don't think I could do it now, ain't got the legs for it."

"You're making this shit up," now the fella sat up straight, challenging, at the same time dismissing the crazy old man and the young, odd kid. "Maybe I should test you on your knowledge of Bull Run so we can all see you're full of bullshit."

There was a smattering of chuckles, a guffaw, and shared looks.

"Nope, was there, don't know all about the whole battle just where I was at," and the old man grinned at the kid who grinned back, because he wanted to believe. "You can ask anything about the left flank. Gotta admit though can't say much about the retreat, we was all just running to save skin by then."

"You'd be dead and dust, gone to worms by now," the bar fly announced contemptuously, giving a half-hearted flip of his hand before returning to a small glass of brown liquid followed by a grimace with a swig of beer hot on its tail.

"Would be if I was you, but I'm not, I'm immortal," he could hear his wife's exasperated sigh from beyond the grave. Could almost hear Her whisper in his ear, 'serve you right if he popped you right between them eyes. Hell, might knock a little sense into that block of mush.' But he ignored Her, though he felt remorse for the doing.

The fella gazed down the bar as if he wanted to say something to put this old codger—who was about his own age—in his place. Get that kid away from him before he bought into this pile, instead he shrugged as if that settled all, returning his attention to the guy shouting politics from the screen and his empty bottle.

"Can I get another round here and ain't there any goddamn sports on?" You can't argue with someone who has lived forever.

"Are you really immortal?" the whisper was filled to the brim with awe.

"So far," responded the oldest person the kid, or anyone, had ever met. Though he wore it well.

"Well, I think you are nothing but an old blowhard filling this kid's head with a shit ton of crap," came a voice from behind the two of them, "and maybe somebody ought to make you either put or shut up." They could hear him actually spit in one of his hands. They couldn't tell which hand though it didn't matter much. "Maybe I'll just toss you out of here."

The old man and kid turned at the same time to see an extremely large man pushing himself upwards from a table with threat radiating. How long had it been? Not long enough. Usually, these wannabes would leave him alone, he was big enough not to tangle with. Not that he was as big as this fella, but he was big enough

The old man slouched on his stool. He did not need this.

"So, you want a history lesson, sonny?" But he wasn't good at backing down. Except from Her, but She wasn't here.

"You going to teach me something ancient one?"

"If needs be," he took a swig of beer.

"Let's see if you can make me learn," the oversized gorilla rolled up sleeves already half rolled. It was a silly, useless gesture.

One could expect nothing less from the type, thought the old man. One would have thought that over the last few thousand years evolution would have weeded out these troglodytes in favor of them with larger brains, but then again, he guessed they served their purpose.

"Think I'll kick a little of that immortal bullshit right out yer ass," as a meat hook made to grab the old man's shoulder.

"Why don't we take this outside," said age as it easily dodged the move, "no need to bust up somebody else's joint." He bowed extending a hand to indicate the door.

"All right," grumbled the mountain.

They hit the door at the same moment, the old man stuck a leg out just enough to catch the other guy's ankle and the mountain crumbled into the open air. Quickly slamming the solid wood door and turning the dead bolt the old man leaned against the pounding from the other side.

"You don't live forever by being stupid," he tossed to the young kid and anyone else in need of learning.

"How you going to get out of here?" snickered the fella at the end of the bar.

"I'm not," said the old one, "I'm going to sit here and enjoy a quiet beer."

"Gotta leave sometime," reminded the casual observer.

"Yup, probably 'bout the time the cops got the handcuffs on," he grinned.

"Yer not really immortal, are you?" the kid sounded crestfallen.

"Sure, I am," now the old man was hurt, "why would you say that?"

"Well, if you were really immortal you coulda fought that guy without a care in the world. What could he do to you? You can't die, right?" it was a challenge and one he'd had to face before.

"Son, there are worse things in this world than dying. Everybody feels pain, death stops that. Now imagine if you could feel it forever," the barkeep set a new beer down pretending not to listen.

"Wow, I never thought o' that," admitted youth and innocence.

"People don't. Hell, I can still remember pain from before Christ was a babe," he nodded acquiescence to the memory. "You don't live forever without some bumps and bruises and a few scars. It ain't for the faint of heart. You got to be willin' to sacrifice.

"It's tedious a lot of the time. Everybody thinks you get to experience all the glory, witness all the comings and goings of the greats of history but, hell, that only happens once in a great while. And usually, you're a thousand miles away. Most the time ain't nothing going on, no excitement. Though to be honest, those epochs are nice. I like the quiet. Some folks thrive on turmoil and strife, not me, just part of the job." He grinned and took a long pull of the bottle.

"I like times like these, ain't much happening in the world right now. Oh, you get the occasional loudmouth ain't got the sense he was born with, just looking for a fight. Me, I'm looking to avoid them, their brawls, and their bluster. Been in too many wars, seen too many die. People what glorifies war, well, they ain't never been. I been in a lot and hope to never see another, though that's holding hope in one hand and a big lump shit in the other. You're gonna get splattered and it ain't gonna be pleasant. Shit, man can't go a decade without some big shot general or dictator starting something they themselves ain't got skin in the game for." Now despondency paid a visit to the old man. He took another long pull on the beer, "I gotta go."

"Ain't you gonna wait on that big guy to be gone?" the kid was scared and concerned, nice kid.

"Oh, he's cuffed and walking to the nice policeman's car right now. Didn't you hear the siren and the scuffle? You gotta learn to pay attention to things if'n you wanna live forever," he smiled threw a twenty on the bar and indicated the fella at the end of the bar with an empty bottle and an empty glass.

He tipped his hat at the mountain sittin' cuffed and in the back of the police car, then thanked the nice policeman for saving him from a fate worse than death. He put on his best frail grandpa guise as he shuffled past the commotion.

He knew he'd made an enemy, what's new? You can't live this long without making a few. The great consolation in life had been that he had never fought for the 'wrong' side. He had always kept his moral compass, his beliefs of right and wrong had never wavered throughout time. He had observed people for as long as there had been people and knew them for what they were. Good, bad, compassionate, cruel, took all kinds to make a world, he could use a lot less of some than others. And he knew he would outlive every one of them, sometimes the best way not to get in a ruckus was to avoid it.

Once out of sight of events he could kick off the frail like a well-worn pair of moccasins. The cops would remember his infirmity and would warn the huge ape to stay away from the nice old fella if he knew what was good for him.

In his younger days, and here he had to laugh, which younger days, the ones before humans had sprawled across the landscape or after, he would've taken the bully apart. That was the thing with guys like that, the bigger and meaner they were, the easier it was to fell them. All you had to do was find the cracks, expose the weak, chip away just a bit and they'd go down hard. Now he just wanted to be left alone. It was the way She'd want it.

She'd seen him get into it one time and She had not been pleased. There'd been two of them making rude noises and suggestions at Her. She didn't care, She'd heard and seen worse, but he was Her protector. He loved Her and would not allow disrespect to this good woman. He'd told them to stuff it where the sun don't shine. She'd pulled his arm for them to leave.

That was where things got a bit dicey. The catcalls increased, the suggestions more lewd, his blood pressure shot through the roof. One of the slimeballs came right up in his face, not an inch away from his nose, saying, 'what's the matter, punk, momma gotta take care of you? Makin' you go home? When we're done with you, we'll take care of her!'

He was in love, hot-blooded, and pissed. They were laid out before She could say, don't. He never forgot the look in Her eyes, the disappointment. She would not be soothed by his protestations of defender of Her virtue and honor.

"The virtue would have been to walk away and not give them time of day. The honor would have been to show them who was the better man," She steamed for days.

She was different than any woman he had known in his life. Most of them wanted him to stand up for them, hell, they instigated the brawl half the time. They wanted a man who could protect them against any and all brutes, to make them feel safe. Had been that way throughout history, long back as he could remember.

Not Her, She was differenter than any other. She was a gentle soul, believed all that stuff about peace and love, treating each other like family. It hadn't been hard for him to jump on board, he knew the truth of it. He'd lived through many lives and saw all creatures was all the same. He knew the fact we was all family. But sometimes brothers wrastled and busted heads 'cause they was brothers. It was what they do, even in nature.

"Wolves do it," he'd explained one time, "all animals in nature butt heads, it's part of the growing, establishing the pecking order. Come into the woods with me, I'll show ya!" he'd offered.

"I don't need to see how animals behave, I have seen it," She had chastised, "we are not animals!"

"But we are," he'd tried to be as gentle as Her but facts was facts.

"No, we have free will, we have intelligence and control. We are not animals," end of discussion.

No way he was going to come out on the winning side here, best to surrender and do what he was told. After the treaty had been signed, She lightened up and things got back to normal. That was Her, never held no grudge, never kept his wrongs in reserve to be used at a later engagement. Once he'd lost the battle, She was magnanimous. She was a damn good winner.

He wasn't, but he was learning. Until, yeah, until he found out just how much losing could really hurt.

He'd promised Her then and every day since he would do his best to control his animal. He would use his brain not his anger. It weren't easy. Though today had been a good day, he knew it would not end there. He was either going to have make peace or revert to his former self. Neither option appealed.

The walk home had been pleasant 'cept for the thoughts. That wasn't true neither, thoughts of Her were always pleasant, they just hurt.

He sat on the porch swing and listened to the night. There was peepers, toads, cicadas, crickets, all kinds of night critters looking to keep the species going. Life was always present. Couldn't go nowhere on this blue marble and not run into it. It reassured, had forever. He knew.

He had his own small glass of brown liquid now, it soothed the nerves, it would help him sleep. He sipped slow not deep. He wanted to enjoy the taste, the burn as it slid down his throat. Eased the thoughts from where they hid in the back of his mind.

There were other immortals all throughout the world, he'd met them, knew most of them. He knew where he came from and why, what he was supposed to do, and he did it well. He knew he had purpose, it didn't matter if'n anybody else knew, they wasn't supposed to. Hell, they wasn't supposed to know he and his kind really existed, they were myths, legends, not real. He was fine with that, most time, just the knowing was good enough. Though it did slip out time to time. Maybe it was just as simple as the world needed those who guide, someone to watch over the children. Well, he could do that, had been since the dawn of time.

This had been their favorite time of day. Just after dusk when the night life came out.

She'd joke, "this is the only kind of night life we get anymore!"

"It's the only kind we need anymore," he'd smile back and pat Her on the knee. He knew it was a symbol of ownership, or had been a few lives ago, now it was just to reassure. They both needed that.

"We're really lucky," She said to the night, Her foot dragging just a bit under the swing, "we have it all, good family, nice joint to lay our heads, the kids," She trailed off with a wince as the sayin' of it had taken a piece of her insides. She'd never been quite right since the boy had died. But it was more, he just hadn't known how much more.

He kept his tongue and just nodded, not trusting his voice, it would betray him sure as day. They rocked in peace, comforted by the night sounds. People who thought the world silent just didn't listen enough.

He thought about the kid at the bar. He been going up there for his two cold ones for a couple years now and had never said a word to the kid. He was like a fixture there, you didn't notice the lights 'til they was either too bright or turned off, guess it was that way with this kid. He was always bustling around cleaning, washing, but you didn't notice him until he, literally, fell into you. He should be more observant of others, especially the invisible ones.

They'd been there all long, throughout time, nobody noticed them until they needed somebody to do something they didn't want to. Somebody to clean, somebody to dig, somebody to grow food, somebody to kill, somebody to die. They were the bodies left on the field when the generals bragged about how these brave boys had give their all, while another big shot pinned medals on them. Weren't no medals for the boys who'd give their all.

Well, he was sure in a happy little place tonight, wasn't he? Maybe he should get to know more about the kid, like his name for one thing. Where he lived, what he cared about or who? Maybe he'd adopt him like a lost puppy and maybe he'd just sit here and sip 'til he fell asleep.

Empty Days Last Forever

∞

He woke up lonely, he always did, it was becoming as consoling as his morning coffee. He needed both to start the day, one to kick start and one to temper. Sometimes it was hard to remember which did which.

He should get a dog; he'd had them at different times in his life. Sometimes for companionship, sometimes as partner. What he ought to do was go back into the mountains, it was where he belonged. He knew that for fact. He knew what he was, knew no matter how many times he would try to be something else, it wasn't him. He should be happy being true to what he had been created for, and where he was supposed to be. Still, he had tried on as many lives as he could over the centuries, dumb. He was just a slow learner. Though he enjoyed the learning.

He'd spent one life, many years ago, as a cowboy. He liked that. Used to tell the kids about it when She wasn't listening. It was solitary work riding the range, not much to do except keep 'em moving during the day and settled at night. Just him and a horse. He liked most all animals, kind of had to, really, they were loyal, kind and didn't talk too much. People liked the sound of their own thoughts. Hell, he knew a guy back in the day who would walk along talkin' to hisself just to make certain the world knew he was there and his brain was workin' overtime. Silly. Couldn't be around the fella for mor'n a few minutes or you'd want to slap him.

She would not approve. Though truth to tell She'd never met the guy either. She might've wanted to slap him as well. And though he'd never done it, the want to was strong. And people claimed he couldn't control his urges!

He had lived many lives as a human. He wanted to know why they were wired the way they were. His people killed for survival, for food, to feed the young. That's the way it was with most species, not man. He killed for sport. He killed to prove something, something that didn't need proven. A bear would knock you around a bit, make a point, but if you were smart enough to know you been bettered, well, that was the end of it. Not with people, they'd hunt you to the ends for fear you'd come back. People lived for fear. Afraid someone was always tryin' to take something from them, land, women, respect. Hell, they was so busy tryin' to keep the other fella from takin' they usually lost it to inattention.

Not much on the agenda today, might just spend it wrapped inside dustcovers and do some travelin'. It was a game they used to play when they knew they had a day to do anything and no want to do nothing. They'd look at each other with guilty pleasure sparkin' like electricity and head to the library. Had to keep yer eyes closed while the other spun you like a top, then you'd stumble over to the shelves and pick a book. Whatever you got, there's where you were goin'. Just fun.

He should get out and trim the yard, it was looking like this house was abandoned. Wouldn't want the neighbors talking, thinking him too old to take care of hisself or this house. They got laws now that they can come and take yer place, sell it, and put you in a home of their choice with your money. Ain't that a slap on the ass? Civilization ain't so civilized sometimes.

Used to be if you outlived your useful you could just get up in the dark of the night when all else was sleeping and walk away. Wander in the woods for a few, get in touch with nature until something in nature got in touch with you. If you lived in the far north, they had icebergs to hop on and ride off into the sunset, or sunrise depending on the current. If you got too cold you could slide off into the water and let hypothermia, exhaustion and lack of air take it from there. They were good ways to slip to the other side without being a drag on the family or village. Everybody respected when you knew the time had come and you didn't whine about it.

People got tired, wore out, the body hurts, the folks you loved most had passed on. Amazing how lonely a body can be in the midst of humanity, but when you don't know nobody, it don't make no nevermind how many of them there are, they's just empty husks.

Yeah, time to do some work in the yard and take the mind with him 'fore it got him in trouble. That was the benefit of keepin' yer hands busy, they usually took the brain with them. No time for this wallowing in the depths. Do something positive and the brain will believe it. Then he could spend the rest the day avoiding any contact with the big bull moose he'd pissed off last night.

He laughed as he gathered his shears and trimmer, that fella was fit to be tied. Guess he was, actually, tied, with them cuffs on and the cops just waiting for him to try something.

The grass was cut, trimmed, and looking like a good suburban yard ought to. Except the weeds, but She liked the weeds. Said they were a sign of a healthy yard. Besides dandelions was good in so many ways. Hell, you do 'bout anything with 'em. Flowers that were just perfect, round, glowing yellow faces waving from the greenery, full of vitamins. You could even make wine from 'em. What other plant had so much going for it? And they grew 'bout everywhere. They was tough and hard to kill, they even grew in the cracks of the drive and sidewalk. Couldn't get rid of the damn things. Yep, he let them be.

She said they reminded Her of him, ornery but they filled the bare spots and in the depth of drought or flood, they survived. He kept a vase of them on the kitchen table, talked to 'em, too. Every morning and evening when he sat down. Sometimes they blocked the TV, but that weren't such a bad thing when he thought about it.

Yep, it was a nice house, craftsman they called. She loved the porch, he loved Her, that was the craft. It was probably his favorite house in history, probably. She was his favorite partner, no contest, and he'd had more'n his share. He'd tell you 'bout 'em, but people got queasy with the real.

The sound of car horn, just a quick beep, roused him. He looked up just in time to see that big angry fella drive by, point a finger like a kid with a gun, shooting him with his thumb. Kind of a childish threat, like you can scare old folks with death. Ha! Guess they let him out on good behavior. He made hisself laugh.

That's one of the many problems with young folks, they scared of death all the time, don't realize later on they'll be looking for the sonofabitch to come rescue them. He held up the trimmer like a long gun and shot back, 'bout laughed hisself silly 'cause it was just as dumb. Sometimes fire and fire can put each other out. And sometimes they just make a bigger fire.

He should try to make it right with the guy, but it went against everything he was. You can't live through a hundred lives with values, morals, ethics and empathy and throw it all away just 'cause some asshole wants to make your life miserable. Sometimes ya just gotta stare the threat in the eyes and dare it.

He grabbed a beer from the fridge, called and ordered a sandwich from the local shop up the street and sat on the front porch swing. If the dumb SOB wanted to make a show of it, well, two could play chicken. Wisdom dictated some backup, so he punched 9-1-1 into the phone, but didn't hit send. Back pocket insurance, if the guy messed with his lunch, he'd call in the Marines. One thing about serving in so many conflicts was you learned when to duck and when to call in air support.

The day was warm on his face as he rocked soft on the porch. The creak of the support chains not annoying today, brought solace, if there was a heaven—which he knew there wasn't—this was close. He had fifteen minutes or so before the sandwich would arrive, so he liberated his thoughts and allowed them free range. There comes points in life when you have to let go, let the spirit stretch its legs, wander the landscape and see what's out there. Today was a good day.

A cloud passed in front of the sun, he could feel the temperature drop a few, it was alright he'd wait it out. The waitin' got old as the cloud remained. Damn! What'd the world cease spinning? Or did the cloud decide to park itself right where he was enjoying?

Easing open his right eye a crack to see if he couldn't hurry the cloud on its way, he was not surprised to see the blockage. The mountain range had moved in front of his peace of mind. This guy was starting to piss him off.

"Something I can help you with, mister?" might's well keep it neutral for now.

"Yeah, you owe me a piece of flesh for taking a night away from me," flat, no anger. Those were the dangerous ones.

"Didn't take nothin' from you, you gave it away. Coulda just sat at the table and minded yer own, instead you gotta jump in and stir shit up. Me and the kid was just talkin'," succinct summation of the altercation.

"You was fillin'g that kid's head with a bunch of bull, talkin' to him like he was normal, making him think he could be good as us, makin' him want more'n whats coming his way. That ain't right mister," this time the old man could feel the anger emanating from this fella like a blast furnace, though his demeanor stayed calm.

"I was sharing stories from my past, that's all. Kid needed calmin' and I figured someone talking to him, treatin' him like a human, ought to be just the ticket. Ain't nothing wrong with letting a person know they can dream." He closed his eyes again, play it cool whispered experience. "Just 'cause someone took yours don't mean you gotta steal all others." Gentle push to see if we can crack this nut.

"You got no right...," began the threat quickly cut off by,

"Sam's Sandwich Supreme," called a feminine voice of about fifteen from about the same distance away.

Half-lidded eyes took in the young woman leaning her bike against the porch. Her own eyes glued to the huge man leaning in towards the old man half reposed on the porch swing. She looked like a chipmunk comin' out of the bushes between two cats, scared and wanting to run.

"Just set it over here on the table, dear, we're only discussing a few things. Ain't nothin' for you to worry," he gestured for her to come around pissed-off mountain and set his lunch down. Reaching into his front pocket for some paper money.

She came around the mountain, set the sandwich down, "six, fifty," she said quiet not wishing to disturb the fragile peace. Only hoping to get out of here with the bill paid and tip.

He handed her a ten never looking up at the big man whose impatience was palpable. She glanced down at the face of the phone and saw the three digits, hers eyes grinned. The old guy had it handled. She hopped her bike and threw a wave his way as she pedaled off.

"Now, where was we? Oh, I was going to take my pound of flesh for you sending me to jail," weight shifted from back foot to front.

"Once again, my good man, I did nothing of the kind, you stuck your nose where it could be disjointed, got tricked, fell outside, so I could enjoy a quiet beer," he counted off the offenses on the fingers of his left hand, "which I am once again attempting. You could have gone home, chalked it up to a wasted eve. Instead, you decided pounding on the door, disturbing the peace of all imbibing within, screaming, and arguing with policemen was a better course of action," he closed his fist around the phone hitting send as he did so, "You sent yourself to jail for an evening! So, if you're looking for payment go talk to the man in the mirror." He picked up his sandwich.

The floorboard creaked, there a rumble of warning before the volcano blew it's top.

"Stop right there, mister," came from behind him.

You could see the conflict in the big man's eyes, should he follow through and deck that cocky old sonofabitch or stop mid-strike. It might be worth the time in jail just to knock that smirk off that wrinkled face. Even bullies have better angels or a grain of sense, that and the memory of cold weak coffee and a dry biscuit for breakfast.

"Can I help you, sir," says the young cop to the old, frail man.

"Don't think so, fella just stopped by to chat and was jest getting on his way, isn't that right?"

"Yessir," rumbled up from where revenge was born. He stepped off the porch, turning his head he muttered, "see you 'round." Before ambling up the street.

"You know that man don't seem to like you very much," the young cop mentioned needlessly, though truth told he was more middle-aged. Perspective changed things.

"Don't seem to, does he?" as he unwrapped the sandwich deliberately.

"This ain't over and we can't always be this near," it wasn't a warning just stating the obvious.

"Yeah, I know."

"Might want to think about getting yourself some protection if you ain't got some already," the cop threw over his shoulder as he made his way back the patrol car. "Be careful mister, that man is real bad news. I'd try to make peace if I was you."

"Some folks just ain't the peacemaking kind," and if honesty is the coin, he had to admit he couldn't certain which one of them he referred to.

The sun was warm on his face as he chewed one of Sam's specials, almost as warm as the beer had gotten in all the jawing. Damn, he hated warm beer, but not as much as wasting it.

Shit, he best call the granddaughter and tell her to steer clear of here for a couple days, least 'til he got all the ill taken care of. Last thing he wanted in life was for his difficulties to come down on her. He pulled his pocket watch, the one with Her picture etched into the back, rubbed his thumb over Her face and turned it over. Hmm, quarter 'til two, Alexandra wouldn't have left the house yet if he called right now, he'd catch her 'fore she did. Tell her he'd be up in the mountains for a few days, she'd accept the lie as it was routine for him to just take off when the missing got to be too much. She knew, just as her grandmother had, how much the mountain healed.

Trouble Don't Need a Reason

Across time he had never gone off in search of trouble, he'd had enough to last him until the end. But trouble, apparently, hadn't had enough of him, 'cause it kept chasin' him down no matter where he went. He'd sidestep it when he could, face it head on when he couldn't. And at times he'd ride it like a wild stallion, holding on for dear life. This looked to be a big stallion and a wild ride, time would tell.

Maybe he should walk away, leave, head out and never look back. Them mountains was callin' to him, maybe he should listen. Yeah, that's what he thought every single time, but walkin' away wasn't in the blood; you just couldn't outrun or hide from trouble when it had your scent. Some folks down here seemed intent on bringing out the miserable. He didn't hate humans as a rule, but some made him think about it.

She told him one time when he'd run into a particular hard patch, "You bring this on yourself. Too damn stubborn, stuck in pride to back down, gotta show the world who's in charge."

"I swear I try," he had mumbled half-hearted like a little kid who just couldn't stay out of mischief.

"You don't neither, you walk head on into it, daring it, provoking it until you tussle," She turned Her back and huffed, making sure he understood Her displeasure.

But he did try to walk away! He did try to avoid trouble! There had been a hundred times he had turned his back on it and walked in the opposite direction. But it always followed him, it always caught him, he didn't go hunting it down, it laid all the traps. And he stepped into 'bout every one of them. Sure had this time.

There was nothing keeping him here, he could just hop in the truck and drive off, never look back. No, that wasn't true neither. He had Her, he couldn't leave Her. Her spirit lived in that house. She had loved it so much he didn't think She could move on. If he wanted Her, to be near what She had meant, to feel Her like his heartbeat, he had to stay put.

He should get a dog.

He required movement, swinging wasn't doing the trick and he didn't want to drive; didn't trust hisself as frustrated as he felt. He should walk around town, no destination in mind, just wandering, trouble can't hit a movin' target, time to get movin'

It weren't a big town, a town center comprised of a few blocks of feed stores, grocery, couple cafes and bars, place to buy jeans, shirts, and a coat, but it had all anybody really needed. Houses held the town upright, sprawling off a dozen blocks in any direction. It was a nice place, well, with a few 'ceptions, he chuckled to hisself.

Before he knew it, he was standing outside the bar, mid-afternoon, he didn't normally drink this early in the afternoon but walkin' had made him thirsty. 'What if that fella is in there?' Her ghost asked him in that tone.

Man can have a beer in this country. I ain't hurtin' no one and ain't lookin' to find trouble, he protested, though weakly. And it's too early for that fella come lookin'!

Humph, She shook Her head, walking right into it head on.

Nope, just havin' a beer. He opened the door, walkin' into the cool.

"Not sure you want to come in here," the barkeep called from where she was wiping tables setting up for the late afternoon rush, "Big Frank usually stops by after his shift out the feed plant."

"Yeah, I know, but it's early and he shouldn't come 'round for bit, wanted to come in for a couple beers, see how the kid is getting along," he sat down the bar from the door where he could see trouble comin' before it saw him.

"Kid ain't here today. You know he's got a name to go along with all the rest," she smiled to take the sting out, "name's Glen, don't know his last, but first is better than 'kid'," she said as she handed him a cold one.

"Dumb of me never to ask, I guess, but I guess even dumber of me never to have hardly noticed him," he took a long pull he and set the bottle on the coaster.

"Nobody ever does, 'til he falls on you," she barked a laugh before straightening up the bar.

"Hell, nobody notices none of us 'til we fall on top of them. Then they either apologize and help us up or want to clean our clocks for livin'. Hell of a thing," the door opened, and they both turned and nodded as the same fella from down the bar walked in and took his, apparent, usual seat. She set him up with a small glass and a bottle.

"Thanks for the drink," he raised his glass in salute and the old man nodded, sipping.

This was usually a friendly joint, no one bothered anybody else. Nobody knew yer name or cared, it wasn't important, they were all here for the same thing, a quiet drink. Which was what made yesterday and the other afternoon so strange. There was a wrinkle in the universe which usually meant something was about to happen, seldom was it something good.

Which made running from or avoiding the inevitable a futile gesture. When the forces of the universe conspired against you, best take the licking, give as good as you got, then go lick yer wounds. Better part of valor was to hope the pain didn't last too long.

And the old man had lived forever so he knew, too long was far too long when you was hurtin', and he hated the anxiety of waitin'. If fate was conspiring against you, best to face it head on—yeah, he heard Her—rather than make it chase you down. All that did was piss it off and things would only go worse for you in the end. She didn't know that, but he sure did.

Fate opened the door and grinned, it was not a pleasant sight, but expected.

"Well," it was all that needed saying. "'fore I kill you, any last requests," he, actually cracked his knuckles this time, sometimes fate was not the least bit original.

"Yeah, you want a beer?" asked ancient, as he nodded to the barkeep. "And how 'bout playin' 'Time to Take Off Them Travelin' Clothes', on the juke, I'll give you the quarter," he grinned.

"Sure, I'll take yer beer," gloating before an occurrence is gauche. Confidence is one thing; you don't have to be an ass about it. "But I ain't listenin' to old, bullshit tunes," some people just born not to be likeable.

"What's yer name," asked the old one buying a little time and a beer, letting the response to Her song being demeaned tamp down.

"Frank, most call me Big Frank," he said standing taller.

"You ask them to do that?" he sounded truly curious, not mocking at all, unless you were listening close.

"Yeah, 'cause it fits, what do they call you? Dead man walking?" he gave a solo guffaw at his own clever.

"Old man, which I am, or Evan, Evan Beach, which I also am," he said extending a hand.

If the big man wanted to be a big man, he had no choice but to accept.

He might beat the shit out of the guy in a few, but courtesy first. He grabbed the old man's hand ready to squeeze until he squirmed, give him a little taste of the main course.

His grip swallowed the old man's hand in his palm, and he immediately began applying pressure. Surprise colored his face red when he felt pain in his own hand. Not sharp though with the promise if he continued. Not one to back down he continued, he had to be crushing the arthritic claw, but the damned grandpa grinned while he glared challenge into his eyes. What the? He applied all the pressure he could summon, and the pain shot from the base of his thumb up into the wrist, along his arm through his shoulder until it coalesced in crippling pain at the back of his neck. This monster had never experienced pain like this, not even when he had snapped his thigh in half down the mill a few summers back. It was piercing and debilitating, he fell to his knees, eyes watering and gulping for air. At long last the old man cut him loose, turning to finish his beer and slapping another twenty on the bar, tip included.

"I will assume we have completed our transaction and are now square," he helped the big man regain his stature.

"How the hell did you do that?" awe replaced swagger.

"I'm immortal, I can do many things you can only dream of," he whispered, so only Big Frank could hear, winked, and walked to the door, "If anyone sees Glen, please tell him I would like a word." He dropped the dialect just for the nonce before returning to form. "Age and experience, folks, age and experience," he chuckled out the door.

The whistle singing from his lips accompanied him almost all the way home. She would have been upset with him for doin' what he did, but what other choice was there? Kill the other guy? Let the big galloot kill him? Not that he could, but still he could cause serious pain and breakage, he dearly wished to keep that to a minimum.

As he walked toward home there was a niggling at the base of his neck, a warning, like an itch you just couldn't reach. Or like someone was following, though not too close. You don't live forever by being careless or ignoring signs, especially those you don't quite believe.

As he turned the corner of his street, he ducked behind a large holly bush to try catch sight of who, or what, might be hot on him. He could peer around the bush just enough to see 'bout ten foot from where he'd come, he'd have ample time to scoot or decide to confront. Honestly, he hoped it was neither.

He almost came out of his skin when someone tapped him on the shoulder.

His first thought was, he hoped he hadn't messed hisself either front nor back. His second was, 'how in the hell did they get behind without him having a clue?' His heart dropped from his throat to his chest, his pulse settled into a high idle, he reassured there was no discomfort in the nethers.

Fine, now who in all blazes, he turned, he was face to face with the prettiest black woman, no, he corrected hisself, the prettiest woman he had ever seen.

Forgive me, he said to Her memory, knowing She would 'cause She was a good woman, honest and had passed.

"Good afternoon, Mr. Beach," she hesitated ever so slight when she said his name as if she wanted to call him something else. "Nice trick back there."

He watched her, wary, as if she might turn on him, before relaxing. If she meant harm, she could've done to him whatever she wanted while his back was turned.

"A little thing I learned in Burma a few years ago," he anteed up.

"Helpful. Why didn't you take him out?"

"I don't like violence, I've seen enough to last," the words were tired, the meaning more so. "How did you know?" Why this hadn't occurred to him earlier showed how he was slipping.

"I was in the bar when it happened, I was over in the dark corner, probably why you didn't notice," she said with a straight face.

He studied her face just to be sure she wasn't just playing with him. He was purty sure he would've noticed her sitting there even in the pitch dark, not that black folks was as rare as Yetis around here, but they wasn't an everyday occurrence neither.

"Can we talk for a few minutes somewhere quiet," she took his arm and guided him toward his house.

They walked the last couple blocks in silence. She biding her time, he not knowing where to begin. Up the four steps to the porch, and the swing. She sat in Her spot. Didn't even ask, just as bold as brass sat where She always sat. Calm down, Evan, said the most familiar voice in his life. I ain't going to need it and she don't know.

"This was her spot, wasn't it," she asked, putting the fib to what She might've thought, patting the cushion, while looking direct in his eye, "Does it bother you I'm sitting here?"

"Yeah, it does, but She don't seem to mind," he responded as if it was the most natural thing in the world. "'course She was always like that."

"You loved her," she didn't need to say, 'a lot', or 'more than anyone you've ever known'. It's there.

"Yeah," tears welled up, but stayed, "I didn't think it possible after all this time, but She, She was the one that completed me." He wanted to spit, 'and She died'.

"Did you think she was like you?" and there it was, not accusation, just holding up the mirror.

"Didn't think, but I hoped," and all the air came out in a whoosh. "God knows how I hoped. Hoping don't make it so. That's the problem with this curse, usually you know right from the first, like I do with you, but there are times when you don't know, there's no sign. Usually that don't make a difference, this time it did."

She wished she knew how that felt, she'd never loved anybody or anything like that. Oh, she loved, but it was always tempered with knowing, not hoping. He was right as could be, the problem with this curse—or blessing depending on the day—was there was no way to know who else had it, 'til ya did. Hell, neither of them had even said the words, he'd called it out and she'd known in the bar, they knew now they was tied together sure as brother and sister.

"Did she know?" now she was curious.

"She never believed. I think She wanted to, in the back of Her head, but it went against everything She had been brought up believing," he stared at the rose, pink and gold on the horizon as the sun began setting, "think it scared Her that it might be possible," he shook his head ever so slight, "and that She didn't have it. She wasn't one of us."

Quiet wrapped them both in twilight and cricket song, he in what had been, she in wishing she knew. Is it better? Neither of them knew and never would, but both thought the other did.

"That's the problem, isn't it? Being here this long. You almost want to be one of them," she sighed the words. She'd been here awhile, too.

"Not really, just wanted Her, alive," and that's it, the thought filled his soul. "I keep thinking..."

"Yeah, we all do," she gazed out over this beautiful world, thinking of the plenty and the scarce, the love, hate, wary and giving. If there was ever a place that screamed disjointed, this was it. "But you love it," she didn't need to voice it.

"You know how many lives I been through?" it was rhetorical, she might've, but it didn't make no nevermind, she'd probably been through as many. "Never paid much attention to humans, didn't seem to have the time. 'Bout the time you get to know somebody, they'd be gone. They'd all claim to be in for the long haul, but they was short haulin' and didn't even know it."

"Maddening, ain't it?" she slipped into the parlance easy as changing socks, it was what they did. They were chameleons, each lifecycle requiring a different costume and idiom. "You feel like we been 'round so long, learned, acquired knowledge, knowledge they should have and most with no want of it. Sometimes you get to thinkin' we should just take over. Run the damn planet for them," she didn't finish the thought, they had all ranted silently a thousand times. Don't do no good. They know what they were supposed to do, what the restrictions were, but it didn't make it easier.

"With Her," he said returning to the micro picture rather than the grand scale, "it felt like forever, in a good way, like this was going to last. She made time even out, Hers and mine. When you treasure every second, it makes it last. And it then it all passed and was gone in a heartbeat." The world closed in for a moment leavin just him and a thought.

"Funny thing is," he started up the engine again, "I respect these folks more now than ever. I never knew intensity of emotion on a limited budget. They don't know how little time they got, not intellectually, but I think viscerally they feel it. And the smart ones don't count the seconds they make them count. She was a real smart one. Damn, I'm sorry, I'm sure this ain't what you stopped here for, listen to some old man whining about lost love." He wiped a little regret from his eye as he straightened up on the swing. "I guess our children are lucky, they got no concept of time, love, or future, they just live. Ain't such a bad thing.

"You want a glass o' lemonade? A beer? Bourbon?" the questions get shorter as the preference comes closer.

"Bourbon would actually be nice," she said coy, "One cube, if you got a big one."

They savored the liquor, he never short-changed on bourbon, life is too short for bad bourbon, even for an immortal. The sky filled with just enough cumulous and stratus to make sunset memorable and satisfy the eye. Neither in any hurry to reboot the conversation, they had all the time they could wish, happy just to sit in the company.

It had been a few years since he had just enjoyed the presence of another of The People without the pressure to talk, to entertain. That's what most conversations resembled, a play, where everybody had to keep the action going or the audience would get bored and leave. Sometimes it was nice to sit in an empty theater and listen to the absence of need.

The tranquility ceased as the squad car eased to a stop in front of his home. The cop sat for several long moments in the front seat as he collected thoughts, or charges against, before he eased the door open. He stood, gazed at the two on the porch before he pushed gentle, leaning on the car door to close it, then made his way up the path.

"Evenin'," good a place to begin as any. He eyed the black woman lounging on the swing. Casual. She nodded, but didn't say nothing. "Sorry to disturb, but we got a complaint 'bout you and I gotta check it out," he sounded like he'd rather be sharing a little bourbon rather than questions.

"Do your duty, officer," Evan tipped his glass in invite.

The cop glanced at his watch, sighed, registered remorse at the injustice of life as he pulled out his pocket notebook. "I'm sure this won't take long," he clicked his pen into action, just like on TV, "you remember a big fella wanted to rip your head off last time we spoke?" You had to give the man points for style.

"I seem to recall something to that effect," can't play checkers with one player.

"Well, he is maintaining that you attacked him without provocation," he pretended to read from his notes, it helped prevent the laugh.

"He said that did he? Or did he get someone with a larger brain to write it down for him phonetically so he could pronounce the words." Evan knew where this was headed or thought he did, and he planned to head this off 'fore it could get a head of steam.

"I guess it don't matter much where the words come from, they been said, and I gotta investigate," the cop wanted to smile but kept professional.

"I know," no need to take out frustration on the man doing his job.

"Gotta ask, did you come up from behind and attack this man?" he peeked at the glass of brown liquor and wish passed across his eyes. "And I need to inform you, he says he's got witnesses."

"Sheriff," Evan corrected his ID of the man now he could see the uniform clearly, "you seem a good, intelligent human being, you really want to ask me that question?" maybe a little frustration leaked through.

"I got to, did you?"

"Nope, he come into the bar, threatened me, bought him a beer, tried to make peace, but apparently I got on his nerve," he chuckled at his own little joke, "he fell down and I left. End of story, anybody says different is a liar and I'll tell them to their face."

"I was there," said the lovely lady sippin' on the other glass, "happened exactly how Mr. Beach said."

"And you'd be?"

"Suzette Otterbein," she held out a welcome and he shook it, "in from out of town, I got no ties to either of the gents involved, just truth."

"OK," he put his notebook into his back pocket, sighed, "try to stay away from him. He's got a bunch of ugly friends just lookin' for trouble and you have become the focus of his life. Not in a good way, case you was wonderin'," one more glimpse at the bourbon, he tipped his hat to the lady, nodded to Evan and walked back to his car.

"You come back when you get off the clock," Evan waggles the glass at him, "it'll be waiting."

He nodded his thanks, took a quick peek at his watch, finished the short walk to his car, got in and drove off.

"Some folks is slow to learnin', and that big man at the bar seems to be in the remedial class," she shook her head, clinked the cube in her empty glass. Apparently, she'd been busy while Evan was visiting.

The screen door squeaked open and then slammed closed before squeaking open again followed quickly by another small squeak of floorboard as he leaned down and poured her a dram or two before refreshing his own and setting the bottle on the small end table.

"We created this," she stated taking in the whole of life, "maybe we should wipe the slate clean and start again, without these," she waved a hand taking in humanity, with a rueful bark.

"They ain't all bad, just a few," he defended what he knew to be true.

People weren't bad, not really, but the bad ones stuck out, that was a fact. And too many times the good ones allowed the bad ones to have their way 'cause they didn't want the evil ones to notice them. It was crazy what folks'd do just to be left alone. Close their eyes, turn the other cheek, walk away, pretend it didn't involve them and hope. He had always thought someday they would come to the realization that we are all relatives and what happened to one happened to all. But slow learnin' is slow learnin', and hard on the whole pack.

"We could get the band back together and do a little head knockin'," that was the bourbon talkin', she was singing a familiar refrain and he wanted to agree. But he knew better, every time they tried to interfere with these problems, things went left and next thing you knew everything escalated, harming a whole lot of innocents. Nope, he had to keep this contained. Not get the family involved.

Though now the subject had been brought up he wondered, maybe the family was already involved. Maybe this big, dumb mountain wasn't moving on his own, but was just a piece on the board sent to start some shit with Evan.

"Does this mischief got the taste of anybody you know?" He'd seen her for who she was and knew for sure they was on the same side.

"Now that you mention it," she was pleased he recognized, "it does have a familiar taste to it, though I can't put my finger on whom. Or, more important, why." Sometimes the family lived among these other for so long they forgot old hurts and psychic debts; and their kind had long memories! She hoped that was not the case here, she hoped Evan had just been distracted by his life; not that he'd gone human. Forgot some slight he'd done to one of the people and they'd waited for an opportunity to cause a little pain. She didn't know his history, and he didn't know hers.

"I might have to do me a little investigating myself." He drained the glass.

Meeting

Evan set up camp at the tree line, no need to go any higher as Yote wouldn't go higher, he'd stay down close to food and people. Above the timberline was neither. Right here was close enough to chase trouble other folk's way and far enough away to avoid detection. This spot should pique interest, but Yote would have to work to come here. Why make it easy on the trickster.

Evan also knew he wouldn't have to go chasin' Yote. If there was one thing Yote couldn't resist was company, especially if'n that company ignored him. All Evan had to do was light up a fire, kick back and relax, and the quarry would come to him. When you know'd somebody since the dawn of creation, you got to know how they thought, Yote was an open book with pop-up pictures. Oh, he pretended to not need nobody else, but he was always close so's to stick nose in where it didn't belong.

That was the thing, Yote thought he was more clever than any of the people just 'cause he liked to affect mischief. Evan knew trouble makin' didn't make you smart, it made you a pain in the ass, and prone to cocky. Yep, that old Yote would come a sniffin' round within a few days to see who, and why, somebody had strayed to the far edge of nowhere.

Meantime, Evan could do a little hunting and fishing hisself. There was a nice size stream back the way he came, looked to have sizable fish, surrounded by berry bushes and, if he wasn't mistaken, a honeybee hive. Yeah, he could use a few days up here away from memories.

He'd hardly left town since, yeah, since, 'cause he forgot about how good it felt to be here. Sometimes a soul gets so locked up in the hurt, the pain, he forgets there are places that can lessen that suffer.

He'd thought about asking Suzette—he'd at long last got 'round to remembering her name—to join him up here. Thought she might enjoy a bit of the clean air and solitude, but then decided against. He could accomplish two things at one sitting. He could wait out Yote and he could maybe wait out some of the pain.

He'd been with females before, lots of them. Some for a night, just to keep a body warm, and some for years. They'd been nice, good company for the most, took away a bit of the solitary without being annoying and fun to romp with. But he was a loner by nature, and nature don't cut you loose.

She, She was different. She made him feel something he'd never known. Real love. His kind had no use for such crazy. You couldn't be expected to be in love forever. Nice concept when you only lived for a few decades or so, eight or ten on the outside if you took care.

That was thing with humans, they thought big, but didn't have the capacity to truly understand. Forever ain't forever when it's only five miles long. People were like goldfish, you kept 'em for a while, but in a week or two they got flushed, that's what it was to immortals.

Not Her, She was a forever fish. It was dumb and unrealistic, but he'd fallen for it. He'd forgot who he was and what She was, nature and the inevitable. Sooner than late Ol' Ma Nature'd come collecting and she always got paid.

Well, he'd paid, he'd overpaid and got no change back. Fell into a hole ten miles deep, dark as the absence of space. A few turns around the sun of heartache, time wasted, but what was time. Just a way to keep track of heartbreak and happiness. Something to mark on a doorframe as the kids grew.

He'd find what he sought up here, where he belonged, solace and retribution. He'd have some fish and a few pounds of Yote for breakfast.

It was the evening of the seventh day as the sun hid behind the peak that Evan caught the scent of Yote on the breeze. It was a distinct smell; you couldn't mistake it for anyone else. It was musky dusty with the sour stink of piss and whatever he'd been rollin' 'round in and scavengin'. Some days he was worse than others, today weren't too bad.

"You gonna hang around in them woods or come in and set," Yote likes to sneak up on people thinkin' they can't scent him out. Evan like to let him know he's wrong.

"Come on, Ev, no need to be unfriendly, ain't seen you in Coon's age, and you know how long he been alive," he waited for Evan to laugh at his cleverness, giving up he came into the twilight. "What brings you up into nature?"

"You," Evan ain't in the mood for tomfoolery, his back hurts from sleepin' on the ground, which should be natural, if he hadn't been so used to his tempur-pedic. He was gettin' soft, being curled up on hard ground and root was takin' its toll on his good humor.

Yote danced over to where Evan sat on a log staring at the night sky as if counting the stars. Yote always danced or skipped wherever he went, thought it presented him as the merry prankster he was portrayed in stories and songs. He liked to keep his image up, even 'round them that knew better.

Yote stuck his nose up in the air sniffing and tasting the wind. He was ruled by desires and wants and right now he desired food and wanted whatever Evan had hid. He knew there was something 'cause he could taste it on the air, question was where was it, what was it, and would Ev share?

"Well, I'm here, you bring anything with you?" if they was bartering then let the game begin.

"Set yourself down for a spell and let's talk, if'n I like what you got to say we'll see if we can't find a little bite with a taste to wash it down," he grinned knowing the other fella couldn't resist food and drink. "A friendly meet betwixt two old friends, right Yote?"

"You know I hate it when you call me that, shows lack o' respect. I got a rep to live up to, people expect certain behavior from me, and regard from friends and enemies alike. If I don't deliver, they lose respect. And you callin' me that don't give me credit where credit's due," he sulked as he sat, knowing he was being played at. Now, he don't mind playin'at others but he sure hated havin' it throwed back at him. "Name's Coyote and you know that."

"Well, if we're going all formal then my name's Evan," said he with a grin. If it was going to be a leg pulling tournament then he wanted a handful.

"Shit, your names Bear, if we're going to hit bottom," and they both shared a nod, a bark of amusement and Bear grabbed the bottle he'd stuck under the log and twisted off the cap. Time to get down to business. He throwed the bottle to Coyote who snagged it out of the air taking a long swig 'fore tossing it back.

"Whatever been done, I ain't done it," Coyote said, wiping the liquor from his mouth.

"Awful defensive for an innocent party," growled back Bear.

"Shit, anytime anybody come sniffin' 'round my part of the world it's only to lay blame for something that happened thousand miles away from where I shit!" he reached for the bottle and Bear hesitated a heart-beat 'fore handing it back.

He couldn't be sure if Coyote was lyin' or truthin', it was damn near impossible to tell with this critter, as he really was the wiliest of all the First People, but he scented of truth. When Bear stopped trusting instinct he might as well just become human. He dug a claw down in the soft earth pulled out a fresh Rainbow Trout, so fresh you could almost see the tail wagging. Coyote licked his lips at the sight.

Normally Bear would've held this in reserve, kind of a promise, you give me what I want, and I'll give you what your heart desires. He knew, hell everybody knew, Coyote was too lazy and unskilled to catch his own fish, usually just dining on other's leavings, so, this would be a treat. But Bear thought it might prime the pump, a gesture of goodwill. He tossed it over, Coyote caught it in his jaws and went to work.

Bear dug his claw back in the loam producing his own dinner. The sound of slurping, chewing, and licking of chops filled the evening air.

"Whatever happened to that young filly you was hangin' with last time I run into you? Shit, what's it been now? This lifecycle, wasn't it?" Coyote was feeling convivial in the company of Bear, a full belly and half a bottle still available.

"Died," flat and lifeless as the word.

"That's the problem with their kind, don't last long. Gotta keep 'em like pets, when they die you just gotta get another one," he chuckled never having been close to a human for more'n a few nights. It gave him the heebies after that. Coyote thought a vulgar thought and was about to pass it on 'til the look on Bear's face. "Hmm, guess you was attached."

"Might say," and Bear took another pull before reaching into his coat pocket for his bag and papers. He was going to need some tempering if he was going to be in the company of Yote without killing him again.

"That ain't what this is about, is it?" Coyote took to rummaging through any and all rascalin' he'd been up to over the last few decades, but he don't seem to remember causing Bear no nevermind. But that's the trouble with having the reputation, everybody just assumes it's all your doin'. "You know I ain't never hurt no one on purpose, certainly wouldn't cause harm to someone you was close to. No need sparkin' malice in the family."

That was the thing about them, they were family, the first nation ever to hold ground. They might not all be brothers and sisters, but they was cousins and that's close enough. Ma didn't put up with no wars in the family, she'd extinct ya quicker than thought if she suspected you was creating discord in the family.

"Sorry to hear about her dying," Coyote put on his best funeral face, "you two was together for a spell wasn't you?"

Bear nodded once, then smiled.

"You met her after all them folks was rioting and starting fires, screaming at each other and them's that was in charge, marching and fighting, back a while, yeah?" he had never heard the story of Bear and his woman after the so-called peace movement turned sour. But the weed was good, the booze was still flowing, and he was comfortable. Tell me a bedtime story. For once it wouldn't be about blaming him for all the unrest of humans, maybe let somebody else take the blame.

Bear considered for a few, then thought, what the hell, can't hurt to talk about her now, might help.

He took a toke, blowing the smoke to the relatives, and started humming an old folkie tune they'd heard together a hundred years ago. Yeah, 'Time To Take Off Them Travelin' Clothes'...it was their song.

"First saw her in a mountain meadow not too far from here," he eased into the reminiscence; well-worn, well-loved. "She was just walking, alone, in the mountains, scent fresh as a new day after an evening rain. Hair down to here, that shone like the sun. Damn, she was pretty, so young. Don't think I been that young since Ma built these mountains and let the water flow. I couldn't help myself, I followed her 'round the forest, meadows, down the river. She never came across as scared of bein' out here alone. Like she belonged.

"You ever run across any of them that just fit out here?"

Coyote gave it a consider before shaking his head. He never had. He'd seen a few that knew how to get around in The People's world, could maybe live out here, but he'd never met one that fit. They's always trying to change things so that the world would fit them. Dumb.

"She felt a part of it all, like she was a cousin I hadn't met, one of the family. I had to get to know her," another toke, another smile, another gift to the relatives. "It hadn't been all that long that I'd come back to me, and I was still a bit skittish," Bear shook off that memory.

"I'd heard you'd gone human for a while. Forgot who you was and all," Coyote gave his own shiver.

"Yeah, I'd got all caught up in their damn wars. A few of them over time. We do some bickering, might be a tooth bared or a claw dug into a rear end, never comes to more'n that, but they hate each other. Hell, they try to kill off whole sections of others just 'cause. Ain't no rhyme or reason. Talk different, dress different, color different, and they lose their fucking minds!" Now both shook their heads and howled or growled to the moon in frustration. "Like as to destroy the whole of the world. It's crazy.

"I got hooked into being human just to see what it was all about, try to figure out why they was always so full of hate and death. I lost myself, my identity. Became human," he whispered as if afraid it could happen again. "Stayed that way for quite a while. 'Til I was at a music fest, you ever been?" he threw to Coyote who only covered his ears and howled, no, into the quiet. Bear knew how he felt, it took a toll on the ears, especially sensitive like they got.

"Well, this fella comes up to me, biggest grin I ever seen on a human, his eyes all big, takin' in the whole of creation, and asks if I want a hit. Yeah, try it and I'll whack your head off if'n you do. Thinking I been hit enough to last a lifetime. War will do that to a fella. He says, 'no, to expand yer mind!' Shit, at that point I got nothing to lose, war been over more'n twenty years, I'm bored with livin' and can't imagine dyin'. So why not? I took his 'hit' and took a few more blows." He laughed from the belly, loud, and slapped his paw hard down on his knee. "Well, it all come back that night. I roamed the universe and flew back to the beginnings of time. I watched the Mother create this world while the Great Spirit laughed and danced all through the heavens. Yeah, that pill took me places I ain't been to since the dawn. Then it took me deep, into the yawning chasm, the abyss of me. Broke down the elements to their basics and then put me all back together once more. I was more complete than I think I ever been.

"Welp, I remembered everything about me, you, all of us. I did the Bear Dance for the first time in I don't know when, every step, every move, like it never left me. Knew right as rain who I was, then saw how the numbers of my children was dwindling and knew I'd been letting my people down. Hadn't been takin' care of them. It's why I came back up here in the first place." He lowered his head in silent apology to the Mother, to those he let expire and to his kind who he almost let go extinct. It was a hard prayer to carry, but it was his.

"You always was one for takin' chances," grinned Coyote appreciably.

"You're one to talk," and they both took a pull. "Then just couple years later I see the purtiest little gal waltzing along through meadow flowers, free as can be. Eyes big as wonder, nose like a black-eyed Susan. Like I says, I followed Her, weren't hard, not with that scent and Her in no hurry. She stayed up in the clean for a couple days to my reckoning. Slept out under the stars, ate berries and what was given, never seemed to note the dangers of the wild. And the weird thing was, the wild never seemed to note Her. Nobody ever come after Her, it was like She was special. Well, She was.

"Then She went back where She come from, and I went into the mountains where I belonged. But She never left me, not for one moment. She was right here," he pounded on his substantial chest and pointed at his temple, "couldn't shake Her." He knew he sounded like some lovesick kid; he didn't care anymore. Man's got to own up to what he is, so does the Bear.

"So, I start prowling round that town down on the flats. Nothing crazy, didn't go in all bear and tear up the dump or nothin', just walkin' round town, seein' if I could spot Her, find out where She lives, ya know?" He gazed up to the stars to see if he could see Her, but he knew better, well his head did, his heart weren't so sure. "One day I bump into Her, just hanging around the park, She's quiet, listenin' to the Ma's music. Birds chirping and whistlin', buzzing of them 'sects, creek burbling, you know the song of life, happy as can be. So, I go up, start conversatin' and it's like we knowed each other since the world got born."

"Was she one of us?" Coyote asked knowin' the answer. If she was one of them, they'd a known right off. They could hide from humans, but they couldn't, far as he knew, hide from each other.

"No, ain't you listening?" Bear could only hold in the exasperation so long when it came to Yote. "She's one of them, but She ain't. She's different. Took Her to see an old folk singer for our first time out together. She'd never heard of him, I had, folks played his music when they come up into the mountains. I liked it 'cause it didn't disturb and the stories ran true. He played 'Time to Take Off Them Travelin' Clothes' and I swore I'd give up everything again just to be with Her." His heart was breaking with the telling, but it felt good to let it out. Hell, he didn't even care it's Coyote doin' the listening.

"I offered Her that I'd change everything about me if She be my mate. I'd quit running up into the mountains every so often, which I had to do for my sanity back then. She said no, She understood. Sometimes you just had to go up into nature, run free, smell the good earth, live off the land. She didn't want me to change nothin' 'cause She loved me just as much." His grin lit the night, his memory lit his life, "She called me Bear, said I was big and cuddly like a stuffed bear She had as a kid.

"Kind of freaked me when She done that, like She knew and wanted me to know She knew without sayin' the words. Like if She said it, the spell would break," story over, silence was the benediction.

"Wow, that is weird and freaky," Coyote reached over for the last of the bottle, Bear weren't going to fight him for it. "You really did love that girl, huh?"

"Yeah, I did. Now She's dead and I got somebody sending a man with a satchel and half full of trouble and a barrel of bad attitude my way. Now I had my fill of killin' in them wars, don't want no more. Hell, I'm damn near a vegetarian as it stands, I don't even go in for carrion anymore. I don't want no trouble, just want to be left alone," he stated the fact and it's final. He won't brook no argument. He's had his fill, but if one more dead body brings peace, then let's get it over with, he was tired.

"I swear, it ain't me and ain't heard tell of anybody wantin' to come at you," Coyote scratched his ass, between his ears and under his chin 'fore getting up to go piss on a few trees, Might as well do some marking while he's up here. "You done anybody a bad turn?"

"None that I can recollect, least not for a few centuries as the humans count. If somebody is holding a grudge that long they is the uncontested world champine and can keep the crown," he stuck his paw in the jacket pocket hoping to find one more rolled and hiding in there. Mother loves him, he strikes a match. "So, if not you, and you got to admit this sounds like your work, then who?"

"Wish I could tell you I knew, but I don't," Coyote nodded thanks as the joint got passed, "I tell you what though, since you been so neighborly, sharing the bounty and all, I'll see what I can find." Bear nodded his thanks, "but I gotta scat and then leave, enjoy the rest of the night." He walked a good pace away from where Bear sat, just to be polite 'fore droppin' trou and leavin' his business.

Bear rolled off the log onto his back starin' up, countin' stars, and rubbing the etched picture of Her on the outside his pocket watch with his thumb, 'til he slept. Morning would come when it did, bringing trouble on its tail. Sometimes a bear could wish to just hibernate until it all went away. But wishing and dreaming was just that and nothing more.

If The Man Won't Go To The Mountain

∞

Another week passed before he could bring hisself down from seclusion, but that was human time, not People's time. You can only hide from life so long, soon or late it's going to come and find you wherever you might have holed up. He kind of hoped he might run into that pretty Suzette 'fore too long. He knew nothin' could happen, she was the wrong species, and he was the wrong heart. But that didn't mean he couldn't enjoy the company.

Sleep was hard to come by since his return to the land of man, he tossed and turned, just couldn't get comfortable. Nightmares stalked his dreams. He woke drenched in sweat. What the hell was happening? He didn't dream, he lived in dream. His whole family were the dream weavers, it was where they resided. They didn't have nightmares they rode them, sent them to rampage through the sleep of humans.

Evan didn't think he'd ever experienced what it was like to awaken and not immediately know who or where you were. To not remember every detail of the night, the dream tantalizing just out of reach. He now spent each night searching for Her. If he couldn't have Her in the day to day maybe he could find Her in the night.

He knew how dreams worked, he was part and parcel, they could be just as good as this reality. Damn, he hadn't thought this hard on Her for a few years. He had suffered the pain, knew it would lessen but never leave. He knew that! He didn't fight it, he embraced it because it was all he had left of Her. So, he loved the pain each day brought as it kept Her in his heart. Now, though, his nights were filled with frustration, hopelessness, and sorrow.

Maybe it was guilt. Guilt for having any kind of thought about any other woman. No, he didn't feel guilt, it wasn't in his make-up. Things was what things was, couldn't change who you were at the core. He'd seen pretty women before, had hankerings, but never this reaction to them. Nope it was something deeper. It was someone doin' this, and he had best find out soon or he was either going to lose his mind or loose himself on this world. And that'd be uglier.

He moved like a spirit among the folks of the town, some said hello, some walked by without a nod. He tried to be in the present, pretend all was normal, but they could see it in his eyes. People being what they was, they just attributed it to an old man who'd lost his wife. They'd seen it before, neighbors, friends, and family. Folks who'd shared a life, one dies, the other just a ghost drifting until time.

Back in the olden times old people who'd reached this stage would wander off into the forests and let Ma have her way. She was usually gentle, caring, she tried to make it come painless. They'd walk 'til tuckered out, lay down to sleep for a few, she brought in a cold front, not cold enough to harm the strong, just enough to allow the sleep to take hold. It was peaceful. Helped keep the bears and others alive in the winter. Everything and everybody served the purpose, kept life moving.

Sometimes Evan would ponder on how life had evolved with people. They lived longer these days, but was it better? They worked so hard to fight off the inevitable, keeping each other on machines. Machines did all the breathing and pumped the blood. They couldn't run in the world or talk to each other, just the beeping artificial life. That weren't life, but to each their own.

Hell, what he was doin' now weren't life neither. He was sleepwalking through and not the good kind. He had to find out who was causing this distress. Damnit, he was Bear, he'd come from the stars. Look up at night and he'd be looking right down atcha. Shake it off, boy, we got shit to do.

Where to begin? At the beginning, of course. Where had this

taken off? At the bar that day. How long he been going in that bar ain't never had lick of trouble, all a sudden he got a truckload of mess dumped in his lap. Time for a beer.

The barkeep turned at the sound of the door opening, saw Evan shamble through, shook head as she bent to grab him a cold one out of the cooler.

"Afternoon," greeted Evan as he took his customary stool down a ways from the door. Old habits. "ain't lookin' for no trouble just a beer or two." He eased hisself onto the stool making a show of age and decrepit.

The bar was close to empty, just him and the girl behind, he should get her name. He had a problem with always getting and forgetting or forgetting the getting', it was on the rude side.

"I'm sorry, but I have never gotten your name," sheepish so she'll know he ain't flirtin', just finally found his polite bone.

"Meg," she stuck out her hand to make if official.

"Evan," he took it, they shared a quick nod.

"Quiet today," if this was gonna turn into a conversation it sure was takin' the long way 'round.

"Yup," she gave the bar a wipe and went to stock beer.

Didn't feel much like talkin' anyway, he consoled hisself. Didn't come here for talking but trying to figure. He couldn't feel nothing in the air, no vibes or mojo, but there was someone messin' with the energy, a blip in the timbre.

There weren't many as could mess with things to this point, could bring such discomfort on another of the people. He could, he supposed, just go huntin' down that list, but he didn't feel like chasin' folks down and accusin' without proof. Nope, best to just wait, see if he couldn't nip this thing 'fore it grew too big to handle.

The door opened and closed, two steps in, stop. Evan didn't have to look up to know who stood there. He could sense the presence. Big guy like that gave off a vibe you could sense within a hundred yards, and he was a helluva lot closer. How in all hells did he always know when Evan was here?

"You got balls," rumbled the mountain, "comin' in here. I got friends, lots of them, make short work of an old man like you." The threat was palpable as intended.

"You thought that last time, didn't go according to Hoyle," Evan took a sip, but still ain't looked at the fella. He didn't have to. "Listen Mister, I don't know why you got me stuck in your craw, but I sure seem to be there, and I don't like it any more than you. Maybe you could tell me why you got a burr under your blanket when before a week or so ago I ain't never laid eyes on you." He thought that a fair place to plant the flag.

"Guess I just never liked your face," a step closer physically and in menace.

"Never's a long time, considering you ain't 'never' set eyes on me neither," Evan was tired and this was wearing on his last nerve.

This wasn't going the way Evan had hoped. He'd thought maybe if he could just talk to the guy, he could find out who set him on this course, but this guy just wanted to go 'round. "Well, you could close your eyes when we meet," he thought it a clever rejoinder.

"I heard tell you been speakin' unkind things behind my back," ah, now we were getting somewhere. "That you was cutting me down, like with that kid, that day. Talkin' shit."

"Mister I ain't never met you before you began runnin' your gums at me that day. Why would I ever say a harsh word to you, about you or even mention you was alive?" Evan could see the wheels start to free up like as they might break loose, but just as quick ceased up again. This was going to be a long day.

The sound of the door, another step, halted again.

"Hey Glen," says Evan without looking up. There's a sadness in his voice that spoke volumes. "Want a beer?"

"Don't think I want nothing from you," and there it was.

Evan turned, still holding his bottle, towards the two standing just inside the door. The mountain was grinning ear to ear, the kid looked, what, pissed, disappointed, sad, all of the above? It hurt deep in Evan's heart while bringing up the internal temperature, his blood hit the boiling point. This was when things would get dangerous.

"So, you turned the kid against me, that what you was wanting to do? Fill his head with lies 'bout someone you know nothing about?"

Evan could feel his grip loosening, red began to tint everything, he could sense his claws digging into his palms.

Please, Mother, do not let me lose control, not here, not now, not with innocents in the middle. He chanted over and over, searching for calm and finding only rage. Glen was a good kid, good heart, simple, innocent, and this sonofabitch was turning the kid's head and heart. It weren't right, went against nature, went against decency, somebody ought to...

His rage was interrupted by the slamming of the side screen door.

"Evening folks," the sheriff nodded the greeting, arms crossed across his chest, hands far from the gun hanging at his side. "Everything OK?"

Evan could feel all emotion drain from him like a plug been pulled. He just wanted to head up to the forest, to run his anger out, to roam and hunt. But he couldn't. He set the bottle on the bar, slow and gentle.

"Thanks Meg," calm as morning, threw a ten spot on the bar, "guess I gotta find another place to have a beer. This joint just don't seem to fit no more, ain't as friendly as it used to be." No more red, just saw blue.

"Good idea, old man," the mountain threw.

"Mister, you ought to thank your guardian angel or whoever called me, 'cause I think that old man would've torn you apart this time," Sheriff nodded to Meg but didn't say another word to the big man and only shook his head at Glen. Who, at least, had the sense to look shamed.

"Mr. Beach," the sheriff waved him back to where his car was parked, "look, I don't know what or why, and that bother's much as anything, but you and that fella is oil and gasoline. I don't need you exploding in my town. You been a steadfast citizen for a lot of years, that buys a lot of trust in my book. I don't know that guy," he pointed back to the bar, "from Adam but I got to treat everybody the same. I'm asking, please avoid that man."

"Sheriff, I don't know much more'n you, whether you want to believe that or not, but something is going on and it ain't good. I came up here this afternoon hopin' to put a stop to it or find out why. Guess I weren't too successful on either count." He rubbed his chin in thought, then rubbed his back on the phone pole behind him without thinking, "I will promise you this, if I can stop this I will. If I find out anything as to what is happening, I will tell you first, but know, sometimes the world spins out of our control."

"I don't much care for things out of my control, kinda comes with the badge and turf. I do know you don't want me and mine in the middle of yours and theirs. Evening."

As Evan walked the half mile to home, he couldn't help but wonder if all this was somehow tied to Her. If not, it was family business and that could get very ugly very quick. Had he done something or said something to one of the other people that kicked off some kind of range war? Or did it go back even further.

Shit, that's problem with living forever, hard to keep track of every little slight, every unkind word done back when Jesus was a babe. There was some, though, who kept track and could hold a grudge like a mother holding a babe to her breast. It would suckle on that hate until it grew into it. Hate was a powerful thing, brought out the beast in man and the man in beast, the two wasn't supposed to mingle.

Back to Her and him. Could be Ma hadn't approved of the mating and was going to make a point about the two kinds of people. Then again, they'd all been the same once, lived together back in the beginning time before humans got it all up their heads they was somehow higher up the food chain. But if that was it, was the kids and grandkids in danger? He should call each of them soon as he got home. Hell, he might want to get one of them cell phones the kids keep haranguing him about. He pulled out his pocket watch to check the time or just from habit, rubbed Her face, and checked time. Might as well he had it in his hand, almost time for dinner.

Decision Made

∞

She was sitting on the swing gazing into the darkening sky. She was a purty little thing, chocolate brown, button nose, and sleek, yeah, that was the term, she was sleek. Good lookin' woman. It's kinda funny, he thought as he made his way up the sidewalk, how The People—and there was a huge difference between The People and people, he grinned—never really noticed color except as a descriptor. Like scent, size, taste, there was color. You could admire a brown cousin, all the benefits it brought, like how well they blended into the woods or how the pure white of the snow rabbit made it almost impossible to see when the snow came. You would never think of using it against them.

Humans was funny. People looked at color as just another difference, something to separate, not be admired, but something to hate. That was the trouble with people, they's always looking for some reason not to like the other. The People either liked or disliked depending on the actions of others.

"Evening," she threw a cheery welcome breaking his own negative, "hope you don't mind," she added gesturing her position on the porch.

"Not at all, you are a welcome sight after another curious day," eased hisself down on the swing opposite and breathed in the comfort.

"Care to share, Bear?" she bided her time, they had, literally, all the time in the world.

So, candor was the coin of the realm tonight, then so be it.

"First a question," she nodded her assent, "what brings you here, Otter? I mean, I been here a long time, this is your first visit. What do you know?"

"I know things is off kilter like an eddy in the river disrupting the flow, and it sits right here. Everybody feels it and it's got all the people on edge," she wrapped herself in her arms for warmth on a warm night, "and you seem to be the rock causing the eddy."

Ask and ye shall receive. One thing about the people they love to dance, they'll dance at the song of bird, the whisper of wind in the pines, the lonesome call of a wolf, but they don't dance around the truth. They treasure it. He thought maybe he should've stayed in his own, then remembered Her laugh. The tear in the corner of his eye proved the lie to that thought. Instead, he laid out all that had happened over the past weeks.

"You got any of that brown liquor?"

"Guess I could find a glass or two," they both attempted to keep it light, but worry weighed heavy. Neither liked what the other had expressed.

They sipped, crickets chirped, peepers sang out by the pond and in the trees, you would have thought it was the most peaceful evening in history. Except the pall that hung over the two on the swing.

"You know, there have been times like this in the past," Evan turned his attention to where Suzette was lost in her thoughts.

"Yeah," she admitted, coming back from where she had wandered, "but it was always just between The People. If we had a quarrel with one or other, we kept it between us, we didn't bring them into it. Now, that has changed. One of us, or maybe more, have infected this fella with a lodestone of hate."

"Two," Evan interrupted.

"What?"

"He's turned the kid from the bar, Glen, against me. Don't know what he said or done, but the kid hates me," he shook his head as if that would push the look in Glen's eye out of his brain.

"That ain't good," she said, though it was unneeded. "And that hate is focused on you. Which means you best be careful, vigilant. You don't know how far this has spread. Bringing others into our disputes can only escalate, leading to an awful bad outcome," she shivered at the implications.

"I gotta break that kid away from that sonofabitch. He's as innocent a soul as any I ever run across. If I can save him, maybe..." hopes and dreams and a bag of nuts, but it was all he had.

"Why do you think this is happening?" speaking of innocence and purity, she was the embodiment.

"One of two things," he counted off two things on three fingers, "one, either I have severely pissed someone off enough that they have held a grudge longer than my memory, which is a feat unto itself. Or, one of us has decided they just want to kick up some shit and hope when the dust settles, they're on top of the pile. Ain't but one or two got that big of an ego combined with the means to try it." He refreshed the glass hoping it would provide the proof to kick start his brain. "Or could be there's something wrong with the balance of the Universe." They both fell silent in contemplation at the implications that exposed.

"Evening folks," voice from the pitch-dark calls, "looking for a fella by the name of Beach, know him? Supposed to live nearby."

Evan turned on the small porch light at the sound of the unknown voice. The small, round man stepped into the dim light, blinking eyes the size of dahlia's, adjusting to the light, the hair sticking out in every direction and from every point on his head gave him a—what did the kids call it? Oh, yeah—a punk kind of look. He wiped his pince-nez on his coattails before placing them back on his beaklike nose.

"I'm Beach, how can I help you?" Evan stood casual leaning against the round wood column, hands in pockets.

"Well, I was passing through the neighborhood," his head turned at the rustle of leaves as a rodent passed through the yard, shrugging remorse that business must come first, "lovely area, quiet, well-kept homes," he sounded like a real estate agent warming up for the pitch, "anyway, were you aware of a small group of angry men assembling at the end of your lane with crude weapons, liquor and growing sense of mayhem?" He turned his head quickly catching the sound of tiny footsteps to his right, another missed opportunity.

"I am not one who wishes to insert myself in the squabbles of others, but also do not wish harm to come to the unsuspecting. Thought you and the lady might wish to make scarce while the making presents itself," a two-finger to the forehead salute and he ambled into the night.

"Don't suppose you'd care to stick around and lend a hand?" shot Evan into the dark.

"I try not to get involved when the battle is not mine, good evening," whistled the darkness.

"You know if we leave, they'll just bust up the house," Suzette sounded conflicted, wanting to protect the home, though not wishing to be the victim.

"Don't suppose you have one o' them cell phone thingys, do you?" hope springs, though not quite as fast as a man attempting to try and save a home.

"Matter of fact," she quipped as they moved through the house dousing all lights and locking doors and windows, heading towards the kitchen and a rear exit.

"Appreciate it if you'd dial 911 and ask the nice sheriff if he'd come over and try to save some of my property," he gently pushed her into the night before rushing back in and up the stairs.

A few moments passed before he exploded out the back door grabbing her arm as they raced towards the back of the property.

"What did you do?"

"Just a little deception, tuned on a few lights in the upstairs, some got timers, might buy us some time if they think we're still inside."

"Sheriff said he'd hurry and bring reinforcements. Maybe if he locks them up for a day or two," she didn't finish the thought knowing wishes tend to be hollow.

"If he does, maybe somebody can bail Glen out," He didn't know where they're headed but he didn't hear the sound of pursuit or destruction. Yet. That was just peachy as he wanted the time to consider the near future and what he could do to change it.

They would need a place to hide for the night, he'd have to call in a favor. He didn't want to as that would drag another innocent into something not their business, and he had no idea how big or ugly it could get. Evan was a man who took care of his own, his own problems, his own friends and, especially, family. Last thing he wanted was to bring trouble down on another's head, and maybe he didn't have to.

He knew of a cabin couple few miles outside of town, up towards the foothills, nobody would be there this time of year. They could be there in no time if she didn't mind changing and riding on his back. Them otters was pretty nimble folk and had claws could hold tight. And he knew where the key was buried. No favor, no involvement, no one the wiser.

They stoked a small fire for light and comfort while checking the cabinets for a little grub. The run up here had put the hunger down in his belly. Beans, spam and a couple M.R.E.'s. It helped to know folks who served.

"This place will do for tonight, safe, but I have got to get some help, see if we can find anyone who knows anything about this whole mess," he was tired, annoyed, and feeling helpless, not his normal state.

"If this is the beginning of a war within the people, why hasn't the Mother stepped in to put it right?" it was good question. One neither of them had an answer for.

The morning was chill, though neither of the cabin occupants noticed, it would take a deeper cold to get through their coats. The eastern sky filled with pink, rose and gold, the mountains still dark to the west. Sparrow sang in the pines. Their scent strong, mixing with the fresh dark earth of the foothills. If sparrow knew they were there, so did others, it was time to head back into town, see the lay of the land.

If he expected the sheriff to have arrived in the nick of time and save the ranch, he was disappointed. It hadn't been burned to the ground or ransacked, but they'd done damage. All the windows were broken, the flower beds trampled—She'd dug those out on Her hands and knees with him turning the spade to help. It had been their first major project together when they'd just moved in. She loved the garden, hell they'd been just kids themselves—and the swing was pulled down. They'd yanked the anchor bolts right out of the ceiling and busted it up. Weren't much more than kindling.

He felt his blood rise, tasted it in his mouth, his thinking got cloudy, all he could see was retribution. He felt Suzette's hand on his shoulder, he turned to tell her to back off, 'til he saw the tears running down her cheeks. She stood in shock. This all was done of mean, there was no reason involved, just pure hate. She had never witnessed anything like this, and she had lived a long, long time.

That was the thing about immortality, she thought, you saw it all, or thought you had. The People hadn't ever acted out of pure malice. Oh, Coyote or Raven would play their tricks, somebody'd get ticked, there'd be a tussle, a bloody nose or lip, maybe a limp for a few days, but Mother would step in and smooth over the rough. Not this, this was a message, an ugly, horrid message. They had to find who was behind this and bring it to an end.

Evan took her in his arms, holding her close, didn't know why, just seemed the right thing. She'd been to this house twice in her forever, yet here she stood weeping over things she'd only had a passing familiarity. She was a good person.

"Let's see if we can find the sheriff," Evan gave her one more hug and a pat of thanks on the back, "try catch him away from the station so we can talk turkey. Let's see if he knows any more today than he did before."

"Do you think..." she began.

"I don't think nothing right now except finding out every little bit of information we can. Then we'll see if we can make a picture or even just a sketch, of what all we are dealing with." He was far less confident than he came across, but he had nothing else. All he knew was ain't nothing you can do with a bag full of empty. He needed facts, information, then they could get to figuring.

Turned out they didn't have to find the sheriff as he was cruisin' slow down the lane checking on the property. They waved him down, he waved them over, and they had a little meet leaning against the back of the car.

"You two want to catch a cup and a bite down 't diner," concern coated the words, he was in protect mode, "Looks like you had a bit of rough night. A hot meal and some stiff caffeine might be just the thing," his eyes finished the question, "I'm buyin'."

"Thanks," Evan's appreciation evident in the want to, "but I think we're all better off with a bit of turf around us where we can see who's listenin' in and who wants to sneak up." He wasn't ordinarily a paranoid individual, but things can change a bear.

"They're all locked up, 'bout eight or ten, depending on who's doin' the counting, all told." The sheriff knew exactly who Evan's concern runs to. "Sorry to say, that kid, the slow one from down at the bar? He was in with them. I never woulda thought it of that one, seemed like a pretty good kid," he was genuine disheartened.

"Well, I think we know why and who turned him," Evan nodded to Suzette, who they now introduced official to the sheriff so he would quit lookin' at her sideways. It wasn't that he was prejudice, 'xactly, just unaccustomed. Humans. "Anyway, could Suzette bail just him out? Don't think it would arouse too much suspicion. Ain't nobody knows her, so they'd not be the wiser," Evan shrugged.

"Maybe true, but she does stand out around here," Sheriff chuckled at his statement of fact. "Problem is if she bails him out, why? Who is she? Why would a black woman, sorry miss," he seemed sincerely repentant that this is the way small town folks can be, but truth is truth, "bail out some white kid she don't know. Too many questions."

"How 'bout Meg?"

"Who's Meg?" Sheriff scratched his head like a dog might. Evan and Suzette share a look then a dismissal.

"Barkeep down 't watering hole where this all started. She seems like a decent sort, likes the kid, bet she'd be all for it."

"Worth a try."

They were all waiting at the bar when Glen got released, knowing he'd come down there as he didn't have no other place to go. Apparently, and conveniently, someone from back east had bought the boarding house he'd been living in and then throwed everybody out, saying they wanted to renovate for their folks or some bullshit. Kid had been shacking up wherever and hanging out with the mountain.

"What's this?" Suspicion, anger, and mistrust collided in a

simmering storm when he saw the welcoming committee.

"Now, just calm down for a second, will ya? Glen, I'm guessing you never hurt nobody in your life, even when they hurt you, ain't that right?" Evan let the sheriff handle this prickly porcupine, sometimes it's best to stay back out of firing range.

Glen gave a surly nod for answer.

"Well, what the hell you doin' bustin' up Mr. Beach's home for? Where you get an idea like that? Sure as hell wasn't yours!" Sheriff ain't accusing, he's sort of excusin', trying to let Glen know they ain't angry, just concerned. It's an old parent trick to get kids to confess.

Glen shuffled feet, eyes flitting like birds caught in a net, almost looked as if he was about to cry, but he held it in. Shame rose in his cheeks, humiliation puddled at his feet. "I'm so sorry," he eked out, words barely fall far enough to hit ground.

"Son, it's OK, well, it's not OK, but sometimes we do things 'cause we feel pressure from others. We feel like we're trapped and can't see a way out 'cept to go along," now it was Evan's turn to sooth. There was no way this young man could be that deep into whatever this was, them fellas hadn't had to time to really make him believe. If nothing else came out of all this, they would save him. "You ain't a bad man," the word used purposefully, "you just done a bad thing."

"I don't know why, I never done nothin' like that. We were havin' beers and talkin' 'bout stuff. They was treatin' me like I was one o' their own. Like I wasn't stupid or slow, I was one of them. I was strong and smart, they told me, they razzed me just like they did each other," now the tears came, "they said I was one of them!" he moaned as realization crashed hard.

Truth sometimes ain't the kindest. His next thought was interrupted by a sound from off in the distance. Glen shot out the backdoor. Evan and the rest following on his footsteps caught him as he stood on the small smoker's deck, head down in concentration, waiting.

Glen's head shot up as he heard the second call, a gurgling groan rising to a whistle from some trees nearby off a side street. He searched the trees trying to see what made the noise.

Interesting, thought Evan, never seen nobody react to Raven like that before, maybe the kid was a birder, who could tell?

Then as if it weren't out of the ordinary in the slightest Glen started to having some kind of spasmodic seizure. He leaned his head back a bit and wrinkled his nose, as if smelling something on the breeze, his ears twitched, and shoulders and arms begin jerking. Almost like he was, nah, stop it Evan shouted inside his head, yer seeing People where only humans exist. Though when he gazed over at Suzette, she had the strangest expression on her face as she witnessed the same before shaking it from her head. Their eyes met questioning before dismissing. They'd know and they didn't.

"Them's just mean and nasty men," Evan had all he could do to keep hisself concentrating while steering the attention back to the issue at hand rather than the birds in the trees. The fact that someone would use this kid like this, knowin' they was going to throw him away when it was all said and done, just wasn't right. "I'll tell you what, you wanna make it up to me, wanna make it right?" He put his hands on Glen's shoulders to try and focus the kid on him, not the damn bird. Apparently, he had the attention span of a Labrador retriever.

The sheriff leaned in a little closer wanting to monitor this and shut it down if he didn't like the direction. Evan met him eye to eye to reassure.

"Here's what you're gonna do. I hear tell you ain't got no place to stay, they took away your roomin' house, right?" his hand remained layin' gentle on Glen's shoulder, who nodded at the truth. "Well, sheriff's gonna take you to collect yer stuff and bring you back to my place. I got a room in the back, with its own bathroom and everything, and you're going to move in with me. You can live there free if'n you help me repair all the damage done the other night. We'll work on it together when you ain't workin' at the bar."

"What am I going to do when them fellas show up again? Or catch me on the street?" fear oozed, he didn't want any trouble from the gang, he'd been beat up enough in his life.

"Well, guess I could take you to work and pick you up, if I can get the pick-up running," he shook Glen's shoulder in a companion way, "and Meg won't let them bother you while you're at her place. Sound like it might work?"

The sheriff gave his vote of approval, Suzette smiled hers. If they could protect Glen physically and spiritually, maybe this would be one that whoever was pulling strings wouldn't get.

And The Wheel Turns

∞

Glen didn't have much more than a backpack and a box, but it was his. His folks were poorly educated, poorly trained, poor people with not a clue how to raise a child with learning disabilities, especially one they had adopted almost off the street. But they had done the best they could with love and caring. They had barely surpassed his development with their own. Children raising children with no preparation or solid basis to build upon. The failures of his life were apparently brought about by genetics and poverty. One tough lifecycle.

Now he found himself ensconced in a beautiful craftsman home with his own bathroom. It was like a palace. His own room, not sharing it with several others who he had no connection to. They wasn't family, friends, or acquaintances, just guys. Guys who would mock him for his slowness of thought, for his goofy grin, who would pound him and steal from him. Not here, nope, this was his!

Well, it was Mr. Beach's, but he had promised Glen he could use it long as he needed, maybe forever. How could he have hated Mr. Beach? Them other fellas, he thought they was his friends, but they wasn't, they just used him. Like all the rest. Well, not ALL the rest, Mr. Beach, Miss Suzette, and the Sheriff didn't want nothin' from him but for him to be happy.

"Dinner!" came the call from the back patio.

There stood Mr. Beach with a goofy apron on, cooking burgers and veggies on the grill. It was like a something off one of them TV shows he'd catch when nobody else was watching in the boarding house. Like Little House on the Prairie or something.

They'd fixed a bunch of the windows, there wasn't nothing Mr. Beach couldn't do, or so it seemed. Glen had helped pick up every piece of the swing. They did it with reverence like it was sacred. Mis Suzette told him it was 'cause that was where Mr. And Mrs. used to sit together. Man, that hit right to Glen's heart, damn near cried pickin' up them pieces, but said a little prayer to whoever with each piece.

"Tomorrow we commence to painting the porch and front of the house," proclaimed the lord of the house, "Once we see how well the colors match, we'll make decisions about the rest from there."

Nobody'd seen any of the crowd from the other night, not down 't the bar nor cruisin' by the house. Shit, from what the sheriff said, nobody in town'd seen hide nor hair since they got bailed and set free. Maybe the night in jail and the warning from the sheriff had done some good. And maybe chickens would fly to El Paso. One thing Evan knew was you couldn't change somebody who didn't desire changing. If they thought they was alright the way they was, they would be stubborn mules when it came to being something else. Them fellas was bent on causing strife to him, and anybody dumb enough to hang around him for more than a pass.

"Here's the burgers, veggies, there's chips in the bag, plates on the table, help yourselves," Evan instructed both the others as he took off the dumb apron, 'Still gotta eat'. And so, life went on for a while.

He picked up Glen at four o'clock behind the tavern in his old pick-up. It was beat to hell, but the tires were good, and it ran like it was off the showroom floor. Though that showroom was a thousand miles and fifty years north of here. Empty prairie now.

It was a short drive from the bar to home, but he was wary, things been too normal last few days. No sightings of any of The People, no problems with humans, hell, the sheriff hadn't even stopped by to see how things fared. Maybe he should swing by and see how the sheriff was doing.

"Going to take minute to pay a neighborly visit to our local constabulary," Mr. Beach spoke as he turned down the street the jail sat on.

Glen appreciated that Mr. Beach didn't talk down to him. He used words Glen might have to look up later that day, but he'd remember them and dutiful look them up. He knew these adults wanted to challenge him, to make him learn, he wasn't going to let them down.

The sheriff's department looked like it'd been abandoned years ago. Windows were shattered, the door wide open, car's tires were slashed. How could something like this happen and nobody said a damn thing about it? Certainly, someone would've mentioned it down at the bar. Apparently, this was a recent occurrence. Evan glanced over to Glen who sat with a horrified expression on his face. He looked at Evan and shook his head. He was surprised as all get out.

They pulled up in front, Evan turned off the engine, shoved the keys in his pocket. Slow and easy, careful they slipped through the open door. The place was a mess, papers thrown all over, desks knocked over, and, shit, the gun racks were empty. That wasn't good.

They searched each room, there were only four counting the front room and jail and a couple offices, and a locked room in the back. Evan tried the knob, nope. And there were several deadbolts running up the side looked to be locked. Whatever was in there the sheriff didn't want nobody getting it. Evan punched the door in exasperation, shit, where were the deputies and sheriff?

They turned to leave when his sharp hearing caught the sound of shoe scrap behind that door. Someone was locked in there and he had to guess from the looks of door, they had done it on purpose.

He banged hard with is fist on the door, "Let's see if we get any response, before we try and bust it down," he told Glen, signaling for him to be absolutely quiet.

Again, shoe on floor, right behind the door, as if whoever was in there was bracing themselves against the door.

"Anybody in there?" Evan spoke close to the door not wanting to shout.

"That you Beach?" came the familiar voice shouting back. The sheriff obviously was reticent about bringing attention to his hidey hole.

Reinforcements had arrived and relief filled his voice. The sound of dead-bolts being pulled back like church bells ringing freedom.

"I never been so glad to see anybody, like I am right now," the sheriff admitted as they sat in the midst of destruction.

"What the hell happened?"

"Your buddy came back to leave a review on the lodging and amenities, apparently he wasn't satisfied," he took a sip off the proffered bottle liberated from the evidence room. "Kinda caught us off guard, I guess, but who woulda thunk they'd attack the damn jail? I mean, really, who in this day and age would actually attack the law?" he seemed less steamed someone had come after him than the fact they had attacked what he stood for. It offended his sensibilities. Evan almost laughed, almost. "I'll tell you what, that is one mean sonofabitch you pissed off. And now he's got a bug up his ass for me!" Infuriation filled very syllable.

"Well, you're alright and the deputies don't seem too much worse for wear," Evan handed the bottle over to the two large men sitting on the desk.

"Yeah, these two, but Jack joined up with them, ain't that a bitch. Lucky these two lunkheads noticed what was going on right away," he tossed them an appreciative thankful nod to take any sting out, "They pushed everybody out, slammed the door, hollered back at me and we grabbed anything worth takin' and hightailed to the safe room. Ain't no way they was going to get in there 'less they had a bulldozer or dynamite!" at this he could finally release a laugh and relax. "We shoved all the guns and ammo we could carry, laptops, whatever, it was still pretty close." He took another hit from the bottle and stood, looked to the two remaining deputies, "Gentlemen, we got work to do."

As Evan and Glen drove to the house, he prayed that Otter hadn't come by while they were out, interrupting any wanton destruction. He had no doubt they would harm her if they found her there. She was his friend, and she wasn't the right color. That was one deadly combination in a situation like this. This was as close to out of hand as he was going to allow. One of The People had declared war, only they neglected to inform the other party, him! And the other party was now pissed off.

Suzette did not like the course her thoughts were following as she floated on her back down the river. She hit the bend climbed out and scurried back up to the drop in point and dove. This was where she did her thinking, though now her thoughts just seemed to be following her route round and round in circles.

She'd been sent to observe, that was her job. They'd had their gathering; most all had come. Not Bear, but he hadn't been invited, now had he? And a few others, the usual suspects, Buzzard, Raven, Coyote, never showed. When asked about it by others they all claimed they had forgot, you know, what with their busy schedules and such. What a surprise! Hell, even some of the eastern spirit animals and water had come. Dolphin, Whale, Panther, had traveled far but they knew this involved them as well. Buffalo, Owl, Eagle, this had been a powerful meet, one for the ages.

They all knew why, an imbalance in the energy, the Great Spirit hated imbalances, the world had been created to be in perfect harmony, it wasn't now. It had begun when Bear had met what was to be his mate. The Great Spirit allowed the meeting thinking they would feel the wrong of it and go about their lives. Either they were blind, or something was interfering, they not only didn't feel the wrong but fell deeply in love. This could not be.

Mating like that had occurred in the past, the way far past, they all agreed but not this intense, this genuine. It could not last. It never had, not for more than a few trips around the sun. This was different, this did not diminish, he did not tire of her. She bore his cubs! That was an abhorrent abnormality, it should not have been possible. If they had not been still born, they should not have survived long. The genetic make-up should have been incompatible, yet they lived. It would seem Bear's seed had transformed, against nature, against the Mother, and the cubs were human. Still the Great Spirit slept, not rousing to put an end to this travesty. Somebody was missing something very important, either the people were, the Mother was, or the unthinkable, The Great spirit was.

The Mother continued her journey and, even though all the people could feel the wrong of this, nothing untoward occurred. It was like an itch you just couldn't reach, if it lasted long enough you got used to it and ignored.

Until Bear's mate died. All had forgotten this possibility, they had all grown so used to the coupling, it had the sense of permanence. If they all had thought the original mating had put the balance in a tailspin her death had broken the equilibrium all together. There was a huge crack in the balance. Those who were prone for mischief had all restraints severed. They were free to create havoc.

Bear was the focal point, as long as he was out of kilter so would the world be. All kinds of disruptions could occur. Humans would have no need to justify, no reason why they did what maliciousness they did or followed those with evil intent, but follow they would. Cursing, threatening, and attacking those who stood in their way. Worshipping lie for fact, false belief for truth, arrogance for empathy. They could justify all deeds as being for the benefit of the whole. If old people, the sick and frail died it was because they were infirm and were a drag on the health of all. They were a cancer that needed to be removed or the whole of humanity would suffer. Sacrifice the few for the many.

It went against all claimed they held dear, their morals, ethics, the purity of spirit, yet they never seemed to notice; thought the opposite, matter of fact.

Buffalo spoke. That, in and of itself, was breathtaking, he may not be as plentiful, as powerful as in his younger days, he was still imposing, and his words carried weight. Eagle and Owl spoke of what they had seen from the sky, others spoke of what they had observed living as close to the humans as they did. Then Whale, Dolphin, Salmon and Trout spoke. They told of horrors in their homes, the filth floating and polluting, still borns, and their children suiciding on beaches all over the world. Most at the gather had never heard these tales nor seen these cousins and were horrified at these stories of sickness and death.

The People needed someone who would not be noticed, who could slip in and out of sight whether land or water to go factfinding. They had all stared at her, she raised her paw, and it was done.

Now, here she was, running and swimming in circles trying to make heads, tails, or fins out of all she had seen, heard, or been told by reliable sources. She had to keep her feelings for Bear separate, for she had come to admire, respect and like him on a level she would not have thought possible. Everyone respected Bear, he was honest, strong, fast, didn't bother anyone who didn't bother him. He didn't eat those smaller and weaker. He was wise. He could be terrible, but made the decision not to, unless pushed too far.

He was being pushed too far, while still carrying the pain, the crushing loneliness, the wound that would not heal. He missed his woman as none of the people had ever missed a mate. He would not care if he finally died, what was immortality but infinite pain and suffering without Her. Even Otter now capitalized in her thoughts how Bear thought about his woman.

They had to discover who was causing the strife. Who had maybe joined forces though they knew better? Why had Raven, Buzzard, Snake not come to the gathering? She knew what Coyote told Bear, but could he be trusted? He was the Trickster, known for his lies and deceptions. She agreed with Bear, Coyote had never purposely hurt another of the People, nor had he harmed humans, but had all that changed? Too many questions and no one to talk it over with, no one with the wisdom, the intelligence to work it all out!

She was just Otter, one of the higher figures on the Totem. But there was no one she could trust enough to bring her worries to. According to what had been said at the meet, anyone could be infected by the crack in the balance, maybe whoever had done all these horrors didn't even know they were doing wrong. Maybe they were like the humans that had followed the false profits and believed they were doing what was right for all, unable to see the destruction they caused. The river was not helping, she should head back to town, find Bear, and tell him all. She had not been completely forthcoming.

Evan and Glen were securing the house when Suzette strolled down the sidewalk. Her look pensive and frightened. Evan attributed that to the insanity and danger swirling around the town. As infuriated by this transgression on his oasis of peace he thought he had built his main concern was the safety of those he now cared about the most. His new burgeoning family.

The children She had born, and they had raised, were well-away from here. The boy long in his grave. The girls and grandkids would have no knowledge of this until it was finished. He feared if they knew they would come running to help, not understanding. Well, the young one would. She loved him above all the rest, she was his anchor to Her; the rest, who knew? They had separated from him by miles, communication, and life. No, they would never understand. Hell, he didn't understand, and he seemed to be the nexus of the whole damn thing.

"Are you alright," he asked seeing the mix of emotions playing across her face.

"No, and neither are you," she took his arm to move him where they could talk and halted. His arm was like steel, the muscle of a young man, not the old man everyone saw. Speaking of which his hair had turned from white to brown with silver highlights, his wrinkled brow less so. A trick of the afternoon light and shadow. "We need to talk."

They sat in the cool shade of the backyard as she briefly skimmed over all she had not divulged to him previous. There was no need nor time for detail, just the facts.

"Hmm," he was pensive, if she thought he would be angry with her, she was mistaken, at least for now. "Really, what we had already determined," he went over again what she had told him. "Though I don't see what my wife's death would have to do with any of this. For one that was almost a decade ago, why would that suddenly trigger whatever this is? It makes no sense."

"Does it have to? What is time in comparison to eternity?" she asked with a smirk, though she found little humor in their predicament. "I don't know, maybe you loved her too much. And maybe a decade is a yawn to the universe, and it just happened to catch up."

"How? How can you love anyone too much?" he began, she stopped his train of thought with a staying hand on his arm, a faraway look.

"I'm not saying her death caused the mêlée we are in the midst of, but it might have caused the 'crack' in the balance." She grabbed the thread dangling on a thought and pulled it close, "Hear me out, what if your love for her was so great," at this he nodded somberly acknowledging the truth of her words, "that when She passed and your heart broke, you being who you are, caused the break. You are one of the strongest of the First People, the Guardian of the People, your strength, both physical and spiritual is renowned," she did not glorify, and he did not bask, what was, was, "and your heart was broken. It didn't just break it shattered. What if the force of that was enough to affect the congruence of spirits?"

Evan was not completely buying into this, though he had to admit when She'd passed, he lost himself in the pain and agony. He had wanted to strike out at the Great Spirit, to make him feel the suffering Bear was feeling. Bear had done all any had ever asked, he had stood guard, he had fought great battles to protect The People. He had done all he could to keep humans from overrunning the habitat. He had stood like a wall of will against the invasion, a solitary creature. He had never asked for anything in return.

Then She came, and he asked. He knew from the moment he saw Her it was wrong, it was against nature and the balance, but he begged just for one human lifetime of joy. And it seemed to have been granted, until She was taken. He had prostrated hisself before the universe, pleaded, promised, to no avail. She died.

He knew She would. Her lifespan was not his. He hadn't asked for forever, he just wanted that moment, that one human lifetime. And it had been cut short. He wanted to grow old with his woman, allowing his physical form to mimic her own. His hair to whiten, his muscles to atrophy so She would never know.

Yes, he had loved Her.

"I never shirked my duties, I always watched over The People," he plead his case to Suzette, to the spirits, to all, "She never asked where I went or what I did. She knew I had an affinity for the mountains, a love for nature," he smiled for his love of The Mother, "She accepted the fact that from time to time I had to be alone, in my mountains."

"She never asked why you would be gone? Wouldn't she wonder why you would be gone for such extended periods of time?" Suzette, caught up in his love and story, wished to taste just a bite of what he had known.

"Time, as you know, is different for us. I could be gone for years to us but a week to Her. Or be gone an afternoon to us and a month to her. We do not have clocks, humans do, we have lived forever, what is time to such as we?" His demeanor grew somber. "But time catches up to us."

"Events catch up, time passes," she squeezed his forearm as Glen came to find them.

"Hey Miss Suzette, didn't know you was here," Glen was overjoyed to see her, his face lit up like Christmas morn. It always did, whether she'd been gone for five minutes or five days. He was always so happy, well, unless somebody beat him into submission or made him believe he had done wrong. She would like to get her pound of flesh from those bastards.

"Snuck in the backdoor 'fore you could see me, like I'm a ninja," back in the parlance of the locality. He giggled, the proper response.

"Hey, Mr. Beach,"

"Evan," corrected Evan.

"Sorry, my ma always taught me to show respect for my elders."

"I know, but I told you if you wish to show respect, then respect my wishes on this. You call me Mr. I sound old," he punched Glen in the arm to show they was friends.

"Where's that dog?" his eyes took in the whole of backyard, the side yard, the empty yard.

"I don't have no dog, ain't got the time to care for one, or didn't," he considers. Dog might be good for the kid to have.

"Strange," says Glen with a confused expression runnin' rampant on his features, "I got up in the middle of the night, couldn't sleep, thought I'd go out on the front porch and set a spell. Yer door was open, I glanced in and there was a big, ol' dog laying on yer bed. Big as all outdoors and furry," he held his arms outstretched to give some proportion to the size. "I thought he might of et you since I didn't see you in there," he grinned at his funny.

Evan peered over at Suzette who stood stock still with a shocked expression. She caught his eye and shook her head; she had no idea.

"Probably just the way the shadows lay, with me wrapped in my brown blanket," he stuttered through the falsehood. "Do me a favor and grab the tools from out front and bring 'em 'round so we can fortify the windows and door back here." The kid took off at a clip.

"There's no way he saw what he thinks he saw, 'cause they can't see. And even if they could, they wouldn't believe it, their minds wouldn't accept. It would mean magic, real magic to their way of thinkin' was possible. And they know that ain't conceivable," he spoke in a forced whisper, urgent, trying to figure this kid. He stared at the spot Glen had occupied just moments before, something happenin' here.

"He sounded positive to me, maybe others can't see, but I think that kid is special. There is just something about him that strikes at the heart," she looked at him for confirmation.

"I told you he was an innocent, pure, in his way, maybe that was why he was so easy turned by them fellas. He trusts everybody. Sure hate to take that away from him, but don't see where as we got much choice," she marveled at the way he could slide in and out of the local dialect. Bears had instinct; they had a way to preserve in just about any circumstance. He was a survivor. They had picked the wrong spirit to start shit with.

"Sheriff's here," Glen set the tools next to the bars they would install on the windows and door.

"Looks like you been doin' some home renovation," the sheriff said as he came 'round the corner of the house and took in the rebar laying on the ground and steel plates leaning against the house.

"None that I wanted to," Evan stuck out his hand to shake the other's.

"Look, I want you to know that we are on the same team here," the sheriff locked eyes with Evan, "I think you know more than what you been tellin' me and I sure would like to know what you're leavin' out."

"You wouldn't, no, you couldn't believe what I would tell you," Evan wished he could bring this good man into the circle, tell him all that was at stake and who was involved, but if he did, the sheriff would walk away and never look back, can't support a lunatic. Hell, he might even lock up Evan for his own good.

"Try me."

Evan thought hard, considering all ramifications, upsides and down, should he take the chance. The sheriff was one of the best folks he'd met, trusting, and not stuck in his ways, but this was so far outside what he could conceive. Shit, in for a penny...

"You sure you want me to try you? You're going to think I am out of my mind, probably lock me up for my own good," he confessed mirroring his own thoughts.

The sheriff crossed his arms and nodded.

"You've lived in this area long time?" Evan asked, though he knew the answer, he had known the sheriff's folks and family for generations, though they wouldn't have ever put past and present together.

"Five generations," was the proud reply.

"You know a lot of first nation folks?" let's ease into this and see what all has to be explained and what might be known.

"Yeah, I've known my share," cautious.

"Well?"

"Well enough," impatience was leaking through the cracks.

"Just bear with me, I need to know where to hop in," both hands up asking for patience. "Did they ever tell you their stories, their beliefs and myths of creation? Where all of this," indicating the whole of the world, "came from?"

"You mean, Coyote, Buffalo, Rabbit, the Great Spirit, yeah, the animal spirits. Mitakuye Oyasin, yeah, we talked about it plenty. What's that got to do with all this?" He'd had friends growing up who talked about this stuff. When he'd hang out with them at the Rez, their grandparents would burn sweet grass, smoke the pipe, and tell stories of the birthing of the world and the First People. What they called the original inhabitants, the animal guides.

"It has everything to do with this, they're not just stories or myths. And this happens to be the epicenter of a feud that, apparently, I am the focus of," he was weary, forever had worn him down. "I am the Spirit guide Bear." There was a brief shimmering where he stood then all solidified again.

The sheriff rubbed his eyes, clearing his vision and what he thought he'd seen. He was either going nuts, a definite possibility after what they had been going through lately, or this guy was using some kind of hypnosis on him. All he knew was, he couldn't have seen what he thought he just seen. He was a man who accepted what couldn't be refuted, but he knew there was a perfectly plausible explanation for what was happening here. He just wasn't ready to accept this one, not yet.

"Well, I'll tell you what, you're right about one thing, I sure as hell don't know what to believe, but this I do know, you are definitely the center point of all that is happening in my town. So, no matter what this entails, gangs, spirits, myths, whatever, I won't let you stand alone, just ain't how we do things," he took a deep breath, more of hard sigh, "me and my two deputies are in with you, what do you need?"

"I appreciate it, sheriff, but I ain't exactly sure yet, 'cause I ain't exactly certain what 'it' is. Even went up deep in the mountains to think and have a look around," Evan scratched his head, then his chin. "What I need right now? A beer, you?"

Glen didn't need the askin', he scooted into the house grabbed beers and was back before Even could've got the askin' out.

"You hunt?" the sheriff shot over the top of his bottle.

"Not really, just like being up in the mountains alone. I wander around, smell the clean earth, the crisp air, the freedom of no people. Sleeping out under the stars, you can hear every critter in the world up there, can feel the Mother breathe," a beatific grin lit his face, "who wants to take gun up into that? Ain't a place for killing unless absolutely necessary, and that's seldom." He took a long draught of his own bottle in thought.

"Not really safe up there without no protection, should at least have a sidearm, case some wild animal takes offense at you stumblin' into their happy hunting grounds," The sheriff's words came from experience, "I got this by stumblin' in on someone didn't want to be disturbed." He pulled up his shirt to show where he had been torn stem to stern, shoulder to buttocks. It was cougar claws what done that, Evan didn't have to ask. "Lucky the fella I was with was a medic in the war. Patched me up and carried me down, got me to a medical team just before my last breath." He took a breath to remember and a pull to forget. "You ought be careful up in them mountains, they'll kill you."

"Nah, me and them mountains, and all who live there, get along just fine. I ain't carried a gun since the last war I fought in, and don't intend to ever carry one again," conviction filled each syllable.

"How many wars you been in?"

"Three, that are worth mentioning." Flat and cold as death.

"Three? Why three?"

"'Cause I didn't believe the first two," he barked a laugh, took a toke, shouldn't've with the sheriff right there, but when in Rome, he passed it over. The sheriff knew he shouldn't, but what the hell, with everything he was living, and stories being told, why not. He took a hit. "I didn't believe mankind could be that cruel. I heard the stories, the tales, the bragging, and the truth. Like when you heard tales of the animal spirits and such. You don't trust the tellin' 'til you witness it with your own eyes. Well, I did, still didn't believe the cruelty. Lived it a second time and thought it just had to be the wrong wars. Where was all the glory? Ain't no glory shivering in a shallow hole in the ground surrounded by body parts and screams. Somebody just waiting for you to scratch your ass so they can blow your head off. Where is the honor of that?" He spit and nodded to Glen, who'd been sittin' quiet and still as a rock not wishin' to be sent away.

Glen went to the kitchen to fetch a couple more for those keeping guard and one for the fella what kept guard on the guard. He hadn't a clue what was happening here, but he knew it was important and he was part of it. These fellas didn't treat him like boy, like he was slow and dumb, like he was less than them. Not like them others fellas pretendin', no, here he was one of them, really, one of them. And he was scared to his bones.

"Shit," it was as if the sheriff just woke from a dream, "what about your neighbors? Shouldn't we tell them to scram?"

"It's a pretty quiet street, ain't but a couple of us left on it, guess that's why you and I never had much need for a run in," he grinned, "folks next door got old. He passed, she was pretty bad off with the Alzheimer's.

Kids put her in a place closer to where they was livin' then startin' fightin' 'bout who was going to get what and how much. Now the house sits waitin' for them to let her go. Folks on the other side just moved out one day, somebody told me he lost his job when the plant up the way closed. Bank don't seem in any hurry to fix it or sell it. Not much else left this far out of town, one of the reason's we loved it here so much. Close enough to walk into town, far enough away nobody ever bothered us."

"Until now," said Suzette pulling up a chair to sit between the two men.

"Well, ain't not much has happened thus far, maybe they got their pound and are satisfied," Evans words don't convince them or him, dumb thing to say.

"Quiet for now," said the sheriff, one hand on knee as he eased himself into a standing position and stretched out the evening, "I still got a town to check on and sleep to find or I ain't going to be worth a shit."

"He's a good man," Suzette smiled her approval as he walked away.

It Takes A Village

∞

The pretty woman stood across the street leaning against an ancient oak with clockfaces stuck about eight foot off the ground, each one facing a different direction. The clocks hadn't started out that high, but trees keep growing and the clocks had grown with it and into it. Evan'd put the clocks in the tree so's the kids could never say they didn't know the time. It was the grandfather clock tree, and everybody knew what time it was when they passed down this lane.

She was stunning in her simplicity. Fringe coat, jeans, short-tousled tan hair—who had tan hair? Well-worn chukka boots and a knapsack that hung casual from her left shoulder. She appeared nothing more than a mid-thirties hippie lost in time and not looking to find it. So, it was humorous she chose to lean against that tree. She had the look of someone wandering through a decision, but in no hurry to come out on the other side.

Then, just like that, she shifted the knapsack, pushed off the tree with a rub of her shoulder and walked across the street. Decision made.

Glen had been watching her for the past half hour, mesmerized, standing at the door afraid to move for fear of spooking her. He had no sense of time or care; his one desire was to stand here and take her in.

Suzette watched them both, riveted by his sheer concentration. She was quite certain not a muscle had twitched in his body for the entire time he stood. She found herself fidgeting, unable to maintain the focus of mind or body, it was not in her DNA, calm had deserted her, and his intense concentration wasn't helping find it. She was a creature of motion.

Her attention was torn between the two, Glen at the door and the mystery woman under the clock across the way. There was something, a familiarity. She knew this woman; she had seen her somewhere. As the woman pushed off the tree, wary, eyes darting left, right, head turning almost completely around to see behind and whipping back to check forward, Suzette knew.

As she climbed the four steps to the porch, Suzette swung the door open and held it with one hand while welcoming with the other. "Welcome."

"Were you expecting company?" a lopsided grin. She had white highlights throughout her mop though not from age more from youthful vigor. Large eyes that took in every movement around her and a slight twitch that gave the impression of a flick of the ear. It was comical and wonderfully lovely.

Now, the woman focused on Glen who for all appearances could not seem to contain his excitement. It was all he could do to stand in place, shifting from foot to foot, as if he wanted nothing more than to run up to greet the woman. Suzette had never seen any human being so excited to meet another.

"Yes, but yours would be far more welcome," Suzette held out a hand, "Suzette, and the anxious young man is Glen." She gifted him with the smile of a mother's love. He gifted her with an embarrassed shuffle of the feet.

"Doerean," the lovely woman stated, taking the other's hand before finally shaking hands with Glen and ruffling his hair. Now, he was beet red. "My friends call me Doe."

"Well, leave us hope we can all refer to you as Doe, then," a tinkle of laughter escaped like crystal wind chimes. Though Suzette was noticeably smaller than Doe they could have been bookends of beauty. "You can set that down over by the chair, if you would like, for now," she pointed at the knapsack and the indicated spot. Though the other woman showed no urgency to part with her belongings. Suzette shrugged, no sense pushing.

Doe startled as the back screen door slammed shut followed immediately by heavy footsteps coming through the kitchen. Suzette gently laid her hand on Doe's arm to settle her nerves.

"It's just Evan, he lives here, this is his house," she smiled, "we are guests here as well."

As Evan came into the front room, he was pulled up by the sight of the woman standing near the door. Sunlight poured in through the opening backlighting her. She bore a striking resemblance to Her, but that would be impossible. It would have been Her forty years ago, Her in the prime of life. His breath caught in his throat; he rubbed the dust from his memory to clear the vision. No, it was not Her, this was one of the cousins, another of The People showing up on his doorstep. The question was friend or foe.

"Evan this is..." began Suzette.

"Doe, if I'm not mistaken," he cautiously held out his hand in greeting not wishing to startle the young woman into flight. She was skittish, though relaxed with his manner.

"You're the one," she uttered bluntly, "I thought you'd be older."

"I am, older than my teeth not quite as old as my gums," he grinned stealing a misquote he'd heard a century before. "Well, welcome, I think. Though you may not wish to hang 'round too long once you discover the threat of being here."

"I have come to aid in any way I can," she spoke formally.

Evan was touched, he knew the courage it would take for her to become involved. "I can only offer my thanks," he said in the formal response.

"Well, I can offer food, drink, a place to rest and friendship," Suzette took her by the arm leading her through the house to the back patio and a cool drink.

"What's going on here?" Glen got up the nerve to ask Evan. If he was going to be included in this, whatever it was, he wanted to be included completely, and that meant knowing. There was some kind of weirdness connecting these three. They recognized each other though they'd never met.

"You got every right to know," Evan gently turned Glen around and pushed him towards the rear of the house, "come out back and we'll all talk."

The small group settled around the glass top table, iced tea, water and lemonade poured and sipped. Evan began to fill in Doe, and Glen, with as much as he, or Suzette, knew about the what, why and when. It was sketchy at best and sounded more like a tale or fable from native myths than something taking place in the present. Glen sat silent, not asking questions, not interrupting, but enthralled, wanting to believe every word. Even though it sounded far-fetched, impossible. Just like when Evan had told him he was immortal, it was ridiculous, but had the ring of true.

Evan knew how it would sound to the kid. He knew how it sounded in his own ears, and he had lived it, but if the young man, he corrected hisself, was to be part of this he had to know the whole of it. Whether he believed or not, well, that would come with time and witnessing.

"So," Glen finally seemed to put thoughts into questions into words, "Yer tellin' me that all them stories I heard when I was a kid, them ones about how the world was begun according to Indian legend, they're true?"

"Well, I can't say all of them," Evan hedged, "some tales have taken on a life of their own, got blowed up out of proportion in a thousand years of tellin'. And some got exaggerated by the main characters to make themselves look better'n they should've, but, yeah, I guess most of them." Evan shrugged looking to the other two for confirmation.

"I knew it, I could feel it when I heard them stories 'round the fire, late at night. Everybody always laughed, sayin' they was just myths and tales the Indians told. They wasn't true, just stories about their beliefs and religion, made up stuff. Yet them same folks believed all they read in the Bible, didn't they? And that ain't no different, stories, so if one can be true why not the other?" He beamed, bathing in the knowledge that he had been right all along to believe; all stories could be true, could be based on actual not made up.

That went better than Evan could've hoped. Now, he had to impress on Glen all the danger they were in. And the fact he had no intention of allowing this to become some raging battle. He had seen enough innocents become collateral damage for somebody else's lunacy. He was not going to let that happen here. He couldn't shove all the dangers and possibilities down Glen's throat, but he could explain over time. He hoped they had the time.

They settled into a rhythm over the next several days, tedium became more enemy than physical beings. Evan couldn't determine if they were being lulled into a false security or if the pressure was building and they couldn't sense it. Right at this moment Evan didn't much care.

He found he enjoyed having these folks around, it was nice for the company, though a bit crowding on the psyche after being alone for so long. Even when She was alive, they led a pretty solitary existence, they enjoyed it that way.

The kids had been gone for a long time, they visited couple times a year, but their visits dissipated with each year after She died. Guess he weren't too good of company since She'd been gone. They had kids and lives of their own. The young girl and her family way out on the east coast—Maryland, he thought—and the elder sis still finding her way after all these years. Though the granddaughter still visited regular since they only lived the other side of town. Some folks took time to figure out who they was, she was a project in progress.

Doe and Suzette had taken up residence in the house the old folks had vacated. Nobody had ever thought to try the door, Doe found it unlocked and the insides dusty but untouched. If Evan had any doubts about the target of the attack this put them to rest. It was in pristine condition. They did a little spring cleaning, and it was livable. Had this been six months ago the fact that it had been open and untouched for as long as it had would not have surprised Evan in the least, it was that kind of town. Until now.

Suzette's thoughts rang in his ears as he sipped his beer on the back porch and looked out over creation wondering. One of The People had decided to take advantage of the crack in the balance. Who? There were People who were known for mischief, causing a disruption in the peaceful co-existence of all, but it was never malevolent. College pranks just to get under the skin for a good story, a reason to drink and laugh. Something to break the monotony. Nothing like this.

The sheriff came 'round the corner of the house, as was his want, pushing Ev's train of thought off the tracks.

"Ya-hey, where's the uniform?" Evan affected shock, though he didn't think he'd ever seen the sheriff out of official attire.

"Just dropping by to check on the boredom brigade," he chuckled shaking Ev's hand. They had all taken to calling him Ev, though he preferred Evan, they didn't seem to care. "You sure all this isn't going to blow over? It's been over a week since anybody has done anything. I haven't seen any of them near town. If their smart they'll stay away!" He rubbed his arm where, a week earlier he'd had to battle for his life in his own damn jail, it still bore the deep bruise where that ass had slammed him with the two by four. His mood darkened for a second before he came out. "Though I will tell you, either you got an admirer or a spy keeping watch on the comings and goings here," he turned his head towards the front of the house.

"Well, let's go have a look," Ev stood up.

"I'd'a asked him what he was doin' out there, but not really here in an official capacity, and, well," he shrugged, "he ain't doin' much but leanin' against that grandfather tree." Things were happening his mind couldn't quite wrap itself around. What with folks coming and going who just didn't quite fit in this man's world. Sometimes it's best to leave the doin' to the experts, just be back-up.

Evan eased up to the corner of the house to have hisself a little peek, no sense rushin' blind into this. He saw a large biker lookin' fella leaning up against that oak right under the clock facing the house. Tree ain't had that kind of attention since the kids outgrew dating, he smirked to hisself. He'd still left the clocks as reminder. He reminded Evan of one of the older girl's old boyfriends, tough guy, but not tough enough to be responsible. This fella was all leather jacket with matching chaps, jeans, black boots, dark grey hair, and beard down to mid-chest. Not doin' nothin' but starin' at the front of the house. One way to find out what he wanted.

"You lookin' to stare this house down or buy it?" asked Evan as he sauntered across the street, sheriff at his shoulder.

The fella took in the sheriff and immediately disregarded him focusing his attention on Evan. They both sized up the other, both deciding talk would be best.

"Is it for sale?" He feigned interest, though just.

"Never." The word did not convey 'for the foreseeable future', but what he meant, forever.

Evan caught the scent, wolf, curiouser and curiouser. He hadn't never had a run in with Wolf, each one of them kept to their own territory for the most part. And if one did wander into the other, they tended to steer clear. Respect.

"Just restin' a spell 'fore comin' over to say hello," he smiled, it was genuine and meant to assure he wasn't here to kick up dust.

"Well, I got cold beer in the back, if you're of a mind," Evan turned his back on the fella to walk back across the street. Trust.

"I got a bottle," said the Wolf pulling his hand out from inside his jacket. The sheriff visibly relaxed, taking his hand from the handle of the pistol tucked into the back of his jeans, happy to see bourbon not weapon. You never could tell.

The embers of the dying fire glowed red and yellow in the dark, flames leaping to life briefly before running out of fuel. The six sat on camp stools or the ground, conversation had settled down with the fire.

The Wolf, Sung, had answered the summons, sensed the tear, and though preferring solitary endeavors, knew he had to come. He was friendly enough, in his own way, though he continually tossed questioning glances in the direction of where the sheriff and Glen sat. Evan couldn't tell if he was bothered by the humans or if there was more.

"Shouldn't somebody be keeping a watch on the front of the house?" asked the sheriff shifting into lawman mode. "I mean, I know it's been quiet, and good Lord willin' will remain so, but wishing is just that. Wherever them fellas went off to they're gonna come back, bet on it."

Evan glanced over where Glen was fidgeting on his stool, clasping, and unclasping his hands, dancing in place. There was something weighing on the young man, but Evan didn't want to push.

"Nah, now that we know the threat is there, we'll be able to recognize a change in the energy should they come close," he wished he felt more confident. Yet he knew that if whoever had started this war was near, they would have the capability to hide their movement until they were right on top of this little band. His hope was, with them all concentrated in this small area one of them would sense the danger beforehand.

"How are you gonna 'feel it'?" People in law tended not to believe anything they couldn't see, touch, or knock down. They had listened to the rantings of too many nuts screaming their innocence because they was possessed by demons. They didn't do nothin' it was the space aliens that forced them to do whatever they'd not done, as they sat behind bars feeling the vibration of evil.

"It comes down to being in tune with life," Sung spoke quiet as if afraid that the sound of his voice would disturb the vibrations most of them could feel. "With the energy that connects us all."

"And all you folks are in tune?" Sheriff wasn't exactly scoffing, but he wasn't near convinced. His gaze took in all seated around him, they wasn't scoffing either, they believed.

"It comes with the turf of being an immortal," It was the first contribution to the evening Doe had tossed.

"OK, now I know you're all just having fun at me and Glen's expense," he pointedly included the young man in his mild accusation.

"Tell you what, sheriff," though Evan spoke to the man directly, his eyes took in the three People. Satisfied with their silent assent, "You want to see for yourself what we have been trying to explain?"

Well, now that put him in a bit of pickle, didn't it? If he said no, he would regret it for the rest of his life. And he would lose the trust and confidence of these folks. Question was, what did Evan have in mind?

"What exactly are you proposing?"

"You and me, I take you to the other side of reality," Evan stated simply.

"This isn't going to involve drugs or anything, is it? I'm still a law-man and I ain't breaking what I'm sworn to uphold," he said matter of fact. "Little toke the other night notwithstanding." There's laws and there's dumb laws. He didn't get to pick and choose, but enforcement was a bit of a grey area.

"Nope. Just the two of us stepping over, do a little wandering, exploring, show you the sights and back again." Like a street hustler trying to sell you on going to see the carnival, "We'll be gone long as you need to convince yourself, but it will only be a few hours here."

The sheriff sat back in his chair, considering, what could possibly go wrong? If they weren't taking drugs to reach this other side of reality, then there was nothin' to fret. And he knew he couldn't be hypnotized as it'd been tried when he was quitting smokin'. He may not know excaly why, but he trusted this fella and was willin' to take this little ride with him.

"Alright, as long there's nothing illegal, yeah, I want to go," he grinned like his dad just handed him the keys to the car. "When?"

"No time like the present," Evan stood and stretched, "Y'all keep an eye on things, if anything don't feel right, you know how to get hold of me."

"We drivin' or walkin?" the sheriff stretched out his own muscles, sittin' too long made him stiff.

"Just goin' over here and seein' where it leads," grinned Evan.

He and the sheriff walked away from the dying embers toward the pitch dark.

Then from behind, "Can I come?"

They turned towards the quiet whispered question. Glen stared into the glowing embers, his face barely illuminated as if afraid to see the rejection before hearing it. Evan took in each of the First People. Suzette eyes spilled compassion as she nodded, yes. Doe shrugged as if to say, 'why not'. Sung was the most thoughtful, he stared at the kid, as he had been all evening, before locking eyes with Evan, a crooked grin twisted his lips. "Yeah, I think you should, might be educational for all involved. We'll hold down the fort."

Glen hopped up from his stool, knocking it over in the process, running over to join the two men before anyone could change their minds. Evan couldn't tell who was more excited, thrilled, or nervous, him or the two humans. Never in his long life had he considered doing anything like this. It wasn't exactly forbidden, and he knew that Coyote, Copperhead, and a few others had done so, but they had done it out of messin' with human's heads, not what he was about tonight.

There was shimmer like a heat wave as they stepped through into twilight. The moon was full here, though only a sliver back home, and they were in mountain forest. Scant undergrowth allowed unimpeded sight lines. Peace reigned throughout the woods; it was hard to imagine that back across the threshold danger camped on Evan's doorstep.

Sheriff John Roberts—yes, he had an actual name, though almost everyone, including his ex and son, referred to him as 'Sheriff'—took in the placid scene. He had spent most of his life coming up into the mountains to hunt, fish, and camp, he knew it as well as any man not 'of' the mountains could. He had no idea where he was. It was wrong, like borrowed clothes, it just didn't 'fit'. The colors were off, more vivid than they should be this time of night. The evening filled with sound, insects, croaking and singing of frog, bird, yips, and howls, he had never heard a forest so full of life. It was as if he could hear the trees and plants conversing with each other. Life didn't just blossom here, it exploded. He took a step back, a deep breath in, turned to ask Evan if this was real. He froze.

The largest grizzly ever to grace the face of the planet stood staring at him. It was ten-foot tall if it was an inch, a thousand pounds of fury and death, stood on hind legs, right paw resting on hip in a pose of patience. Sitting next to the bear was a mutt, tongue lolling out of the mouth, smiling, tail wagging.

The bear turned his head, saw the dog, did a double take, and said, "Well, I'll be." It was Evan's voice, the sheriff was good with voices, he knew. It was impossible to discern who was more shocked as the three stood/sat glancing from one to the other.

"What's the matter?" asked the voice of Glen.

"I didn't know," said the bear gesturing where innate Glen sat.

The dog stood, backing up several steps away from the monstrous bear. Things had certainly changed.

"What the hell?" Said canine Glen.

"Indeed," said the bear.

"Somebody has got some big time explaining to do, and I would suggest it start before I either shit my pants or pass out," Sheriff John gave his all to sound light, humorous, but there was no way to cloak the fear and confusion.

"This is who I am," explained Bear, "those who are sitting around the smoldering campfire back at Fort, same, only they are Deer, Otter and Wolf. We are the First People, the animal spirits that guide, not just our people, but all the inhabitants of this lovely garden." He swept his great paw to encompass all the earth. "We are immortal. We can still experience pain and suffering, joy, empathy, compassion, love, dislike, not hate, we are supposed to be forbidden hate. We do not believe in inherent evil, for instance, just a spirit that is out of whack. A thing that can be set right." He glanced at Glen, his dog face contorted into confusion and anxiety.

Sheriff John nodded his head in acknowledgement but didn't quite trust any of his senses right at the moment. Maybe there had been something in the beer, or the bourbon, but, no, he didn't 'feel' anything out of the ordinary, just seeing things that could not be.

"Why do you keep staring at me?" asked the voice of Glen from the mouth of mutt.

"You don't remember, do you?" The voice of the bear at odds with his appearance, it was gentle, compassionate, understanding. Hadn't he lost hisself in the world of humans for a time. It was that hit of acid that brought back who, and what, he was. "You are Dog. Not one of the First People but of a later generation, and welcome addition." His smile was of gratitude and warmth.

"I'm not a dog, I'm me," Glen said taking inventory. "I'm the same I always been, though the sheriff is right, you, on the other hand, are one big freakin' bear. I don't remember fallin' 'sleep, but I must have 'cause this is one weird damn dream."

"You will never appear different to yourself because what you see is your true self, at your core," he touched paw to head, heart and soul, "but come with me and we'll see if I can show you who the sheriff sees."

All three walked down the mountain where Bear knew there to be a small reflecting pond. He would have to be tender, easing Glen to see, without shocking. As they walked, he could see the sheriff struggling with new concepts and realities. This was a lot to take in in such a short period, but they didn't have the luxury of time. He needed the sheriff to adjust and come to terms. He was a good man, Evan trusted him to assimilate.

"So, what's going on, and why is it happening in Fort? Why my town?" The sheriff had to shake himself physically while they walked.

Speaking of out of whack, here he was talking to a bear that was a man while a dog who was a kid from home was coming to terms with his own readjustment. If this ain't a dream, then he was having a nervous breakdown with hallucinations. Maybe if he concentrated on collating information, the problem at hand, the burgeoning war in his town, maybe he could find some solid ground.

"I'm afraid that would apparently be me. We are categorically not supposed to intermingle with humans. Nudge, send messages, lead, act as guides, but not become physically entangled. There have been instances where Coyote or Raven will use someone for their own purposes but it's rare and usually benign. I broke that rule, smashed it into bits. I committed the ultimate sin, I fell in love," he sighed as a tear rolled down his snout.

"I didn't just fall in love, infatuation, youthful dalliance, I immersed myself in Her soul. We are beings of pure spirit, I never realized what that meant until Her. We merged into one. Physically, mentally, spiritually, we were love. I should have walked away. I couldn't." he stared hard at memories, the breeze kissed his face, he held Her hand. His heart shattered just like it always did when he couldn't keep Her away.

"When she died, I lost control. I was mad at the Great Spirit for letting Her die, at the doctors for letting Her die, at the universe for letting

Her die, at me for living while letting Her die. I am a strong spirit, one of the strongest, truth be told, strong enough that when my heart splintered into a million pieces, I cracked the balance of the Universe allowing what had been unthinkable to become, to coalesce." He stopped for a moment gathering thoughts. "One of the First People has taken advantage of that crack and now is trying to destroy me, you, all of us, to realign the power structure. The evil we don't believe in doesn't care what we believe."

"So, who is behind all this? Why can't we just stop them now before this goes any further?" the way you solve a problem is to eliminate it at the root, every person involved in keeping the peace knew that.

"Well, there is the crux of the issue, we don't know who that is. They haven't shown their hand, they are working through these puppets. That's the trouble with deception, they deceive." Evan's botheration lay heavy on the admission of helplessness, "Not much we can do until we discover who is at the crux or repair the crack."

"Can you do that?" the sheen of hope glistened on each word.

"Not sure," Evan admitted, "but sure am gonna try. Come here Glen, I want to show you something," the Bear led the Dog to where a glistening pool of water reflected the beauty of the forest surrounding it.

Bear knew these woods, they were his home, had been, literally, forever. This was where his peace lay, this was where he came to reclaim hisself when She told him he needed the mountains. She knew, he didn't know how She knew, it was not what he did, but what he was, what his soul craved and what he required for balance. She could sense when he was out of sorts, when he just didn't fit, and She'd send him away. To Her he'd be gone a few days maybe a week, to him it might stretch to a month or six, time was a funny thing. There's human time and there's immortal time. The latter was the better, more malleable.

"Look around, Glen, breathe in life here. Can you scent others nearby? Can ya feel the world around you?" Get in touch with your senses was the silent commend. "Close your eyes, block out everything except what you can smell, what you can taste in the air." He waited.

Glen gave him a suspicious once over 'fore following instructions. Eyes closed, head tilted back, deep, slow breaths. His eyes shot open, pleasant surprise evident by the dropped jaw and look of wonder.

"It's, it's," he searched for words, for a way to describe.

Evan stood patient, knowing, and hoping. The sheriff adrift on the lake of confusion without oar, outboard or clue. There was no point of reference for him to grasp, he could but bear witness to something beyond his comprehension.

"It's like I can 'see' everything around me, but with my nose? Does that make any sense?" How do you describe beauty to blind folks? "I can taste the trees, the dirt, the leaves decaying on the forest floor, scat over there, pee, another bear has been marking this territory." He grinned satisfaction at his analysis. "There's three squirrels in that pine and a honeybee hive hanging in the hollowed-out tree stump. Deer passed through two, three days ago, and, and," the images flooded his mind, sensing with nose rather than eyes, opening up a world he had never known existed. Or had he.

Fear crept into his joy. Why could he all a sudden do these things? What was he, some kind of freak thing?

Deep breaths, Glen told himself, look around you. He tried to focus, tried to grasp a handful of solid, the world is solid, he said over and over in his head. This was still the mountains near the town where he lived in the real world, though it wasn't quite, was it? It wasn't in color, he had failed to notice, it was like somebody stole all the color leaving just black and white. 'Cept when he closed his eyes. Then it was more brilliant than it had ever been. The colors, textures, it was like a sharp 3-D world with his eyes closed. His head swooned, he needed to sit for a minute.

There was a fallen tree trunk next to the small pool, he sat. His head dropped until it was between his knees, breathing in through the nose, out through the mouth, tasting the surroundings, rubbing his temples with his paws. His what?

His eyes once again shot open, and he stared at the reflection of the large dog gaping at him from the surface of the pond. With a gasp, he fainted.

Cold water revived with an assist from gentle shaking and pats on the back. Well, that was weird, Glen had never passed out or fainted in his life, no matter the provocation, (a former word of the day) but the world would soon be in focus, and all would be right again, thought the dog ogling from the pond. Alright, this might take a few minutes.

"Close your eyes, try to remember. How far back do your thoughts go," the bear, resting on his haunches, concern contorting his features, spoke just above a whisper, soothing tones, "how far back in time do you recall? Think of what seems real enough to touch, can you do that?" He pushed gentle, mollifying the obvious fear radiating from the young man.

"I don't know, maybe, I remember Fort, but nothing before it, guess I been there my whole life," Glen was trying but exasperation clouded his mind.

"Do you recollect when you was a boy playing with your friends? Do you recall your teachers at school? Or going on vacations with your ma and pa."

Tears welled up, spilling down his snout into the pond.

"No."

"Do you remember the folks what raised you?" Evan felt fear creeping up his back.

This was going to be tougher than Bear had imagined. It was becoming obvious that some catastrophe or injury, a blow to the head maybe, had induced amnesia. Definitely above his healing skill set, maybe one of the guides back at his house, maybe.

The sheriff found himself a nice boulder overlooking a deep valley and peace, seeking his own place in this parallel world. Knowing how he was clinging to a sense of reality no longer in vogue, weeping like a babe crying for its momma in his own head. He didn't care, he wanted his old reality back. And he wanted it back now!

What Is Reality?

∞

The last embers of the fired glowed red beneath the charred remains of the fire, if only just, not providing illumination nor heat, just a hint of what had been. Suzette thought it appropriate.

"What do you think Bear hopes to accomplish?" she asked the night.

"Who is to know the workings of the mind of Bear?" Doe replied in her best misterioso voice. She attempted spooky but only brought laughter from the other two.

"I think he is trying to impress upon our good sheriff the level of danger involved. That he is now dealing with forces that, up to this point in his life, he would've considered to be myth and insane. He needs to comprehend the unknown nature of what is happening here. Personally, I concur, no matter whether the sheriff comprehends immediately. At the very least, he will have the knowledge lodged in the back of his mind," Sung spoke not taking his eyes from the dying cinders. "What I am most curious about is our young Glen. There is something about him, something that makes it impossible to determine his nature. I know you all believe him of this world," he pointed at the dim glow of the town in the near distance, "But I feel like there is some force shrouding who he is. I fear he may be, and pardon my euphemism, a wolf in virtuous attire. I don't sense danger; I don't sense anything. He is like a blank spot in the world. That concerns me."

"Now that you mention it, there is something to what you say. It's almost as if every time you try to watch the boy, or concentrate on what he might be doing, an energy or pressure pushes your attention away," Doe said realizing what had been standing right in front of her.

"I think you two are reading way too much into this young man," defended the motherly Suzette. "I have been around him longer than both of you and have sensed none of what you are saying." Anger suffused her defense though she couldn't explain why. What a strange reaction.

Like a sign from beyond the pale the last embers extinguish on wisps of smoke, the scent of the burnt wood filled nostrils and eyes, a haze hung over the group. Instead of muddling their vision it cleared. Each gazed at the other with the same thought, Bear is in danger, though none can name it. And worse, can't say whether the danger emanates from here or the other side. Is it happening now or prescient of the future? In the huge oak across the lane a crow called in the darkness. It is wrong, wrong in the bones, wrong in nature, crows don't call when they roost. And this isn't a roost but one lone crow, one lone crow in a tree calling out to someone they can't see or sense. It is a spy.

Sung motioned to the two women they should go arm in arm, like old friends, to the house of the old folks where they are staying. They should talk and laugh, make it known they are turning in for the night. He will creep like the night, stalking the crow, to see if he can hear any response to the call, any motion of predator hoping for surprise. Wolves almost always hunt in packs, not Sung, he is the lone wolf, he is legend. If there is nothing, he will return for the two so they can go to warn Bear.

On wolf's paws he moved from shadow to shadow, his grey-black coat blending into the changing hues. He appeared as nothing more than shifting outlines, bushes blowing in the gentle breeze, shadow in motion, of tree leaves against the ground.

The crow called out again, then to the north maybe a quarter mile distant another, a response, just on the cusp of his hearing. Interesting, they were relaying what the spy was spying. Just then the crow leapt from the branch into the night. With the wolf's keen eye, he could see it against the underbellies of the clouds as it circled the house, the backyard, the neighborhood before disappearing into the dark.

Once assured it had well and truly gone, he trotted across the street and knocked quietly on the rear door of the old folk's house. Doe cracked the door open; he saw Suzette peering around her right shoulder as they both visibly relaxed. The tension almost sparking in the pitch dark.

"I think we need to go find Bear, now!" he growled as they slipped out the door. "Any idea where he would head?"

Realization smacked them immediately between the eyes, all their desire for solitary existence might have served their psyches well but for something like this, damn, they hadn't a clue where he might wander.

"Let's head back over to his house, spread out around where he shifted over. See if we can scent anything. If we can cross over near where they did, we should sense the sheriff or the boy if nothing else," it wasn't much of a plan, but it was all he could come up with on the spur of the moment.

It was Suzette's acute sense of smell that caught the whiff of the sheriff's aftershave on the Rose of Sharon, they crossed over one at a time. If there was something waiting, the other two would feel the vibration and come around another way. They had all, in their own way, played at this when they were pups at the founding of the world.

Clear, the twilit scene as peaceful as death. They stood motionless and strained to hear anything that might give away the location of the others. Nothing, not insect, night predator nor prey, not a leaf or twig, silence. That in and of itself was disconcerting, the forest was never completely at rest, never silent.

Off to the right, a cry broke the silence, an exclamation, then silence, three pair of eyes as one turned downhill. Wolf was first to react with Doe and Suzette right on his tail. They bolted down the hill without concern for their own safety, coming up short at the sight that greeted them around the placid pool at the bottom of the valley.

Bear lay motionless on the ground, blood streaming from his head. The sheriff was holding a mad dog at bay while it snarled, attempting to rip out his throat. His arms straining, shaking as his strength began to wane. There was no sign of Glen. Wolf sprang from where he stood knocking the vicious dog from off the top of the sheriff, his own jaws clamping on its neck. He had no idea what had happened but this dog's part in it was about to end.

"Stop," the voice weak, yet with enough force Wolf lessened the pressure, though keeping teeth firmly planted. "That's Glen." The sheriff rolled over slowly rising onto knees and hands, coughing, spitting out exertion, dirt, and blood.

Suzette and Doe ran to his side, checking the severity of his wounds, satisfied, they helped him to his feet, before Suzette scooted down to where Bear lay motionless.

She checking to see if he was breathing and for a pulse. On this side of the barrier wounds could become perilous. Assured, she tried to roll him over to examine the head wound. She was a small woman and a smaller Otter, push and prod all she wanted she would never move the thousand-pound Bear. With help from the exhausted sheriff and Doe the three finally repositioned him enough they could see the wound.

The blood on the rock, the position of his head and the scuff marks in the dirt told the story. Her guess was something or someone, probably that dog, had startled him, he'd lost his balance, slipped, and whacked his head on the rock, knocking himself out. But that didn't explain the dog, Glen, and the sheriff. They would have to subdue the dog, apparently without killing it, to find out what had taken place.

Wolf knew exactly where to apply pressure to cut off circulation to the brain until the dog passed out. It would not be adversely affected, he assured them, except a massive headache. Now to see if they could revive Bear and find out what the hell was going on.

Cool water from the pond, a bandage fashioned from the sheriff's undershirt and time combined to bring Evan back from the brink. The dog would not be the only person awakening with a massive headache. Slowly they pieced together what had happened from Bear's account and the sheriffs two cents.

The sheriff used every faculty he possessed to force a sense of normalcy onto the scene, failing miserably, he sat back to observe. An interrogation was being conducted concerning the previous events with a Bear, a Wolf, Deer and Otter doing the conducting. The boy who was a dog did not help dispel the sense of twisted fantasy. Hey Disney, I got a movie for you, but you would never believe it.

Once the facts were laid out in sequence of event the story began to come into focus. All were taken aback finding Glen was not human but one of them. The only one who didn't seem taken aback that Glen was the spirit of Dog, was Sung. Bear, whether it was the knock on the head, or just general confusion, couldn't quite grok how the kid had been hidden from all of them, even himself. He had never heard of any of the People with the ability to perform such a thing.

"Have any of you ever heard of this before," Bear asked to shaking heads.

Though Wolf was thoughtful, had he heard rumor of someone with this capability? There was a memory niggling at the back of his head, from a thousand years ago, of one of the People dabbling in distorting the essence of People, but the problem with rumor was it was seldom based in fact. The facts pointed to amnesia so complete it hid Glen from them as well as himself. It wasn't magic.

"We don't have magic!" insisted Doe, "not that kind." She specifically spoke to the sheriff, "We are not magical beings, just immortal," as if that made everything normal. "When Sung says we can sense things, it is not magic, just a heightened sense of danger or each other's presence. Like how animals can tell when there's going to be an earthquake, or a fire before humans can see it. Though they can't outrun it," on the verge of tears she stepped back, "and we are even more so connected to the energy, the spirit, the whatever you want to call it, but it's not some weird supernatural power, just natural." She was spent.

"What she means, Sheriff," interjected Otter taking over to explain the unexplainable, "is, we aren't sorcerers or witches, warlocks. We can't pull bunnies from hats—though why anyone would you want to—or make things disappear, create forcefields or make someone standing right in front of you appear to be a hole in the fabric." She collected thoughts attempting to put them together in a coherent concept, "we are the spirits of our cousins, we do our best to protect them from harm, to allow them to survive. To protect them from the encroachment of man," she shrugged the truth of it, "Sorry, but your people are extremely destructive to us, the mother, and anything that gets in your way."

"Though even with that," proceeded Sung, glancing over to get her permission to pick up the thread, "we don't hate humans, in fact, if people, tribes, cultures, individuals, believe in us, we try to help them as well. We guide, lend strength, moral compass, healing, health, all within limitations, but we do what we can to assist. Even if sometimes it is only comfort in a time of pain and suffering."

"So, how was someone able to do whatever has been done to Glen?" One thing about the sheriff he adjusted on the fly and accepted what he could not deny. That served no one. Facts and evidence were facts and evidence whether you liked them or not.

"We don't know," whispered Bear before closing his eyes. "Though I am becoming convinced it's some sort of amnesia. I'm thinking if he didn't know who he was then it would stand to reason neither would we."

Glen stirred, moaning, paws pressed to head to alleviate the pain.

"Or, maybe some kind of glamour, would be another guess," Doe spoke the conjecture out loud, "Oh, my children have been used as spirit guides and gods for witches for thousands of years. I would never believe such a thing possible, as have never actually seen an actual glamour, but it might be possible to dupe the subject if they were gullible enough. You can make folks believe just about anything if they've a mind to," she added.

They all regarded Glen. His memory was gone, he could recall nothing past the last several years. He had never been child, teen, been in love or a dog. The sight of himself in the mirror of the pond had set off some kind of reaction, he flipped out, Bear had tried to restrain him, slipped on the mud. The sheriff had jumped in to calm the kid, who was now in a blind rage. Thinking the sheriff was attacking him, Glen turned on him. They had arrived just in time.

Otter swam to the other side of the pond, climbing up onto the bank and gnawed off several large chucks of willow bark. Back on the other side she presented a chunk to Bear and one to Dog.

"Chew it," she insisted, "we all need clear heads."

"We should head back," Bear sounded as weary as any man in history, "We've all had enough shocks to the system, surprises, and exercise for one day."

"That's a damn fact," maybe the sheriff could top Bear for having had enough.

"I'll help the kid, might be best if we can get him back in a body he recognizes," Wolf felt an affinity for the young man he wouldn't have thought possible. But, then again, weren't dogs the cousins of wolves?

They were all going to have to help each other, lean on each other if they had any hope of preventing the breaking of the world. Bear knew these folks were all keys, they had to be, you don't just show up after a thousand years without purpose, but hadn't a clue where they fit in. He traced Her face on the time piece in his pocket for reassurance, to center hisself. He felt every curve, every line, he could scent Her perfume, how fresh She smelled in the morning, how...forget it old man, he silently chastised, keep yer mind on the game at hand.

With Doe and Suzette on either side of the sheriff, Sung carrying the semi-conscious Glen, Bear shifted them from the dream state to Fort and bed.

Picking Up The Pieces

∞

With the sun peeking over the Great Plains painting the sky in pastels of rose, pink, yellow, gold on a canvas of white and blue, it looked to be a perfect early fall day, as long as you didn't look to close.

Coffee was brewed, poured, drank, brewed, and poured again. The concept of a good night's rest got lost in the reality. They had each taken a turn watching over Glen, who was their number one concern. Evan might have taken the brunt of the physical cost, but it was Glen who had been battered psychologically and spiritually, though the sheriff was a close second. He had his world turned upside down almost as completely.

Each of the spirit people could, in some measure, relate to what Glen was experiencing. Each in their turn had lost their true selves for short epochs in humanity. It was easy to fall into, to forget what you were when you were surrounded by those who weren't. The concept of immortality became foreign as you watched those around you suffer and die. The forever of the dream state became the nightmare of the dream. But none had ever so completely forgotten who or what they were. Somewhere in the back of the mind they knew; it was truth, it would find a way. Though Bear had come close.

Not Glen, he was as lost as any of the People had ever been.

Sung and Suzette sat on the back patio allowing the crisp morning to snap them from the stupor of a sleepless night. They might be immortal spirits but when in human form you lived as human, tired is as tired was. Doe was taking her turn sitting with Glen. Bear returned from the house with another pot.

"This is uncharted territory, it should be impossible for him to be that far gone, that lost from who he is," Bear shook his head. "I really thought if he saw his true self, the reflection of who/what he is, it would shatter whatever psychic block had been put in place."

"Well, that didn't work. How's the head," Suzette asked.

"Still attached, though there were times last night I wished it wasn't," Evan chuckled.

"Here are our priorities for the nonce," Sung brought them back with his deep intonation, "we have GOT to find out all the parties involved. Shit," he turned to Evan, "I forgot to tell you about the crow. We got spies flocking around here, spies with a network to pass on info." He quickly related his discovery of the previous evening to Evan's complete lack of surprise.

"I guess I would be more surprised to find out Crow wasn't involved, and his murder weren't spying on us," he explained, "sloppy on my part not to take precautions." He was going to whack hisself in the head in an act of self-chastisement before reconsidering. No sense doing more damage to the loaf than had already been incurred.

"Well, now we know, and can all be much more cautious," Sung ended the self-incriminating line of thought, "We need to investigate whether there isn't something you can do," again to Evan, "to repair the damage to the balance. It is my belief that only you can fix what you broke," there was no insinuation only statement of fact.

"I think you are right," admitted Evan, Suzette settling her hand on top of his. She was the epitome of compassion.

"And we need to find a way to bring Glen back into the fold," Evan continued as he sat thoughtful for several quiet moments, "It's dumb, but I wonder if this would explain the explosion of unwanted canines throughout the land. Not having a guide, a spirit to watch over them, they just get lost," he shrugged, "something to think about. Because we don't have enough on our plates right now!" He laughed, it hurt the coconut, but it was needed.

"We never have so much to do that we forget to watch out for our charges," soothed Suzette.

The sheriff sauntered 'round the corner of the house with a peculiar expression riding his face. "I don't know what kind of tree that is across the lane but it do bear some interesting fruit. Maybe it's those clocks," He scratched his head. He'd gone into town to make sure no other trouble had taken place during his interesting evening. You could take the lawman out of reality but you couldn't take the lawman out of the man.

Evan was quite certain he had never met a more resilient human being since the dawn of time. The man accepted whatever came his way, he had an uncanny ability to tolerate any reality thrown at him. If he saw and could not deny it, it was true, and he accepted.

What now? Thought Evan as all three got up to investigate.

"Mind if I tag along?" asked the sheriff as he reversed course, "never a dull moment around you folks, is there?" He guffawed not attempting stealth, why bother?

Even if Evan hadn't known him for centuries, he would have known him by reputation and attitude. No one, not of the People nor human could carry arrogance like Coyote. He didn't lean against the oak he lounged as if he owned it.

"Ya-hey Bear," he endeavored to convey casual friendly. He came across as trying to pick-up your wife while you were peeing. "Hey cuz," he tossed Sung's way. His eyes sparked and he oozed slimy suggestiveness when he noticed Suzette, "Well," he reeked of creep, "what have we here? How is it we have never met?"

"I don't frequent cesspools," she shot back.

"Is that anyway to greet family? Thought you folks would be overjoyed, an old cousin stopping by. Hmm, and is this your human?" condescendingly referring to the sheriff, who, like a good lawman, ignored the taunt.

"What are you doing here, Yote," Evan was in no mood.

"Ain't too friendly for someone what asked for some help," Coyote taunted, but only just as he was not blind to the vibe. "I thought you should know, ain't nobody talkin', but everybody is skittish, on edge," his own skittishness betraying whatever bravado he was trying on. His eyes darting left, right, his nose scenting every hint on the breeze, feet dancing as if they wished to be on the other side of the world from here.

"I coulda told you that," said Evan dismissing the canine, knowing it would push the Coyote's pride enough that he would spill whatever tidbit he didn't want to say.

"Look, something ugly is comin' and it's comin' soon, and nobody wants no part of it. They think if they can stay on the sidelines, when the dust settles, they can just go back to being what was," there was more Evan could sense it. Patience wasn't just a virtue; it was a tactic.

"Thanks for info, I'd invite you over for a bite and sip but am guessin' you don't want no part of any of us right now," Evan turned to leave. "If you run into any of them that thinks things is just going back to what was, they better stop and think again. Ain't no sideline sittin' when it comes to this time around, you're on one side or the other, or about to get run down, that's it. Thanks for the update," he said over his shoulder. Sung was about to say his piece, but Evan's sharp glare stayed his words.

"A drink would sure calm the nerves right now," Coyote licked his chops, "and I been so busy runnin' for you I ain't et in a spell. What the hell, People already don't trust me, or much like me," a rare moment of honesty from the deceiver. "I mean, if you don't mind."

Evan had never known Coyote to be scared, to have lost his confidence, but the world was turning on its head, you couldn't tell what might be real.

"Come on," Evan knew also that a little kindness, a little charity could go a long way to prying loose that tidbit.

It was late morning and the bottle had been passed, most between Ev, Sung and Mika, Coyote's human name. The companionship began to work loose the reticence of Mika's tongue. No matter what People thought, even the lone trickster and grifter wants companions to alleviate the solitude, even if they ain't friends but acquaintances. Lonely can wear on a soul.

"I been thinking hard on this," he jumped in after a long pull, "you gotta separate what you know about people, then tie it in with what you seen happening 'round you."

For once Mika was making sense, Evan threw a quick glance to warn the others of patience. Let him talk, he seemed to say with his eyes, he wants to impress us. Not that they needed the warning. Doe poked her head out and mimed that Glen was still out, Evan nodded and turned his attention back to where Coyote was sweeping all his thoughts together.

"Here's what I seen," he began, "there is more than one or two of the People being manipulated by and then manipulating. The question is who is at the center of it all. Who has the knowledge, the expertise to control so many at one time?" another pull on the endless bottle in the silence of late morning, "anybody here might could pull a couple few together to cause a stir up, but here, in this disruption—though I don't know exactly who all—there are a bunch doin' the biddin of one.

"Crow, fer sure, and by the scent of death waitin' you gotta assume Buzzard ain't far off, Raven ain't been seen, and Rattlesnake just to name a few. And who got the wherewithal to be everywhere at once and ain't nobody the wiser?" He glanced at each one of them to see if they was following his perfect logic.

It was time to lay his card on the table, show them just how clever he had been. "Who spins the web? Who controls humans, sorry sheriff if I offended previous, but who finds it just so damn easy to control humans to her will and wish," he sat back, waiting.

It was Evan and Sung who both blurted simultaneously, "Iktomi!" You always forgot about the small but mighty.

Suzette clapped her hands as she had come to the same conclusion a second behind. Who else, indeed? No one else could control so many like a puppet show. Making all dance to her silent tune while running in circles chasing their tails, blaming others aways two steps behind and on the wrong track. Evan shot a glance towards the bushes, the downspouts, the corners under the eaves, everywhere Iktomi was known to hide. Damn, how had he missed it?

"I don't mean to be dense, but my learning on Animal spirits, myths and legends seems a bit on the meager side. Who, or what, is an Iktomi?" They all gave Sheriff John points for getting the pronunciation close.

"The spider." Suzette enlightened, "the spinner of webs and

known trickster."

"Well, I don't want to burst no bubbles, but this seems a tad bit beyond tricks," the sheriff wasn't quite ready to buy into a spider causing all this trouble. "And spiders ain't 'xactly mighty creatures to be orderin' around huge fellas like the one that's been comin' round here."

"You have to understand," Doe had noiselessly come down to where they sat around the small glass top table, "when it comes to us," she drew a circle to include present company, "size doesn't matter." She glared daggers at their adolescent titters and snickers. Geez, the world was coming apart at the seams and immaturity was supposed to be the savior. Great Spirit help them all.

"What you see physically is only a representation of what we are," she continued, "just because one of The People might appear substantially small, the power of their spirit could be massive. A tiny spider, such as the Brown Recluse, has a bite that can be extremely harmful to your people, whereas a very large one, such as the Wolf Spider is ten times the size of the Recluse but not dangerous in the least. Size, in this case, gentlemen, doesn't matter."

"Be that as it may," was the sheriff turning red in the cheek and neck? "I still ain't getting' how a spider can control something a thousand times its size!"

"You like spiders?" queried the Wolf.

"Not particular," answered honesty.

"Afraid of them?" nudged Sung.

"Some," admitted a candid man.

"Most people, most humans," Sung corrected himself, "are unreasonably terrified of them. Ninety five percent of spiders are beneficial to your household. They eat bugs, lots of bugs, and they don't bother nobody while doin' it. But fear can be a great motivator, especially when it comes in the night. And Iktomi can ride the Mare bringing fear and terror to your dreams while sending her minions to make your skin crawl. Panic can drive folks to do most anything," he sat back on his chair as the sheriff digested simple fact.

"OK, so, we can make a reasonable assumption that Iktomi is behind the disruption caused by the crack, what do we do now?" Evan took a hard chug of the brown liquor emptying his glass.

"And with whom?" the sheriff's skeptical kicked in.

"What are you getting at?" Suzette thought she might know the road he was headed down but wanted to make sure before turning.

"Well, you just spent half a mornin' explianin' as to how this trickster, this being that is the epitome of hoax and sham is makin' puppets out of my folks and yours, how do we know who we can trust?" opening his arms to include all.

"Man's got a point," Doe shrugs.

"I mean, correct me if I'm wrong as my grasp of Native lore is a bit tenuous, but, fer instance, I seem to remember that you," he pointed direct at Coyote, "and, now that I know who this Iktomi woman was, was tight, weren't you."

Mika sat up to protest before slumping back into his chair, "Yes, we have had many adventures together, but I ain't in on this, I promise," he held up his right hand to signify.

"How do you know?" Again, the sheriff wasn't going to let loose of this bone. "Don't seem like the folks being led around by the nose is all that aware of the leading," he finally took a sip. "You think that fella from the bar, who you never seen before, knew why he was so pissed off at you? You think all them fellas what attacked me and my men few weeks back knew what they was doin'?

"Hell, I went to school with two of them, that's how they took us unawares, I trusted them men," his words were like an open wound. This was a man to whom trust was almost everything and he had been betrayed.

Silence met his rundown. That was an aspect none had taken a moment to consider.

"Speaking of which, what about the boy?" the sheriff didn't want to throw the kid under the bus, but... "According to the last few days, and if I am to believe my own two eyes, arms, and witness, he ain't quite sure who he is. Somebody been messin' with Glen's mind," he shook his head, helpless. He liked that kid, he really did. He was kind, loyal, happy, nothing seemed to bother him. Had been like that ever since, when? He couldn't remember when and under what circumstances Glen'd showed up.

He hadn't grown up here, had he? The sheriff began to question his own mind.

"I had a dream last night," the familiar voice interrupted the mental wanderings of all. "I dreamt you were all plotting against me. You were going to hurt me, lock me up, you were all sitting around this table just like you are, plotting," he didn't project anger or seem upset, just stating facts. "I tried running from you, to get away from all of you, to escape before you could do what you did before," Glen looked directly at Evan who met his gaze head on. "You wanted me to believe something that could not be."

"I couldn't move, something held me in place, tied my legs and arms, covered my mouth so I couldn't speak; or breathe. I was suffocating, I was dying," tears flowed down his cheeks, he gasped for air, no one moved. From her seat Doe caught Evan's eye silently apologizing.

She had gotten distracted by the conversation and overconfident that Glen would not awaken. She couldn't stop him now, no one could, they would have to wait and see where this train came to a halt.

"I didn't want to die," as if it needed to be said, spoken matter-of-factly, "I fought, fought with every ounce of strength I could muster, fought to live, to not let you take me away, let me die. Then you came," pointing at Doe, "then you, Suzette, you both told me you would protect me, that you loved me like your own, you wouldn't let anyone hurt me. Then you both told me a secret, you showed me who I was, the truth, of what I was, just like Evan had tried. And told me I couldn't die, I had to protect my children." His smile was pure joy, "I didn't know I had children. I have many," and they nodded their assent. "I am Dog, thank you all."

Well, that was unexpected, Evan smiled, had the Spirit guide actually come around or was he being guided to by whoever messed with his head in the first place. Shit, shit, shit, now he couldn't trust nobody, there were times he hated people, this was turning into one of those times.

Though if he was to be honest with hisself and protect all involved, it was peculiar that Glen would see the light and accept this new, very bizarre reality overnight. Yes, we are beings of dream and light. Yes, we are used to a mutable reality. And as immortals last night could've lasted a week in dream state as time means nothing when away from humans. But still, Glen would have to be watched.

The others accepted the transformation without comment or disputation. If they had reservations, they kept them well hidden. Except the sheriff, who was suspicious by nature and apparently not a very good poker player. Though he did not raise any alarms, it was evident he was not buying the overnight conversion any more than Evan but chose to keep his own counsel for the time being.

The three of the subfamily Caninae talked and joked among themselves welcoming Glen back into the fold. There had always been tensions between these and others of the species, quarrels, territorial squabbles, and such, but what family didn't. Wolf didn't appreciate Coyote sending his children to poach where wolves should reign, Dog, now fully engaged and remembering, warned Coyote about poaching his children. Coyote feigned innocence but Glen stood his ground. Coyote's children were well-known for hunting the smaller members of Dogs family. Until Evan interceded. These disputes could be addressed once the upheaval had been settled. And yet, he was pleased beyond tickled that Glen did seem to be remembering and engaging with the other two. Maybe.

"We have to assume we are constantly under surveillance if Coyote's suspicions are correct," Evan spoke quietly, then added to quell any protest before it began, "and I am inclined to buy into his hunch. Especially considering we know Crow is in the trees."

"That's great, but where do we go from here?" Doe stated the obvious. "We still have not clue one as to how to conclude this without great destruction. I know the humans Iktomi has manipulated cannot kill us, but they can inflict much pain and suffering I would prefer to bypass. Plus, I don't think we want to start culling the herd." She mellowed the meaning for the benefit of the sheriff, though he understood.

"If we commence to eliminating all those we consider a threat, Iktomi will only bring more players in. She cares not one whit about how many get hurt, just so she wins," Sung refused to dance around candor. "It would be an endless exercise in slaughter."

Though wolves were purported to be viscous killers they killed for survival only, not for pleasure. That was the main difference between animal and human, the former never killed for sport or indulgence.

"Then it would seem we have to extinguish this threat without violence, to us or them. But how?" Suzette had summarized the quandary succinctly.

"Two things have to happen; I have to heal the crack, though I don't know how. And, we have to find a way to distract Iktomi enough that she loses her grip on those she has spun into her web," Evan was not the portrait of hope, "And that is assuming we have deduced correctly." Silence greeted the plan. "And here's the really hard part, as Suzette has stated we have to do all this without escalating the violence level, without anyone getting killed on either side." He shushed the growing argument, "The only thing killing does in bring more killing until it never stops, trust me, I know."

"I agree completely with Ev," threw in Sheriff John, "I been doin' this job a long time and he's right, one death leads to ten to more blood-shed than anyone could ever want or would ever satisfy the lust once it's begun."

Coyote had a strange, contemplative countenance watching Glen, he was considering something though Evan could not conceive what. Making his decision he spoke to Glen as if he was the only one there, "When was the last time you ran just to run?"

It was an odd question on the surface, especially in the midst of this discussion, though from a canine perspective as normal as hello.

"What?" Glen seemed stunned by the abruptness of the question. They were smack dab in the middle of some kind of meet about an oncoming war and Mika wanted to go for a run? Yet, it appealed.

"Just admiring the wide-open spaces and my legs are itchin' to be stretched out, thought you might like to come along," he grinned the challenge.

Glen looked to Evan for permission, he wanted to. Evan tried to figure every angle of what and why, but there was no ciphering. Whatever Coyote's game, Evan knew he wouldn't harm Glen, well, he was pretty sure, and that was his main concern. He would pick the kids brain when they returned. Right now, he had other things on his mind. Nodding his assent, they took off at full sprint. Might be best if Glen was out of the way right now anyway.

Evan pulled his prized pocket watch out of his jeans pocket, though whether to tell the time or glance at the picture not even he was certain. He could feel the pull on his heart, the sadness that weighed him down. He should call the kids. It was early afternoon here; the elder's girl would be done with lunch, and he should tell her he was going to be out of town for a few days or a week. The daughter would understand, he had disappeared in the mountains from time to time her whole life. The grandkid thought he went there to talk to her dead uncle, he let her believe. He didn't need the granddaughter coming over in the middle of this skirmish. The youngest and her family on the east coast would not be serving dinner just yet, he could talk to the other grandkids.

Funny, he had been so preoccupied with all that was happening he hadn't thought about his kids and grandkids much, he sucked as a parent. Had his Granddaughter been by while he was chasing phantoms and fights? Yeah, he needed to call them let them know he'd been crazy busy and to tell her not to come over 'til he told her to. There were just so many 'other' children to be concerned with. When this was over, he'd make it up to her. He'd be a better head of the family, maybe take them all up into the mountains for a few weeks, just him and the grandkids.

He prayed she would listen.

The phone calls had gone well, the youngest, Alexandra, wanted to come over to make sure he was alright. She was the one, the best of her grandmother, she deserved better from her folks. Her father had split almost 'fore she was out of the birth canal and her mother had gone is search of herself with booze, drugs and men, never quite finding who she was or what she sought.

He made promises, assurances, swore up and down they would go to the mountains together, every little lie he could pull out, finally she acquiesced. Time to get down to business.

While Evan had made his phone calls Sheriff Roberts thought he should check into the office and give his deputies as much information as he could, without sounding insane. They had repaired most of the damage done to the office as it weren't that big of a place to begin with. Small town, small budget, small force, it was now down to him and two deputies. Which in normal times would have been plenty but weren't nothing normal in these times.

He thought he should follow Evan's example and check in with his own son, just to say hi and inquire after his health and well-being. Though he was as divorced as his old man, no kids, thankfully, but he'd taken to drinking away the lonely. John really should head over to Grand Junction.

"What the hell is going on?" he had hardly made it through the door before the deputy's question knocked him back.

"Gee, Sam, whatever are you talking about?" he tried to make light.

"Funny, Sheriff, but we're right smack dab in the middle of this war, or turf skirmish or whatever and haven't a fucking clue what this is! We deserve to know what's on the line," he looked at the other deputy for confirmation.

"Yeah, guess you're right, has been more'n a little crazy round here of late, ain't it?" The sheriff sat on the edge of a desk, the only available spot, dancing in his head in an attempt to find a way to make this all seem within the realm of possible, make a pill they could swallow. "It would seem our little burgh is 'bout in the center of some kind of turf war. Which is interestin' as it doesn't have a damn thing to do with us in the slightest." He gathered together a few more facts.

"If it's got nothin' to do with us, why we in the middle?" both men nodded.

"Cause by virtue of the fact it is happening here, it puts us in the middle," irritability seeping through his impotence to control the situation, "it's our job to protect this town these people."

"Just don't see why they can't take their turf war to another piece of turf," Sam had never shown any sign of being squeamish before, why did John get the feeling he just wanted to get in his squad car and keep driving?

"Well, Sam, I am guessing you are going to get ample opportunity to ask them that question," the sheriff had had enough. They had a job to do, and he expected his men to do their job, no questions asked. "I would think big a fella like you might want a little comeuppance fer the way them fellas treated you, me, the office and your honor the other night! Don't that frost you in the least?" Now the anger was growing. He had never been heated with his men; they had never given him cause. What the hell had got into them now?

"Just thinking, that's all. They seems to be a truckload o' trouble comin' this way and only three of us to off load it, maybe we should call in the Marines, or something," now sheepishness replaced nervousness as shame crept into the bargain.

"Ain't you never seen High Noon or Tombstone? Any of them old time movies where the lone sheriff and deputies gotta stand up 'cause they're all that stands between the town and evil, well, son, you're living it right now." If you can't fill them with confidence, baffle them with bull-shit, "you can either stand on the side of right or walk away," it wasn't much but for some of these guys appealing to their Randolph Scott was all he had.

"I still don't like it," a word from the mute one.

"Shit, Ray, ain't nobody likes it, but it's all we got, each other. I'm going to tell you all I know, who is the good guys, who is the bad. The most important thing you need to know is, we are going to do everything in our power to try and not get anyone, us included, killed," the one thing he could be certain of is, escalation of the dead count served nobody's purpose. On that he and Evan were in complete agreement.

Now, if he could only get the other side to see the brilliance of that.

Doe, Suzette, and Sung had retired to the old folk's house to lay out their own participation in whatever might be coming. In the dining room center of the house, they sat around the table, the knights of the rectangular table. You don't live forever and not pick up a few fables.

"I don't know how you both feel about it, but I agree with Evan and the sheriff, we cannot, at all costs, trigger a blood war," Suzette took the initiative, "there can be no deaths. Injuries, I would guess, are unavoidable, death is not."

There was an attraction to the dark woman that Sung could not deny, or disregard. It wasn't her physical beauty, though that could not be refuted, it was her strength of character, her intelligence, she was small in stature but commanded respect. He liked her.

"I am guessing you have never been in a battle before," he did not mock but asked sincerely.

She shook her head, no.

"'When the heat of the battle rages it is all one can do to avoid one's own death, trying to be cautious of causing another's can lead to mistakes," He spoke from experience, blood sport was primal, kill or be killed.

"Nonetheless, we will have to use every skillset we have to avoid it. Each human life taken, especially as we are assuming they are not in control of themselves, is a pound of flesh from our own spirit," she spoke softly, but with force, "and will only escalate fury which leads to more and more death. We have to find a way to neutralize without causing permanent damage."

Wolf wanted to argue but couldn't, she had valid points, they would have to find another way. Another way without taking all the blows themselves.

"I know your children have suffered from attack, have you not felt the agony?" Sung almost whipered the question.

Suzette nodded once, wincing with the memories. "It is our burden, to know, to feel, to sooth their pain. It is what we were created for."

"If you have suffered for them, imagine how much you will suffer for yourself. We cannot be dispatched permanently but we can suffer forever. And if one of our own extinguishes this form, yes, we will come back, reincarnate, but while we reconstruct our children will be unprotected," the Wolf looked directly into her eyes, "you know what that means."

Again, one nod, "The possibility they could become extinct while we are unable to protect them." The tears flowed down both cheeks, but she would not allow more to show.

"But that's the most puzzling thing of all," chimed in Doe, "Iktomi must know all this, why would she take the chance? It would not serve her, her children, The People, why?"

This whole thing stunk of lunacy and madness. The only explanation was the crack in the balance. If that was so, why didn't the Mother step in? Or the Great Spirit? No one could imagine there was any issue more pressing on their schedules. If they expected the animas to repair the damage, wouldn't it behoove to give a hint or two?

There's More at The Door

∞

The knock on the door was tentative, almost questioning, then patience. Again, a tap, tap, tapping on the window of the front door. What the? Evan had come close to not bothering, assuming either the small chain that usually held a plant was swinging into the window or it was a salesperson too timid to knock. Not what he needed right now.

Peeking out the front window he saw the small, rotund man who had warned them of the impending attack several weeks back. Hmm, interesting.

Opening the door, Evan grinned welcome, "I hope you are not the bearer of ill-times on the horizon once again," he held out his hand inviting the small man in.

Large eyes blinking against the sunlight the stranger welcomed the more subdued interior. Pulling a pair of pince-nez from somewhere inside his jacket and resting them on his beak-like nose, he gazed around the hallway and adjoining rooms. As if assuring there would be no tomfoolery for which he was ill equipped.

"Mr. Beach, I assume," he dipped a short bow in Evan's direction.

It was all Evan could do to stifle the laugh caught in his throat. "Again, yes, can I help you?"

"Possibly, though I am quite positive I can be of assistance to you." With that declaration he moved swiftly, though smoothly, through the vestibule towards the kitchen and the rear patio. "I prefer the outdoors," he explained as they exited the home into fresh air, "too cramped in those boxes, can't see the sky."

Taking a seat at the small glass top table he patiently waited while Evan sat hisself after getting both an iced tea.

"All alone, Mr. Beach? I would not think that advisable considering the circumstances," His eyes never ceased motion, his head constantly swiveling side to side. Evan would not have been surprised had the man's head turned completely around.

"Are any of us ever all alone," asked Evan philosophically.

"I have heard word that you believe Iktomi to be at the root of this unpleasantness and that you believe you the root of the crack, the unbalance, as it were, therefore the solution, is that correct?" Well, he didn't beat around the bush, and succinct, but a question first before the answer.

"Who told you?"

"Pardon?"

"Who told you that I think Iktomi is behind this and that I am not just the problem, but the solution? There were only a few of us here and you wasn't one of them, so I ask again, who told you?" Evan was a gentle man, not prone to threats, but his tone didn't know that.

"Let's say a little bird told me," he smiled at his own inside joke.

"Let's say you tell that bird if I catch it I will eat it live," not threat, more promise, "Mister, I don't like being spied on whether it is to help or to harm, if someone wants to know my thoughts they can be honest enough to come to my door and ask, like a civilized person," he grinned a toothsome confirmation.

"Point taken," half bow of apology, though he was not flustered, "be that as it may, I am here to offer my assistance to rectify this situation."

"And why would you do that?"

"Because believe or not, I care about how this will affect the People, actually how it will affect the People and the humans as all are necessary for the balance of this world," he spoke slowly, without emotion.

"So, you come in peace? To bring same to me and mine, and I would assume you'll take what we say to Iktomi and see how Spider weaves it?" part of Evan wanted to jump at the chance to nip this before it could take root, but it was in the minority. Suspicion was set to full, there was too much at stake to believe in fairies. And he wished to see if his accusation of Spider would be denied.

'Mr. Beach, I am not here on my own. I have been sent as a representative of the little people, those whose voices are not being heard, those who will indubitably find themselves in the middle of this conflict through no fault of their own," his expression one of magnanimity and self-sacrifice.

Well, he didn't deny.

Up until this moment Evan never knew The People had anything resembling lawyers, they had never been needed. Apparently, all things evolve including the definition of predator and prey. Here was the embodiment of the predator without the need for claw nor beak to shred the intended to pieces, though he possessed both. Evan had run into his ilk previous but only in human form. He was disappointed to find one who flew in the pure air, as he would have thought it would have been one who slithered. Such are misconceptions!

"What is it you propose, Owl," No sense pretending we didn't know who we were.

"I would suggest an amicable divvying up of the assets where each party would have domain over certain territories, the borders clearly defined," eyes, though at half mast, huge through the bi-focal pince-nez.

"So, you suggest Spider would rule over some and I would rule over the other. Is that it? All others would be subject to our every wish and whim? To sell the freedom, the equality we have all enjoyed since the birthing of this world, for peace?" he kept his tone soft, even, as if considering.

"Exactly. Peace for all so we can return to normal activities without threat," he nodded his head once, slowly.

"You fear if this escalates your normal activities will be restricted, is that it?"

"Well, mine and all else," Owl defended, not wishing to appear self-serving.

"As the 'innocents' will be scarce, hiding, keeping out of sight, if this thing gets out of hand, is that it?" Evan leaned toward Owl but thinking of rodents.

"Well, yes, I suppose that would occur," he stuttered out.

"And YOU wouldn't have the capability to feast on the weak and petite?" Evan had not fed on live game since meeting Her, he'd lost the taste and desire.

"It is the natural order, sir," Now Owl had his feathers all a flutter. How was he supposed to sustain his life if he could not feed?

"And I would be king, or emperor, lording over my subjects," now the indignation began to seep through, "my former friends, those in the other house, perhaps?"

Owl's eyes now had purpose as they scanned every inch of the property and surrounding area, escape. This man was becoming irate. "I came here in peace, to make peace, not be threatened," righteous indignation made an attempted entrance but was blocked by truth.

Across the lawns Suzette walked by the side kitchen window, she stopped in her tracks. She knew that spirit sitting and chatting with Evan, knew him well. All this talk of battles and blood had stirred her own. As she took in the spirit sitting, casually conversing, she thought it might be nice to have a little piece of Owl for lunch today.

The backdoor of her house slammed against the porch rail as she stormed out the door making a beeline directly towards where Owl and Evan sat. Both turned, startled at the sharp retort. If Evan thought Owl's eyes could not possibly grow larger in aspect he was mistaken. At the sight of Suzette advancing across the lawns he took on the demeanor of a creature about to take flight.

"I want a word or two with you!" her voice even, not screamed, which only augmented the threat. How one could stomp on grass without making a sound yet drown out all other, would have to be explained by physicists.

But he was gone by the time she arrived. Evan had never seen any creature move with such alacrity. He had to laugh. The extremely angry brown woman glaring at him caused a cessation of humor.

"What?"

"That sonofabitch had better tell his damn children to stop feasting on my babies or there's going to be a war the likes of which this world ain't never seen!" If Evan had thought to pacify, his better angels told him to shut it.

"What did he want?" Suzette regained control of her emotions, sitting across from Evan, and wondering where that bottle had gone to.

"To bring peace to the world," he dismissed Owl as the other two strolled up.

"And how did propose to do that?" quipped the lovely Doe.

"By making me king of my domain," Evan replied with a mixture of sarcasm and majesty.

"Nice," Sung joined in, "did you accept?"

"I didn't think any of you would obey if I did. It would require far too much time and effort to tame all of you. I think I prefer my life as an ordinary Bear," he said bowing from his sitting position. "Though if I was to require obedience, I would command someone to bring the bottle from inside so I would not have to bother myself with such mundane chores," he suggested in his most regal tone.

"Ask and ye shall receive," surprisingly it was Sung who took up the crusade.

The sheriff turned the corner of the house just as glasses were being poured. Sung and Evan had bourbon, Doe, and Suzette tall glasses of iced tea.

"I'll have what they're having," Sheriff John requested indicating the tall glasses.

"You look beat," Evan said with concern.

"'Fraid the boys ain't 'xactly excited to be part of the saving of the world," he said matter of fact., "guess I can't blame 'em after the ass whoopin' we took the other night, but still...," he let the thought slide.

"If it's of any consolation, I will do all I can to shield them from the worst of it," Evan's word was gold to any who knew the Bear.

"What did that fella want?" the sheriff shifted gears pointing over his shoulder to the front of the house, "he lit out of here like a bat out of hell. Thought he was going to take off flying!"

"Wanted to make a deal."

"Take it you didn't like the terms," he could read faces.

"Didn't like him or his terms." Owl's visit had put Evan out of sorts. He couldn't say exactly why, besides the obvious, but there was some unknown variable just below the surface, an itch that would not go away.

Owl was feeling him out, but about what? It wasn't like he was hiding anything; everyone knew exactly where he stood. And he had to've known the answer to his stupid proposal 'fore he ever stepped out of tree this morning, so why had he come? And why would Iktomi send him in the first place? She wouldn't, Evan was pretty sure of that, hmmm and hmmm, again.

"Where's Glen?" The sheriff tossed to anyone who wasn't distracted.

"Him and Mika went for a run," Sung replied.

"Never hit me as fella who went for that sort of thing, but I guess you can't always tell by lookin'," Sheriff paused, "Guess there's a whole slew of things I didn't know about 'til about a week or so ago." It was hard to tell if the grin he wore was in appreciation for the knowing or a wish he'd never had to find out.

"We all thought it a good idea, let him run off some of the disorientation he's still feeling." Doe expanded, "He appears to be coming to terms with his loss of memory, though I think he still feels like a boat without a rudder. Sometimes a little physical exertion is the perfect medicine. I find a good long run clears the mind and sweats out the frustration of life sometimes."

"Ya-hey to that," Sung concurred, "it's the being alone with your thoughts. Even when you're running with a pack, nobody talks, they are all concentrated on the physical, heartbeat, breathing, so the mental is free to roam."

"I am not one for running, not built for it," Suzette joined the fray.

Sheriff John nodded though he thought she was built just fine for anything she chose to do. He had not known many black folks in his time, a few fellas back in the Navy, though had never been close to them, but he wasn't no bigot. Everybody got the same treatment, man, woman, black, red, white, brown, yellow, orange. And it wasn't that he had what they called 'jungle fever', or so the fellas in the Navy did, but he sure could appreciate a pretty woman.

"More of a swimmer, ain't nothing like a good swim down the river to clear the head and if that don't help, then you got to turn it around and swim against the current!" She may have been being literal, maybe figurative, but the sheriff thought that applied to a lot of things in life.

"Maybe I should go for a walk as that's about all these knees are good for and see if I can't shake something loose up here," Evan thought out loud pointing to his temple. He could use a little movement, he couldn't shake the feeling he was missing something important, a huge piece of the puzzle. Everything had fallen into place too easily; it was too convenient. Something was wrong, maybe a walk through the farmland was just what the psychiatrist ordered.

As he got up out of his chair Mika and Glen came jogging up, both breathing hard but not winded. They nodded their hellos to all concerned before plopping down on the grass. Laid out and looking up they appeared two brothers taking pleasure in long lost companionship.

"Good run?" Sung tossed over.

"The kid has some stamina, especially for someone who hasn't been running in a few years," Mika's admiration and respect were showing.

"You carry enough beer cases from the cooler out back into the bar every night, it does a job on the legs. And arms, really, it's a complete body workout," Glen grinned.

"Yeah, well, youth don't hurt either," a tinge of jealousy stuck its head out.

"Time for me to stretch a few muscles as well, I'll be back," Evan said over his shoulder and headed towards the lane and the farm fields across the way.

"You gonna be alright all by your lonesome?" The sheriff shouted after him, never can be too careful he thought to himself.

Evan waved.

"Guess I should be getting back to work as well," Sheriff John let the words get him out of his seat.

"Protecting the good citizens never ends, does it," Suzette smiled to take out any sting.

"Someone's got to do it," he tipped his hat as he turned to leave.

Distraction and Destruction

∞

It was early fall, and the land had the scent of it, smoke, fields plowed under so the decaying plants could feed the land for next year, leaves and the leavings of crops decomposing in the fields. It was, with spring, the time of year when the perfume of the Mother was its most pungent, heady, and exquisite. She had always loved those two seasons the most, and so he had as well.

He thought back to an autumn a thousand years ago, or so it felt from where he now stood. The days had grown shorter, sunset came too soon, chill filled the sunshine not the heat of summer. They sat outside having a sip of wine after he had finished chopping a couple cords of wood. They were set for winter. Yes, they had a perfectly good gas furnace, but sometimes they liked to set it low, pile a few good-sized logs in the fireplace and cuddle up on the couch. And it came back to him, a favored moment.

She gazed out across the prairie to the east, the shadows stretching halfway across the country, the sun setting on the mountaintop behind, and sighed.

"How can people hate this?" She asked so She could hear the sound of his voice.

That was one of the million things he loved about Her, spending time with Her, just the two of them. She would say something or ask a question that needed not be answered as She already knew but asked anyway knowing he would pontificate on it. She said She just loved to hear the sound of his deep, rumbling voice, his passion when he spoke, it was comforting to Her. She would lay her head on his chest to feel the rise and fall, the rumble of his voice.

Evan knew what She meant about the season. They'd had this discussion a hundred times, but he obliged.

"They don't understand it, and people always hate and mistrust anything they don't understand," he began the familiar oration, "They think everything dies in the fall and they fear death. They misconstrue the meaning, taking what they witness out of context. Fall isn't the worst time; it is the best.

"Things don't die now, they actually die in winter, but winter is beautiful, all coated and dressed in pure white. How can you hate purity? The clean scent of a freshly fallen snow, it promises rebirth, a blank canvas. It isn't bare trees, the trees are clothed in white, everything is. It is quiet, waiting for the hand of the Great spirit to come along and create new. It is hope for a new beginning, new life." He sighed, he caught a glimpse of Her out of the corner of his eye and he smiled.

"I think this is beautiful," she whispered not wishing to break the spell as he spoke but wanting to cash in her two cents.

"I agree. It is beautiful and restful. That's the thing about fall, it isn't death it is a time to relax, put away the tools, the food stores having been stocked, the logs laid up, the work complete. A time to sit and be grateful, thankful for another year. It's a little retirement each year," they clinked glasses, shared a kiss, before he went into the house to retrieve a couple blankets so they could sit out for 'just a while longer'.

It had been a few weeks since he had taken the time to think of Her, really think of Her. To remember. He loved remembering Her, the feel of her hair on his arm, the warmth of Her body spooning next to him on the couch or in bed, the way She'd frown a tut-tut and share an exasperated sigh when he'd start in on another tall tale of his life immortal. She hated when he said that because She thought someday, he'd begin to believe it himself. She'd told him more'n a few times 'if you say something often enough, you'll come to believe it, and then you get reckless'. It was Her fear.

She was afraid if he believed it to be true, he would take chances, live too close to the edge. She was terrified of the thought of outliving him, thought it would kill Her. She'd made him promise over and over that'd he'd let Her die first so She wouldn't have to bear the sorrow. He was stronger, he could handle it. Well, She'd got her wish, though She may have overestimated his might.

At first, he thought it was raining, but there wasn't a cloud in the sky. 'Course, wouldn't be the first time some weird freaky nature thing happened out here. Then he realized, he was crying.

He hadn't cried since, yeah, since, well, that explained it. He refused to relive it, bad enough he had to remember how much he loved Her when she was breathing and moving. He couldn't bear to think of Her in that damn box. Humans had this bizarre need to preserve their earthly remains in a box in the ground and put a big stone on top of the spot so they wouldn't forget. How do you forget someone who lives in your heart?

Might as well told folks he lived on the moon as tell them you live forever, She used to say, 'bout as likely. She was not a religious person, She went to church out of routine, it was what one did of a Sunday morn. She didn't believe in any kind of forever, kind of made him sad. He snorted in recollection, if you only knew.

If he disliked anything about fall and winter it was the short days, always seemed like you was getting bilked out of half a day. But the sunsets couldn't be beat, he thought, as the current one caught his attention. Shit sunset, how long had he been wandering? Who cared, getting home could wait a little while longer while he enjoyed the show.

The sky rode from azure to light blue, painting the perfect background to the white and black cumulous clouds, with rose, pink, gold turning to purple underbellies. One of the prettiest sunsets he'd seen in forever. They'd probably been more, but he hadn't taken the time to look up. Only took a second to notice the beauty of the world, why didn't he do it more often? She'd a chastised him 'til his ears hurt if She knew he wasn't takin' a few just to appreciate what the creator done created. Yes, he would have to do this more often.

He heard the twig snap behind him. He took a lungful of air, releasing it gradual, relaxing muscle, clearing brain. There was at least one, could be more from the feel of the air, turn slow.

Four, not bad, they was big in every aspect of the word and had weapons intended to inflict. Hmm, two by four, several foot of pipe, shit, that fella got a hammer? Interesting. Going to be a ruckus, sure wish he could share the fun with someone, anyone, but he would have to stand alone. He was too old for this shit.

"Hey grandpa, old man, you wanna tell us one of your tall tales?" Smirked the mountain from up 't the bar.

He was one mean and ugly piece of work. Whoever had his hooks in this fella sure picked a prize bull to ride.

"You don't have to do this, you know," might as well try.

"Yeah, I do. You made me look pretty stupid and weak at the bar, that's been with me ever since," unconsciously he rubbed the wrist Evan had tried so hard not to break, "People kinda been raggin' on me 'bout it, bustin' my balls and such. I lost a lot of respect. Seems I got no recourse but to get it back. One piece at a time." He took a step towards Evan as the others spread out to surround him.

"I really wish you would reconsider," began Evan as the big man swung the two by four, and it was on.

Evan could sense the attack coming, self-preservation was a powerful emotion, and his was as powerful as any being on the planet, but he didn't want to kill nobody. And he didn't want them stompin' him either, this was going to be one helluva balancing act.

He ducked under the two by four and swung up landing a blow on the big man's chin and knocking him backward just as the pipe came whistling through the air, missing Evan's shoulder by a quarter inch. Without looking he kicked out and got lucky, hearing the grunt, he turned and saw the fella behind him grab his knee, Evan kicked again and watched the knee buckle. Welp, there was one.

The hammer took him in the left shoulder, that was going to leave a mark. The pain shot direct into his brain just as the arm went numb. The good thing was he didn't feel the two by four break the arm. Nope, wait a minute, the numbness was temporary, he felt it head on.

The pain tripled and he fell to one knee. He recognized the swirling in the pit of his soul and knew. He could not let this happen, the fury was building, coalescing with loathing, pain, death. He had to stop it. He had to maintain control. He could not let it take over or there would be only death. It's not that he would become the Bear, that could only happen if he consciously made the decision. But the spirit was just as dangerous as the physical. The two by four landed again and a kick to the solar plexus knocked the wind out of him.

He was down on the ground; he didn't remember falling or being beaten down. He thought of Her and a calm came over him. Get up, She plead from beyond the grave, save yourself. They were about on top of him when he came up good arm swinging wildly while he kicked out trying to maintain balance.

The sight of a man they thought dead rising like a Phoenix from the ashes caught them completely by surprise. Fear, followed surprise, with pain on the end of his one good fist. He got lucky again and landed square to the temple of the smaller of the three still standing and he went down like a bag of potatoes, the other two stepped back out of range and reconsidered their naked assault.

One on each side, the big guy still holding half of the now broken two by four, apparently broken on Evan's back and the other fella swinging a tire chain, this was going to hurt.

They took one step toward him to, hopefully, finish off this old man. He was one tough S.O.B, they had to give him that, but tough or not he was going down. The sound of a gunshot brought the action to a halt.

"Enough," the sheriff commanded walking slowly over to Evan's side, the gun swinging carefully between the two assailants, "drop the weapons, NOW!"

He turned his head slightly to speak into the microphone at his shoulder, his eyes never leaving the two men. "I'm out in old man Whit's south pasture, about a quarter mile in off the south road, NOW!" his attention returned to the two, "Alright gentlemen, on your knees if you please, let's not have any unpleasantness." Both men obeyed without comment, though they did not look happy about it.

"You alright Evan?" he asked as he pushed the first guy down on his face in the dirt, knelt on his back and applied handcuffs.

"I'll live, though I can't guarantee that's a positive, hopefully won't take long to heal," his arm hung limp at his side, a large, blue/black bruise was growing on the side of his face, and he limped hard when he tried to walk, unable to put much weight on his right leg.

"Soon as we get these two taken care of, I'll get you home," The sheriff had an unreadable expression as he glanced over at Evan, as if he wanted to say something but couldn't right now.

That was just fine with Evan as he had no desire to talk right now, he simply wanted to find a place to set his tired aching body down with the possibility he would have the ability to stand up again. He would have to wait until the deputies showed up so he and the sheriff could get to the squad car.

Thank all that we hold precious the deputies were relatively close and both had arrived within five minutes. Of course, it helps when you can run lights with your siren blasting and cherries on fire. Each one of them took two of the assailants, the two still standing and two who were coming around to consciousness. The deputies asked about an ambulance, but the sheriff didn't think either of them had life threatening injuries. No sense dragging the EMT's out of their chairs. Evan might have taken a beating, but he'd given almost as good as he got.

"Please give these gents a nice comfortable place to sleep tonight," he told the deputies, "and have the doctor come over and check out the two who were clocked."

He came over to lend a shoulder for Evan to lean on, "Can you walk to the car?"

"I'll get there."

It took a while, as he couldn't hardly walk and it was hard to lean on the sheriff with as much pain as he carried, but they made it. No one was in a hurry.

"Maybe we should run you into town so the doctor can have a look at you as well, you look like shit. How big was the truck?" The sheriff attempted levity, but quick gave it up as a hopeless exercise. Stupid of him to try.

He eased Evan into the passenger side, he'd have more room in the back, but thought Evan would be worse for the wear if he had to ride all the way home on that hard-plastic seat. The front was at least padded, he'd just take it slow.

Fifteen minutes later after doing his best to avoid the worst of the holes, cracks, and uneven pavement they pulled up outside of Evan's house. Sung, Suzette, Doe and Glen were standing on the front porch waiting, and immediately made for the passenger door.

"They're the ones who called and told me you been gone all day, they was getting worried. With just cause, it turns out," the sheriff said as he exited the car to come around and stay out of the way of the mob.

Between the worried, relief, scolding for going so far alone, not taking the flip phone Suzette had bought for him, not telling anyone where he was going, comforting murmurs, cooing, mothering, he was glad to be in the company of People. They knew, they understood and would know what needed doing.

They got him inside and comfy on the couch, well, as comfy as he was going to be for quite some time, and a little glass of pain relief. He downed the bourbon holding out the glass for a refill. Sung brought the bottle, someone had been thoughtful enough to buy a fresh one. They knew what to do.

"Same guys?" asked Sung.

"Yes, four of them," answered the sheriff, "but we have them safely locked away for now."

"Where did they come from? To surprise you in the middle of the field?" He couldn't tell which woman spoke or if it was both.

The questions came like lightning, the answers slow and a little slurred now, but he'd sleep. That was what he needed most right now, rest. The badgering tailed off finally as they realized they were not helping the matter.

Before Sheriff John walked out the door, he hesitated, turning to Evan, he had one more question but didn't know how to ask it, Evan saw.

The man had saved him from a worse beating than he'd ever had, he had right to ask.

"What is it, John?" He had never referred to the sheriff as anything but. Well, he was a friend now. He'd showed up when Evan needed him most.

"If what I saw up in the mountains was real, and I gotta believe my own eyes, well, why didn't you, what about," he just couldn't say the words because that would mean he believed in fairies, goblins, and animal spirits out of myth.

"Why didn't I turn into that huge bear?"

John nodded once.

"Not allowed, not by me," he straightened up where he sat, "you see, if every time you get into trouble you pull your gun and start pulling the trigger, each time it means less. Each time it gets easier until you don't think about it at all, you pull out the gun, point and shoot."

John wanted to argue the point but couldn't, it was known in the business as having a happy finger, and it wasn't a good thing.

"So, I don't. Imagine if folks commenced hearing stories of a man who turned into a bear. At first, they'd laugh, mocking anybody who told them. Tell them to come back when they was sober or down from the drugs. But then if the stories keep gettin' told, by more and different folks, maybe folks they trust, they got to reconsider. They start believing, next thing you know you got bear hunters coming out the woodwork, people not trusting each other case they might turn into a huge bear and eat 'em

"The Bear has his place, but it ain't in this world, it's in his. I'll heal, but there won't be any stories we have to deny, I won't have to move, and maybe, just maybe, them fellas'll have a little more respect for old people from now on."

The sheriff laughed hard as he stepped through the door. "Ya-hey to that!" Shit, was he goin' Native?

The Crowd Thickens

Within a few days some of the pain had subsided, not all, but it was bearable. One of the great benefits of being an immortal spirit animal was any physical injury tended to heal quickly. The Mother did not want you suffering as that would radiate out to all your children, causing them pain, shortness of temper and fighting. She hated belligerence and combat, it was destructive to the soul, harmed innocents, threw the balance in a tither and devastated beauty. It always made him wonder why she suffered humans.

For more than a week he rode the couch, reading, talking to the others, trying not to think of Her. Every so often he would slip across where he could heal for a few weeks there, but it would only be a couple hours here. Over there he could think of anything he wanted, as he had the time, here he couldn't 'cause he didn't. It wasn't that he didn't want to, he most certainly did, every thought of Her would distract from the pain in his shoulder, arm, and leg, but he had to concentrate on the tangle at hand. He apologized to Her memory knowing She would forgive.

They were thinking of this whole thing wrong; he knew it to the soles of his feet. It fit together too perfectly; it shouldn't be this easy to pin it on someone who trafficked in deception. Plus, the offending party had been brilliant in disguising who they were and what they were doing, now all had been handed to him on a silver platter; he didn't like it. When he explained his discomfit to the others, they put it down to his pain, the attack, the fact he had too much time to think.

"Why don't you try to walk down the lane a few houses, try to stretch out some of those atrophying muscles before you're a cripple," Suzette cajoled.

"She's got a point," echoed Sung, "I could go with you, just in case, you know..." he refused to speak their anxieties out loud. Even spirit animals can have superstitions.

"Or you could take Glen," Doe piled on, "he's been a bit surly since Coyote took off," she gazed towards the back of the house as if she could see him through the walls sulking out back.

"Where'd Coyote go?" this was news to Evan.

"Where does Coyote always go? Who knows, to bother someone, boink some pretty, young coyote, get drunk with folks down Mexico way. He took off and never said to a word, to no one," Doe made sure Evan knew the implications.

"Glen!" shouted Evan in his best commanding tone.

The screen door opened and slammed shut, footsteps, painfully, slowly made their way into the front room.

"Yeah," he may not have been a teen in number, but attitude made up for a lot.

"These nannies believe I need to exercise these muscles and don't feel grandpa can go it alone, would you care to accompany me on a stroll down the block, not far, so I don't fall down and hurt myself?" He put on the frail so all would know his displeasure at their mothering. They did not care.

"Sure," enthusiasm was in short supply.

Glen helped him to his feet, and they gingerly made for the door. It was a bit of a project to get Evan down the four stairs and headed in the appropriate direction. He hated to admit it, but they had been right, too many hours on the davenport made a bear stiff, sore, and wobbly. The three inside pretended not to be glued to the windows.

As they strolled—an extremely forgiving definition of the action—down the lane Evan had to admit once the stiffness and sore lessened he began to enjoy the physical activity.

"Feeling a little abandoned?" He didn't bother to glimpse over;

he knew what he would see.

"He didn't say nothin' just took off," there was no need to explain who. "I thought we was friends. We ran together every day, didn't have to talk or explain nothin' just two guys sharin'."

It hit Evan, Glen had no friends, nobody to hang with, talk to, just be with. Here he was in the middle of some kind of reawakening, finding out who he was or wasn't, and he had no one to confide in. And this change of life was huge, this wasn't hormonal, this was mind blowing. Coyote would have been the perfect companion if he hadn't've been Coyote.

"Coyote is like that, it has nothing to do with you. I think he does like you, it's just his nature not to get too close to others, he is a loner and likes life that way," Glen had to understand the inherent character of the immortals. You couldn't judge them by the same metrics as humans, they were NOT the same.

"When you have lived since the dawn of time and will continue until the end, the concept of time means nothing," he tried to impart the difference in concepts, "and when you're as erratic as Coyote, time means even less. He becomes bored at the drop of a pin. He has to keep moving for fear he is missing something. He has no idea what that might be, he just knows something is going on somewhere and he wants to be a part of it. He assumes y'all will just pick up where you left off whenever he gets back." Evan peeked over to see if Glen was soaking any of this in.

"I guess," well, it was a start.

"He doesn't' mean to be callous, he just doesn't think about it, he assumes we are all the same," at that Evan had to chuckle, he had never tried to explain Coyote, or any of them, to an 'outsider' before, it was an interesting exercise in thought problems. "You have to understand it is his nature, he can't change who he is. I guess the rest of us have been around him so long we don't take offense if he takes off in the middle of a sentence, we know he'll be back, usually with an entertaining story or two." He shrugged; how do you solve a problem like Coyote?

"I guess," but Evan could see the wheels turning as Glen was coming to grips with his new reality.

"Things, life, the whole of reality has changed completely for you." Evan spoke knowing the words were pointless "It's going to take some time for you to come to terms, luckily you have all the time in the world. Literally!" He guffawed and slapped Glen on the back to reassure. He'd be alright

Coming up the steps was easier than going down, Evan was pleased to discover. He assumed it was because the muscles were in a little better working order than they had been on initial motion. He would be alright. Back to working out the bigger puzzle at hand.

The concern he had was not that some aspect of this whole craziness didn't point to Iktomi, it was that every single thing did. And she would not have been that sloppy, she was too smart. Oh, she loved to spin her web, playing puppet master, make everyone dance to her tune, but not this.

Evan didn't know her well, mostly by reputation, but he couldn't make himself believe she was the center of it all. Hell, he couldn't make hisself believe any of The People were, but facts was facts, someone was. First, he would have to clear things up with Iktomi, and soon.

Banged up as he still was made heading up the mountains extremely difficult if not impossible. He wouldn't be up to the trip. This would require him to leave the body behind in stasis while his spirit did the traveling. Unless anyone looked too close, they would assume he slept. He didn't want anyone, human or People, discovering he wasn't here.

He could make the trip and back in one night assuming nothing went screwy. What could possibly go wrong? He was going to strip down to his essential state, beard her in her home, surrounded by her minions, have a nice chat, some tea, and bid her a fond adieu. Right.

The couch was lumpy, which was homey, but not always comfortable. He would sleep in the queen that he had shared with Her. It would bring luck. She would not allow any harm to come to him. Hadn't She come to him when he was getting his hide tanned?

Sleep came hard, he knew it would. Anytime you had to get some rest the mind run in fifth gear and the tach would pin. It never failed. He closed his eyes, relaxed his body, and the brain flipped the switch. It raced through all that occurred over the past months. A simple story in an almost deserted corner bar had led to a confrontation which was now out of control. What had been said? What had triggered?

Nothing, that's what, his brain shouted, this is being stoked by outside forces, not you! You are not the center of the universe! Though you play an important role in this vignette, it had to concede. His broken heart, his grief, his strength, and lack of control. Who among the people would have allowed themselves in so deep? To truly join souls, to become one with a human. None, that's who, just the dumb old bear. This was why we are not permitted the mating for life humans are. We could destroy the world with our pain. The animal kingdom don't mate like that, they breed, and we represent them.

Although, some do, came the thought. What species mate for life? He would have to investigate once he had gotten a sense of where Iktomi stood. Hmm, interesting side road of thought.

His body finally sunk into a restful state giving the appearance of sleep. His consciousness separated from the body crossing over the territory of dream and spirit. He knew approximately where Iktomi's lair was, as he had slid by it once or twice in his travels, though had never stopped in; who would?

It was dark forest seldom covered by any who were not hopelessly lost. What he sought was a cave entrance surrounded by rock, like a gash in the granite in a crevasse hidden by pine. She was not a sociable creature, preferring her own kind rather than the companionship of others. Fine, he wasn't seeking friendship, just answers.

Sunlight now blocked by towering pines told him he had entered her territory. A shiver ran down his back though in this phantom state there was nothing she or her children could do to affect him, still...

The scene resembled the yard of someone way too far into the Halloween vibe. Cobwebs hung from every tree, like fresh snowfall. Evan was certain that if sunlight could force its way through the pines this would be a wonderland. Though the thousands of insects captured, half eaten, and decaying might be off putting.

The grandest web he had ever witnessed announced the

entrance. He saw thousands of spiders skittering along their own webs, each connected to hers, a massive highway system so all would know what one knew. Watching the trees and all between come alive did little to reassure one was safe from harm and was enough to give the boldest creature night sweats, not solace. In this parallel world he might not be physically here, but he was solid enough to detect web on skin, feel claw dig into soft soul, the scent of death.

He plucked one of the mooring threads to announce his presence, though he knew she knew, still it was always more polite to ring the bell rather than come busting in. He took a step back and waited, she would want to force discomfort, unease by putting off her entrance. Evan took a breath and sat back on his haunches.

"Well, Bear, what brings you to my neck of the woods?" came a pleasant, sultry, hypnotic voice. The hollow of the cave amplifying and echoing her words.

"Was hoping to have a word or two about a matter of grave importance," he responded honestly.

"The crack and ensuing malice?" she knew but remained coy.

"Of course."

"Why would you come to me?" there was a playfulness in her question. She toyed with him but did so out of mischievousness rather than ill will.

"I think you know what people are saying, your spies surely have informed you of goings on and the lay of the land," if she wished sport he would oblige.

"People say too many things," she scoffed, "they are bored, lazy and like to gossip, I pay them no nevermind."

"Can't say as I blame you, though with the discord, the fractured sides, the animosity, I'm afraid what they say gets blown out of proportion and a simple prank becomes war. I fear for The People," Evan thought it time to give a nudge, "all fingers keep pointing in the direction of the weaver."

"I am an easy target, because I tease and sometimes feelings get bent," a snicker echoed.

"Still..."

"It does sound like me, to an extent. It is awkward and clumsy, and I have been known to be clumsy, sloppy," the silk vibrated with movement, a soft hum filled the air, the mocking tone aroused her children. The children of Iktomi buzzed and chittered almost out of Bear's hearing range. "Clumsy like a ballerina!" she danced across the fine thread, pirouetting, a twist, flip landing in front of the large spirit Bear.

"I am known for being subtle not crashing through the bushes like some bull moose or stampeding like an animal!" the insult to her cleverness, grace and finesse enraged her. She threw the insults back like daggers, "I am delicate and wily, AND I DO NOT HURT OTHERS!" all eight eyes bore holes in his lowly two.

"I am not here to accuse, but to ascertain truth," Bear would not be intimidated. Not by her, nor her numerous children. "There is something horrible occurring, it seems to be concentrated around me, and I want it ended before anyone else gets hurt!"

"People have been hurt?" she was genuinely concerned.

"So far only me, but it will not remain so if we don't work together. I told you all fingers pointed to you, and I have to confess, I thought so for a while until I took the time to consider," his tone was apologetic, offering concession, "I discovered my foolishness. You would not be so clumsy or sloppy. It was a nice package all wrapped up, tied with a bow, ready to be gifted. You would never be so stupid."

"Thank you," she was sincerely grateful he was here to apologize, her ego assuaged, her anger tempered. Though, there was more. "What is it you want from me, Bear?" Time to get down to parleying, "I know you didn't come all the way here chew the fat, make nice and apologize."

"It is becoming obvious that I have to figure a way to mend the balance, as, I guess, I am the one who broke it." There was no mirth. "I was hoping you would ask your children to watch," he didn't want to imply spy, "and tell me of anything strange, meetings, any of The People acting suspicious, or more suspicious than normal. Who is interacting with whom, where and what might have been said," he knew he was asking the world, but without it the world might end.

"I will," she eyed him suspiciously, "are you going to tell me who you think is trying to pin the coming unpleasantries on me? I do have a right to know," she pushed.

"As soon as I have more information, proof, whatever I can find, I will tell you. Until then we have wasted enough time chasing phantoms and accusations, I see no reason to lay guilt on another without rock solid proof," he would say no more. Meeting concluded.

He knew as he awakened in the dark, he was putting much on the line by trusting Spider, yet he knew it was right. Spider might be a trickster, loving to have her fun at the expense of others, especially if she could tweak the noses of those who thought themselves mightier People, but she wouldn't put the fate of the world on the line. Though he had thought the same thing of Coyote, now he wasn't so positive.

That was the fly in the ointment, he had no idea who he could or couldn't trust implicitly. Doe and Suzette surely, but could he trust Sung? He hadn't known him previous to this emergency, hadn't had much interaction before now, hadn't needed any. Though, to be honest, he hadn't known any of them well before now. He wanted to scream his impotence. He got up to face the day and he needed coffee.

Was he siding with the females of The People because he was biased that way? Did he really believe that females were less prone to mischief than males? And, really, when it came to The People, the representations, such as he, were whatever they were at that moment. They could be male, female or a combination of both. He was the representation of all his children, not just the males. So, why would he be more trusting of those who represented females at this juncture.

Her. That was it, part and parcel. She colored his decisions, shaded all his thoughts. He had to be more self-aware, understand why he reacted as he did and guard against his own prejudices.

All he wanted to do at this moment was romp in the forests for a few years. Eat berries, grubs, and honey, lounge in the sunshine and hibernate for a few winters, was that asking too much? Right now, yes, it was. He had to concentrate on the chore at hand, then maybe.

He must have been lost in his thoughts for longer than it felt as the sun was now a quarter of the way up in the sky and beams streamed through the half closed blinds and door window.

"Grandpa!" came the scream of delight as the door swung open and she was in his arms.

She shouldn't, couldn't, be here, he had to focus on too many things, he'd told her explicitly to stay away from here, yet here she was wrapped in his love.

He was attempting to weed out who was pulling strings, who was in league with whom. How could he repair the damage done to the balance of life? How could he protect those he had come to care about while restraining those who would destroy? How was he to save the world while playing grandpa to a young teen he loved dearly.

But here she was, he could deny her nothing. She was the best of Her. Her heart, Her compassion, Her empathy, Her understanding, the way She just knew. She even had Her eyes, nose, but most of all Her smile. He loved this child, maybe she was safer where he could keep an eye on her to protect her. Maybe.

"Oh honey, you shouldn't be here, it might get dangerous," he hugged her close. Yes, there were other grandchildren and his two daughters, you should never favor one over another. Yes, you shouldn't but he did.

She was the one who came over to listen to the stories. She who made his lunch, peanut butter, and strawberry preserves on homemade wheat bread with rippled potato chips, his favorite, or so she said. She believed, she who defended him, who loved him unconditionally. She who inherited his personality and loyalty. She who now had sole possession of his heart, and therefore, was the biggest threat to him. She was a weapon they could throw at any time. Still, he was gladdened to hold her in his arms.

"Then you need someone to care for you!" she stated with finality, examining him with her eyes, "looks like I am not a moment too soon."

With the sound of doors crashing open, excited conversation the rest of the house came alive and rushing to see who might have broken in. Frantic excitement turned to bemused interest as the others rushed in ready for battle and instead found the young teen scolding her grandfather. They stood outside the door attempting silence and invisibility far too late.

"As much as that might have had some embarrassing overtones," Sung mused in a hushed tone from behind a strange envious expression, "I find myself wishing, for a moment, to share in the love."

The squeak of floorboard and voices caught the attention of Grandfather and granddaughter, as if the cacophony earlier hadn't, twisting their attention to the three at the door who could only smile, half-heartedly waving away their slight fluster at being caught eavesdropping.

"Who are these people," whispered the girl, eyes wide with wonder. She did not appear frightened nor shocked to find three folks jammed into a doorway in her grandfather's house, just curious.

"Well, hon, these are friends of mine visiting from out of town," he stammered, "that tall fella with the shock of black hair sneaking through all the grey on top is Sung," who tipped his imaginary hat, "next to him, the young fella is Glen, he's from down t' bar I like to have a beer at," Glen gave another awkward wave with a sheepish grin, "and the pretty lady is Suzette." Who kind of curtsied, stopped herself, then one nod of the head.

"She's just lovely," said with hushed awe.

"Lady and gentlemen, this is my granddaughter, one of the finest folks you're ever gonna meet, though she doesn't listen when her grandfather tells her to do something. Alexandra."

"Interesting choice," issued from somewhere behind the wall of people.

"I thought you were next door resting," A stern Suzette reminded the visibly tired Doe.

"Did you think I wouldn't hear all the commotion? Did you think I would roll over and go back to sleep not wondering what might be taking place over here," a joyful tinkle of laughter escaped the lips of the other most stunning woman Alexandra had ever laid eyes on. They were like two sides of the same perfect coin except one was light, one was dark and a bit of a height difference.

"What did you mean, 'interesting choice'?" Interrupted Glen.

"Her name, it is Latin, though I am quite certain whoever named her did not realize it," she bowed slightly from the waste in apology to Evan, "it translates loosely as 'the helper' or 'defender of man'." She could not take her eyes from the girl, there was more to this than she was voicing, and Evan couldn't wait to send Alexandra to safety so he could speak with Doe.

"She will have to defend man some other time. It is very late, and she needs to be safely tucked into her bed and sleeping," he attempted firm reprimand, yet only love showed.

"The sun is barely up!" Bear glanced out the window at his mistake forgetting he had been on a mission while others slept. "I wanna stay here!" Her voice perfect petulant teen, "You have all your friends over, I shouldn't have to go," she begged in a pouty tone used specifically for grandfathers.

"I told you, there are things, maybe dangerous things, going on around here and I have to focus on those, not be worried about you," his eyes begged her understanding, but today, her eyes chose not to see.

"They know, don't they? The animals know. It is why they are here. If they can stay to help you then I am staying," feet firmly planted on floor, arms crossed across chest, the dare had been thrown. "You need me, mom doesn't, she doesn't even know I'm gone. Most of the time she doesn't know where I am, she doesn't care," there was no seeking of pity nor denial, just facts, he knew the situation, her mom. She spoke the truth; she would not be missed.

But he was supposed to be the adult in the room, yet he wanted her here, he needed her strength. And here he would know where she was, they would have to come through him to get her. She was right, she was better protected here than at her home with her mother passed out on the couch.

Wait! What had she just said? 'The animals know?' What the hell had she meant by that?

Alexandra swooned, her head swimming, the world spun fast and loose, as did reality. The lightning bolt of realization struck, she blinked once, twice, slowly attempting to bring the world into focus. What had she meant by her declaration about what the what knew and what the hell had she seen?

She had said what she saw without thinking that she couldn't have seen what she thought she saw. She stared hard at those in the outer room, her grin growing," Oh my," she breathed. She took two, then three steps up to where she could look right into their eyes. All four now frozen, afraid to move a muscle. What was she seeing? Alexandra stepped back, "Oh my," tears of joy, a small squeak of awakening, comprehension stole across her features. "Oh my," she giggled, clapping her hands while her feet did a jig and she turned to her grandfather. With the largest smile he had ever witnessed on a human face she shouted with glee and threw herself back into his arms.

She hugged him as hard as she dared around his thick neck, burying her face in his thick black hair. She pulled her head back ever so, staring, 'shouldn't his hair be white?' a voice in the back of her mind spoke with uncertainty, before moving onto the matter at hand. She looked intently into the deep, brown wells of his eyes. "Oh my" she hugged him again.

"They're true, aren't they?" she hushed into his ear, "the stories, they aren't stories, they're true." And the tears flowed like liquid love. She knew it, she knew it all along. He was immortal, and these were his immortal friends. She wept joy, ecstasy, and the certainty of the righteous before...

The tears abruptly ceased; the breath caught in her throat as she pulled back from the tight hug. A quizzical glance and her world shifted, changing, morphing into something unrecognizable but wonderful. Reality did not come crashing down around her, the fog lifted, all she had ever known became crystal clear. She had been blind, but she was blind no more.

"She knew, did you know she knew?" She shook her head at how dumb the question was, "No, of course you didn't. Grandma knew," he shook his head, gently dispelling any notion she might have had about Her, but she held his head in both her hands and held his gaze with her own. "Yes, she did. She never once denied your stories. She never said I shouldn't believe them. She asked me not to. I told her once that I loved your stories, she said I should, but she begged me not follow you. She was afraid if I knew, if I had faith in the truth of them, I would want be like you, but she knew. She never once told me you made them up, never once called them lies or fairy tales, she always told me they were your stories because she knew."

Oh my, the two words shot across his brain like sizzling hot pokers. He staggered, catching himself on the doorjamb before he toppled. Was it true? Did She know? Did She become upset when he would tell the stories because She knew and realized She would not be there for him. It must have tortured Her with the pain of knowing, knowing She could not follow him on his forever path. Oh my, how She must have loved him to let him wander the mountains by himself, because She knew he would suffer so without it.

Did you know, my love? I am so sorry. I would have taken you with me, I would have shown you all the wonders of this world and the parallel. I would have given you the beauty and magnificence of two worlds.

As he considered Alexandra's words, he knew the truth of them. She had never denied the veracity of the stories, not to him, not to the children, not to the grandkids. She had always asked them not to judge, it was OK to let the imagination run a little wild, but they shouldn't follow too close. For they couldn't. They were not like him, they would not live forever, and the knowledge would eat at them every day. As it must have eaten at Her.

Oh, Great Spirit, silent the words spoken from the heart, sent on the soul, please let Her know, please tell Her, it was and always will be forever.

"I did not know She knew," he wept into his granddaughter's hair, "I swear I did not know."

The others made themselves scarce, disappearing into the backyard or over to the old folk's house. Sung grabbed a bottle, Glen the glasses.

"How did you know about the others?" it finally hit Evan, she had seen they were not human, she should not have had the ability, not here.

"I don't know, just when I saw them, they were kind of fuzzy around the edges, like a picture out of focus. So, I screwed up my eyes, like you showed me when I was a kid," she grinned, "and there they were. A wolf, a deer, an otter and a kind of a dog, but there was something wrong with him, I don't know, just out of focus."

A Gathering of The Family

∞

Time will allow healing; however, time and healing don't always move at the same pace. Evan was stiff in the mornings. If he turned too quickly or reached the wrong way—too high, too far left, or tried to tie his shoes—sharp, stabbing pain would shoot through his body like an electrical shock knocking him to his equally painful knees until he could regain his breath. He'd be fine, if only he had another lifetime or two, but he didn't.

Sung and Suzette worked out a stretching regimen to begin his day, which helped to a degree. The only stretching he wanted was the long, deep stretch that followed a few days nap, such was life. He could move with less pain every day.

Alexandra refused to leave, telling him if he demanded she go, she would not go home, but would hang around outside to keep watch. She was safer, he hoped, in their company. They called her mother to let her know, though neither could tell if she understood. She had either just woken up or was in the bag at eleven in the morning. He'd made some mistakes with that girl; mistakes he couldn't go back in time to repair. He sincerely wished he could.

Wouldn't that be a nice power to have? To move freely through time, fix a little misstep here, put a patch on hurt feelings there. Nothing big, nothing that would change the future of the world, just simplify, create a more pleasant now for some. But would that be all that would happen? The beating of a butterfly wing becomes the hurricane. And not even an immortal can move backward in time.

"Has anyone seen Mika of late?" Asked Glen as he walked through the house, apparently with nothing to do and seeking a companion to not do it with. "I thought maybe..."

"It would appear he can only suffer our presence for limited periods, then it is time for him to go cavorting through the forests and towns seeking his own entertainment," relayed Suzette.

She liked the free spirit yet found it impossible to trust him completely. Maybe it was reputation, maybe it was the way he always seemed to be looking sideways at people, the way he was always seeking that edge. She knew he was not working with them so much as working for himself and using them to his advantage. None of the rest came across that way.

Sung came into the kitchen fidgeting with some mechanical thing no one else could discern, busy work, he set it on the table, nodded to where Glen sat in a morose state, and scrounged in the fridge for something to gnaw on. He, like all the rest, was growing more anxious and agitated by the day. There comes a time in conflict when you wish whatever was going to happen would quit screwing around and get to it.

"Glen," he said to the inside of the fridge, "I'm bored out of my skin, you wanna run?"

Glen's eyes lit like spotlights, his head bobbing yes, finally realizing the wolf couldn't see him around the fridge door, almost shouted the word, "Yes, dear god, yes, please!" He hadn't run since Coyote's disappearance. The strange thing was, he had never been a runner, had never taken up any kind of exercise that he remembered, now it had become as much a part of him as breathing. And right now, he needed to breathe.

"Think Evan would mind?" he turned to Suzette.

"I think he would be jealous," she considered for a moment, "though not as jealous as he would be if he knew you were taking a nap."

Sung and Glen scooted out the back at full gallop seeing who could outrun whom. Boys and their competitions, smirked Suzette.

The knock on the front door startled all concerned, as they had not been expecting anyone. Well, they had, but knew those whom they expected would not be ringing bells or knocking to announce their presence.

"Shit, with my luck it is probably either Jehovah's Witnesses or the Fuller Brush Man," Evan shambled to peer through the blinds, "though I'd rather the Fuller Brush...Interesting, curiouser and curiouser."

Doe and Suzette followed close behind, they would protect the rear. Alexandra peeked out from the kitchen, if she was needed, she could be there in four steps. Everyone was on alert; she had been informed of all she should know; and nothing more. Evan had no idea why or for how long she had had the ability to 'see' The People, but she shouldn't have that ability. No human should, it was perplexing to say the least. Maybe a skoosh of his DNA had leaked through after all.

The three large men stood in a small semi-circle behind the petite woman, hands clasped at their waists attempting to give the impression they weren't there. It was comical, yet you could almost taste the threat.

"May I help you?" asked Evan as he opened the door. He had thought about just cracking it a few inches but just as quickly reconsidered. Number one he didn't want to give the impression of dismay or weakness, number two he wanted them to know they were welcome. He stood in the wide-open door, holding the screen almost as if it was yawning.

"Hey Bear," said the large man to the woman's right.

"Elk! I almost didn't recognize you with that damn suit on," japed Evan.

He could tell by the way the large man fidgeted and pulled at the sleeves of suitcoat and shirtsleeves he was uncomfortable. "Why don't you all come inside where you can relax, kick off those shoes and those coats, and we can share a sip." He waved them in.

Alexandra stood in awe, not believing for a second these huge animals would squeeze into the hallway, and if they did, how much damage would they cause. They came into the kitchen on their way out back nodding to her as they passed through. She gaped at the hallway, not even a vase knocked akimbo. She scooted out back, she was NOT going to miss a second of whatever was taking place.

Evan sat on an up turned log, the guests tested the strength of the outdoor furniture, well, except for the small woman with the over-sized ears. She stood with the air of authority yet ready to be off at the snap of a twig.

Alexandra huddled just inside the corner of the porch, protected from the chill breeze running down from the north carrying the promise of winter. Heavy clouds skittered across a lapis sky carrying winter south, she could feel the shovel in her hands and the bite of frost on her toes. Yet, that was only in her head, she could feel none of the chill where she crouched out of grandpa's notice.

No introductions were necessary, they all knew who each other was, if not personally, by reputation and scent.

"I thought Wolf was hanging around here," said Elk, "been a while since we crossed paths, was hoping to say hello. We've had our differences," he grimaced at a harsh memory, "but Mother is the one who made us as we are." He was rambling.

"He is out for a run with Glen," replied Evan. There was more here than was being voiced, it was wrong. The People did not dance around truth, they lived for it. Now, all were being cautious in all they said or inferred.

"Alexandra," so much for keeping out of the notice, "in the cedar chest in the hallway, up against the stairway, under several blankets is a long wooden box, would you mind making yourself useful instead of pretending to be invisible?" Love and a gentle tone took any hurt out of the words.

A minute later she was handing him the box. It was maybe two-foot long, four inches high, and eight across, she had a thing for measurements. It was dark brown with carvings of the sun, moon, stars, and animals covering the entirety of the surface. It had heft but was not heavy. She scurried back out of the line of sight.

Evan opened the box and pulled out what resembled three wooden pipes, one with a carved stone fitting perfectly on a notch on top of it. He assembled the single pipe, murmuring a prayer while the others remained silent. Next, he lifted the cloth insert, hidden underneath was a leather pouch filled with, what she was quite certain from the look of it was tobacco. Pouring enough to fill the hollowed-out stone he set the rest aside, cinching it with his teeth, all the while continuing his prayer. Flicking a wooden match on the stone at his feet he lit the tobac.

He held the smoke in his mouth for several seconds before allowing it exit. He did not puff like one does with a cigarette or cigar, merely opening his lips and allowing the smoke to leave of its own accord, while he brushed it against his face, neck, and pushing it down to his chest. He passed the pipe to the small woman sitting quietly next to him.

She repeated the ceremony before passing the pipe on to Doe who then repeated before handing it to Suzette, she passed to the next who repeated, passing on to the huge man to his right, who methodically repeated with a prayer before passing it on to the last who repeated the ceremony before passing it to Alexandra. Her eyes grew wide, staring at her grandfather, what was she to do? She'd never smoked anything in her life, surely, he didn't expect her to smoke this pipe.

Evan sat silent, eyes 'closed', meaning he could see her and waited.

"You are one of The People," spoke the woman in a muted tone, "if you wish to remain you must bathe yourself in the smoke to guarantee you speak the truth."

Well, she had every intention of remaining! She glanced at her grandfather one more time before setting flame to tobac, he mouthed, don't inhale, as he puffed out his cheeks. She mimicked what the others had done and passed the pipe back to Evan. His pride was evident in the respect with which he received it, and his smile.

"So, cousins, what brings you here?" he quipped as he lovingly dismantled the pipe and placed all back in the wood box.

They snorted, except the petite lady who barely wriggled her nose at the jape.

"We do not want war among the People," Alexandra guessed the woman had been chosen as spokesperson as the others remained stoically silent, nodding heads in agreement.

"No one wants war, we have never had war among The People," agreed Evan, "I do not want this war, but someone seems awfully intent on bringing it to me."

"You still have no idea who?," rumbled the huge man sitting on the right of the woman, his face a conflict of consternation and empathy.

Alexandra squinted her eyes to see true and they popped open, she was quite certain there was an audible pop as all gaped her way.

"What is it, child?" asked the small woman. Alexandra wished they had exchanged names. She didn't wish to keep thinking of people by their description. As if hearing Alexandra's thoughts, "I am Willow." She held out her hands so Alexandra could walk into her embrace. It was the most natural thing she had ever done.

"I did not know," she began.

"You did not know what," prompted the woman.

"I did not know who you all were, I am sorry, I should show much more respect," Alexandra bowed, curtsied, stumbled, and sat.

"And who do you think we are?" asked the man to her left, a whimsical, curious expression dancing about his eyes.

"You are Elk, the noble and majestic, he," she said pointing at the man in the middle, "is Frog, of hidden beauty and peace, you," she giggled, but ever so slight, delight not mocking, pointed to Willow, "are Rabbit, the joyful, intelligent, known as Steps through Fear, and he," she pointed at the massive man with the smirk and kind eyes, "you are Buffalo," an awed whisper, "the sacred."

All eyes turned to Evan who sat, once again, taken aback in mild shock at this child. Had she always had this ability? They were going to need much time alone with a thousand questions to be answered.

"And these others?" Willow prodded.

"Oh, they are Otter, Deer, and my grandpa." She grinned ear to ear, "he is Bear."

"You have an interesting child here," Buffalo rumbled, "I am guessing by your expression, you did not know." He quipped, thoroughly enjoying Bear's discomfort.

"Well, now that we all know who each other are," Evan, with a shake of his head and blink of the eyes attempting to reorient, changed the subject back, "may we get down to business. You are here to avoid war within the People, how can we avoid conflict when we have no idea who that conflict is with? Or, for that matter, why?"

"You are no closer to discovering who?" Willow's tone was pensive as she repeated what Buffalo had pronounced, "We were hoping you had made progress on narrowing down the suspects. Though we all have our suspicions."

"On that I believe I have made some progress. I have come to the conclusion I was running down the wrong paths several times. First off it is my opinion that Iktomi is beyond suspicion."

"Really? She would have been my suspect number one," said Willow.

"She was in my top five," scoffed Evan, "But after having a sit down with her, I concluded this ploy was too obvious, too clumsy to be her. Everything pointed at her, she was a known trickster—though starting a war is beyond the pale of trickery—which should have been the first warning. Spider might be many things, but she is not stupid nor sloppy, nor is she, at heart, mean enough to want war. Too many of her children would die, and say what you will about our Iktomi, she is not cold-hearted when it comes to her kids."

They all nodded their ascent to his line of thought.

"And Coyote?" Frog threw the obvious.

"He would be the most natural next suspect." Willow glanced at her companions to see if they were in accord, "He has always been jealous of others, and loves to tweak noses to prove how much smarter he is, and can have, when push comes to pissed off, a mean streak."

"Ya-hey, true as day, but I don't think he would push it this far. We have all been the object of his wicked sense of humor and deceits, but he has always pulled back before any real damage can be done." Evan looked each in the eye until they grudgingly agree, "Yes, he is a pain in the ass, but I don't believe him evil. And this is evil." He waited.

"This is evil in a human way, not a People way," Evan shrugged a slight apology to his granddaughter, who shrugged truth back to him. Though he was not so certain she fit so neatly not that category, "this has the scent of human on it, with an assist from one of the people. Or one of The People manipulating humans and possibly others of The People. And the only way one of the People could be involved in something so destructive, is if that person is corrupted. There would have to be something horribly wrong, a sickness of some sort, a malignancy of the soul."

There, he'd said it, he said the words that were impossible. One of the People would have to have been twisted spiritually, to have a cancer of the soul. How that was possible, well, it wasn't, but there was no other explanation. Humans could get all twisted up in jealousies, envy, hate, but The People suffered none of that. They had squabbles and a few played their little games but nothing to contort their spirit.

"We were hoping if we showed up in strength, in a show of unity, maybe, just maybe whoever was corrupting the will of the Mother would realize how hopeless their position was. They would back down, climb back in their hole and leave the rest of us alone," Buffalo's deep, sonorous voice vibrated chair, glass and hearts. Then as if realizing, bowed an apology to Willow, not all who resided in holes were evil or to be looked down upon.

Willow smiled, "We can see that tact will not succeed. If the corruption is severe, they may not even realize what they are doing," she sat back in her chair, staring at the ground in contemplation of her last statement, before raising her eyes to the sky, right hand on chin, foot tapping, "Is that even possible?" She voiced to no one in particular.

"What?" Asked Doe.

"Could one of The People be so diseased of the soul they are causing this without realizing it?" She glanced from person to person, waiting as they considered the matter.

"It would have to be one with great, strong spirit, I suppose," chimed in Elk. "Or else none of this," he flicked a wrist to indicate the troubles, "would be possible. The fly in the soup is, if they are that strong of spirit how could they be corrupted in the first place?"

"The crack in the balance is affecting all in some ways, maybe this spirit is more susceptible than others. Maybe whomever was leaning in this direction previously," suggested Suzette.

"We are some of the strongest, but I do not think any one of us could affect others in such a way," Frog spoke in a professorial tone as was his want when he was proselytizing. "The concentration of power would probably kill whoever attempted such."

"I don't think you are correct," breathed Suzette, "the crack in the balance of life has never, to any memory, happened before. There is no way to tell how it would affect one of base intentions. I honestly believe the rupture is where the corruption comes from and where it must be healed."

"But, if one of us was so corrupted, wouldn't the others see or feel that corruption. Especially if the two were close in proximity." Doe couldn't help but believe they would know; they would have to.

"I don't know. Do any of us know the others so well we would note a change in heart or spirit? We believe we know the feel of our own but do we really? The rupture must be healed if we have any hope of avoiding war or keeping it contained," Suzette looked to the others for agreement.

They all turned gaping at Bear.

"It is true," Evan said as he closed his eyes in remorse and guilt, "though I never had any intent, the damage has been done. Until recently no one knew what had happened nor by whom, not even me."

Alexandra ran the few steps to where she could nestle in his lap, hold him tight around the neck. To protect him from what they all knew.

"But, again, who would have the strength?" Rumbled Tatanka the Buffalo. "You are talking about someone with enough power of spirit not just to control several, or a dozen, human's will and actions, but who could also be affecting the behavior of several species of The People. Which up until now, I would have thought impossible."

"There are several occurrences of the past months I would have considered impossible up 'til now. I think they might be improbable, but no longer use the word impossible." Evan could feel the weight of the task that lay before him and the guilt associated with the need. His bones ached, the eons stooping his shoulders, the want to curl up and wait for it all to go away. Though he knew it wouldn't. Not until he fixed what he'd broke.

A deep breath, straightening of the shoulders and time to take charge. "It strikes me that we have two distinct chores to accomplish, and that they may not be isolated," the others began to talk at once, their voices increasing in volume and passion. Two? How could he possibly narrow it down to two chores, there had to be a thousand things to do before... Evan shushed with a placating gesture of hands and pleading, "Hear me out."

"None of this had ever happened until I cracked the balance, true?" he glanced from face to face, all nodding their assent. "Now things have been torn asunder and we believe there might be one of The People whose spirit has been corrupted, yes?" They nodded yes, though with not the same fervor as before. "So, if we wish to avoid an all-out battle with whomever is the core of the problem and whoever has also been corrupted, as well as an unknown number of humans, then we have to approach this from two completely separate fronts. I have to figure a way to heal the True Path, and that means while I am busy saving the universe, you all have to find out who is corrupted and find a way to put a stop to whichever spirit is behind this. If they can't be stopped then you all will need to put him or her down. Those are our choices."

He could hear a leaf move under the front porch, the small spider cease spinning its web, the breath of the snail as it stopped for rest. The world was silent. No one had honestly considered the idea of ending one of the spirit animals of another. It would mean the species would become extinct.

"What do we do?" resignation filled Frog's words, backed with steel determination.

"What I am praying you can do is find out who, without who finding out about you," grinned Evan. "That way maybe you can take turns watching, observing, to find out who else of The People might be under their influence."

"Do we need to intercede with all involved simultaneously? Or can we split off some here and there, taking them out of the conflict without ending lives, but lessening their numbers before going after the central problem?" Tatanka calculating numbers in his head came to no conclusion as there was no way to know how many.

"We haven't got a clue, as no one has ever faced this sort of crisis before," Evan had hoped maybe one of them would suggest a solution, but they were as stumped as he. "I do know this, violence only escalates more violence, and death escalates all. It is my ultimate wish that once I figure out how to heal the balance it will have some effect on whoever. And then we, in a concerted effort, can heal the effected party before any more harm comes to any more people, human or spirit."

They all nodded at the wisdom of this approach, the last thing any of them wanted was to eliminate one of The People which in turn would extinct their kind. All must have had the same horrible concept occur to them at the same time, as a shiver of despair flowed through the assembled.

"Iktomi, will you side with us and lend your multitude of eyes and web?" Evan called to the sky.

"She says yes," whispered Alexandra gaping at the large black spider resting on her shoulder.

"Please relay what we have discussed to your people, and remind them, we wish no harm. We wish to avoid any kind of battle, fight, or brawl. Innocents cannot be brought into this, cannot be injured by recklessness, they must be protected by The People," Evan would brook no discussion of the point. They would hold true to their nature, to their beliefs, to their core.

"What will you be up to while we scour the world seeking the needle in this infinitely large haystack," Suzette put to him.

"Not much, just seeking The Mother, a solution to what I have done, and saving the world," Evan sighed, rubbed his not quite healed shoulder, arm, leg, and ego. It was going to be a very long inquisition.

Alexandra had been forgotten in the immediacy of the moment. The spider rubbed up against her in thanks, well, someone noticed her, before disappearing in the eaves. She knew if she asked, her grandfather would demand she remain here with the animal spirits, but she couldn't. He would need someone to watch his back, and all the rest would be busy, she was the only one available. The simple solution was just not to ask.

She was terrified at the prospect yet thrilled at the adventure. She had never told anyone about her ability to see things others couldn't, well, not since trying to explain it to her mother. Who immediately told her she was never to mention that to anyone, especially her grandfather, or people would think she, her family, and especially her grandfather were insane and would be locked away forever! At times she believed she had lost the ability by forcing herself not to see until she had forgotten the ability. This confluence of events had awoken it with a vengeance. And these 'people' were pleased, certainly they did not act like either she or grandpa were nuts!

She would use this capability to watch over and help him. She just wouldn't mention it to him or anyone else.

Plans Become Motion

∞

Alexandra shadowed her grandfather through the next several days, she slept when he slept, or so she thought, ate when he did, staying just out of sight. After the big meet a couple days previous had concluded, Sung and Glen returned from their run, not even winded, smiling like they'd just come up the walk from the car. They appeared unconcerned they had missed all the talk, the meeting, the decisions come to, and the breakdown of duties. Evan informed them of all that had been said and planned, both agreed it was as good a plan as anyone was likely to have, but they were glad they had chosen to run.

The sheriff stopped by later that evening with a nice bottle of bourbon, "Figured I'd drank more'n my share of yours, ought to replace a portion," and they commenced to put a large dent in the new one.

It was funny, Alexandra thought, that no matter how much beer, bourbon, or other liquor they consumed none of the Spirit people ever showed a sign of being inebriated. The sheriff would slur a word, stumble a bit, they'd let up on the pour, bring him coffee and some other concoction that had a miraculous effect on sobering him up, but none of them ever seemed to take note of the booze. She had to assume it was their constitution that was somehow different, booze was just for the taste and to be social.

Willow had moved in with Suzette and Doe, while Tatanka, Elk and Frog occupied the other abandoned home.

"Looks like yer getting' a real neighborhood going here," remarked the sheriff after being introduced to all.

"It's comforting to be surrounded by friends and family," responded Evan.

"Bet it is," confirmed the sheriff. "You know, I still don't believe all that stuff you showed me up in the mountains. And the farther I get from it the more I doubt what happened, like as you let me in on a dream or something," he kicked a little dirt, "but still..."

"Ya-hey, that's how it goes, one day it will seem just like a fantasy, but for now, I just need you to believe for a while longer."

"Though after meeting the kinfolk here," Sheriff John took in the assembled, not cutting bait," it feels a bit more real and solid than it did on the drive over." His bark of laugh was tinged with giddy.

What Alexandra didn't know was that Evan had told Suzette to keep an eye on her. He knew she was planning something, and he didn't want her getting in the way. Problem with having a loved one so near to danger was usually the wrong person got hurt. So, Suzette, Doe and Willow took turns on guard duty.

They quickly settled into routine, once again, and companionship. For individuals who had spent the better part of eternity as loners—oh a skirmish here and there or an alliance when needed—they found they meshed well when forced to work together. They found strengths and weaknesses, some of which overlapped, some which enhanced the others. They discovered they enjoyed each other's company. Even that of the human sheriff.

"I'm just curious," said Frog one day as he and the sheriff listened in on the police scanner, keeping an ear out for anything out of the ordinary, "is it that you no longer note the differences between us or are ignoring for the purpose of working together?"

John—another bizarre occurrence was he began to think of himself by who he was rather than his title—sat back and considered the query.

"Don't know 'xactly, I guess a little of both," he scratched his day-old beard before removing his hat and applying the same treatment to the top of his head. "It's like all a dream, none of this is real, well, until somebody whacks me in the head again or I'm running for my life. Reality is shifting, I feel like I am standing on a beach with the waves washing away the ground beneath my feet. I am just hanging on by doing my job. Sometimes it's all you can do," he shrugged his impotence at the situation.

"Do you believe we are real?" Ever the professor seeking to know.

"I know you are real because you are sitting next to me talking to me, but are you human or animal spirit? That begs the question, am I experiencing life or insanity? Am I talking to an inquisitive fellow while monitoring the scanner or a frog who embodies all amphibians?"

"Just the Anura," he corrected.

"Whatever," barked the sheriff, "Maybe we're all insane locked up in asylum somewhere, I guess right now it doesn't matter what I believe, half my brain tells me I am living in a fantasy of spirits and magic, the other half tells me to watch my back because I am in the middle of a turf war without a clue who is who."

"If I may advise," said Frog and the sheriff nodded, "I would hold tight to both, as I think by the end of this, they will both serve you well."

Sheriff John decided he might wish to recruit a few more able-bodied folks in case they required greater mass than he had at his disposal. He only had his two deputies, whom he regarded as trustworthy, though skittish. They had never questioned his authority or orders before, the fact they had last week left him less than completely certain. He expected that when the rubber hit the road, they would stand with him, but who knew who might have been corrupted. They would be normal until they weren't, this kind of thinking could drive a man nuts!

There were a couple folks in town he knew and trusted, that he considered solid, the barmaid where this had begun. She was sturdy, used to handling drunks, and could bust a head if needs be. Van from down at the garage, he was a strapper and could handle a wrench, yeah, there were a few. He could deputize them, read them the riot act, and pray they didn't fold. He wished he knew who they were fighting, how many of them there were and would he need the actual Marines. Bringing in a couple townsfolk to a huge brawl where they might get killed wasn't exactly playing according to Hoyle. He should rethink the whole damn thing. Where the hell was that bottle?

Willow caught Evan as he completed his checklist before heading into the mountains.

"Got everything you need?" she asked noting he had nothing, not a bag, a jacket, a blanket, nor food.

"I go to talk to the Mother, I have no need of anything except a clear mind and humility," his smile crooked, thoughtful. "Please watch over my Alexandra while I'm away. She truly is the best of her grandmother, the best of all I am. I know we are not supposed to have get with humans, but She was more than human, and I loved Her deeply. This child is all of that in its totality, it would destroy me if anything happened to her."

"I am still not sure about her genetic make-up," Willow watched the child as she played with Glen out in the yard. "They are both so innocent, children mixed in their heritage, confused by this world, not knowing where they fit in. It makes me sad. Yet, here, together, they are as happy as any two children have a right to be. Sometimes you just don't know."

"This ability to 'see' us as we are, especially here, is astounding," Evan shook his head in wonder, "Why would it take so many years to reveal itself?"

"Maybe it didn't," Willow said, "maybe she has had it all along but had no one to tell it to. Who would understand? Her mother? You told me she hated when you talked about being immortal, that she thought you crazy for believing such. Her grandmother? Again, she would become discomfited when you told her or the children your stories. She feared you would come to believe and become reckless, could she worry less for your scions?"

"And yet, now, it would seem mayhap She did believe, She chose to pretend for Her own sake," heartache rolled down his cheek, he didn't bother to wipe it away.

"I am beginning to think there are many things in your life which are not the way you thought them," Willow hugged him close, the promise to watch over Alexandra sealed. "Please be careful. There is obviously much more going on than we are privy to. You may be immortal, as far as that goes, but suffering in agony forever doesn't hit me as a wonderful life." One more hug and she pushed him on his way.

Alexandra watched as the two separated, she wanted nothing more than to run up to him, throw herself in his iron grip and beg him to take her with him, but she already knew the answer. Let him go then, she would find a way to follow.

Bullshit! She ran as fast as her feet would carry her and jumped into his arms; he had no choice but to catch her. She'd known that! She hugged and hugged as tightly as she could, "I love you grandpa, I love you more than anything. You are all the family I care about if anything happened to you, well, just don't. I couldn't begin to think about that. Just be careful." She hugged him one more time for luck, "I'm certain my guardian angel will watch over you."

There was something in the way she phrased that last that gave Evan pause before he turned and walked toward the open field, it would deposit him close to where his search would begin.

"Who was that?" came an unfamiliar voice startling all who stood nearby.

How in the hell could anyone sneak up on this group? Weren't they kind of supernatural? Didn't they have extraordinary powers? Not really, just immortality, and a little mojo and magic. Just enough to lend an assist when needed. They had been distracted by the leaving.

The tall, magnificent woman standing nonchalantly several feet behind with the bemused expression, bobbed her head once in 'hello' causing her mane to come alive. Yes, thought Suzette, that was the only way to describe the long, flowing, brilliantly shining thick sunshine bouncing with each movement. The woman was stunning, proud, yet didn't flaunt. The rest was only a reflection of her true self.

"Sorry, didn't mean to surprise, guess I didn't understand how intent you were on the elderly man," she flicked her hair back, "somebody special?"

"That was Evan, in whose yard we are standing," Sung sauntered up, charm on high, "he owns the house, we are but guests." His smile would have been amiable had it not been for the predatory gleam in his eye.

"Sorry I missed him," she gazed at the empty spot recently occupied, "he looked, tired." Her tone one of disquiet, strange for someone who had never met Evan.

"He's had a few hard years," defended Alexandra.

"And you are?"

"He's my grandpa, I am his granddaughter," the pride, love and honor carried a power all could feel. She didn't know why the woman's tone bothered her so. I mean, really, she hadn't said anything horrid, just that he looked tired. Well, he was. And she wasn't going to listen to anyone disparage her grandpa, she stomped off into the house.

Tatanka and Elk came out of the house next door to see what had caused the disturbance. Yes, all had felt the rancor.

"I beg the forgiveness of all, I meant no disrespect, quite the contrary he is who I came to pay my respects to," she apologized to each, "and offer my meager services."

"Equine, how lovely to see you," bowed Tatanka, "hope you aren't out hunting," he teased, but only just. He loved horses when man wasn't involved. He understood it was the humans who forced the horses to do their bidding, but still, he could outrun a man easily enough, the horse changed everything.

"Peace, brother," she curtsied, "you know if they would leave us all to ourselves there would be no animosity."

"Truth is fact," rumbled the huge man, "I have lost so many children over the ages, I thought we would soon be gone. There was a time, in the long ago, when I was the one of the mightiest of spirits, now I am but a shadow." The pain and sorrow in his voice was enough to affect all.

Though Suzette, pretty, petite Suzette, had to wonder how large would he have been before if this was but a shadow? She had never had any encounters with the grandest of the North American spirits. She'd heard of the Elephant and Whale but could not condone the teller or the far-fetched tales. And still could not, for who could be grander than he who stood before her?

"It would seem all The People's representatives are gathering," murmured Sung to Doe.

"We shall see who does and who doesn't, the attendance will be telling more than any other facts," though she didn't sound as certain as her words would indicate.

Alexandra had stomped off in a huff, as would any normal teenaged girl whose feelings had been hurt by some unthinking adult. She had used the perceived insult as an excuse to be alone, she knew it would work to her advantage. Everyone would leave her be, thinking she wished to sulk by herself. And she could go to sulk in her grandfather's room, what would be more natural? It would serve her purpose better than her own on the second floor. That would entail sneaking out and crawling down the latticework without any of these sharp-eyed first people noticing her skedaddle. She would just have to be patient.

While she pined away the few hours until dark, she wondered if she had made a mistake by not hot tailing it out right on grandpa's heels. He could be anywhere in the mountains by the time she tried to find him. How was she going to track him down in the Great Rockies?

She would find him, she could feel him, how could she forget her close tie to the man? They had always been two peas in a very exclusive pod. Not even grandma had been allowed entry. They shared something special, something unspoken, a bond between people, souls, spirits, whatever, that she could always sense where he was. She knew by closing her eyes and concentrating on him, and him alone, where he was. She'd never needed the ability more than now.

Slipping in and out of sleep only made the wait interminable. She'd fall asleep, then jerk awake to find few minutes had passed and the cycle would begin again. She was exhausted when the time finally came, and all was quiet in the outer rooms and yard. She knew someone would be walking the outer perimeter of the yards, but only one. She could watch for a few rotations and get the timing, then make her break for it. Excitement replaced exhaustion, her senses keen.

Sometimes the gods love you and care for you. The night was pitch black, the sliver of moon covered with thick cloud cover as she slipped out of the window and silently to the ground. She kept low against the dark siding of the house, dressed in a black hoodie, black sweats, and boots, she was a shadow in the night. No one could possibly see her. She would blend into the darkness until she was across the street, just before she ducked into the corn. If she did this right, she would only be visible for several seconds, not even immortal animal spirits would notice that. Then on to find her grandfather.

It was the flicker of shadow that caught at the attention. She lifted her head, a slow intake of breath, now, still as death, the only movement her eyes painstakingly seeking any motion. When your natural element was the wide-open plains, every motion was suspect and a threat. It had been near the corner of the house but all that remained was shadow. Where would a specter get to if it hadn't wished to enter the home? She focused her eyes and ears on the other two homes, easily visible in the near pitch black with her acute sight. Nothing, hmm, maybe she had been mistaken.

Across the lane a shadow moved silent as night until she stood just this side of the stalks towering over her. She checked one more time to assure she wasn't being followed before ducking into the corn field.

There it was again, that slight flicker of motion, this time over across the lane by where the late harvest corn still stood. The stalks moved as if tussled by a breeze, or the passage of someone trying to avoid detection. Well, this could be interesting. Now the question, to raise the alarm or follow. Curiosity is a powerful motivator, when sense demands you turn back, curiosity pushes onward and so Equine followed.

Alexandra hadn't thought her sketch of a plan through, therefore had not a clue how she would find her grandfather, all she had was a belief she would. She concentrated on him, trying to think like him, where he would go. If she was to have any chance of finding him, she had to immerse herself in him. What would be the quickest way into the heart of the mountain forest. She knew that was where he was going, but where was the heart. Any time she had ventured up that way it had all looked the same to her, felt the same, but there had to be a heart. That was where she had to go.

Concentrating with all her will she walked what she thought would be the path he would. He would follow his heart. It came to her. She had heard of the Red road, the true path north, that was what he would follow. Blocking every distraction from her mind, Alexandra thought only of her grandpa, his face, how his whiskers tickled when he kissed, her, the strength of the old man, she did not notice the shimmer, but she certainly noticed the change in terrain and temperature.

There! Just to the left and about a hundred yards ahead, not a flash but a shimmer of night, like heat waves, then nothing. Ah, Equine knew who and where and could guess at the why. She should go back and tell the others, but was afraid if she did, she might lose her quarry.

Elk watched from the deep shadows on the dark side of the house, as the statuesque woman made her way across the lane, obviously stalking something or someone. He kept close tabs on her in case she might need his assistance, or to see whom she might be meeting up with. He didn't know Equine, had not had run ins as Tatanka evidently had, therefore couldn't be certain whose side she was on. There was the rub, they had no idea who might or might not be on their side, or what constituted a 'side', the situation was more fluid than any could hope.

He thought about following her to see who she followed. It was becoming quite obvious from the way she moved she tracked, not meeting another. Interesting, he should follow, or at the very least alert the others. The problem was, he was the only sentry and that would mean leaving the houses unguarded. He hoped she knew what she was doing.

Hmm, but just in case. The short snort he gave through his vocal cords was a high-pitched squeal, staccato, that any would understand as a call for assist, though not loud enough to alert Equine she had been spotted.

"You wish assistance?" Frog squinted up at the much larger man.

"It would seem our new acquaintance has gone off in pursuit of a mystery into the cornfield. I thought it would be best if others were made aware as I am engaged at the present time," they knew most preferred the jargon of the First People, but these two had studied and educated themselves over the centuries so preferred more formal language.

"I shall inform les responsables," Frog was conversant in eight distinct languages, Elk in six, they enjoyed the banter, it allowed practice. He smiled as he turned to report to Suzette, who appeared most responsible and in charge.

Suzette ran upstairs to check on the whom she immediately knew Equine was following. Who else could it be? She knew before she pushed open the door that the room would be empty.

"Shit! Shit, shit, shit!" how could she have been so stupid to leave the girl alone. Alexandra had set them up perfectly with her little hurt feelings act. Now, the Great Spirit only knew where in both sides of hell she could be.

"How long ago did Elk see Equine tailing someone?" She threw the question at the diminutive Frog. She knew the blame fell on her shoulders, if anything happened to the young woman Evan would need look no further. Hope sprung for just a moment as she remembered the girl had gone to Evan's room.

Racing down the stairs two at a time she nearly knocked Sung over. He had come to the bottom of the stairs to find what the commotion was about just as she had come barreling towards the bottom and taking the corner. She was through Evan's door before Sung could get a word out. Empty. Shit, shit, shit, she knew it would be, but she had hoped.

"Alexandra has escaped the coop, I believe she has gone in search of her grandfather," she explained to the Wolf.

"Well, then she has to be close," he calmly responded. Then added before compounding Suzette's scandalized expression, "He has gone over in search of the Mother," he answered her unasked question, "Where else could he go? The girl certainly cannot follow him without someone to take her across the divide."

They walked, gathering the others, towards the backyard, the official meeting place as it provided room for all, "If she has gone in search of Bear she cannot follow him," Sung stated to all as if it was the most obvious thing in the world, "she can't follow him there." He gestured with both hands, " She can't go across without someone to take her, therefore she has got to be close by." He gazed at the others, "To the cornfield, use all senses, silence unless you hear or spy something." They all nodded their approval.

"I sure wish we had someone in the air," muttered Suzette to Doe as they made their way across the lane.

Four hours later, frustrated, and ornery from wasting a night, they settled into the backyard once again. They had found two sets of footprints, one clearly Alexandra's, the other they had to assume was Equine's. Both ended abruptly, though not at the same location. Either something spooked Equine early or she had lost sight and scent and took a leap of faith. What to do now? How was it possible that Bear's granddaughter had crossed the boundary without one of the People to escort her? It should be impossible, though Suzette was beginning to believe that with Bear and his get, nothing would be impossible.

They didn't want to lessen their forces any more than they already had, especially to send several on a wild goose chase looking for several needles in an impossibly large haystack. The girl, Evan, Equine, could be anywhere. No one knew for certain where the Mother's spirit would be at any particular moment. She was of all so could be anywhere or everywhere. Bear had believed he could find her as his need was the greatest, and need, counted for much when it came to discovering where certain spirits might be.

It was decided that until more reinforcements showed, they would have to stay put and hope for the best.

Alexandra was lost immediately. She was in mountain forests, that she knew, but trees were trees, scrub was scrub. She'd been up in the woods with friends during the day, screwing around, a little drinking, a little pot. But she was from the plains, she preferred sightlines of more than a dozen feet in any direction. Forests always made her feel claustrophobic, even here, where there was little ground clutter. The thick canopy of pines did not allow enough sunlight nor rain to seep through, ground vegetation couldn't take hold.

She knew little of the forest and what she did she had learned from the stories her grandpa had told her since she was a child. She loved his stories, he made the animals, the woods, come alive as if each was just like people. She hadn't realized until the last several days why. Now she knew, because they were.

Fantasies, imagining people who were not people and animals who were, no matter how real they seemed to her, she had been told all her life these were figments of her imagination. Make-believe planted in her mind by her farcical grandparent. She was no longer a child, she should stop buying into what the old man told her, her mother had scolded over and over.

He had never done the things he talked about. Never traveled the Rockys when they were just hills, nor swam across the plains when they were ocean. He had not helped carve the Great Lakes nor hung stars in the sky, and he had never danced with The Buffalo Girl by the light of the moon. He had never been friends of First Nation people before the white people came to this land. And he had definitely not danced with Elk, Buffalo, Cougar, Eagle, Coyote, and a hundred other animals while they each sang songs and the earth made rhythm before there were human beings. These were the fanciful dreams of an old man.

Even grandma had cautioned her against falling in with the old man's tales, but she had never denied them. Alexandra had never thought to listen carefully to what grandma said. She had told her granddaughter not to be taken in, not to follow him down the rabbit hole, but she had never actually told her not to believe. She had only asked Alex to be critical, to think through what he said, to assess for herself whether she thought it plausible that he was immortal, and what that would imply.

Truth, that was what it implied.

These were the thoughts that kept her company as she wandered lost in the forests. Moonbeams showing her little except more of the same. She thought it apropos. This was stupid, how could she have been so rash, so dumb, coming to the high mountain woodlands without a clue where to begin her search for him and now finding herself hopelessly lost and afraid. And how had she come here? She hadn't walked nor flown; she had wished herself here. How was that possible? It wasn't, this was dream, though she couldn't seem to wake herself.

She thought of him, begged him to come find her, begged anyone to come find her; just not kill her.

Equine wavered into the dense forest, immediately finding her sense of direction completely useless. She, like Alexandra, was of the open plains and prairie; it was her natural habitat where her speed and agility suited the terrain. She could navigate the trees, brush, winding streams and rocky terrain if she had to, but it was a slow, ponderous crawl. And she could negotiate the paths far easier with someone to guide her, four eyes better than two. She should've known this would be where Evan, and therefore, the girl would come. This was the heart of the world, the Great Mountains.

You could feel a presence that dwarfed your own. You might be the grandest mare to have trod the soft earth and grassland but here, you were the mouse. She listened, ears flickering to catch any sound that might lead her in the direction Alexandra had taken. Of course, on this side she was in her natural state, a large Appaloosa with pale mane, she blended in with the trees, that should work in her favor.

The girl could be either on the other side of that large copse of trees, six feet behind her or ten miles to the Northwest. If only she could have come in at the exact same point as Alexandra, they would have been within calling distance. She would have to try and figure where she had come in, then approximate where the girl had come in and start from there.

The main drawback with that brilliant idea was they had been skulking through a corn field and now were hip deep in the mountains. Add in, that distance and direction in the human world did not always translate, and you had despair. Luck would be her best option. She took a deep breath, settled her nerves, and slowly began to walk in what she hoped was the direction the child had taken.

Evan sat on a large boulder overlooking a wide, verdant valley, it was peaceful. Though darkness had settled, the moon lit the landscape brilliant enough for his excellent night vision. He wished he could stay here forever, away from whatever threatened the peace back home, away from the pain, away from people, but he couldn't. He had done the damage; he was the only one who could repair it.

And then, there was her. He loved his granddaughter; she was the best of everything he had hoped to accomplish. Not that he had set out to accomplish anything. He had merely been ambling through the forest thinking about fish and a nap. And then She wandered by, and all life changed.

There had been no plan, you didn't plan on falling in love. You were ambling through life, not paying attention, stumbled and fell into it. Yet he had known the moment he saw Her wandering free as any spirit across that mountain meadow. His chest hurt as his heart tried to force its' way out. Emotion took over where common sense should prevail, his mind had shut down as well. What reasoning should have done was stop him from attempting what his heart proposed; it was forbidden, it was impossible, it was against nature. He was of the First People, they did not cohabitate with any, not even those like themselves.

First People were where all the species of the world had originated. Though once created and set loose, their progeny would hence forth be born into the world. From that instant on they changed, genetically, physically. They had lives that flew by in the intake of breath, that was why so many were necessary. Why their main purpose was breeding, if they were to keep the species—and thereby keep the animal spirits of the First People strong—then they had to keep their numbers strong and plentiful. Evan's people were immortal, they had no need to procreate, they lived by the energy and life their children created.

Evan had lived millennium without a single thought of mating with a female, there was no need and without need there was no want, until Her. He thought, like most of his kind, he knew what love was. He loved the Mother, his children, and their scions. He loved a full belly, though, again, it wasn't need it was pleasure. He loved the feel of the hard rock and soft ground under his paws as he roamed, ran, and wandered this earth.

Ah, but the love one feels for a mate, that is something quite different. He'd never wanted it, never wondered at the mating cycle, never knew lonely, until that moment. It should have been completely and irrevocably unfeasible. It should have been.

But the heart of the Bear is immense, his soul vast, his capacity for this new emotion unlimited. And now the balance of life, of spirit, of existence was cracked and all hell was breaking loose. Shit, shit, shit, shit.

Does a Bear shit in the woods? In this instance, yes! He had to find the Mother, and soon.

Laying back on the huge boulder he gazed at the night sky trying to find hisself. One of the many marvels of the great outdoors were boulders. Put one in the perfect spot and it would absorb the heat of the sun all day long. Now, when the chill of the night was upon the land, it gave that heat back to any who might be lucky enough to stretch out on her surface. He was the chosen one tonight.

Evan loved being out here, alone—as alone as any could possibly be surrounded by nature—with his thoughts. They swam through his mind demanding his attention, he brushed them away like bothersome flies. Not now, he told them, there will be plenty of time in the morning, let us enjoy some peace.

Staring at the stars and ignoring the buzz, his thoughts at long last left him to the void. He could sense everything around him. Life exploded even up this close to the timberline. Nature never sleeps, it abounds in energy round the clock, simply different at night than the day. Nocturnal hunters silently close in on those who believe themselves safe in the dark. The owl hunts from the sky seeking any movement in leaf or twig, bats consume insects as they swarm the heights. Sometimes the hunter becomes the hunted down among the brush and rock. He could see it all in his head as the sound told the story.

His mind rode the breeze, he hadn't been this relaxed, this free of spirit since, yeah, since. The equilibrium shifted with the thought, as much as it hurt inside his chest, he pushed the vision away. At this point in the cycle, She was a distraction, the greatest distraction imaginable. Now what he required, a clear mind, was the necessity. He focused on Dubhe, the star in the middle of his back about halfway up from the horizon in the northwest sky.

It was the brightest star in the constellation, always drawing his attention as it pointed towards the small bear. There, in the northern sky, containing the Little Dipper. Ursa Minor was his favorite constellation, he loved it even more so than his own. There was consolation in having another bear to roam the cosmos with for eternity, or as close as anyone was likely to come.

He smiled. It was seldom he thought of time, honestly. Until Her he had never understood the concept. None of the First People had, they had no need to count days, months, and years. What is time when you have forever?

But She had taught him different, time meant everything, he understood that now. He fingered the pocket watch he kept on him constantly. He could see the sketch of Her engraved on the outside cover. He had scratched it there himself one night while staring at Her while She slept. His focus lost, he wept. The boulder lost its warmth, the night sky fell into chaos. How could he heal the balance when he could hardly maintain hisself.

Sheriff John Roberts patrolled alone through his town, and it was his town. He hadn't been born here but he had become a man here, moving into town from the farm lost to big agribusiness. His father never complained, if he carried anger, he kept it buried, he did not strike out verbally or physically against those who had withheld the lifegiving waters.

He sold them his family land, packed the trucks, and moved here to begin anew.

When John would ask him about it, the old man would simply say, that was the way of the world. The rich and powerful always won in the end. Some folks could hide from reality for a while, sometimes the world would pass them by, for a while, but soon or late it would find them. The object in life was not to let it crush you, it could beat the hell out of you but don't ever let it knock you down. You were at your weakest when laid out on the ground. He worked in the packing plant until it killed him. John would not let the plant or anyone or anything crush him. He hoped his deputies had the same intention.

Their grumbling bothered him, not that they'd ever had to face anything as outrageous or dangerous as what they did now, but the fact they questioned the necessity of their participation riled him. They were sworn officers of the law! Simple as that. If they didn't agree with the laws of the town, county, state, or Fed, they were free to voice their opinions in open forum, council meetings, committee meetings, boards whatever, but when the rubber hit, they were expected to do their job. High Noon played in the back of his mind, "Do not forsake me oh my darlin'." He chuckled.

The light turned red, and he glided to a stop, the car behind him tapping his bumper, what the hell? How drunk was this guy that he would hit a sheriff's patrol car? Wasn't like he was plain clothes or driving his own truck. He looked in the rearview as he slipped the gear shift into P before getting out of the car.

Hmm, nobody sitting in the car, his spidey sense kicked in as he eased the shifter back into 'Drive' automatically locking all the doors. Holding the microphone for the radio in his right hand he clicked the button as he surveilled the empty streets and sidewalks of the intersection. He set the mic on the seat next to him so he could unstrap his sidearm. Nope, he didn't like this at all. It was night but not midnight. All the streetlights were blazing, the streets should not be deserted, not completely. Folks kept early hours, but they didn't go to bed right after supper.

Movement to his right as a pickup eased into the intersection blocking that road, then another to his left stopping to block any chance at escape. But no one directly in front. Seems someone wanted to herd the quarry before releasing the trap. He once again pressed the button on the mic but did not raise it to his lips.

Speaking from where he sat, "Anyone listening right now, we have a mayday, mayday in progress at the corner of Center and Elm, mayday, at the corner of Center and Elm. Sure could use some back-up right about now, Mayday." He released the button, static.

He sat at the intersection awaiting their next move. If it were only these three, yeah, if was only, but the best way to make a guy show his hand was to play possum. He checked the rearview again, still no sign of occupant, looks like that was parked there to block any thought of re-treat. Neither the truck to the left of him nor the truck to the right were in any hurry either. He would've thought if they wanted to play like the movies, they'd be stompin' on their gas, tauntin' him with air horns and screechin' tires. Instead, there was silence, except for the sound of en-gines idling. Maybe he should try the radio again, could be those guys were taking a shit or something. He pressed the button, the radio squealed, and the brick shattered the passenger window.

Broken glass littered the inside of the patrol car, but he was un-touched. Now the engines roared to life and tires squealed on pavement, John was not one to waste time. He cut the wheel to the left as he slammed the gear shifter into R and stomped the gas to the floor. His tires spun as he caught the truck behind him at an angle so the inertia would push the vehicle out of the way rather than straight behind. It jumped the curb hitting the corner of a nice, solid brick storefront and John whipped around the catty-cornered pickup before winging the wheel in the other direction while jamming the gear into D.

You had to love a well-built cop car, solid, big, heavy and an en-gine that could pull an ox out of a mud pit. That and the extra nudge bar forward and aft might just have saved his life. He pulled the mic close to his mouth as he raced around the streets of the small town. He could've gone back to the office but reconsidered, that would be where they would expect him to go. They would be waiting, maybe they were already there. Maybe that was why the deputies hadn't answered, he prayed they were not harmed or worse.

Where to then? Where else. Slowing down to lessen the sound of tires on concrete, he began slipping through the back alleys behind the bars, stores, and small warehouses. Now, he wished he was in his own truck, shit a bright orange Mustang wouldn't stand out as much as this cherry top.

He wound his way to an abandoned garage he knew about, an old friend had died and left it to no one. Swinging in quickly he eased out of the car and slammed the garage door down. The sound of his heart pounding in his ears almost drowned out by his panting. He put his ear to the door and held his breath. Nothing. Sometimes you're lucky.

Popping the trunk, he pulled out a bag he carried with a change of clothes, civilian clothes, and changed. Reaching in the passenger door he unlocked and released the twelve gage he wasn't supposed to carry and the spare shells out of the glove box. Back to the trunk he grabbed the duffel with the extra boxes of 9 mm shells for the Glock, shoved in the shotgun shells making sure there was nothing of any use to anyone left behind. He snuck out the side door and began a zigzag pattern that would take him to the old man's house. He prayed—he was doing a lot of that today—that either he or any of those who knew John, would be there.

Down The Rabbit Hole

∞

Glen moped around the house not wishing to talk with anyone. He thought he and Alexandra had become kind of friendly if not friends. Yeah, right, if they were friends why had she taken off without a word to him? He could've come along, protected her, guided her. He had no idea where she went or why, but he should be with her, that was all he knew. She needed him, whether she knew it or not.

Damn, that was two 'friends' in less than a week, both had deserted him. He hadn't done a damn thing to warrant it, neither. He didn't know which one pissed him off more, Alexandra or Coyote. He just knew he was pissed.

Suzette watched the boy sulk and knew the reason. Alexandra was a pretty little thing, with a stubborn streak a mile wide and a wild streak twice as long. Boys liked girls who were a challenge, they would never admit it to themselves or anyone else, but they did. Oh sure, the easy girls were popular with most of the boys. They'd laugh with them, drink with them, have a little fun and give too much of themselves to them, then the boys would leave them, heading out to newer, fresher pastures. It was the way with boys.

But boys who were going to be men wanted a girl who made them work for what they had. And what they had was self-respect, a plan in mind of the kind of life they expected. And that didn't always involve babies, washing dishes and laundry. They realized early on they didn't need a man, if one wanted to tag along that might be fine, but don't think you're running the show. Alexandra was like that to a T, and Glen was smitten.

The problem was, yeah, that was the problem.

"You OK?" Suzette sat down next to where Glen was noodling in the dirt with a stick.

"Sure, why wouldn't I be?" spilled all the youthful angst, arrogance and surly one man/child could contain out onto the ground in front of him.

"Just thought you might be missing someone and want to talk," easy girl, easy, don't push too hard or you'll spook him.

"Nah, if she wanted me with her, she would've taken me with her," moody with just a dash of bravado.

That was it, wasn't it? She should have taken him with her, into her confidence, into her secret, into the grand plan, but she hadn't. She had kept all the thoughts to herself. He could understand if she hadn't told any of the others, they were bona fide adults, but he was different. He wasn't like them; she should have taken him into her confidence. He thought she liked him as much as he liked her. Suzette thanked the Mother and the Great spirit she wasn't born into the family of man. Glen may not have been born into it, but he sure had become part and parcel, things might change if his memory completed itself, but until then...

The others came together slowly in the backyard, it was time for some kind of plan. They had to face the fact they were short on recruits, with most of them undersized and not experienced in battle. For Frog, Doe, Suzette, and, up until this point, Glen, escape had been the foremost means of survival and though they wouldn't mind continuing the tradition, they came to the consensus they were not being given that option. It was time to consider all options.

"Can we call in all available cavalries?" Frog proposed.

"I certainly think all the others should be apprised of our situation, which, in a nutshell, is their situation," Suzette spoke thoughtfully, hand on chin, gazing at all the questions the sky could hold, "Certainly most if not all can sense the wrongness, the lack of harmony, they have to be wondering why if they don't already know." Helplessness overwhelmed; her head swam in the opposite direction as her insides. She thought she might be drowning. Impossible, screamed her innate instincts, she could no more drown than fly. Whirlpools were fun rides not treacherous whirligigs.

"I could sense it and came," said the tall grass to her right side causing her to jump, just a little, in her seat. "It's like a huge glowing arrow is pointing at this house, the others will come as well."

Suzette looked directly into the eyes of the snake gazing up at her from the safety of the groundcover.

"More will come," it said as it transformed into a small, wiry, athletic woman looking as fresh as if she'd just stepped out of the shower. "I thought they would already be here as they have legs which should provide more mobility. Though how one uses that mobility is their choice, is it not?" She said as she stretched out muscles. "As is whether they come or not, many choices," she shrugged a shoulder.

Suzette settled back into her seat and skin. Couldn't the woman have rattled or something so a body would know she was there?

"Yes, but the question is, whether they come to the aid of all good men," Frog/Flynn nodded an apology to Suzette, Doe, and Snake, "or whether they come to do battle."

"It is insanity we fight," put in the short round man whom Suzette recognized from his previous visits. Owl. He nodded to her as he came around the corner of the house, joining the conversation as he settled himself into a chair, "with the dissonance increasing, it will be difficult to recognize friend from foe." His spikey hair sticking out at all angles framed the round face and pince-nez.

"What are you doing here? I thought you didn't want to be involved except as an intermediary." There was bitter accusation attached to Suzette's words.

"Sometimes it is not what you wish but which opportunities are forced upon you. There comes a time when you have to choose a side, whether that side remains static, we shall see," he half bowed his surrender to the inexorable.

"What are you getting at?" asked Doe as she took a seat.

"It is my considered opinion that as the dissonance grows, 'sides'," Owl emphasized with air quotes, "will be determined more by the waves of imbalance than by loyalties." The statement was met by blank stares. Hmm, more explanation necessary.

"I think I see clearly, what our friend is attempting to explain," Frog picked up the thread in what Suzette had come to understand was his professorial tone, "What is taking place is not a stable fracture. This is the universe we are talking about, and it is anything but stable. It is its instability that allows it to exist at all. If it were a robust, unyielding entity it would shatter with all the forces yanking it in every direction possible. So, the 'crack', as it were, is not stable either. It floats along a kind of fault line in waves, affecting the matter and space, and behaviors, of all within. Where it happens to be at that moment, do you see?" His eyes begged understanding.

"You're insinuating that reality is malleable, yes?" spoke the athletic young woman.

"And you are?" asked the rotund little man, holding out his hand in introduction.

"Cynthia," a slight lisp on the sibilant.

"Oscar," he shook her hand, found it disconcertingly cool, clammy, but not completely unpleasant.

"Well, Cynthia," he concentrated to assure no lisp, "reality has always been malleable, there can be no absolute reality. Consider if you will our world compared to the mirror world of man," he shrugged, she nodded.

"So how will we know who is friend and who is trying to take our heads off?" Wolf's attempt at levity might have worked in more glad times.

"And keep in mind Evan has begged us to use constraint. As he stated violence leads to more violence and death escalates to the point of no return," Suzette reminded, "maybe he knew this was happening and why he was so adamant."

"And where is the beloved Evan?" Oscar still carried a wee bit of animosity from his discussion with Evan days before and a certain wariness as to the temperament of sweet Suzette. Though if he were to be honest with himself, he could understand their attitudes.

"He has gone in search of knowledge," Tatanka replied, now more concerned than previous. "He seeks to repair the damage done, or, at the very least, minimize. I would guess he will attempt a healing, as it were."

"He is not here?" Oscar was taken aback, expecting to find all parties on the front lines and preparing for whatever onslaught might be amassing on the other side of the looking glass.

"No," Doe stood, as if physically holding her ground, "he left us here to hold the fort until his return."

"And if he doesn't?"

"If you are suggesting that he might abandon us while he skates away, I would remind you, and all engaged," the fire in Doe's eyes burning into each spirit assembled, "there is no escape from where we stand. Nor from where he has gone, we are all related, as are our lives. We fight the same battle, we hold together to heal, our strength is our numbers, our knowledge, and our willingness to hold together. And this is Bear you speak of." She hadn't known this man long but his, obvious, slight towards Evan riled her as nothing had in eons.

"I meant no offense," hands up to ward off the vocal assault, Owl continued, "I merely implied as he was the acknowledged leader of this small company." He cleaned his spectacles on his tie, "We would not wish to lose our captain, but if we do, then what?"

"We do not have a captain, per se," rumbled Tatanka, "We are all responsible for our own people, the idea is for all of us to work in concert as a herd, or flock, if you will. Watching each other's backs and supporting where needed, not to tell each other what to do."

"Though I do think co-ordination between species, as far as strategy, will benefit all," kicked in Lawrence the Elk, also of the herd.

Suzette could see where species think could create massive glitches in co-ordination. She, Doe, Evan were solitary creatures, relying on family or themselves, not the herd mentality. They tended to be independent, free thinkers, actions could change in an instant and they had the ability to change with them.

The others were herd animals, even Cynthia. Though most thought of snakes as solitary creatures they were prone to nesting with hundreds, if not thousands, entwined. Yes, they would need come to a meeting of the minds if they were to have any chance of success. They should find each other's strengths and play to them, not try to put a herd animal into an independent hole.

"I've had a thought," she interrupted the burgeoning squabble, "what we need is to figure out where each of our strengths lie, as individuals and as a group, so as to use them to our advantage."

The appreciative silence was gratifying, no one had considered the concept before. They had found, over the last weeks, that as individuals they could work together, it was personal, friendly, convivial, but could their children? Each species thought different, fought different, ran from or into danger differently. This would require massive adjustment.

"It would seem you have hit several nails on several heads, my dear." Oscar bowed low in acquiescence to her brilliance. "And you say you have no experience in matters of hostility?"

"None, and I hope to never have another beyond this engagement."

"Who's getting engaged?" The sheriff chirped in as he swiftly turned the corner chancing a glance to his rear.

"No one," Suzette glowered, "You look like shit, what's wrong?" You couldn't miss his furtive glances in all directions, she had never known the man to be edgy, he was now.

"A little tiff back in town. What's going on here?" he took in all the new folk as well as the old, "Who are these folks?" he asked pointing to the new faces, "and where is Evan?"

"That seems to be the million bison question." Tatanka responded, "We believe him to be in search of answers which will provide solutions. Our task is to keep a lid on whatever is happening here until he does. I am Tatanka," he bowed lifting a hand in greeting. "These other three are Willow, Finn and Lawrence," he introduced Rabbit, Frog and Elk. "Oh, excuse my rudeness, this is Cynthia and Oscar," he seemed genuinely embarrassed.

"Pleasure, as we have heard tell of the good Sheriff," Willow held out a small hand which he eagerly grasped.

"We were discussing a new wrinkle in the battle plan, something to add a bit more danger, just to make it interesting," smiled Suzette. "It would seem the distress in the universe is not stable so it will be difficult to tell friend from foe at times as alliances can change without notice. Also, wondering how we will know of Bear's progress." She sketched him up to date, though he may have preferred ignorance.

"Of course, that begs the question; how will we know if or when he has found this solution?" Doe brought up.

"You'll know." Oscar nodded knowingly, "Oh, you'll know."

"I hate to interrupt the summit, but you are running low on time, if what I just slipped through in town was any indication," John gave a quick synopsis of what had taken place, his escape, and what weapons he had brought with him.

"I appreciate the back-up, sheriff," Suzette spoke kindly, softly, "but if you remember, Evan believes, and I think all of us have come to the same destination, including yourself, that escalating violence serves no one's purpose and death the least of all."

"Yes, I thought so, for a minute, but these folks ain't plain' around, they mean business and we have to be prepared for whatever happens," the sheriff was visibly agitated. He was out of sorts between Evan getting beat, him getting beat, the deputies acting scared and about to mutiny and now getting chased out of his own damn town, yeah, he'd had about his fill.

"You think you can fight a war without casualties," Sheriff John Roberts had heard some doozies in his time, but this one was the top of the mount, his position having altered. "Well, explain that to the people who keep beatin' the shit out of us."

"John, you ain't acting right," Suzette put her hand on his knee and he jumped, startled, and spinning seeking the attack before Suzette could calm him.

"What is wrong?" She held him close, calming, rubbing his back, soothing, until his breathing returned to normal, and his muscles relaxed.

"What the hell just happened?" he came back to himself.

"A prime example of what the wandering wave of the imbalance can cause, I am guessing," replied Tatanka thoughtfully.

"I'm sorry, I don't know what... where that came...that wasn't me. I'm sorry, you're right, all of you, no deaths," he sat hard on the ground trying to find his own equilibrium.

"We think we have to find a way to incapacitate without causing irreparable harm," Oscar corrected, he said cleaning his pince nez, which seemed to help him think.

"Have you come up with any kind of plan on accomplishing this?" John was back in sheriff mode.

"Well, now that you're here, I, we, are hoping you might have some miracle in your rear pocket," Suzette couldn't have been sweeter if she were a statue of sugar, honey, and molasses.

Reality is an ugly thing. "Oh, I got something in my rear, though not my pocket." What the hell had he got himself hip deep in? Shit! They had to understand the difficulty of what they asked. Yes, he agreed with the concept, but the doin' was the hard part. "If I had a month with nothing to do but think on this and read every treatise on the subject, I don't think I could come up with nothing. War ain't about not killing people, just the opposite. The whole idea is to hurt the other guy, so he'll quit trying to hurt you," there was no way this was going to end well, he had to make them understand that. Silence wrapped the rapt audience as they awaited his conceding.

"Alright," if he was going to die, these were as good of 'people' as he could think of to die with, and as good a cause, "anybody know the town at all?" Hope springs, and is answered, Glen's hand shot up. "Ah, Glen, damned if I didn't forget about you."

"It happens all the time," sulky hadn't taken a long break.

"I'm sorry, I really am, my fault of overlooking a prime asset and I been kind of off my feed. We should all keep that in mind, me especially," he stood, walked over to lay his hand on Glen's shoulder, gave it a shake of apology, "Here is what I need for you to do. There's a garage halfway between Grand and Elm, the side door off Elm can be jimmied with the screwdriver sitting behind the metal garbage can next to the door. Here are my keys, here is what I will need," he gave Glen a list of non-lethal armaments tucked into the trunk. "Bring them all, can anyone go with him to help carry?"

"I think Glen and I have shown we can run together," Sung stood up stretching his back as he did so. "I will be his deputy. If he knows of what you speak, he can give me the orders and we will bring back what you wish. If that suits you," he said to Glen.

"I couldn't order you around, you, you are Wolf," Glen said the word with such respect and awe, Sung bowed.

"But in this you are the expert," he gave another perfunctory bow, "I subordinate myself to you."

"You folks always talk like this?" It was not what John had expected.

"Only between ourselves and those we trust the most," Suzette patted his shoulder. "If you'd prefer, we can go back to talkin' like y'all," she laughed kindly.

"No, wouldn't want y'all to dumb it down fer the likes of me."

"Sheirff, ain't nobody got to dumb nothin' down for you," Said Doe, "We put ourselves in your hands as an expert on military matters,"

"Excellent," said Sheriff John as he considered the others. Suzette was right on the money about finding strengths, weaknesses and working them together like a puzzle. "While you are running that little errand, we will try to figure out how we all stand here." They asked the unfeasible, it was up to him to make it so.

If what Evan had shown him was true, and if what he had been told of the breaking of the universal balance, then maybe this was the only way. You didn't heal with blood, anger, hate, and death. He would need to find another way.

"Do we have any concept of who is for us and who is against us?" best to know the lay of the land and troops available before concocting a strategy.

"As the lovely Suzette mentioned we were discussing that as you entered the fray," Oscar waved to include all present. He gave the sheriff a brief rundown of all they had been discussing.

"You mean to tell me we have no idea who are the good guys or who the bad guys are in this?" the jolt to his plan to plan left him slightly devastated.

"Not only that, but we can't guarantee that just because a species starts out on our side they will remain so," added Doe. "We believe that was why Evan strongly advised against taking lives and avoiding as much damage as possible. The one you hurt now might be your ally in ten minutes, or vice versa."

"Fantastic!" he didn't know if these spirits or whatever the hell they were understood sarcasm, but he was going to give it a go anywho. "We are engaging people who might be spirits or ghosts who might or might not be on the same side and if they are or aren't might not remain so, do I have that right?"

Tatanka nodded solemnly, "Unfortunately you have summed up the crux of our predicament."

"And there is no way of knowing?" There had to be some way to tell if the person next to you that had your back just a minute ago was now going to stab you in it. "This is so far above my experience and knowledge I'm drowning. There has got to be some kind of weathervane or windsock or energy barometer that could give us some warning when this wave or front is happening."

Suzette and Doe shared a look, "Give us some time to consider."

"Aren't there plants that give off a scent or try to protect themselves from danger?" Suzette thought out loud, "You know, to signal others of their kind, give them a heads up." She searched the faces of the others for confirmation but found only blank expressions.

"I think you might have something," quipped Willow, "I seem to remember something..."

"Yes, yes you're right but which and how?" Joined in Doe, "We should do a little research."

"Now, if someone wouldn't mind," the sheriff turned to Finn, Lawrence, Tatanka, Oscar and Cynthia, "or all of you, can you give me a concise summary of any weak points you might, as animal spirits, have." Once again, he couldn't have said he honestly believed everything that he'd been told or that he found himself in the midst of, but when all you have are shadows and fantasy you deal in shadow and fantasy.

All five shared glances of suspicion and reluctance, to share or not to share, that was the question. How far could they trust this human? They knew Evan trusted the man, but could they trust Evan?

"This is nuts," spoke Cynthia as she paced in thought and decision, "we either have to begin from a point of trust or we are all doomed." Silence with a dollop of embarrassment greeted her pronouncement, she took it as consent and continued, "I apologize, sheriff, for our restraint, but we are cautious, as any would be, of showing our frailties, especially to one who not of us." Her face scrunched in a 'what can you expect?' expression.

"I understand, but if you wish me to find a way to incapacitate without causing irreparable harm, I need to know weaknesses. Is there a way to knock one of you unconscious if only for a moment or preferably longer? Are you physical or spiritual or both? If I trap you, constrain you, can you just make yourself ethereal and walk away?" he searched his brain for any and all eventualities. What were the restrictions? What were the tricks? What the hell was he doing?

"Excellent questions," growled Tatanka, "ones we have never ourselves considered previously. We have never had need as we have never meant to harm or constrain another of our kind. Though there have been instances where, of necessity, we have attacked one and other, it is usually solitary. A fight for survival, food, territory, never one species against another." A grimace of mental anguish clouded his face, the sheriff could tell this pained him beyond what he had previously experienced.

"Forgive me, the last thing I would wish would be to cause you distress, but we have no other options. We are attempting a holding pattern against forces that are, apparently, in the control or lack thereof, of forces beyond my comprehension," John shook his head and spread his arms in a gesture of powerlessness. "I understand the want to do the right thing here, the necessity of nonaggression, but I still have to figure out the how."

"The problem you are encountering," Lawrence the Elk stood in order to pace his growing anger out, "is that you are thinking of this in a white way. The way your culture has appropriated ours and attempts to put your stamp on our spirituality."

Sheriff John stood to apologize for his ignorance, but before the words could form, "I know," Lawrence shushed him and gestured for him to sit, "We all do, you are a good man, but even the best whites always see things through white eyes, it is the way of all men. You can't see it through the eyes of others, as you are not of them. Even those with the greatest empathy towards others just don't have the life, the experiences, the bigotry faced, the denigration, poverty, the whole of the other to call upon. It is not your fault, it is nobody's fault, it just is. You can't know something you have never lived, not completely. We appreciate what you are trying to do, this is your world too. But you can't think of it through a white mind, it won't work that way."

"You see," tempered Doe, " we are not 'animal spirits' that is just a term that makes us easier to understand. We are guides, messengers, sometimes we are Gods who can help in minor ways, but we don't save your soul, we don't make promises if you love us enough. We try to protect those who love us as any would."

She seemed to run out of words or concepts as quiet wrapped the gathering.

"Yes, we have some 'tricks' to distract from the suffering of life. We have lived forever so we know how to reduce a fever or clean a cut, so it doesn't get infected, and a thousand other things but we ain't magic, we are just immortal. The guise you see us in from time to time is who we actually are, we represent the animals of this world. We try to keep them strong, healthy, to let your people know they need our people as much or more than you need each other." Her eyes pleaded with John's, "do you see?"

"Not yet," he could not lie to her or the rest of them, he had asked them for honesty he owed them same. He'd need an epiphany, something to build on, "But I will try my best to see, to understand, to learn, if you will let me."

Doe hugged him close, "We will help, maybe together we can help Bear, maybe we are all needed to help him heal," she closed her eyes in prayer to the Mother pleading.

"Ya-hey," came the response from all.

It's All in The Learnin'

∞

The information they passed along to him were treasures, gifts. They had given of themselves, to an extent he didn't believe any other being ever had, he thanked them profusely. It had taken trust, an openness of heart, and a level of honesty he didn't remember ever receiving from any human being. He was honored more than words could convey. Now he would have to prove his worth.

It was interesting how wrong he had been in his assumptions about Native culture and belief. His concepts of religion were based in his limited Christian sect. There was a time when he thought all Christianity the same, he had been a child. Christianity was as diverse as human beings. There were dozens of 'mainstream' Christian sects and subsect upon subsects. Each convinced only they knew the way to interpret the same book. And don't get him started on how little he understood about Muslims, Jews, Hindus, and Sikhs. The level of misunderstanding in the world was infinite. It was why he had fallen out of favor with religion while still in short pants and before girls.

His understanding of Native spirituality—as it was more that than religion—had been twisted and turned by an overzealous mother, an absent father and a hundred different interpretations. Theirs was a simpler view of life and soul. There was no evil as such, only spirits that were out of whack. They explained that was how the Universe was right now. You just had to adjust the spirit and the person would be alright. A belief that all things are truly interrelated. Mitakuye Oyasin, they called it, We Are

All Related, it was a wonderful way to look at the world. He wasn't sure he could, but he liked the idea.

Then there was these folks themselves, and those that would be coming. They weren't some kind of mystical, supernatural fairies, they were merely the physical representations of those they watched over and protected. Simple. They were immortal, at least until those they loved and cared for were no more. There were no spirits of creatures long gone into extinction. No spirits sitting around the bar recalling the old days, better times when they and theirs roamed the earth. Turns out immortal ain't all it's cracked up to be.

But it was what he needed to know for now. He could consider all the ramifications of religion, belief, and the afterlife if he could avoid going to it for a little while longer.

One of the best things he learned was that the humans, who might be bent to the will of those who spirits were twisted, would be the only ones with weapons, and those would be limited to basic. Rocks, two by fours, pipe, these folks didn't care for man's more destructive inventions, therefore shied away from their use. He guessed that was one of the reasons why they had reacted so strongly to his bringing the twelve gage and boxes of ammo. They had rules and he had to abide. He hoped the ones on the other side were just as persnickety.

This, of course, would help him to set up nonlethal defenses. The concept to disable until such time as the skirmish could be ended. Nice concept, they would see how well it played out.

Now the question was, where in the hell was Glen and that Sung fella? If they followed his instructions, they should have been back half hour ago. He didn't like tardy, tardy meant something hadn't gone according to plan. And things that didn't go according to plan were not good.

Sung and Glen loped the half mile into town, running through neighborhoods, back alleys and, when necessary, along the side streets and across intersections. They zigzagged, stuck close to cover whenever they could, avoiding detection from all sides.

It was a half block from the garage that things went haywire. The hitch in this kind of plan in this kind of territory was you never knew who was on your side. They had run past a couple of female teens five minutes before and thought nothing of it, until they saw the pickup trucks full of puffed-up young guys cruising the roads of small-town America.

There is one thing when you see a truck full of young fellas out for a good time and quite another when they are armed with boards, chains, and hate. It didn't take a genius to figure who they were looking for. The issue at hand was, could the quarry evade the hunters when there was so many hunters and so few hidey holes.

"This is your town, Glen," whispered Sung into the young man's ear, his breath sweet with the scent of blood, "I would prefer to avoid any confrontation if possible." His voice was calm, his breathing slow and steady, but Glen could feel the ferocity straining to be released.

Glen leaned against the brick, struggling to calm his own breathing, and not succeeding. He had to think, he couldn't let Sung down, there had to be..."Wait here," he said, gathering himself together, straightening his clothes to appear normal.

"Glen, don't do anything rash," Sung didn't like the look in Glen's eye, "there's a good chance we can sneak passed them, get around them, and scoot back to the house."

"I'm tired of running from guys like this," as he stepped out of the shadows and onto the street.

"Shit! This ain't no time for the Alamo or John Wayne," but it was too late the truckload had spied him walking with his hands in his pockets down the side street. What the hell to do?

Well, wasn't that nice, someone had conveniently hung a fire escape to the side of the building across the alley. All Sung had to do was get a little running start and he could easily jump the four feet he would need to catch the bottom rung. Ah, the joy of immortality, you never got old, just lived with all the aches, pains, not muscle deterioration.

He scurried up the iron ladder to the roof of the three-story building. Now, to get back to where he could see what was taking place on the street all he needed do was hop back across the alley to the roof of the two-story on the corner. Nothing to it, he hoped.

The pitfall of living forever was you began to believe your own hype. He barely caught the edge of the stone parapet, damn, another foot he'd have made it clear. His arm ached as he pulled himself up, his boots scrapping and sliding off the side of the building, there being no footholds, until he threw himself over the edge, landing hard on the tar roof. Dummy!

He scurried on hands and knees to the edge by the intersection and peered over the side. They had Glen surrounded with the apparent leader of the small-town gang pushing and poking Glen's shoulder trying to make him take a swing. Glen, head down, looking for all the world like a puppy being scolded for pooing on the floor, took it, poke after poke. Sung found his chest swelling with pride at the young man. He knew Glen wanted nothing more than to take that swing, to knock the smug expression right off the bastard's face. And from what Sung had now witnessed of the strength and agility of Glen knew he easily could, but he waited.

Sung had to use the time being given him or Glen's sacrifice was all for naught. He hung himself over the side of the building until he could let go landing in the alley. He hurried to where the car had been hidden, slid in the side door and popped the trunk. Grabbing all that the sheriff had asked for he made ready to go save Glen. His eye caught the cannister tucked into the webbing on the side of the trunk. He threw it on top of the box with all John had asked and pushed his way out on to the street.

Setting the large box in the alley where he could easily come for it, he walked onto the street towards the corner of the building. There were eight of them, not counting the girls who had snitched them out. Not bad odds, though he would prefer a clean getaway.

"Howdy, boys," he nodded to Glen, who appeared relieved yet a little miffed he had come, "Seems a bit one sided here, eight to one, not exactly macho odds." He sneered at the ringleader. "Now, four to one sound much more fair."

"I don't think you want any of this, old man," ah the arrogance of youth rears its pretty little head.

"Jervis, that's the guy that was with this one when we saw 'em," drawled one of the girls, though which Sung couldn't tell and didn't care.

"Then I guess he can come to the party," Jervis guffawed his own brilliant humor.

"Really, I would love to, but you see, Glen and I have an appointment and just don't have the time," casual as asking the time of day.

"Guess you're going to have to make time, old man, time for an asswhoopin'," maybe this kid had been dropped on his head too many times, but whatever the reason for his inanity he was getting on Sung's nerves. Time to end this stupidity.

"Comprehension not your strong point, is it son? OK, let me make this perfectly clear, you and your band of idiots can either get in your trucks and go play in the mud somewhere or you can stay here and die," he pulled the cannister from his jacket with a finger through the ignition ring.

"Crazy bastards got a hand grenade!" screeched one of the less macho.

"You have until three to get out of my sight," he glanced back at Glen who stood cool as can be against the side of the storefront. Again, he felt pride in the young man.

"Don't move, he ain't going to do shit," Sung had to give the kid points for cajones if not for brains.

"One."

"You don't want to die."

"Two, I ain't going to."

"You will if you lay that thing down," the problem with youth is you think you'll live forever.

"Three," he pulled the pin and allowed the fuse to spring.

And if you want to live forever, then don't do anything stupid.

The kid's eyes popped open as he instinctively fell to the ground. The rest of the gang scattered like chickens being chase by a hatchet. Sung casually tossed the 'hand 'grenade' under the kid's shiny truck where it popped, fizzled before spewing clouds of black smoke.

"Let's go," Sung motioned in the direction of the hidden container lay.

"Just a sec," Glen walked over to where the bully lay in a pool of his own piss. "Why you gotta be such an asshole?" He brought back his foot to land a kick direct to the temple, the kid on the ground pleaded with his eyes, before Glen did a little jig and whacked him on the ass. "You should change those," he joined Sung at the corner of the building, grabbing the other side of the box.

They dropped the large box in front of where Sheriff John sat, their breathing hard but not wheezing. The container was a load, even between the two of them.

"You OK?" Sung asked Glen as they caught their breath away from where others could hear.

"Yeah, I been pushed a lot harder than that pussy could ever do," he smiled. They hadn't knocked him down, that was the victory. "Long as I keep my legs apart and my feet mobile, they can't make me go down. Something I learned long ago," he stopped mid-thought, "though I still don't remember where or from whom." Concern and confusion crashed across his face before he could collect both and push them aside.

"Thought I saw what you were doing, so, I hurried quick as I could," Sung's tone contrite.

"It was good, it was fun watching him getting more pissed 'cause he couldn't make me swing at him," the grin split his face igniting the twinkle of mischief in his eyes.

"I woulda decked the sonofabitch," Sung admitted.

"That's the hardest part," Glen said soft, almost to himself. "The easiest thing to have done would've been to strike back, but I couldn't, 'cause that's what he wanted the most."

"That is one tough fella," Sung said to no one as he walked past the group seated throughout the backyard.

Sheriff John looked over to see who he was talking about. Glen sat on the lawn lost in his thoughts and rubbing his arm. It would seem Glen was made of sterner stuff than Sheriff John had ever thought. Hmm, guess he was going to have to give the kid more props than previously thought. Looked like this whole group was going to be one surprise after another.

He still had to figure out the best course of action without too much action. Though discovering these wasn't magical sprites was reassuring.

"Just to reassure myself," he said to Lawrence and Tatanka, as they seemed the most reticent about their answers therefore probably the most honest, "you can't just leave this body and reassemble into another one somewhere else, right?" He knew how it sounded but he had to get facts straight in his head.

Lawrence considered the question, the questioner, and his answer. He wasn't certain where the sheriff was headed with this, but honesty, he knew, was paramount.

"That's right," he said, "though on rare occasions and if the need is great, we can change from this body into our natural form. The metamorphosis being physical and within the bounds of this world. Our spirits cannot leave these bodies even to become ourselves somewhere else, all stays put." Funny how he had never considered the concept before, though there had never been necessity.

"But keep in mind," Tatanka quickly added, "if we do morph into our natural state all the strength and agility comes with it. I may appear large and powerful here, but if I were to transform into true, I would dwarf what you see." The levity of his tone belied the weight of his words. "And sometimes that can be 'difficult' to control." It was a warning of caution to be careful of what you ask for.

"Though if the need is great, we can. Say, if you have use of a small creature that can get into and out of certain situations," grinned Suzette walking into the conversation.

"Or two," grinned Willow, pretending not to notice the scathing look from the woman next to her.

The More You Know

∞

Suzette, Doe, and now, Willow hit the books to discover if Suzette's concept of a plant-based warning system was feasible. Doe seemed to recall just before some impending disaster took place certain plants would attempt to protect themselves, either by turning in on themselves or by shedding the weak so the strong might survive. If she was correct, and they could detect when the plants reacted to a change in the direction of the flow of energy, that might give a moments heads-up to be wary of friend or foe. The other question was whether all plants would react or only certain species, and would they react to this threat, the change in energy. She had to hope with this much of a differential in the intensity and flow all plants would react immediately. It wouldn't be much, but it might be all they had.

Sheriff John took the 'warriors' off into the fields where they would have the least chance of detection amidst the tall cornstalks. Oscar could keep an eye on those who might attempt to spy from above. His keen eyes and knowledge of the skies would provide early warning, his sharp beak and talons would keep them away. He had no compunction about morphing to protect the greater good.

Then the hard part, how to turn what he knew of battle, learned from time in the Marines and Navy, as well as his decades as sheriff, into non-lethal combat. The difference meant fighting instinct and sense to make moves which went against their nature. Instead of backing away, for instance, your best course was to lean in, or even to rush in, to surprise or cause a blow to go wide while you were now in a better position to retaliate. If someone had you in a tight grip the instinct would be to struggle to freedom whereas the best course of action was to remain calm—the announcement greeted by shock and howls of laughter—to try to control the hands of the adversary while allowing them to wear themselves out. It was not the fastest way to win out, that would be to avoid in the first place, but it could save your own skin.

He pulled out the array of non-lethal weaponry Sung and Glen had rescued from the cruiser. Two tasers with extra charges, netting, used for capturing wild game that had inadvertently wandered into town, rifles with hypos of tranquilizers, for the same purpose, and some flash bangs. The military had sent them along to many law enforcement agencies throughout the country. John had never imagined he would need them.

Sung took over when it came to explaining and demonstrating where pressure points were located on each species. Where, if you applied the proper amount of pressure, it would cause each adversary to lose consciousness. That was the concept, to disable without dispatching permanently.

But with all the knowledge they could assemble it was still one on one, victory could only come with numbers, and numbers they did not possess. If the opposition—they did not want to think of others as enemies, they were friends with disorders—brought overwhelming forces they were in trouble.

"But what if we just disable our cousins?" Suggested Finn, his voice croaking, always seeking the intellectual solution. "The thought is, if we disable one of our own, would that not put the children of said spirit without a head, so to speak? They would have no spiritual guide, no focus or no entity directing their actions, they might just fall apart as a unit."

John's astonishment exploded across his face, "Is that possible?"

His exclamation was met by blank stares. No one had ever considered the possibility, and it frightened to the core.

"Although if that was the case, wouldn't they be left to their own when you sleep?" reality reared its ugly brick, hope was waning, and the straw John held tight was slipping from his grip.

"If we slept," replied the Wolf.

"What are you getting at, of course you sleep, I've seen all of you in states of unconscious," John's confusion swirled inside his head, dizziness threatened.

"No, you have seen us rest, our physical bodies need to regenerate, though while they are recuperating our spirits roam the other world, we never are completely at rest," Sung explained, "we, our true selves, have no need for it. We cannot, it is necessary for us to be ever vigilant."

"So, theoretically this might be possible," the sheriff pushed, "maybe as a last resort, if we can't accomplish our purpose in any other way," he looked to the others for confirmation.

They grudgingly concurred. Though none would commit to being the example that proved the theory.

"As an absolute last resort," Tatanka said, though it bore the weight of command.

"Promise," a word is a vow when spoken in truth from the heart.

There are promises made between The People that are carved in stone and there are promises made between humans which are like water. All in attendance would like to believe this promise was carved, but humans were humans, and all needed to be watched with the eagle's eye. Now, they had to hope they could trust the Eagle!

Either way this was where it would stand as they had no other choices, none of them could see any clearer path to follow. They would have to hope their trust was not misplaced.

Sheriff John would also have to trust, though with the ever-changing climate of friend and foe it would not be easy. Trusting plants to indicate ebb and flow of energy, an energy he would not sense in the slightest, was asking that he put his life on the line for a theory. Something he was not inclined to do. He wanted something solid, a friend, an ally, a person to whom he had been in scrapes with and knew they had his back. This ethereal concept of battle was idiotic.

He knew they didn't have utter faith in him, how could they? They hadn't met him before a few weeks ago. Yet they were willing to place, within reason, their lives, and the lives of those they represented, in his hands. That was huge. Still, how did one fight a war without death? How did one engage an enemy while attempting to cause the least amount of damage? How does one sheriff get himself involved in such insanity? He had thought he could spend his pre-retirement years locking up drunks, breaking up high school pranks and handing out speeding tickets. Shit on a stick!

Bear had fallen into a fitful sleep filled with doubts, outcomes that were less than satisfactory, and disaster. He wished his night had been filled with visions of Her but wishes don't run the world. There were just too many variables and nothing concrete to grab hold of. He had to dig up some nugget of information as to who had started this horseshit, though he was beginning to think he knew.

He was aware the others were attempting the same, but they would be distracted by the need to prepare for the oncoming skirmish. He also knew the discovery would be of the utmost importance as then he would have an exceptionally good idea how to stop this war before it could get a good foothold. Right now, he had to find the Mother and find out why she had allowed all this to get this far.

His thoughts spinning their wheels in his rock of a brain were interrupted by the sound of scrape on rock. Someone was attempting quiet when quiet was not their nature. It is near impossible to sneak when you are geared to barging, whoever this was they would never be a thief in the night.

Equine's hoof slipped on the scree causing her to catch her balance for the umpteenth time before she became a splat on the hard rock two thousand feet below. Horses were supposed to be surefooted, and they were, when the footing was sure. Plus, she hated heights! Her kind was more at home on the wide-open flats rather than the steep inclines. But when wide open wasn't available, then caution and slow-footed pace would have to do. She rounded the rocky outcropping and almost completely lost her footing as Bear stared her hard in the eye.

"Becky!" Bear caught at her shoulder as she teetered on the precipice. She had come close to toppling off the edge at the sudden appearance of Bear coming round the outcropping, almost walking head-long into her.

"Ayi!" Quoth the equine in lieu of curse, "What the hell are you doing here?" It was a dumb thing to say as her purpose in coming had been to find either him or his scion, but she had been badly startled by the near collision.

"Just wandering around enjoying the sights," a little levity can go a long way in soothing the nerve.

"Well, you ought to be trying to find whatever happened to your girl child," Equine was not in the mood.

"My what?" Now it was his turn to be startled.

"Your girl child, your, what do you call them? Your, granddaughter, she's out here somewhere wandering about, lost, one can only assume, seeking you," there that ought to put everything in succinct order.

"My granddaughter is supposed to be back at my house being watched over by Doe and Suzette!"

"Then somebody took a nap while on duty or was distracted by events. The girl seems to be quite clever when she is of a mind," Equine spoke admiringly. The People prized clever.

"Where is she?" his anxiety seeping through his attempt at calm.

"If I knew that she would be sitting comfortably on my back and we'd be wrapped in a joyous reunion," she shook her head, her blond mane waving in the breeze. "Do you mind if we continue this conversation somewhere with more stable footing?" she nervously took a peek over her right shoulder to the sheer drop-off.

Bear took several sure-footed steps backward before finding room to turn 'round and lead her away from the cliff.

"Tell me everything," he said, pacing in the small clearing near the tree line.

She gave him a brief synopsis of all that had taken place since his departure and the escape of his grandchild, her attempt to follow, coming across too soon and losing the girl in the transition. She was trying to find where the girl might have wound up, but, off course, time and space, landmarks, did not always match up. She had gotten herself slightly lost in the mountains and fortuitously had run across him.

"So, you're telling me she came across by herself?"

Equine nodded.

"With no help from you?"

Nod.

"Nor anyone else?"

"Yes," exasperation filled the word.

"All on her own." Now it was a statement of fact, accepted.

Silence as realization filled the mountains.

"Damn."

"Yes, that is exactly what I thought, so came in pursuit," how could she remain so calm, so accepting? Oh, that's right, she was not intimately involved with humans.

It was impossible to explain to most of The People the relationship humans had with their children and scions. Each of The People watched over so many of their own children. It was unfathomable to think of concentrating on only a few. When your family numbered in the tens of thousands or millions you couldn't know all their names, though many tried. When you had but one or two, just a few, they were precious in their rarity.

"We have to find her," now that the obvious had been stated, all they had to do was figure out how.

Bear knew the scent of her as well as he knew the scent of any creature on this earth, almost as well as he knew the scent of Her. Now, all he had to do was catch that scent on a breeze, a leaf, a tree. He would have to be extremely meticulous in his search. Equine could help, though her sense of smell was not near as acute as his own, it would be beneficial. Her keen sense of hearing might be more beneficial as they closed in, he could but hope.

The biggest positive they had in their favor was their location. This far up in the mountains and on this side of the boundary she would be the only human, she should be easy to find. Well, until one took into consideration the millions of square miles surrounding. The other positive is she would be seeking them with the same intensity they sought her.

Alexandra was tired, more tired than she had ever been in her life. She was lost, hungry, thirsty, and as pissed as she could be for being so stupid as to come wandering into the mountains without friends, without her grandfather, without thinking.

Oh yeah, she was going to come to his rescue, watch over him, have his back. What she hadn't considered was, who would have hers? Who would come to her rescue? Nobody, that's who.

She sat on the ground. It was hard, rocky, uncomfortable. It was cold, cold as her future. She saw the rustle of the bush, almost as if a breeze, but there was no breeze. Something was in the bush; the question was what and how big?

Should she move? There were plenty of trees, but could she make it to the closest one before whatever was there caught her.

The large cat edged out from behind the bush, looking everywhere but at her. Almost as if reassuring itself they were alone; they would not be disturbed. Or, should it say, it would not.

This was the largest 'cat' she had seen in her life. Easily eight-foot long and almost as tall as her, not that she was a giant, but when a mountain cat can stare you right in the eye, it gives you pause. It smiled, she had never seen a cat smile, as it lay down several yards from where she sat, almost as if daring her to make the attempt at escape.

"What brings you to my home?" he asked. She now saw it was a male.

"I'm looking for my grandfather," she replied as if speaking to a large cougar—yes, that's what it was—was as natural a thing to do as walking down the street whistling a favorite tune. She could almost believe herself even with the shaking in her voice, almost.

"And who would this grandfather of yours be?" he asked while licking his crossed paws.

"His name is Evan Beach, from down in Fort," she added though she couldn't say why she didn't tell this cat who her grandfather really was. Something in the back of her mind told her it might be prudent to keep one's secrets close to the vest for the time being.

"And why would Mr. Beach be this far up in the mountains? Why would his little girl be searching for him? And most important, how did you find yourself on this side of the barrier?" He stopped licking his paws and glared into her eyes.

"My grandfather," she emphasized the importance of the word, "comes up here to relax, to get away from the stress of the world. We are having a small emergency back home and we need him desperately. As to how I got here, I have no idea. Oh, I know how I got into the mountains, I used to play up through here when I was a child," her attempt to sound grownup failed miserably, "so, mother sent me here to find him." That should answer all questions for the moment, oh except, "and the only barrier I came through was from pavement to forest."

"I see," again searching the nearby for any sign of company, "it would seem you are quite alone and defenseless," he stood, stretching to his full length. "You may have made a mistake not bringing along a companion or three. I'm afraid you will have to pay the price, as all of nature does, soon or late."

She considered jumping up, sprinting to the nearest tree, but what was the use? She was the mouse, and the cat was huge, fast, and deadly. She was done for. Stupid, stupid stupid!!!

If Alexandra had never seen a cat smile before she had certainly never seen a spider wink. Today was a day of interesting twists, turns and discoveries. The small, black spider sitting on her hand seemed to be attempting to tell her to sit still, not move a muscle, wait.

"Did you not study nature in school, dear?" the cat began a steady, prolonged pacing, circling around her. There was no hurry, the girl could not escape, he almost wished she would try. It would certainly make the kill more exciting, more challenging, though only just.

Alexandra clenched her teeth to keep them from chattering. If she had ever been more terrified in her life, she no idea when that might have been. She could feel the cat's presence, its' might, smell his breath, sweet with the aroma of death, sense the threat and the final conclusion. She would die, here in the forest, the forest her grandfather so loved. Her youthful arrogance would be the end of her. Why hadn't she told someone, taken one of the others with her, Glen would have come. Yeah, right, and then he would be just as dead as she.

"Nothing to say?" The big cat was growing weary with this one-sided game, it was time to end it.

Alexandra heard the buzz nearing, though from which direction it came she couldn't tell. Nor if it was actually heading toward her or just passing nearby. The cat heard it as well, it distracted, if only for a second, now would be the moment to make a jump for the tree.

She tensed her muscles ready to make one futile attempt at life when the spider tapped with all its might on her hand. She glanced at the arachnid to see it caution patience.

The hell with that, the damn cat was distracted the tree was right there, it was time for scootin'!

The buzzing grew louder until the small clearing was alive with the sound of it and the air filled with wasps, hornets and a hundred stinging, biting horrid flying creatures. But they weren't horrid, they were saving her life! They didn't bite or sting her, only the big cat, who jumped and howled, tried to swat the insects away, rolled on the ground before finally jumping up and tearing off into the forest away from the torture.

"You tell your grandfather when you find him what happened here today. Tell him Iktomi wishes peace, this is a down payment," the spider, stared into her eyes before it hopped from her hand, disappearing into the undergrowth.

Alexandra couldn't move, astounded, shocked, by all that had just happened. Had it? Well, she was alive, alone and knew she had to get moving if she had any chance to find her grandpa. It was well past discovering where he might be. She hadn't concentrated as she needed, she'd been distracted by the mountains, the sights, fear, remorse and a hundred things she should've done.

Sitting on the hard ground, the sun well past its zenith, she closed her eyes, blocking out sound, smells, discomfort. The singular image occupying her every breath, heartbeat was her grandfather. If she focused, she would feel him, know his presence. Run straight as an arrow into his arms, if only she could give every ounce of attention to that one purpose.

Evan's home had taken on the appearance of an armed encampment, though with hardly any armament. More of the People had begun to arrive, Sheriff John recognized pretty much all species of them, though one had to be careful of where you stepped or sat. Adjustments were made and other than a few bruised egos and appendages, and a plethora of apologies, all got along well. You could tell where traps had been lay and new ditches had been dug or fences erected. But, as he had explained in minute detail to all, those were not really the true defenses, those were distractions.

Someone seeking to mount an assault would be wary of the poorly hidden new protection, therefore would not be as likely to note the well-hidden ones laid where, hopefully, they would traipse to avoid falling victim to the obvious. Hope would be their best weapon.

Hope Evan would find a way to fix that which had been broken. Hope they could mount their own battle without causing irreparable harm to any friend or foe. Hope that Equine would find and keep Alexandra safe. Hope, hope, hope and a hand full of wish made for a poor game plan, but it was their game plan.

"How many do we have living in these homes and the adjoining lands?" he asked Suzette, who had taken on the position of tracking all their assets. She had a mind for detail and minutiae that astounded him. She was not just attractive of physique, but her mind was a wonderland he hoped he could explore when, yeah, when. Keep yer head on straight and yer thoughts on the challenge at hand.

"Two thousand, three hundred and forty-two," she threw offhand the number from the top of her head. "If you count all the bugs, crawling and flying, and you'd better, burrowing critters, flying, swimming and those of us that just creep around on all fours," she laughed, and the universe chimed. It might have been the most beautiful sound he had ever heard, or it might have been the circumstances and geography.

"I wouldn't underestimate the need for the little ones, sometimes they are the most necessary," he grinned the implied compliment to her.

The sound of engines roaring, glass packs backfiring while tires squealed interrupted the pleasant exchange as reality walked back through the door. "Sounds like we got company," grimaced the sheriff, "would you mind seeing who is available for a welcoming committee?"

She patted his arm in a gesture of compassion and caution as she went off in a hurried, though not running, pace. The last thing she wished to convey was fear or anxiety.

As Sheriff John Roberts came around the corner of the craftsman home, he saw a dozen or so pickup trucks, with a half hundred surly athletic looking meatheads aboard, idling on the lane blocking traffic in both directions. Glen had arrived seconds before and stood, hands on hips, where the verge met the road, a big grin splitting his youthful face.

The sheriff reached up to click on the mic at his shoulder before realizing he was in his civvies, he was not a representative of the law here, just a guy in the middle of something he wished he weren't. Bullshit, the word raced through his head, a lawman is always a lawman. He walked over to where he could stand next to Glen and crossed his arms.

The big kid who had assaulted Glen —or had made the attempt— while he and Sung were in town, hopped down from the driver's side of the equally big four by four, strutting over to where he could tower over the two by the side of the lane.

"Looks like you're a little outnumbered," his malicious grin threatened.

"What?" shouted Sheriff John.

"I said, it looks like you're a little outnumbered," he raised his voiced over the noise emanating from the street and gestured to the truckloads of good ol' boys.

"Sorry, what are you saying," Sheriff John now yelled cupping his hand to his ear.

The big kid threw up his hands yielding the point as he turned and gestured for the pickups to be shut off. Glen and John managed to stop themselves from laughing.

"I said," he yelled before coming to the realization volume was no longer necessary, "you seem to be outnumbered." He attempted to maintain the bully aspect, though had lost ground when he'd been forced to turn off the noise makers.

"Yes, again," Glen spoke softly, almost inaudibly especially after the racket of a few moments before, "but that is how things started last time, wasn't it?"

"Yeah, well, you ain't got your buddy with you this time, do you?" Bravado resumed.

"Nope, but he does have me, Jervis," the sheriff, still with arms crossed over his chest stared the boy in the eye, "your daddy know what yer up to?"

Jervis shuffled feet before looking back and taking courage from the couple dozen fellas with two by fours, pipe and ax handles standing behind.

"What my daddy knows and don't, don't concern you. I'm my own man, growed, and of age to do my own thinking and doin'," Now, the former athlete stood up to his full height.

If he thought to intimidate the sheriff, he obviously didn't know the man.

"Son, you might want to rethink this before you get hurt," the sheriff almost whispered, Jervis had to lean in to hear the words.

He grinned, two against more'n twenty times that many, yup, this would be fun. Sheriff or no. He turned as if to say something to the large beef truck behind him when he about-faced and brought the two by four he was carrying around to take out Glen. Glen had anticipated the move. The kid was big, but smart hadn't entered into his strategy.

Glen stepped into the move, just as the sheriff had shown him, so the wood came round behind him, and he was able to trap Jervis' arm while bringing around a punch to the temple. He gently lay Jervis' body on the ground and threw the weapon up towards the house.

"Nice," the sheriff was genuinely impressed. He really needed to re-evaluate his thinking on young Glen.

"Lotta beer cases, kegs and garbage," Glen shrugged. People didn't know how much work a barback does in one night, multiply that by a few years and, well, there is some muscle growth. Now, throw in a few years of manhandling and bullying from these same toadies and there is some extra added atonement. Glen hated to admit it, even to himself, but it felt good to get an ounce or two in change.

There was a bit of murmuring among the remaining, without the head the beast it had no focus. No matter where things went from here, it gave Sheriff John some hope their plan might work. And as quick as thought, the murmuring stopped. As one they turned in the same direction, the direction of Glen and John. All attention fixed and centered on the purpose at hand, as if some great puppeteer had pulled all the strings tight and now held command. Apparently only the small head had been severed, someone was still in control.

Sheriff John and Glen stood their ground, though some of the newly acquired confidence had leaked out. They could but hope the cavalry was on the way. John took a quick glance behind him to the very empty ground between him and the three, apparently, empty houses.

"Not sure what's happening," he confided to Glen, "but we might have to hold the fort for a bit. Looks like the reinforcements have lost their way," he shot another peek to their rear.

"You don't think they'd just leave us out here, all alone, just the two of us agin all these others, do you?" now a hint of nervous coated Glen's words though his outward appearance was calm and confident.

"Nah, I'm purty sure they're just cooking up something special to make certain these goons don't ever want to come back and bother us anymore," he sounded far more cool than he felt, "we just got to hold tight for a few."

The many began to move in on the few. Well, if they were going to go down, they were going to go down in epic fashion. Glen and the sheriff moved back onto the front lawn of Evan's home, getting beat on grass didn't sound as painful as getting beat on concrete.

"What's the matter, punks, afraid of getting' an ass whoopin'?" spoke the large boy who took fat for muscle.

That was the thing about meatheads like this, thought John, their lack of originality, just too dumb to come up with an actual clever quip. All muscle, no cranium, and with this one, lotta gut.

"Nah, just don't want you scrapin' a knee on the pavement, though your momma ain't gonna be happy 'bout scrubbin' the grass stains out of your purty jeans," Glen rolled up sleeves and stood with feet at shoulder width, just like in the movies.

Well, it wasn't brilliant, thought John, but it was all Glen. He found he was as proud as a father standing next to this young man. He hoped he would live long enough to tell him so.

The circle began to close in as John took one more hasty peek to the rear. He was shocked to see Sung, Suzette, Lawrence, Finn, Tatanka, shit all of the others, standing, watching out the front windows. Nice, at least they got good seats for the beating.

All he could hope was whatever they planned it had best start soon; and decisively.

When it did.

Was he hallucinating? The ground was coming alive. This was the plains at the foot of the Rockies, as solid of ground as there was in the world. They did not have earthquakes! Yet the earth was clearly undulating as if becoming liquid right before their eyes.

Though not where he and Glen stood, that was terra firma.

That was when the farm boys began to dance. Fear became terror as realization crawled up their legs. They swatted at the living, crawling horror coming up from under the grass and dirt.

Bugs! Sheriff John realized exactly what was happening and why the others hadn't come to their aid. They were using the littlest soldiers on these human targets. Humans had an irrational and perverse repugnance to tiny, crawling things. And the ground was alive with them. Beetles, moles, grasshoppers, praying mantises, ants, and cicadas climbing, chittering, though not biting, not stinging, not harming, just annoying and getting into the psyches of the assembled. Snakes coiled like living rope around ankles and calves, pulsating, terrifying.

The farm boys began swinging, swatting, pounding here and there on themselves trying kill or dislodge their attackers. As blows began to land on the tiny soldiers, injuring and knocking them from the jerks, the air became alive with the buzz of bees, yellow jackets, and hornets, distracting the louts from attacking those who could not defend themselves to those who could not be hit.

The big, bold, brave locals ran for their four wheelers, not bothering to climb the small ladders into the cabs, they jumped and vaulted over bed sidewalls to escape the terror. The creepy crawlers sliding and jumping to the ground, not wishing to go for the ride.

As John stood marveling at the use of fear over violence, thereby negating harm to either party, he smiled. Until he felt the flutter of tiny wings and the grasp of minute claws on his legs. He gazed down where he could see the ripple flow up the inside of his pantleg. Deep calming breaths pushed down all repugnance, mind over anxiety to overcome revulsion. He had never feared insects. Like many a small boy he had toyed with them, but the concentration of hundreds crawling up his bare legs was quite different.

They scuttled out onto his arms where they could look him in the eye. He nodded his head in thanks, what else could he do? They had saved him, at the very least, of a horrible beating and possible hospital stay, if not a visit to the morgue. How do you thank a beetle? Let it scurry around you for a bit and then move on.

Suzette met him at the door and wrapped him in her arms. She stroked his back, arms and back again, letting him feel the warmth of mammal over insect. She was proud of him, not for his willingness to stand up and protect, but for his willingness to allow the tiny soldiers their respect. To meet them as equals, she knew it couldn't have been easy.

Humans just didn't see the rest of the world the way The People did. They saw themselves as apart from it, not related to each species. It must be a lonely existence believing you are superior, separate from an entire world where you live. Let's admit it, though, she thought, no one wants to be inundated by hundreds of creepy crawlers.

He realized that the big kid, Jervis, was still laying on the lawn out by the lane. John should go help him up and back to the world. He turned just as the kid came to. He shook his big empty head and focused on where Glen stood with his back to the kid. He saw his chance. Jervis came up with a speed that surprised Sheriff John. He wouldn't have believed it if he hadn't seen the kid come to and take off like a big defensive back right at Glen.

Glen saw the shock in John's eyes and turned at the last second just as the kid hit him. Glen braced, rocked, and came up standing, but wrapped in the arms of Jervis. John took a step towards the boys and then stopped.

He saw Glen visibly calm himself. He didn't try to get away, he just gave in to the bear hug Jervis had him in. He became a dead weight, rag doll. Jervis tried to throw him down on the ground, but Glen would place a foot here, bend a knee there and remain upright. The only struggle he put into the fight was working himself slowly around so he would be facing Jervis rather than away. Mission accomplished he resumed his slow breathing, relaxed dance. Jervis was getting tired wrastlin' someone who refused to wrastle back. His energy soon waned from struggling with inertia. At last, he'd wore himself out and collapsed on the ground taking massive gulps of air while attempting to regain his equilibrium.

Glen gazed down at the big mound on the ground, straightened his shirt sleeves, tucked the shirt tails into his jeans, and shook his head. "Don't you get tired of losing?"

The sheriff came over to where Jervis lay panting on the ground and between him and Glen, they were able to help the kid back into his truck where he could rest more comfortable while regaining a modicum of dignity.

"You get home to a hot bath and some rest," suggested the sheriff.

"And if you'd ever want to make friends instead of actin' the dope, let me know, I'll buy you a beer, if'n yer old enough," Glen closed the truck door without slamming.

As they walked back towards the houses Sheriff John slapped him hard on the back almost knockin' poor Glen out of his shoes. "Hey, careful, I've had a day," Glen steadied himself.

"Yeah, you have," said the sheriff, "where'd you learn that little trick?" he asked pointing to the sight of less than mighty struggle.

"Something you said about wasting energy in a fight. You said if you knew you couldn't win, don't waste what reserves you have, let the other guy tire himself out. And when the opportunity arose, that's when you strike," he smiled bright as daybreak, "I'm glad I didn't have to."

The sheriff wanted to hug the kid right there, but thought he might be embarrassed by it, so he punched him, gently, in the shoulder.

He felt the pressure on his feet as if someone had laid a heavy hose across the tops slowing his steps. Now what? He looked down and almost fainted. If there was one creature John hated, or feared he guessed was the right word, it was snakes. They terrified him to the bone and there were two, no, three curling about his feet, ankles, and shins, not threatening, just kinda huggin' him.

First, he had to concentrate on not shitting his pants or pissin' himself, wouldn't want to do that in front of the womenfolk. Then, maybe, he could figure out how to extricate himself from the embrace of the serpents. Out of the corner of his eye he saw Cynthia standing smack dab in the center of the picture window. Well, he couldn't kick them or shoot them, which would be his first reaction. Damnit! But if you want trust and respect it has got to be earned. And these folks was going to make him earn every ounce.

He bent over in an easy, cool manner, soothing the screaming, wailing, weeping child inside his head. When he had been a small child some of the bigger kids had stuck him in a box full of snakes, closed the box, and began whackin' it with sticks and rockin' it. He had shit his pants back then, he wouldn't now. Breaths, deep, cleansing, relaxing breaths. He let his hands fall toward the ground and the serpents coiling there. They tasted him, rubbed their heads against him, squeezed his calves. He wanted nothing more than to run, kick them away and run hard and fast, his hands tried to recoil from the soft, smooth skin, but he held firm. Earn it, John, earn it.

The snakes slid off into the fields and John took a long, fierce breath so he wouldn't fall over and came up slow.

"I didn't think you had it in you," said Cynthia from his side, "Thank you, you are one helluva human being. I thought you might faint or do something horrible. Sorry, I had to know."

"So, did I," John replied with relief.

From his safe nook down the lane in the copse of bush and tree he watched with intense interest as all events played out before him. The gambit with the insects and snakes was interesting, one he never would have thought of, and though it might have succeeded where humans were concerned it would fail miserably where The People were.

And what was going on between Otter, Snake, and the sheriff? Intermingling of species? He didn't get it. It would seem now certain members of The People wanted to find what ol' Bear had. That was the trouble with folks, they simply focused on what they wanted, not the cost. Oh sure, Bear and his woman had had a lot of good years, human years, but what was that compared to forever years? And look what the 'great love' had done. The world, both sides, were now in peril and war between the People was as close fresh scat. And that had never happened before. Yeah, love was wonderful, until it wasn't. It had hurt ol' Bear until he damn near destroyed the balance of the whole damned universe. What good was love if it could do that?

Nope, he'd stick to his own kind. Well, unless he needed some humans for his own purposes. They did have their uses. A fun night in the sack, as pawns for a particularly nasty little ruse when one wanted to remain as an innocent on the sidelines, as suckers when the fighting began. Fodder for the war machine so those of greater import could stay out of the fray.

They all thought themselves so smart and yet the answer they sought was literally right in front of their noses, if only they could see that far. He chuckled to himself. By the time they figured out who was behind this little action it would be well past the time of reconciliation. It was not that he wanted to rule the world, just control those parts he thought important. Maybe show them all what and who was important in the great scheme of things and mayhap in the process garner some respect.

He'd seen all he required. It was time to make the final plans. They'd be expecting some kind of ultimatums, he'd not make a one. No, he would wait until victory was his and then walk in to save the day. Even in defeat they would never know it was he who had been behind all this, they would think he just happened to show up when they needed saving and hand him the world on a platter in gratitude. It was brilliant.

Small Victories, Future Worries

∞

That evening the representatives of The People and the few humans involved met in the adjoining yards behind Bear's home. The few humans did not include Sheriff John Roberts as he had gone into town to check on his deputies. He had attempted to contact them several times to no avail, and now he was concerned. There could only be a few reasons they would not get back to him when the call had come through, and none of them was good.

Meg had come down after her shift at the bar on request of the sheriff. He had told her what he could but knew she would never be convinced just in the tellin', she would need to see and hear. Even then it would be even money as to whether she bought into the whole ball of shit. Hell, he'd been involved since the git-go, and still couldn't make himself believe it all wasn't some kind of weird dream or hallucination/hypnotic meltdown. But she was a levelheaded girl who would believe her own eyes and ears. Or so he hoped.

The strange addition was Jervis. After Glen had bested the kid a couple times now, he seemed joined at the hip with him. Kind of a, 'if ya can't beat 'em, join 'em' kind of thing. After the day of the insects Jervis had gone home and cleaned up, while doin' so he, apparently, had a long talk with himself and decided change was in the wind. Jervis had been beat fair and square, now they would be friends forever. To be honest with himself, he was tired of bein' bested. He hadn't a clue what he'd got himself in to, but he didn't care, his friend was here and that's all he needed to know. Maybe he'd be a decent sort after all. And Glen needed a normal friend, not someone who would take off on a whim without a word.

Suzette was proud to be associated with such fine people on both sides of the great divide. She laughed to herself. She had never had much use for the humans, they had hunted her children for their coats, for their meat. She blanched for a moment, her head swam, that was how the humans referred to her children, as meat. She felt her blood rise, a churning in her belly, she took in the few humans in the yard and settled her anger. These were not those people.

As a matter of fact, most humans today had not committed those sins against her family, but when you are immortal, memories run deep. Suzette could still feel the bullets, the knives as they carved the hide from her children, slaughtered by the thousands, heartlessly, without thought. But these were not those humans.

These were good people, they had their faults, their quirks, and warts, but who didn't. The People were not perfect, they just were. They existed, and that was enough. She just wanted it to continue.

"Suzette," Glen's insistence yanked her out of her reverie.

"What is it, Glen?" she asked, knowing there was some minute detail that needed her attention so the meet could be started.

"Shouldn't the sheriff be back by now?" He wore his worry like a veil.

"John will come back when he is done with his chore," she was concerned but not to the point of worry, not yet. She wished the sheriff had taken some back-up with him. Yes, they had dispersed the 'gang' but there was still that mountain of a man who had it in for all of them, and he had friends. "If you are that concerned, I will send someone inconspicuous to check on him."

"I could go." Glen danced in place needing some kind of activity. Suzette was suddenly overcome with the idea of throwing a stick or a ball, and then immediately shut it down.

"They know who you are and will be looking for you. No, I think we need to send someone they don't know and wouldn't even if she was standing on the top of their heads," She turned surveying the crowd,

"Fiona, could I have a word with you?"

The small woman, almost the same size as Suzette, with up-turned eyes, stealthily slinked through the assembled to Suzette's side. Glen thought she might rub up against Suzette's leg, though she stopped short. She was Cat and though he was Dog, he felt no need to chase her. He liked her.

"Think you could steal on into town and check on our illustrious sheriff," the two women stood face to face, hands in hands, "Glen, and I am in agreement with him, thinks he should have returned to our loving embrace by now, and he has some enemies. We would like to be reassured as to his safety and time frame."

"I keep forgetting that these folk have a great concern for time, it's like a chain they drag around with them. Minutes, hours, what are they but grains on the ground?" Fiona stood silent wrapped in thought.

"Um, yes, well, we can wax philosophic when this is all behind us, but for now we would like to know our friend is safe," Suzette had lists that begged accomplishment. She required the assistance of her general and friend.

"I'll return momentarily," Fiona grinned at her little time jape as she turned to take the straightest line to where the sheriff's destination. She stopped short.

"You should have a local guide," Meg stood before her blocking her path, her eyes darting between the woman and the meet. Meg really wanted to know what this was all about, but the sheriff was a friend. If he needed help, she needed to go.

"I appreciate you wanting to help, but you would only slow me down," Fiona spoke soft, almost a purr, "I find that I work best alone. Like many here, I find that other's presence only complicate matters."

"OK, I'll just tag along then, shall I?"

Bear crashed through the woods, Equine in his wake. He had the bearing of a creature on the most direct course to where he could sense his granddaughter's presence. She was not the only one with the ability. Evan had always known where she was if he'd take the time to think about it. She was that itch at the base of his neck that would never go away. Well, now that itch was like a homing beacon that would lead him directly to her.

If Becky had thought herself fleet of foot, she had never considered the speed of Bear through brush and scrub, especially when he had the scent of someone he loved in his nose. She was spending some small effort keeping pace with the large bear, though he cleared everything that might obstruct their progress.

She had never known the love he had. This young girl represented all that was good about that love to Bear, and he would protect it like any other mother bear. One thing she was certain of is, they would encounter no others out here as the racket of Bear's passing would scatter any in their way.

The shriek of joy, relief, love, and gratitude shattered the cacophony Bear generated. The young teen threw herself into the grasp of the humungous bear who, in turn, cuddled her close to him as gentle and soothing as a mother to her babe.

Equine felt water running down her nose. It was odd as that had never happened in all eternity, she believed the humans referred to it as crying. She found she liked the sensation.

"What were you thinking coming up here all by yourself?" he demanded as he checked every inch of her to reassure she had come to no harm. "How did you cross the threshold by yourself? Why didn't you tell someone you were going to do this? They are probably worried. Worried for you, worried for what I might do when I get back, worried for themselves. What were you thinking?" He finally came full circle.

"That you might need me," sheepish and on the tip of a tear, she hugged him close.

What could he say? "I love you. If anything had happened to you..." he couldn't finish the thought. He clung to her swearing on all he held dear he would protect her with his very last breath, which was an extremely long way away. She would not leave his side now or ever. And would have to come live with him when this was finally over.

Though what Evan knew in his soul he should do was to send Alexandra back to the house in the company of Becky, but he also knew she would not leave his side. And he didn't really want her to. She had proven quite pithily that he could not protect her down there, or anywhere, unless it was by his side. Facts was facts. So, the plan came into focus, he would keep Alexandra with him in his search for The Mother while Becky galloped back to inform the others of where things stood in the upper elevations. 'Course, the question was, what would the Mother think of Bear showing up with his get in tow.

Parting was quick and thankful. Becky had done her best to watch over the precocious child, though success would have to be graded on a curve. Alexandra lived, which was the important detail, and was now in the care of grandpa. The teen and equine women had come to know each other, though only just, and so there would be no tears, no long hugs, just a thank you and a wave of energy.

"Now, we have work to do," Evan the Bear spoke to the comparatively small teen, "I still need to find the Mother and find out what she wants of me. How I can repair the damage I have done. How to return life to normal if that is even possible." He spoke with a confidence he knew did not exist. What he hoped to accomplish was impossible or at the very least, improbable, yet he had to try. The question remained, where do you find the heart of the world? For that was where she would be waiting for him.

"I am curious how you were able to come across to find me?" he asked as they strolled through the forest. He had no direction in mind, aimless he hoped some solution would come to mind. Sometimes you had to let fate take your hand and let your feet lead you where they would, and hope.

"I needed you," she said logically. "I needed to find you, to come to help you. All I thought about was you, I knew I would find you." Confidence is a great back-up when you have no other plan, he should try it sometime.

Hell, he thought, there is no time like the present! Time was running faster than he could. He'd tried everything he could think of, maybe out of the mouths of babes.

They came to a clearing on the edge of a drop-off into wide open valleys and rivers thousands of feet below. It was breathtaking even for

Evan who had been here many times, had sat on the edge to contemplate, to recharge, thousands of times over the centuries. It was one of his top ten thousand favorite places to admire, to appreciate the beauty of this world. It was perfect.

"You aren't afraid of heights, are you?" he asked just a moment before too late.

"Not that I know of," she pronounced bravely before taking a step back from the eternity.

Alexandra hadn't realized how high in the world she had come or maybe been dropped off upon entering this parallel world. From where she stood, she could see her future and her past, both went on forever. An optical illusion, she was quite certain, though never questioning the sight.

The peculiar thing about the teen years in humans is they accept experiences without a second thought. They believe anything is possible and therefore it is. Experimentation is necessary, it is where knowledge lays hidden, waiting for them to discover. Fear is to be conquered not succumbed to. If she was terrified to be standing on the edge of the rocky outcropping the solution was not to step back away from the fall, but to take another step forward.

"Steady," says the Bear, "unnecessary risks are not worth taking."

They sat on the edge of the cliff, feet dangling over the precipice, swathed in beauty. Neither said another word while the world continued on its way. Sometimes quiet says so much more than meaningless words. Sometimes there is just nothing to say for the moment. They waited for the words, in no hurry for their arrival.

Birds flew by and waved; Bear waved back. A rabbit stuck its head out from behind some scrub and Bear said hello. The rabbit blinked as if it had never been greeted by a ten-foot bear before. It made to run until Bear softly told it that he was pretty much a vegetarian, and the rabbit relaxed, nibbling on what little green grass was still available.

"Think anybody's missin' us yet?" Bear asked as he adjusted his seat.

"Ain't nobody missin' me," replied Alexandra with just a hint of sad, "only person who cares is sittin' next to me." She smiled.

"How long you known about me?" Evan was curious. He had never suspected she might know about him or who he truly was. She'd never let on.

"Guess always," she scrunched up her face in thinking of the past, "when I was little, I thought you was a big, old cuddly dog when you wasn't a person. I remember thinking you was the most magical person in the world, but nobody seemed to know it but me." She giggled.

"Whyn't you never say nothing?" This was truly what had got his curiosity piqued.

"Well, I thought it was kinda like your stories. Weren't nobody supposed to believe them. Grandma made sure all the others, her kids and all the grandkids, knew they was just made up. Like I said, she never actually said they wasn't true, but she sure hinted hard. But I knew different. And if she knew but didn't want nobody believin' what would she think if I told her about you?" she sighed and rubbed her hands on her thighs in thought, "I didn't know if she knew that part or not, but if I tried to explain and she didn't know, there'd be a whole peck and half of trouble for me. I knew what ma would say, so there was no reason to bring it up to her and the rest of the kids would mock you and say rude things about your stories, so I sure wasn't going to tell the likes of them."

"Why did you never ask me about it? Or mention that you could see?" One would have thought, he finished to hisself.

"Well, I figured since you ain't never told nobody about it, far as I could tell, then you must want it to be your secret. And if you wanted to keep your secret, it was yours to keep, not mine. If you wanted me to know, you'da told me. So, I kept my mouth shut with my own little secret hidden up in my head," she was so proud of herself for not tellin' and so pleased that she had this wonderful secret and never told nobody, Evan had to laugh.

"The other kids would make fun of my stories?" he asked, his feelings hurt, but only just, "I thought they enjoyed the tellin'."

"Oh, they did, but then Buck got older and decided he could prove it by mocking you and your stories 'cause he was too sophisticated to believe in childish things," she didn't much care for her cousin, and it showed in the bitterness when she mentioned his name. "If it makes you feel any better, he's the one who ruined it for all of us about Santa, the Easter Bunny and the Tooth fairy."

"Least I'm in good company," he laughed.

"Nah, you're real," and now they both shared a long laugh.

"What are you looking for, grandpa?" she'd heard some of the others talk, but she was confused on exactly what he sought.

"Well, the balance of the universe, for want of better term, has a crack in it making everything off kilter, whacky," the bear waggled his paws to illustrate. Alexandra held her laughter at the silly visage, he appreciated the effort. "Anyway, I don't know if you remember when your grandmother passed," he turned his gaze on her to see her reaction.

"Gosh, grandpa, the whole world knew when grandma died, you could feel it like a big ol' cold front coming through," she shivered in remembrance.

"You felt that?" would this child never cease to amaze him? Not any time soon, he replied.

"Don't you remember? I showed up at your door within ten minutes of her passing. I knew you'd need me. I remember as I rode over on my tricycle that I couldn't understand why no one else seemed to have noticed. The feeling of her passing almost knocked me over," a tear escaped as she rode down the same path.

Bear had forgotten. He had been so deeply immersed in his pain, in the insanity caused by Her passing he'd forgotten how Alexandra had just showed up, as if she knew. She had. Now he remembered her coming through the door, this tiny child, and jumping into his lap, holding him, refusing to let go while he grieved. She had been so strong, supporting him emotionally, not crying, not falling apart, but holding him together. This little child, so mature beyond her years, so caring, so different than any child he had ever known. He had no idea at the time just how different.

"Well," he continued, "apparently you, The People, and the universe felt it as well. I went a little crazy for a while. I lost myself in grief, I loved Her so, so much. Well, I kind of lashed out at everything, and I'm pretty powerful, so I kind of broke the universe, in a way. Now I need to find a way to repair what I broke. See?" It was everything in a nutshell.

"So, what do we do?" He picked her up and held her to his bosom and hugged her for a long time. Of course, she would ask, that was who she was. And, he realized, it was why she was here.

Fiona had considered sauntering into town like she owned it, that would be her nature, and no one would know who she was. It was one of the reasons she had be asked to check on the sheriff, the other was that she was exceedingly smart. Smart enough to know that would also set her up as a target in a small town like this. They had an inherent distrust of outsiders and in this town, at this time, any person unknown would stand out like an alien from outer space. She saw the wisdom of having Meg at her side, as if Fiona was a cousin or someone just in from out of town.

It was quiet on the street and peaceful from all outward appearances, though appearances could be deceiving. Meg led her on a circuitous, meandering route to where the sheriff's office sat; just two girls out for an afternoon stroll. They stood in the alley, hugging the brick of the store on the south side. They could stay out of sight while observing all who entered and exited the jail. A few minutes here could save a great deal of running, dodging, and bruising later.

Within moments Fiona was glad they had waited. Coming out of the jail were the two deputies. Meg almost ran to them to ask if the sheriff was alright, almost. Their furtive behavior, eyes darting to the left and right, searching the surroundings for any movement or any sign of people where there shouldn't be. Satisfied they got into their patrol cars and took off in opposite directions.

Softly they padded over to the front window, attempting to appear as natural as any humans walking down the street peering in the front window of the jail could. It looked abandoned. They slipped through the front door closing it behind themselves. Fiona listened. All quiet on the jailhouse front.

The almost imperceptible moan from the rear of the building caught Fiona's keen ear. Moving swiftly towards the sound she found the crumpled figure of who could only assume, was sheriff John Roberts. She called Meg back and her reaction confirmed Fiona's suspicion. He lay on the frame of the hard metal bed, the thin mattress having been pulled out and thrown in the corner of the room. He had been beaten, badly. The door was locked.

Visually scanning the walls for keys, they found only empty pegs and let-down. The damn keys had to be here somewhere; you didn't take keys for a jail cell with you. She searched methodically through drawers and cabinets, nothing. Meg searched the other offices, nothing for her either. Where would you hide keys that would be close but not obvious. She saw the coffee can sitting on the table by the old-school percolator. She opened the can. Shit, coffee grounds. What about the? Just as Meg came out of the side office Fiona picked up the percolator and shook. They heard the keys banging into the side.

"Hang on, we'll have you out of there in a few," she called in a low tone.

Meg had no idea how long they had. She wasn't certain how long they'd been here, but she knew they weren't leaving the sheriff, even long enough to go find help. They had to free him and get him out of this building as quickly as possible, but how? He wasn't huge but he was large enough it would present difficulties for two petite women to carry him down the street. They had to get him upright and carry him between them. It wouldn't look good for the drunken sheriff to be manhandled by two women, then again, it might buy some respect.

Fiona may not be magical or have any kind of superpowers as many attributed to Spirit Guides, what she did have was righteous indignation, backed by an extremely pissed off bartender, it would suffice. What they both desired most to was stay here and kick some ass for what had been done to this man. What they knew they had to do was get him out of here, back to the house where he could receive proper, or proper enough, care. She unlocked and swung open the door.

He heard the squeal of metal hinges and tried to raise his head. He couldn't get it much off the hard surface of the bed, but what he could see reassured. There was an attractive, diminutive, Asian woman coming to his aid with Meg by her side. He had no idea what angels should look like, but these would do.

They attempted to lift him off the bed, but his broken ribs screamed in protest and agony. This would not do. They would have to immobilize what they could and drag the rest. Meg found where the sheets were kept and ripped them into strips she could tie where bones were broken. The last thing they wanted to do was inflict more damage. Grabbing two more of the rough sheets Fiona tied him into a poorly constructed travois praying to herself that it would hold long enough to get him away from this building. Between the two of them they should be able to keep the bouncing and banging down to a minimum.

They eased him onto the sheets, clutched the corners and tied them, each grabbing a corner and wrapping around hand and wrist. Time was wasting when it wasn't climbing up their back. Damn!

They dragged him out the back door and into the alleyway behind. Though speed was of the essence, care was taking over first place. No sense killing yourself to save someone only to kill them in the process. If they could find a vehicle maybe Fiona could pull up some memories from when she was hangin' around with those cats back in the fifties out in LA. Wasn't there a way to hotwire a car?

The going was slow, try as they might, they couldn't avoid all the bumps, curbs, cracked sidewalks, and potholes. This would not do, it was taking far too long, by the time they got him to help it would be too late. They needed a miracle.

And there it was. A Ford pickup sitting outside the grocery store with the engine running and the owner inside making a quick purchase. They would borrow the vehicle. Well, it wasn't stealing, was it? Meg said she would bring the truck back to town and leave it somewhere close by once they delivered their package, so the fella wouldn't be without it long. Their need, right now, was greater than his ride.

Meg backed the truck into the drive and yelled for help. Tatanka, of course, was the first to come with Lawrence right in his tail. One look and they needed no details. Each taking a side they hammocked the sheriff into the house and onto Evan's bed. Now, what to do?

"I gotta take the truck back to town. I kinda borrowed it without asking," Meg took the blame while attempting to appear sheepish, smug was a poor substitute. "Want I should fetch the doctor?"

"Please, and be very careful, obviously we are dealing with some vicious individuals," Suzette's concern wore on her like poison ivy, she'd never satisfy this itch.

The two deputies stomped around the empty sheriff's office smashing whatever they could get their hands on out of frustration. Some sonofabitch had come and stole the sheriff right out from under their noses. Why hadn't they thought to leave one of them there while the other ran around getting everything ready for them fellas from the city to take down the Beach house. Probably where they took the damn sheriff!

Well, they'd made their deal with the devil and whatever happened from here on out wouldn't change a damn thing if they lost this battle. Not after what they'd done to John.

"Maybe we shoulda not been so rough on him," Sam said to no one but himself.

"And maybe we shoulda just let him get us killed fighting who knows what," Ray was not in the mood. "He wasn't going to tell us everything he knew, just going to let us walk into a turf war with all these sonsabitches we din't know and was none of our business. I didn't take this job to get killed by a bunch of bikers and gangsters," Ray had found out what the sheriff had been holding back, and it pissed him off royal.

How could a man you'd know'd for so many years keep this info from them? He'd had to find out from the fella down't the bar. Hell, he'd never met the guy before, and he was more honest than his friend of the last fifteen years. How'd you like that? Couldn't trust nobody no more.

Lucky he met the guy, too! Sittin' there havin' a beer and this fella, out of the goodness of his heart, tells Ray that he can't believe he's just sittin' there havin' a beer when all of hell is about to come down around his head.

"What in all blazes you talkin' 'bout," Ray turned on his stool to face the fella. Big biker lookin' guy, though no colors, so he ain't associated.

"Heard through the grapevine there's gonna be a hellraisin' in this town over the next few. Bunch a city folks havin'a dispute and decided they'd rather tear up this nowhere town than their own turf," he shrugged as if it weren't no nevermind of his. "I figured if I was going to get through this town before shit starts splattin' off fan blades, I'd best get rubber to road. Figured I'd stop by for a burger and beer on my way through while there was still a town to stop in. Good thing I run into you if you didn't know nothin'," he tipped his beer to the deputy. "Matter of fact, on my way outta here now. You'd be smart to do the same."

Ray agreed to meet with one of the opposition that the biker knew. "Just trying to help avoid a lot of innocents getting' hurt," he'd said.

"They're bringing a lot of drugs into our city," the guy had told Ray, "and sex trafficking, kids, man, little kids, can you imagine?"

Ray was flabbergasted, "You shitting me? Kids? And drugs?" These were the biggest buttons on Ray's pissed meter. He'd seen what drugs could do to a community and trafficking in kids was the absolute lowest rung on the crime ladder. Fuck those guys, he'd be happy to help these fellas stomp them out.

Ray had brought the news back to Sam and they'd confronted the sheriff this morning. They didn't like his answers or his attitude. Throwing around words like duty, honor, and oath, what the fuck did he know about any of that? He's the one 'bout to hang them all out to die. And for drug pushers and child sex traffickers, over Ray's dead body!

That's when the arguing started. The sheriff was the first one to push, he'd said his last piece before he fell to the floor. They'd locked him nice and secure in the cell, and now, here some sonofabitch had let him free. Didn't much matter now. They'd both decided that after they'd set everything up for those that come to parlay, they'd hightail out of town. They'd got the info the gang that was trying to stop the traffickers wanted, made certain nobody from any other law enforcement would interfere with their operation, now it was time to head to the hills.

They'd just hang out in the mountains 'til everything blowed over. Then they'd call in the Staties and let them clean up the mess. Neither of them had liked the look of the crop of folks growing around the Beach house, looked to be nothing but trouble. Bikers and bitches, huge guys who just emanated threat, scum of the earth types, nope. Sam and Ray had no desire to be between them and those the two of them had made their peace with. Best to save the skin on your own back.

Meg parked the truck in front of the store she'd taken it from, dropped the keys on the mat and eased her way out of the cab and into the alley. As she crept through the town making her way back to their encampment, she saw the two deputies leaving the sheriff's office. They slunk around back where their vehicles were parked and followed each other in the direction of nowhere and mountains.

Hmmm, she thought, should she follow or take the info back to Suzette? She headed back to the house. If what she'd garnered from bits and pieces of conversation and what Sheriff John had said, no matter where these two were headed the family would know exactly where they were.

Curious Bed Fellows

∞

Equine strode up to the house, which was a hive of activity. She smiled at the recent memory of Bear finding her in the mountains and the reunion he'd had with Alexandra. It was a wonderful relationship they shared and filled her huge horse heart. But the funny thing was, what she thought of fondly was his shock at seeing her and calling out her name, Becky, nobody but Bear would call her that. She wasn't sure anybody else knew, and that was fine. It was for her and Bear, it was nice to have shared secrets.

If Equine thought she had been gone on a long trip up in through the mountains she had no idea how long. The house was now abuzz with People she had never met, hadn't seen in a very long time, and with some she could do without seeing for a long time again. She and her family had always had a tenuous relationship with insects of any kind, but some were worse than others. She thought she might have to do some bug stomping when out of nowhere Suzette showed up, wrapped Equine in her right arm and directed her out the back door.

"I know what you're thinking," she cautioned companionably, "many of us had the same thought but we have learned they have their uses. A truce has been established, you will find," she soothed, "they are amenable as long as we don't squash them, they won't bite us."

Equine was dubious, though Suzette was an honest sort whom she trusted would not lead her astray, especially when it came to biting insects.

"You have been busy," Equine remarked looking at all the changes and 'improvements' around the perimeters of the backyards. She could only assume the same had been accomplished around the front, but she had failed to notice in her delight to be back on the flat land.

"Most of these ideas were Sheriff John's," Suzette's admiration was poorly concealed, "it turns out our sheriff has a pretty good military mind especially when handed the impossible."

"And which impossibility is that?" Asked with a nudge of humor in whatever direction Suzette chose to take it.

She, being a lady and of The People, chose to ignore the implication. "How to wage war without killing anyone," matter of fact.

"And how is that working?"

"So far, so good," but there was something in her tone which betrayed the anxiety and fear she harbored.

"You're not telling me important things, things I might wish to know," Equine charged.

"Sheriff John was ambushed by his own men two days ago in town. His own deputies!" Suzette's ire was barely contained. The other woman was surprised by the intensity of feeling.

"Why would they attack him? I thought they would be aligned with us. I thought their loyalties would lay with the sheriff and no one else," she eyed the petite woman who stared into loathing, something Equine would never have thought possible. "Apparently I thought wrong."

"They had been fed a pack of lies about us, about what we are doing here, about everything," now anger fused with aggravation, "and the deputies believed it. I don't care that they judged us as immoral or odious, they don't know us, but they knew the sheriff! Had known him for years! And out of nowhere people whom they've never met before start telling them lies and horrible things about a man they had trusted, a friend, and they choose to accept the words of strangers over family." Now her disgust found full fury. Betrayal of any sort was the worst sin any of The People could imagine. Which was why so many had come to the aid of those determined to make a stand in the backyard of this beautiful home.

"Did you find Bear? Alexandra? Where are they? Are they alright?" the questions came fast and furious as Suzette realized she hadn't asked a one yet and she required a change in subject.

"Yes, yes, still up in the mountains, and as far as I know," answered Equine in order. She then spent the next several minutes telling in more detail what had happened and what Bear and Alexandra were up to. Well, what they had been up to when she had departed and as far as she knew what they intended from there.

People passed nodding their hellos to Equine, welcoming her back.

"What can I do to help?" she asked gazing around and not seeing much which needed doing. "Though I seem a bit late to the trough, it would appear you have all in hand."

"Well, you can give an old friend a hug hello and let Suzette get back to her patient," Tatanka's deep rumble of joviality lifted any despondency. "I'm certain she would like to check on her sheriff as she trusts no one else to nurse him back to health."

Suzette blushed, but only those with the keenest vison would have noticed, before excusing herself.

"Would you like to see all we have done in your absence?" Tatanka asked convivially, though the air was tense between them.

She was remembering his accusations from their previous meeting. Though how mankind had used and abused her children could hardly be laid at her feet. He seemed to be attempting amends and was now pushing freight overboard to lighten the load.

"Of course, I would," replied Becky. She didn't know why but at that moment she wanted to think of herself as Becky, the way it came off Bear' tongue. "You seem different than the last time we were together." She stuck a toe in the water.

"Different? How?" Tatanka did not do coy well.

"I don't know, friendlier," she ventured though she left out 'overly'.

"One can only hold a grudge for so long," he let the thought peter out on its own, "I guess I was too lost in the far past. You know, with us the past is as close as yesterday, when you've had so many yesterdays, they can get intermingled. Some are so fresh you can hear the crunch of the snow under hoof on an eighty-degree day." He still was smiling though she could not discern any humor.

"Where are we going?" completely back in the moment Equine realized they were out in the middle of a farm field, alone.

"Just for a walk," he said grabbing her by the arm.

"Let go of me!" She screamed. She was strong but the strength of Tatanka was legendary. There would be no way she could break his grip unless she adopted less than respectable means.

Terror can be a great motivator and adrenalin multiplies the muscle depending on the threat. This threat was real, life threatening and immediate, she kicked out with all her strength landing a blow square to the groin. No matter the species a good kick in the nuts will get the attention of the receiver. Air whooshed from his lungs, he let go of her to grab that which had gained in importance, and she turned and ran blindly away.

Tatanka fell to the ground, vison blurred by pain. A pain so intense it cleared the fog from his mind. What had just happened? What the hell was he doing? He couldn't be certain, but he knew he had to head back to the house and explain.

Wherever Equine had run she hadn't come running back to the house, there was no sign of her anywhere and he had failed to note the direction of her panicked flight. For now, that was good. He could warn all the others before she came back and told her version of what had happened. He would prefer the story come from his lips first.

By the time Equine found her way back to the fortifications the word had been spread what had happened. Surprisingly, she thought, it was the truth. What she didn't know was the why, she was about to find out.

Tatanka, surrounded by many of the others, Sung, Suzette, Doe, Glen, Cynthia, and some she didn't know, met her as she came into the house. Before she could holler, scream, or protest they had her sitting in a kitchen chair and Tatanka was apologizing and explaining and apologizing.

"It has begun," he finally stated solemnly, "I swear on the Mother and the Great Spirit, I had no idea what I was doing until you roused me with your well-placed kick," he wanted to rub the sore area but would not in front of the ladies. He was back to himself.

She stared hard into the eyes of all present to gauge the truth of Tatanka's words. Satisfied she allowed herself to relax, though only just.

"If I can be affected so completely, and I say in all humility, I am one of the strongest of the spirits, then we are all in danger. From now on, no one is to be left alone," all assented, "I think we travel in threes just to be sure our backup has backup. If you notice anyone acting suspicious in any way, a look, being somewhere they shouldn't be, behaving differently in any way, get assistance immediately, preferably in numbers."

"How do we know that all three will not be affected at the same time?" Threw in Finn from where he crouched on the floor, always the meticulous one.

"We pick three who are not alike in the least," thought Sung out loud, "it would seem the safest, sanest way to assure. We are not all the same, in fact quite different, to control three divergent minds at once would seem near impossible."

It wasn't much, but once again, it was all they had.

Bear and Alexandra sat on the edge of magnificence gazing into forever talking soft, not wishing to disturb those around them. One thing about nature, she defends her own, sometimes with force, sometimes with a sting, a bite, quickness, Bear didn't want to disturb anyone into taking action. He wanted peace.

And that was the thing, wasn't it? That was all he wanted out of life right now, peace. He had lost his mind and half his soul when She passed and been wandering in a haze, lost ever since. Just ghosting through life. An immortal who'd had enough. He thought he was through.

Not by a long shot. His reason sat next to him, legs crossed at the ankle, innocent as sunrise over the mountains, damn near pretty as her grandma in her prime. Yeah, if he'd been looking for life, to sense the pounding, vibrant, heart and soul, the energy of eternity, he'd found it in the form of a young teen who was also searching. A young teen who would never fit in with the world she had been born into. He would have to find a way to fit her into his.

"You know what, grandpa?" she threw the brake on his train of thought. Then, without waiting for any response, "I think I'm more similar to you than anyone I know. All the kids at school, their parents, the folks I meet at the store, see on TV, they ain't like me. They come across as silly, wrapped in things that don't really seem to matter. Well, not to me. I just want to look at them and say, 'you know, you're only here for an instant, why you so worried 'bout things that'll pass before you're done thinking of them?' But I know that ain't right.

"I know you shouldn't shove their limited existence in their faces, it's not polite," she continued, "but sometimes when they're being really mean, either to each other or me, I just wanna tell them that I'll be here long after they're gone and if they aren't nice to me or the weaker kids, I'll make the lives of their great grandchildren miserable." Her ire spent she sat taking in the beauty of the world laid out before her. She laughed at the silliness of her own shallow vengeance, "I apologize, that was wrong, and I shouldn't think that way." She sighed shaking her head as if chastising herself internally.

What a sweet child, Evan thought, what a sweet, sweet child. And then it hit him, "Do you think you are going to live a long time?" prodding with care.

"Just forever," she said so sure of the fact it almost made him burst out in laughter.

He stopped hisself just before, "What makes you so sure you are going to live forever?"

"Because I am like you and you already have, so why shouldn't I?"

Bear almost fell from his perch. Did she know something he didn't? None of the other children or grandkids had shown any inkling they carried his genes. Shit, he wasn't certain he carried genes. He wasn't of that side of the world. He was spirit, though quite substantial, physical, but he had been created of the Mother, not of others. It was an interesting conundrum; one he would have to look into when this unpleasantness was brought to conclusion.

"I want to try something," the thought came a fraction of a second before the words, "close your eyes." Glancing over he saw her follow his instructions. He was glad she didn't ask why, or any other questions, as he didn't think he could answer. He wasn't certain what it was, exactly, that he was proposing to do. He closed his own. "Now take a deep breath in through your nose," just above a whisper, the words almost tickling her ear, "hold, now ease it out through your mouth. Again, slow, and easy. Try to clear your mind of everything, no thoughts, no memories, no questions, allow your mind to float, like it is drifting down a tranquil river, forget where you are. Let yourself drift."

Alexandra did as he asked. He could hear her breath slow down as the intake and exhale were deeper, longer in length. He could almost see her enter a R.E.M state while sitting on the edge of forever. He reached over with his right paw and laid it gently on her leg. She hesitated for a split second before relaxing back into her long, slow breaths. She wouldn't fall. He relaxed.

His body melted away, a little more with each breath, until he was ethereal. As he expected, and hoped, she stood beside him, awe and joy adorned her features. She stood on nothingness and gazed at the universe spread out before her.

"Want to do a little wandering? See what creation is up to?" he grinned, a tingle of excitement, ecstasy ran down his massive spine.

"Can we?" she whispered as if she would break the spell if she spoke out loud.

He took her hand gently, but firmly, and they flew like dolphins swimming through the ocean into the blackness of space. He took her to the birthing of planets and the dying suns; they traveled the astral plane. He wanted her to see, to experience what immortality encompassed. Specks became planets, asteroids flew by and through their ethereal forms. She was certain they had flown forever with eternity in front of them, though it felt a moment.

Before she could process a millionth of what they had encountered she found herself walking side by side with her grandfather, the

Bear, down a beach, waves lapping at their feet, the sun brilliant and dancing off the waves. She noticed the two shadows moving down the beach and was taken aback they were both shadows of bears, one huge and one quite small.

"Is that...?" wonder giggled and bubbled in the question.

Evan was as surprised as she, "I would have to say yes," he answered to the little bear walking along side. Two sets of bear paw prints being washed away by the ocean.

"Where are we?" Asked the little bear.

"On a beach," answered the huge one.

"But where is the beach?"

"Next to the ocean," Evan smiled.

Alexandra realized it didn't matter, she was with her grandfather, and they had the world to themselves. Well, here they did, and she was content. Somehow the discovery that she was a bear did not surprise her in the least. She might have been more surprised to discover she wasn't.

Since she was a little girl, she had known she was different from other children, other people, she didn't know how, but she knew she was. As she grew older, and especially now in her teens, the knowledge was reinforced by her total lack of concern for anything the other kids thought was world shattering. She was consumed with the environment and how it affected the weather, food production, health and, of course, animals, especially, and here she had to grin to herself, bears. She was mature beyond her years in many ways and yet immature in others.

She had no interest in boys, sex, dating, who was the latest heart-throb. She cared little about her clothes, makeup nor much of anything maturing young women were supposed to care about. She had always liked animals, the supposed beasts. She thought, no, she knew them better than people, whom she judged cruel, shallow, and too cliquish by a country mile.

Not that animals didn't have a tendency to attract their own kind, but it was different. Animals never went out of their way to harm others. Oh, if they were hungry, they would kill to eat, that was the way nature had set things up. A bear's gotta live, don't she? But they never hurt something just to hurt it, to watch it suffer, to hang its head on a wall somewhere.

She probably came upon these concepts by hanging with her hippiesque grandmother and grandfather. They had been more influential on her life than any other living beings. Now she knew why.

"Was gramma an immortal?" She knew the answer before asking, no, of course she wasn't, she had died. "I guess I mean. I think she had to have known, on some level, 'bout you? Didn't you know she would die?"

Simple questions sometimes are the hardest to ask and even harder to answer.

"Yes, I knew, but, you see, love doesn't always care what you know. There's a reason they say love is blind because it can close your eyes to reality. It makes you wish things weren't as they are. You think if you love someone hard enough, deep enough, you can change reality, but you can't. You can't make something different just 'cause you want it to be so," the sorrow almost overwhelmed him before he caught hold of his emotions. He couldn't get lost again, not now. Control, he had to maintain control. "We should get back; I think I know how we can find the Mother."

Ray and Sam set camp up near the timberline. They didn't need much, a tent, supplies for a week, maybe two at the outside, there was wood enough to keep them warm at night and cooking what they caught. It was dry as kindling so it would light quick and produce very little smoke. It was perfect up here. Them fellas should be able to clear out the nest of pervs and scum within a few and then they could return to civilization. 'Til then they could just do a little hunting, fishing, set by the fire and watch the stars, no one would be the wiser. Well, long as the good bikers took out the sheriff along with the rest.

Both were experienced back woodsmen so they knew they could survive for as long as needs be. They got comfy and settled in. No one would ever find them up here.

They failed to notice the hundred eyes on them. Even when the forest seems devoid of life it fairly teems with it. All the small critters, the game, the prey, knew how to stay out of sight and these particular critters had been assigned an important job. Keep an eye on these two so when time came, the others'd know just where to find them.

The war council was meeting as usual in the backyards, it now took all three to hold everyone, spilling into the fields behind, when Coyote showed back up. He came up all chummy to Glen, but Glen was having none of it. It wasn't so much that Coyote had taken off, Glen was now well acquainted with the spirits reputation, it was that he never said nothin' to Glen 'fore he took off. That ain't the way friends is supposed to be to each other. You should say goodbye, so long, see ya in a month or when I pass this way again, but Coyote hadn't said one damn thing, just gone. Ain't what friends do, he said to himself.

"Well, look what dragged itself back down here with the mortals," Sung had never been much of a fan of his cousin and his treatment of Glen had not changed his assessment. "Where you been Yote?"

"Takin' care of business, like I told Evan I would. Where is he?" Coyote asked looking about, "Don't seem to see him here. Ain't everybody here?"

There was something in the way he phrased that got Sung's hackles up. Coyote wanted everyone here for a reason; he always has a reason.

"Well, lookie, lookie what we got here, the celebrity!" Doe sidled up next to Sung. "Seems you been the topic of much conversatin', yer ears burning?" She kept her arms folded just below breasts almost to lift and show them off. Give Coyote a glimpse of what he ain't never going to see or hold.

"Don't much like me, do ya?" Coyote could feel the animosity emanating from both, like standing in front of an oven with the door open.

"What's not to like?" Suzette made three, "A 'friend' who shows up when he wants, seems to only be in this world for his own entertainment, runs out on a friend without so much as a word," now Coyote shot a glance Glen's way. "Yeah, you were missed, like a toothache. What brings you back?" If animosity was a commodity, it had just shattered previous records on the market.

"What's everybody so pissed at me for?" Coyote was truly mystified, "I been like this since the dawn of time! I ain't apologizing to nobody for being who I am, you don't like it too bad!" Now he glared at Glen, yet there was a strange sensation down in his belly that filled damn near to his throat. Maybe he wasn't so certain he felt like he said, but he wasn't going to let these fools know it. "Where's Bear?"

"He ain't here, he's takin' care of what he needs, and we're charged with holdin' down the fort." Glen's tone was terse and strained, "Now, why don't you tell us whatever you come to tell Bear."

He glared at all assembled for a heartbeat or two before, "Alright, here's what I know, there's been a ruckus down 't jail, it's a mess and the sheriff can't be found, lotta talk but nobody seems to know anything, and the deputies have taken off somewhere as well. So, we'll get no help from the town itself. And it would appear as if the war is upon us and the fluctuating wave of energy has begun. Some of the people are acting very odd, though it doesn't seem to be affecting humans, but with them it's hard to tell. Also, did you know there is a door in the side of that great big tree across the lane? The one with the clocks?"

"Old news," sniped Sung who was allowing his hostility free rein, "we know about the sheriff and the deputies, they are hiding out up near the timberline and thinking themselves quite clever. We have witnessed the free-floating energy wave firsthand and are now on the watch for it. And, yes, again we knew about the door, the tree and the Spirit who you saw come out of it." Taking away Coyote's thunder was just the ticket to lift Sung's spirits. He had seen the Beaver spirit same as Coyote as it had exited the door, how it knew about the door but nobody else had, well, Beaver's and trees, he guessed.

Mika felt the wind leave his sails as he deflated in front of them. If he had thought they would be grateful, praise him for his sleuthing, and hail him a hero, he was sadly mistaken. Respect would not be easily gained from this group and his supply of good will was in short supply.

They all knew him! They had known him forever; this was how he was made up. It was who he was, they couldn't expect him to just change because some dog might get it's feeling hurt. I mean, he liked the kid and all, but Coyote was a loner, it was part and parcel of his mystique! Damn it all to hell.

"Look, I'm sorry, but you can't expect me to change overnight," he said to Glen's back, "I like ya kid, I really do, but I gotta be who I am. I can't just change for one person, I got a reputation," if he thought that would buy him some cred he was as wrong as he'd been about the respect.

"I thought we were friends," Glen's hurt was palpable, "we ran together!" As if that was the most important thing in life. It might have been to Glen.

"I truly am sorry, I guess I didn't realize what all this meant to you. I'll try to do better in the future, OK?" Mika found he did care about the kid. Maybe it was because they was cousins. Maybe it was 'cause he liked having someone to run with. Maybe he was tired of being alone. And maybe, he was succumbing to the energy of the broken balance, and it was an empty promise made to buy time. Did it matter?

"Looks like I am a few days behind on the info side of this, so what do you need me to do?" he was back to his cocky self like flipping a pancake. Coyote could not change what the Mother had created.

"We are told the humans are planning on moving on us again, and soon, we thought it might be fun to disrupt those plans," Cynthia was quick to forgive as her children had borne the brunt of blame, suspicion, and dread since humans had put that story in their book. She knew for a fact it had never happened, but it was easy to impugn the reputation of snakes. Maybe it was just as easy to impugn the rep of the canine.

"Thought they had stopped by already,"

"Hmmm, for a guy that hasn't been around much you seem pretty well informed, even if a few days late," Sung's tone was suspicious, his attitude intimidating.

"I like to keep up-to-date, even when I can't actually be present," Mika was cocky and self-assured. "Don't much care for what you are insinuating." He stood not two feet from Sung facing him dead on as if daring him to try something.

"I don't much care what you like or don't," Sung made to step closer.

"You're pretty good at tricks and disruption, from what I remember," Suzette eyed him as she stepped between the canine cousins and attempting to lower the temperature between the two, "maybe you could help come up with some deceptions to cause confusion." She threw him the bone and he was quick to snag it.

"Do we know how they plan on arriving? And what they plan to do once here?" here was an activity he could sink his teeth into. "Was I told the bugs and ground dwellers were your first line of defense last time? I don't think you can count on that working again, they will have their own defenses in place against it."

"Remember, no one gets harmed more than absolutely necessary, and no deaths," reminded Tatanka as he joined the group. He was still off his feed after the incident with Equine. He was a man of honor who would no more harm another of The People than he would his own. The episode would weigh heavy on him for centuries. She might have forgiven him, but he never would. "Has anyone seen Lawrence?" Right now, he could use some bucking up from the Grand Elk.

Evan and Alexandra reanimated the two bodies sitting on the edge of forever. She remained motionless as she regarded what lay before her across the vast open valley before, finally, bringing her tear-filled eyes around to his.

"It is magnificent, isn't it?" she whispered. Though whether she referred to the valley or their trip around the universe was anybody's guess.

"All of the Mother's creations tend to be so," he agreed, thoughtfully until, "Let's try another experiment."

"Are we going flying around the universe again, that was wonderful, glorious," she giggled in anticipation.

"Not this time, this time we are going to keep ourselves firmly planted right here, waiting," he took a long inhale, holding his breath as he had the smoke in the backyard ceremony, before allowing it waft out.

"I want you to look out on the grandeur that lays before you. Don't think on it, don't comment even in your own head, just let it enter your senses. Your eyes, your nose, scent everything coming up from the valley, listen to each chirp, creak of branch, babble of creek, taste the life that fills this wonderland, feel the rock underneath, the breeze on your skin. Allow yourself to experience it, immerse yourself in it physically not intellectually.

"Deep breaths again, like before, in through the nose, out through the mouth. Now bring up a joyful memory, something that fills your heart, brings a tear of happiness to the eye. Some moment in your life that you cannot stop smiling when you remember," Again his voice was hypnotic, calm, the breath of life in her lungs.

"I know what you'll think of," she barely allowed the words to slip past her lips.

"So, do I. The question becomes whether I can hold the joy without the pain." He spoke quiet, as if in dream, she should know, "You see that is the difference between human and Spirit People, time. We have no sense of time, how can we, there are no markers. No births, no deaths, we do not change with the seasons we blend with them. There is no day or night, the sun and the dark are always present, it depends entirely on where you are standing. We have no need of clocks or calendars, we just are.

"As I was until," the valley before them shimmered ever so slight before Bear regained control of his emotions, "pain keeps track of time. When it happened, how long it will last. When it begins to dissipate, it keeps track of the hours, minutes, days seconds. I never knew that before; I know it now. When you are immortal the pain never dissipates, it is forever. I must find a way past the pain, suffering, to remember Her with bliss not aching."

"Can you?" she asked, concerned.

"I don't know, I haven't yet," was the honest reply, "but I really need to right now, so, yes, I think, with your help and Her love, I will be able to."

Alexandra knew respect and awe.

"You've had a lifetime, albeit a brief one thus far, to know how to deal with disappointment, pain, physical and emotional, to know soon or late everyone you know will cease to exist. You may not realize it, but you are born with that knowledge. It is ingrained in your souls. You know your time is short, you know all of this," he stretched out a great paw to take in all that was before them, "was here before you and will be here when you are gone. Death, old age, the passing, is part of life; you can witness it as it is happening. Watching parents, grandparents, friends, idols, growing older, some dying before their time, you accept it as part of the deal. Or you have until now, apparently, but you retain that knowledge and that is what I need.

"We do not." He said with some finality.

"That's sad," she spoke in an analytical tone, "Yes, it's hard to watch people grow old and die, but that's what makes them precious, time. Knowing you only have so much yet not knowing how much. You have to learn to treasure it all. You can't hate forever, I don't think it's possible, we're not that strong. You can't stay mad at somebody forever; we need each other too much. Immortality might be nice for a while," she grinned at her miniscule play on words, "but you need the pressure of time to make life special.

"You're immortal, there is no hurry for you to forgive grandma for dying. There is no pressure to move on from the pain, you have all the time in the world." From the mouths of innocent children truth shall flow like rivers.

How was it possible for her to understand so much in such a brief period? Yes, he thought, she was truly mature beyond her years.

It begged the question, the soul-searching reflection, had he clung to the pain, to the anger? He knew he felt cheated, cheated out of the small amount of time She was supposed to have. The time that had been cut horribly short. But that wasn't Her fault. She hadn't wanted to suffer, to die. NO! She wanted eternity with him as much as he wanted it with Her. He had never felt pain before, he had no idea how to overcome, to process this horror.

"Who am I mad at?" he asked hisself, the words foreign in his ears and bitter on his tongue.

"Maybe you're mad at you," she said.

"But why?"

"Because you let yourself be fooled by want and love. You allowed yourself to believe it could be. She could live forever with you because everything you have ever known has. You told yourself if you loved her enough, wanted her absolutely, you could make that happen," she sat there, legs swinging over the edge, crossed at the ankles, eyes closed as if she could see the world better that way.

Who was this child? Where had all this wisdom come from? It was as if she had existed throughout the ages, as if..."Mother!" he blurted the honorific as realization almost knocked him over the edge.

"How long have you been in possession of my granddaughter," now surprise and shock became indignation. How could she possibly think taking over the child was right?

"Not very," said the voice of the wind from the mouth of the babe. "It was necessary to get close to you without you knowing. She really is quite a special child on her own, which she shall be once again, soon." Alexandra's face grinned.

"Why?" it was a thousand questions boiled down to their simplest form.

"I had to know if you were stable, if you could overcome the pain, to think clearly. I had to see how damaged you were," her tone sympathetic, though would brook no argument. "We are attempting something that has never been done, has never had the necessity. I had to know if you were as broken as the balance. I believe, as you do, that you are intimately tied to this, it is your heart, your strength that is needed."

"And?"

"And you will have to trust yourself as well as my belief that your heart is true," that beatific smile reflecting all that was true. He was well and truly her champion.

"So, that was your shadow on the beach? That was you who allowed her to see all of us as we are?" Evan didn't know if he should be pissed or relieved that it had been the Mother not Alexandra, meaning she was still just a normal teen. He had to know.

"Actually, no," Alexandra's face scrunched in puzzlement, "it would appear we both discovered secrets along the route. She is a Spirit Child, though there has never been one before. I have no idea how this came about, but she is part of you, maybe mostly.

"We will have to figure this out after we correct the problem at hand,"

Alexandra stood on the edge of eternity before turning to him, "come we have much to do and only you can do it."

"Why?" the word plaintive, the meaning, this time, was singular.

"Why did I let her die?" Alexandra gazed back over the world, "I didn't, there are just some things that cannot be changed. The cycle was put in motion back before even you and I; we are as bound to it as any."

"There are times when I wish I wasn't immortal," and at that moment he meant it.

"You're not, no one, nothing is. You, me, the others, just seem to be compared to everything else here," she sighed, "but the sun will die, so will I, the universe will not cry. That's the beauty of the whole damn thing, we are all filled with our own importance until we find out we are just specks of sand waiting to be washed out to sea." Her laughter was joy. "Hey, you want your granddaughter back?"

"May I?"

"Yeah, she won't know any of this happened. To her she will have fallen asleep. I really have not been here that long, though with us what does that mean?" There was the shimmer as Alexandra wobbled for a split second before righting herself.

"Who's the lady? And where did she come from?" Asked the girl from dream state to the spirit of the Bear about the striking woman standing next to him. "Guess you put me to sleep talkin' that way you did."

"That's who we came to find," Evan hugged her close before setting the young bear on his back as the three of them turned to make their way through the forest.

She faced the vision standing next to her grandfather and held out her hand in greeting, "I'm Alexandra, nice to meet you."

The area surrounding the three homes erupted in humanity. Every testosterone laden under twenty-five-year-old within a fifty-mile radius had shown up, whoopin', hollerin' ready to kick some hippie pervy ass. It was as if every guy who'd peaked in high school now wanted an ounce of flesh for not getting his just reward of fame, fortune, and young babes.

One moment peace lay across the farmland in all directions and the next the thundering horde descended like a plague across the land. Once again, The People and their allies had prepared. The burrowers had been diligent and efficient. Tunnels, some cavernous enough to swallow a four-wheeling pickup, some just deep enough to trip up the leading edge of forces, disguised with a thin layer of sticks, leaves and dirt, collapsing with the first footfall. Those following close behind would follow suit, tripping and falling on the fallen until they had built a wall of tumbled humanity. Any strays would be subdued with the beanbag netting, tazed or dazed and confused by flashbangs.

They had come as John had predicted, when the sun was low in the sky, just above the distant mountain peaks, in the hopes of blinding the occupants of the homes. Iktomi had sent her spies to confirm John's suspicions.

Now chaos ruled the plain as twisted ankles, snapped tendons and shattered shins threw every aspect of the planned attack into disarray. The sound of shrieks, howls of frustration, and moans filled the air. The battle had hardly begun before in came to a disheartened conclusion. It is impossible to win against those who know more about what you are attempting than you. Spies make the difference.

"That's it?" Jervis sounded disappointed that he would not be given the opportunity to collect on a few debts from the far past. "We don't get to bust a few heads?"

"The idea," explained the maturing Glen, "is to stop this before it can escalate. Small injuries easily healed leave less animosity after the battle. Hate to tell you but now we have to help them, bind wounds and set bones. They're gonna be back to normal and won't remember how they got hurt, we gotta help them."

John grinned, proud of the student. Glen was growing into a fine man, now that had been given the permission to become one.

Jervis wandered off into the field across the street checking for stragglers. Maybe he could still get a poke or a kick in before it all ended.

Sheriff John stood on the front porch of the craftsman, mostly so he could hold the railing, while he watched the debacle. He loved his town and her people, but they were not trained soldiers and many of these boys were not from town. And whoever was leading, controlling, this cluster wasn't trained in warfare either. They should have known, especially since they were of The People, how easily their forces could be spied on and prepared for. This had been a rout of epic proportion; it was almost as if they didn't care how many people were hurt or killed. They had thrown them against superior forces and been destroyed. Well, harmed, they would heal, but out of action for the time being.

It was then he heard the sound of thunder coming from the plains. Interesting as there wasn't a cloud in the evening sky. A beautiful sunset, pale yellows turning to gold, pink and rose transforming to mauve, the white underbellies of the clouds darkening with, oh dear God.

"Everyone in the houses or get up in the trees!" he yelled at the top of his voice.

Suzette, Doe, Sung, Glen, Cynthia and Tatanka picked up the refrain. Tatanka frantically searching for his friend in the midst of chaos, where the hell was Lawrence? Even someone as large as he would be crushed by the onslaught, they all could not miss the thundering herds, careening their way.

"Where in the hell is Lawrence?" rumbled the call from the great Buffalo.

"Get up here and out of the damn way," Finn had him by the arm pulling, yanking, pleading with the great one to save himself, though Frog to Buffalo was not an even match

Tatanka tilted his head back and with a mighty breath letting loose a series of loud grunts as he walked over to where all stood hugging and hanging on to each other on the porch. He called again this time louder and more insistent. Sung leaned his head back and howled, long and plaintive, and again, and again. Suddenly the air was filled with the sound of calls from a thousand beasts.

As all made the porch Glen looked out across the field to see Jervis frozen in horror at the impending living wall of death. He couldn't move, but Glen could. He flew off the top porch step and ran, ran as he had never believed possible to his one friend. It would be a race to see who got to the large young man first, Glen would not be beaten. Without slowing he reached one arm around Jervis' waist and threw him, firefighter style over his shoulder before skidding and turning back towards the house.

"Shit!" Screamed the wounded sheriff, as he eyed the rapidly approaching cloud of dust and the mass of humanity laying immobilized in the path. He might be injured but not wounded enough to stop him from leaping from the porch, hobbling and lurching across the lawn and diving headfirst into a pickup truck parked in front of the home. As quickly as a torn-up man can move he turned the key and started the motor, slamming the gear shift in drive and pulling it over in front of where the formerly attacking line lay weeping, shrieking, and moaning on the ground. They had no idea what was coming from the plains, laying where they had fallen, waiting for someone to come to their aid. He had.

Sung seeing what the sheriff had in mind pulled on Suzette who snapped into action as both jumped into trucks of their own and pulled them nose to tail with the sheriff's. Glen threw Jervis into the cab of the next and hightailed to join the blocking line. Meg not one to be left out of the action jumped in her own four by four adding another twenty feet of protection. She may not have gotten to knock heads but she sure as hell was going to play a part.

Within minutes a line of vehicles was barricading the wounded from becoming the dead. There was no sense attempting to get out and make it back to the relative safety of the houses, they would have to stick it out in the vehicles and hope.

"What the hell, man?" Jervis had finally woken up from his terror induced stupor

"I don't know, I knew I just couldn't let you get stomped into the ground," Glen's breathing was hard and fast. He remembered hearing about mothers lifting cars to save their children and firefighters jumping from buildings, he had to assume he found the strength in adrenaline.

It was impossible, but John swore he could hear another rumble of thunder coming from the other direction, only louder than the first which had become deafening as it closed in on the doomed.

Tens of thousands of hooves pounded hard on the packed earth, autumn barren and devoid of crops, which might've slowed them down from the east. And thousands pounded their way from the west.

"What the?" He stuck his head up above the dash where he could see Suzette bouncing up and down in the cab of the truck in front. "What the hell do you see?" the sheriff yelled with everything he could muster. All he could think was there was a giant pincher coming together and they was the nut about to be crushed.

Sung was shouting something back but there was no way the sheriff or anyone could hear what he was saying. Though the look on his face told all they would need to know. The cavalry had apparently arrived.

John tempted fate by sticking his head up higher to try to get a glimpse of whatever it was that had Sung so excited.

The sight of hundreds of buffalo charging from the west, followed by thousands of horses, and hundreds more wolves was awe inspiring. Hundreds of thousands of pounds of animals coming to meet the wall of elk, mountain lion, cougar, beaver and who knew what else descending on them from the east. If they met where it appeared they would everything within blocks would be crushed under the weight and force of nature; people, trucks, animals, houses, trees, all.

The bison arrived first taking up position across the lane from the houses, fifty or more across and three deep, backed now by wolf and horse. Who would be dumb enough to try and break through a wall of meat, thirty feet thick, eight foot high, with horns.

As it turned out, no one would. The huge herd of elk, cougar and beaver turned at the last meter before crunching headlong into the assembled. Like a river rushing around a massive boulder, the animals wove, danced, and split before they could be broken on the solid wall, missing the great oak tree, and the blockage of vehicles.

The stampede dissipated as it lost steam on the other side of the, now, circumvented battle. Without the cohesion of the rampage, purpose slipped off, they meandered. What had been controlled now was confusion.

"Elk!" shouted Tatanka, his voice rising above the fray, "Elk!" He jumped from the porch, running with reckless abandon towards the large man standing alone in the trampled field, disoriented, as if waking from a nightmare.

Tatanka tackled him where he stood. This creature had been his friend since the dawn of time. They had roamed the plains and mountain valleys together. And he had turned on Tatanka, had come to kill him and his children. Elk put up no fight as the great Buffalo began to pummel him about the head and chest. Elk made no move to defend himself. It took several of the People to get Tatanka off the bleeding and battered man, but they did.

Tatanka rolling over on his back huffing and puffing, weeping, and crying out for the Great Spirit. They appeared two old men laying in the dust of time, wondering how they came to be here. Realization came to both simultaneously, they had both been played by the same enemy.

Tatanka rolled over, laying on the ground he reached out to his friend, their hands touched, they grasped each other close. Elk in shame and humiliation over what he had almost done, Tatanka in the knowing having lost himself so recently with Equine. Forgiveness begins in the heart when we forgive our own failings.

Buzzard flew high above observing the happenings on the ground, laughing to herself. Dumb bunnies, that's what they was, she thought to herself as she took in the crazy dishevelment. Humans strewn like cords of wood knocked over, The People rushing to and fro' like chickens at feed time. Big ol' Tatanka blamin' Elk for it all, it was comical. She called loud, screeching as the sky soon filled with feathers turning the daylight to night. Avian bodies filled the sky so completely it appeared as if one huge-feathered blanket was about to descend and smother all. Buzzards, crow, ravens, every bird of black blotted out the heavens.

Not one of them thinkin' to look up. Including her.

Owl came like a bullet out of the black of the sky and whacked Buzzard right behind her head. He wasn't worried about hurting her she was too ugly, she spiraled out of control heading straight for the ground. Ten foot above Owl caught her with his talons putting on the air brakes and gently landing between the two old spirits and the growing entourage of onlookers. He squeezed ever so gently as Sung had taught until the revolting creature lost consciousness, releasing all she ruled. The sky cleared.

This had to stop, someone was going to die, maybe a lot of someones.

Out behind the bushes, safe from the sight of all the two sighed. The best laid plans had fallen short. And if Bear repaired that which had been broken, they would probably never get another golden opportunity to control. That had been their one hope, one was smart, one could control, the imbalance provided opportunity. It was going to be a long eternity. They could but hope no one would be the wiser, let the others blame Buzzard, Cougar and Elk, these two would slink under the radar.

"Bear, this is going to take everything you have; I am not going to lie to you," said the Mother as she stared into the emptiness of space. "I hope we are not wrong about you, your heart or your love. You cannot falter," she spoke it like prayer.

They stood at the very peak of the mountaintop; darkness had overtaken the entirety of creation. Alexandra fought with every ounce of energy to stay awake, but time and adventure had taken its toll, she was too exhausted. She lay on the ground, listening to the soft murmur between her grandpa, The Bear, and The Mother of Earth. She could smell the freshness of spring, the blooms of summer, the dank, dark decay of autumn and the crisp of winter every time the woman walked near to her. It was as if every scent of the planet wafted around her or emanated from her. She was the most stunning person Alex had ever seen. As if every race of man lived in her and only the finest qualities showed through. She wasn't white or black or brown, red, or yellow, she just was. Every plant, every animal, every insect, and bird could be seen in her ever-kaleidoscopic appearance. You could only look at her for a few moments before the dizzy would begin. No wonder Alex was so tired, concentration was hard work.

She'd tried to watch the woman setting up their little camp, lighting the bowl of the pipe from the flame snapped to life by her fingers, letting the smoke flow of her. Alexandra could see her future and her past in the woman as if she were a screen in the movie house. But none of it was solid, her life changed and flowed like streams, rivers, and ocean waves, and it was alright. Alexandra had no need to know.

"You know, it wasn't supposed to happen," she said to the night, "you falling for Her."

He grinned as he distinctly heard the capital. "I didn't intend for it happen neither, just did,"

"The Great spirit and I talked about making it end," it was a time for truth, a time for confession.

"Why didn't you?" He was truly curious, maybe it would've hurt him some but not enough to completely bollox the damn universe.

"He thought it was nice," she laughed, " I know you don't realize it, but the Great Spirit has a lovely sense of compassion, of love. He said that none of you had ever known true love, He wondered how it might change you, affect you if you knew it with a human. He is a hopeless romantic, and a bit of a scientific maven, always wanting to see what will happen if he allows this or adds that. I guess that's evident in all he does," She shrugged. "You should know I argued against it," she looked at him with half lidded eyes.

"You probably were right," he coughed a cry.

"Anyway, by the time He realized it was a mistake it was too late, we had to let it play out," she offered no apology, facts were what they were. The past was.

"Did you give Her the cancer," he had to know.

"No, we would never do that," he thought she might protest further, or maybe weep at the inequity of it all, she sighed, it was hard to tell of sorrow or resignation, "no, that happened on its own. There are some things that are part and parcel of life. Humans get sick, they wear out, they catch a bug, they die. So do your children, that's why we made you, to soften the blow, lessen the pain," a hint of anger found its way into her words but only for a moment.

"Yeah, I get it, but I don't think you should let others experience what I did, it could kill or harm an awful lot of children," he stared at hisself in the dark sky, then gazed over at the little bear not far from it.

"You know, you might have to give up more, something dear to you," she glanced at Alexandra gallantly fighting sleep.

"I will not harm that child, not even to save the world. If that is what it would take, then this world should be allowed to die," Bear was quietly adamant.

"Do you know how many children die every day on this world?" she asked still not looking at him.

"They die not for purpose; they die because people don't care enough to save them. They die because of human greed, selfishness, they die to satisfy the need for power. They die for hate, they die for no purpose," he sighed, "I cannot save them, not even by sacrificing this child. I will not, not for any purpose harm one hair on her head. If that's the only way, then let the world save itself."

"What if you don't have to harm the child, per se, not physically. What if it means you have to give her up, never see her again? What if it means you would be wiped from her memory?" now The Mother stared hard into his eyes, "would you?"

Evan could feel the tears roll down his snout, could feel his heart breaking as it had broken before, could feel the last breath leave his body. She was all he had left. She was all.

"What if it came down to that?"

"I don't know," he answered honestly, "I don't know."

Somewhere right at the timberline the cork came out of the whiskey bottle and a copious amount was poured between two glasses. The two deputies were bored, lonely, and just wanted this whole thing to be over. They sat on each side of the fire, not talking, but thinking, drinking, and brooding. They tipped glasses to each other and drank deep.

"What do you think is happening down at Fort?" Sam asked the fire.

"Should be about over," replied Ray spitting into the dark.

"Maybe we should head down in the morning, have a looksee," Sam took a large mouthful of whiskey before swallowing it and lighting another smoke. He knew pot was kind of illegal, but he liked it.

Ray took the proffered joint and sucked the smoke down into his lungs, he enjoyed a hit from time to time as well. "Guess we'll finish off this bottle get some shuteye and check it out, I've 'bout had 'nuff of back to nature." He threw the still burning roach into the woods, "that ones for the spirits of the forests," he spat out a bark of laughter. "Time for bed."

The small ember burnt through the paper and into the pile of dried leaves. The dried leaves set the small dried out pile of decaying tree limbs afire, within seconds the trees surrounding their campsite were ablaze. The two passed out deputies in the cloth tent never felt the fire as the smoke smothered them as they slept.

"Can you sense the imbalance from where you sit?" asked The Mother, "Can you feel your paw print upon it?"

"Yes," said Bear from far, far away though he sat not three feet from where she did. "And I think I can heal it." There was hope and relief.

"What do you need?"

"Quiet and to concentrate."

She sat down next to the sleeping child and stroked Alexandra's hair, watching him intently.

Evan could sense the crack but couldn't see it, not in his mind nor in his spirit. And that was the reason for the concept of the crack, it made it possible to visualize. If you thought of imbalance, or disturbance, or some kind of variance, it just didn't jibe with 'seeing' it in the mind. A crack he could fix.

He had to think of the universe as a giant pot or vase with a hairline fracture, a fracture so minimal he would require a magnifying glass to find it. Yet it would be enough to throw the waves of energy off balance. It was an interesting dilemma. Which was why he had to think of it the way he had conjured. Find the crack, meld it with willpower and duct tape and pray for the best. Simple. He was a potter, he would use his hands, his mind, to smooth the 'crack', his love to seal it, but it would be his need that found it.

If only he could puzzle out where it might...You stupid, stupid bear, he almost shouted to the world so there would be no doubt. Now, where in the universe would a crack created by the Bear spirit exist? Almost of their own volition his eyes looked to the North-Northwestern sky about forty-five degrees from the horizon. Ursa Major, The Bear.

How many times had he gazed up at the night sky since Her passing, to reassure, to find comfort in the familiar, the known, hisself? Yet had been blind to the obvious, but he was blind no more. There it was between the two stars designating where his heart was, of course. He could sense the wrong, like rubbing his fingers over a mirror and finding the imperfection. The flaw, his love for Her, and its destruction.

Bullshit! Cried Her memory in the back of his mind. 'Our love was perfect; it was NOT a flaw! Maybe it was not supposed to happen, but it did, and it fit, like a finely honed diamond fits into the cradle created just for it, and it alone. Never think our love was wrong, look at what was created. She cried.

And almost destroyed, he replied fighting the sorrow in his heart.

Almost, says She, but look at the child asleep next to you, she would not have been possible without 'Us'.

Point, to Her. I have been so lonely. If I had never known love before, I certainly never could have conceived of loneliness. It is horrible.

"Bear," her voice remembered, soft on his skin, and Her love pulsed, the heartbeat of life, of the universe, of him, "you are the strongest being ever. You hold the universe together with your kindness, your honor, your character, humility and love, you will survive this and be even stronger for the love we knew."

There was disruption in the vision, he cried out, don't go, don't let this end! She held out a hand and desperation made him whip out a paw and grab hold, just as the scent of smoke reached his nostrils.

Mother smelled the smoke at the same instant. Alexandra slept sound at her grandfather's knee, she would be safe with him. Gaia ran through the forests, she had to find where, which direction, and how many of her children were in dangers path.

The fire raged out of control, the forests parched and dry, the trees exploding and showering sparks and creating new fires wherever they landed. The wind kicking up as the inferno created its own weather system. Fire tornadoes would soon be born. She had to get her children racing in the right directions or tens of thousands would die.

Flying from den to hole to burrow, from cave to treetops, crying the alarm, barking orders, pushing, and prodding as many of her children as she could force into motion. They ran, jumped, carried their young, drove their elderly, the large animals grabbing the smaller to escape. It was madness and chaos, but she finally got all, or as many as she could rouse, fleeing in the right direction.

Bear had to pull hisself out of this rapture, pull hisself from his stupor, there was fire, and he was high in the mountains, with Alexandra. But that meant letting go, letting go of the dream, letting go of Her hand, letting go of Her forever. He screamed his impotence, his helplessness, but he had to save the girl. Alexandra was all he had left of Her in this world, he loved this granddaughter. The child with so many hidden pieces parts and secrets. He could not let her perish in a damn fire.

He let go. For the second time in his life, he knew the searing pain of heartbreak. He didn't have time to weep, the intense inferno surrounding he and Alexandra. How in the hell was he going to escape with her?

"Come on, honey, time to get up. We need to get moving, and now!" he gently shook Alexandra's shoulder to no response. He shook her harder, but she wasn't coming around. "Alexandra!" he roared, nothing.

He soon realized she wasn't sleeping, she was unconscious. He checked her as quickly and thoroughly as he could but found no injuries. Maybe all of the last few days and weeks had been too much, it had finally taken its toll.

He could feel the intense heat on his fur, patches beginning to smolder. Hell had arisen around them, and he could see no exit. They would both burn to death if he didn't come up with a solution immediately. A tree exploded to his right, tinder dry pines were enveloped in scorching flames within seconds, falling as if a giant ax cleaved through their bases, spreading more sparks and flashes bursting into new infernos. There was no way out, he knew a fire like this was so intense it would be burning on both sides of the boundary.

He had no choice, he had to save Alexandra, at all costs. Theoretically on this side of the barrier his spirit status should provide a certain amount of protection. He would have to lay on top of her, like a shell, a barrier to protect her from the searing heat, flames, and smoke. Maybe, just maybe, The Mother would come back before both were consumed. It was all he had.

He dug his claws into the soil excavating a sizable depression, big enough to provide some safety for Alexandra. He would lay on top and absorb what he could, he was done with this life. Too long, too much, too lonely, enough. He lay down to die.

"Evan, Evan," the call soft yet strong. "Evan please give me the girl."

It was Her voice. He was going insane before he died. Well, why not?

"Evan look up, Please Dear spirits, lift your head and look up here," She plead, weeping, begging.

The dead couldn't weep, could they? He raised his head, blinked open his eyes clearing his vision. There, just above the roaring flames, she stood, arms outstretched as a mother demanding the return of her child. She waited, patient, he had to find the strength, to rise from the grave, to raise the physical body of this child and hope the specter of his dead wife could take her to safety. The absurdity of the idea gave him the heart to try.

His legs buckled as he tried to rise, the heat had done its work, sapped his strength, dehydrated him, his muscles cramped. With his massive arms he pushed himself up, ignoring the pain, the cramping sinews, rising to his knees, could he stand? One way to find out, he pulled Alexandra to his chest and with every last gasp of energy, one final thrust, he stood. It would take the end of his strength to hold the child out, to extend his arm for Her to take Alex from his paw. He knew this would be his last. He brought her back towards his face, kissing her gently.

"I love you more than life," and lifted her to the specter, if this was the bargain then let it be sealed, one life for another. This would end his pain; he would suffer no more.

She took the unconscious teen into her arms just as Bear fell back to his knees, her hand holding onto his paw for a few moments, but it was enough. For just a breath, a moment, the pain was gone, the searing agony left his body and instead he felt her love. He smiled; the girl would live.

The trees collapsed, one after another, falling on top of him and burying him under tons of burning timber. Purifying fire, like the intense heat of a cosmic kiln, melting his soul, reforming, acting as adhesive, liquifying and reforming the energy at the crack, smoothing, healing, restoring. Peace settled across the land. One life in exchange for many, the sacrifice complete.

The wave of healing energy washed over the battleground. A cry rose from the throat of every spirit, each singing of the sacrifice of Bear. Each calling to their children to remember, to tell the story, to remember in their bones and their souls, to sing to their children and dance the bear dance. The wail, roar, chirps, croaks, and bellow lasted well into the night until all fell, exhausted.

John understood what they had said about the connection of all, Mitakuye Oyasin. He felt it to his marrow, he wept in the arms of Suzette, Sung, Glen, Doe and, surprisingly, Coyote. Jervis sat mute on the lawn, lost without knowing why. Tatanka and Lawrence were helped to the house by Finn and Willow. Bottles were opened, pipes were lit, weeping, howling and laughter filled the night. The towns people were attended by the uninjured and the small medical staff of the town. Generations would remember the great earthquake that had struck without warning. The only time in history such an event occurred, and all prayed it would be the last.

Alexandra didn't regain consciousness until she found herself in a hospital bed and learned what her grandfather had done. Wolf and Otter had crossed over to find her and bring her back at the insistence of The Mother. They found her unconscious on the rocky outcropping she had shared with her grandfather. Except for slight amnesia she was unharmed.

Those who told the tale could not fathom how Evan had gotten her away from the flames. How he had performed the impossible and saved her life. They only knew he had given his life for hers and hoped she would understand the love that took. She should always carry that love with her, carry her grandpa in her heart. She wept for a week without cease before deciding it was up to her to carry on for him.

She would be the spirit of the Bear.

Meet The New Bear, Same as The Old Bear

∞

Alexandra made the decision she would leave the dysfunction that was life with her mother, she would move into her grandfather's house with her 'aunt' Suzette. She sued for emancipation and easily was granted such, as her mother hadn't bothered to even make an appearance.

She would make her new life at his house that was now was her house, her heart lived there. She would attend and graduate from the same school, it was part of the court judgement. Her 'aunt' would supervise and raise her. The courts didn't care, she was now out of their jurisdiction.

As she walked up the front path leading to grandpa's house—which is how she would always think of the perfect craftsman that had held so much love over the years—the silence crackled like heat lightening. As if every creature within miles held its breath in reverence.

Those who had known her grandfather, those who were closest to him or had become so, stood on the porch, or sat along the railing. Suzette stood at the top of the four stairs leading from walkway to porch. Next to her was Doe and Sung, Glen sat on the swing with a young man Alexandra didn't recognize. Tatanka, Elk, Finn and Cynthia lined the railing. And off to the corner of the porch, standing alone on the grass by the corner of the of the porch, was Equine. Becky her grandfather had called the woman.

Alexandra walked directly to the woman and wrapped her tightly in both arms, laying her head upon the tall woman's chest as a child to a mother. They stood rocking in embrace for several moments before Alexandra let go taking a step backward so she could see the totality of the woman standing before her.

"Thank you," she said simply though so much more was implied. They shared a tear, another embrace, and the knowledge they were the last two to see her grandfather alive. Alexandra walked back to the stairs to take in the assembled.

"There are not words to thank all of you for what you have done," she began before melting into a weeping, sobbing mess.

All the Spirit guides looked to each other, not knowing what to do. They were not used to such emotion especially from one who, apparently, was one of their own. She would have to learn how to be one of them from them, and they could learn how to be more like her from her. It was good.

From behind her she was once again wrapped in the loving embrace of one of The People. Shock was too mild of a word as she turned and gazed into the eyes of Coyote. He wept with abandoned, wracked with remorse and sentiment neither would have thought possible or possessed.

"Your grandfather was the only one who ever believed me. In all of time he stood out as a bearer of truth, honesty, and kindness. By The Great Spirit, I will miss tweaking his tail and nose and the feel of his forgiveness," it was all he had before dissolving into emotional wreckage.

Though the collected spirits of the Earth attempted to project a staid exterior, they failed miserably. Bear had been well-loved by all.

"You must excuse our inability to respond in a steady, composed, modest manner," apologized Finn, ever the analytical, "but your grandfather became quite a symbol to many, admired by all, and by all accounts the first of our kind to meet his demise. Certainly, in such a magnificent manner. At least in recent memory. Our kind do not 'die', as you will discover, and certainly had never in the service of another. Your grandfather's sacrifice with be sung about, remembered in story as long as there are People, humans, and our children. He will live." Silent consent from the congregation. "You carry a heavy burden of responsibility but know we will all always be by your side and will aid you in all ways."

Suzette descended the stairs and stood before Alexandra, the two women taking each other's hands while losing themselves in the depths of friendship born of shared grief.

"Thank you," said the diminutive Otter to the young Bear, "I will always be here for you. You honor me by your choice to be your mentor, second mother, and friend." They embraced. Time has no meaning when you are Immortal.

Some of The People stayed for several weeks, some for several moments, all would be connected through the rest of time. Tighter than they had ever been, now realizing how they needed each other, were interconnected, the weaving of the Great Spirit evident in all of them and their children. Mitakuye Oyasin, indeed!

Time, whether noticed by immortals or not, continues and it had now been ten years since the passing. Alexandra still wept from time to time, but time had lost most of its meaning. She discovered that talking to him each night helped ease the pain. Though the world believed him dead, killed while saving her, she knew in her heart he could not die, he was too powerful a spirit. He had to be somewhere; it was his nature to dance among the stars. And he was! She could see him every clear night, forty-five degrees up from the horizon in the north-northwest sky.

The People still came 'round when they were in the general vicinity, to talk, share a cup, teach her ways to help her people, catch up on stories and songs, then they'd move on. Glen had stayed. He and his friend Jervis were inseparable until Jervis hitched up with a girl from town.

Alexandra had taken what little money her grandfather had saved—apparently in an effort to have something to pass on to her cousins and her, but they had enough and didn't care about him—and bought the other two houses—no one else wanted them and the bank was happy to divest itself of the one and the family of the other—and some acreage behind to allow it to revert to plains. It would give The People somewhere to camp when they came.

She completed high school and took college by mail and online completing her master's in Environmental Science with minors in Philosophy and Biology. She should know how to help the People in this new world of technology and data. She was a new Bear.

Glen lived in the old people's house contentedly learning what he could to help his own children. He would disappear for weeks on end and then show up with a passel of canine's yipping and yapping to distraction.

"Where'd they come from?" she'd ask.

Always the same answer, "From God, it's our job to watch over them and care for them," he'd smile. They'd keep a few and he'd adopt out the rest to folks he knew needed companionship and love. One thing about his children, they knew love. Jervis had a half dozen himself. He and his new wife—the girl who had ratted out Glen and Sung years ago—were expecting their first child.

Alexandra became known as the crazy lady with the dogs. The folks around here might mock her a bit, but it was with love, for they knew if anybody ever needed anything, Little Bear, named in honor of her grandpa, would be there. She'd deliver a meal, a house payment, money to pay the gas and electric, an ear, shoulder, and an open heart. The money coming from donations. People who had heard the story of her grandfather, and wanted Alex to continue good work, sent cards and letters with fives, tens, and twenties. Alex wanted for nothing; immortals didn't need much. Turned out it took less to live forever than it did for just a few decades.

"That girl is a giver," they all agreed, "got it from her gramps!"

A movement grew up around her, she hadn't meant for it to start it just kind of organically cultivated. They were known as the Ursa Society, a loose benevolent group dedicated to helping others. Not a fraternal group, it was an inclusive organization, all were welcome, all were equal, all participated. They had places they met called Bear Lodges, named in honor of Evan. It was easy once the nickname She had given him came out.

They raised funds for medical needs, had food drives, took in and doctored injured animals and people. They were the epitome of the do-gooders, the true good Samaritans. They asked for nothing but gave it their all. Alexandra could not deny them the use of her grandfather.

A few years back, the mountain side began to heal, new sprouts and more flowers every year, saplings growing taller, stronger, and more plentiful, stretching towards the sun and pure mountain air. Young pines and juvenile spruce finding the burnt soil fertile, the cones taking root. The Ursa Society decided to have a yearly pilgrimage, as it were, to the place of passing. It was as peaceful as any place on Earth, almost sacred, if you believed in that sort of thing, and the perfect place to meet, commune, share stories and ideas, and frolic in nature. Alexandra had attended every year out of respect for their passion and to remember her grandfather.

Suzette came each year, always accompanied by Sheriff John, Doe had come the last two, Glen, of course loved to run and play in the new forest, Jervis, as always by his side, now accompanied by his wife and newborn son. Lawrence showed up this year explaining he had tried to get Tatanka to come but he was a plains guy, not a mountain spirit. They had laughed. Sung and Coyote rode in together with Equine! Now, wasn't that a tribute to Evan! It would be a banner year, she would get to visit with The People who mattered most. Well, a goodly portion of them.

Small fires popped up as the twilight covered the mountain on the third night of the gathering. Small, well-banked, well-tended, with rock perimeters, all cognizant of fire and this sacred spot. Someone started singing along with an acoustic guitar, it was song she didn't recognize but it fit the evening. A single voice carrying love on a breeze with lyrics so sweet she wanted to cry. Her grandfather had always loved a well told story song. He and Gran had a song that was their own. It was a love song, though she couldn't remember the name or how it went, but he said it meant more to him than any song ever writ. It epitomized their love. She loved her grandfather, she loved the mountains, and she loved this mountain above all else.

The sing-a-longs slowly died out in the night as silence wrapped the hundreds in comfort. A slight breeze brought the scent of new growth, pine, and wildflowers, fresh turned earth, life. Far away in the darkness, riding that same breeze came the plaintive baritone.

There was a time, a long time ago Solitary man wore these trav-elin' clothes

Wandered this earth lost and alone Searching for something he'd never known

All in the camp stopped breathing. It wasn't exactly on key, the voice breathy yet full, love acting as Auto-tune to the heart, if not the ear.

A man of spirit a man of soul She smiles, and life explodes

A brilliant future true love unfolds Flying higher than both had ever known

All turned this way and that, eyes searching, ears attempting direction.

"Who is that singing?" asked Doe, wonder and joy filling the question. She like every other within hearing wanted to follow that voice to its source yet fearing to move. Afraid any movement, any other sound, might break the mood. The singer might cease, and that would be a travesty.

For those who had never known love, true love, the total gift of soul, mind, body, and heart, they knew it now.

With one touch she made him whole Time to take off them trav-elin' clothes

The smile started in the pit of Alexandra's stomach. She could feel it grow, filling her chest, her heart dancing in rhythm to the song. She knew. She also knew she had to wait, to be patient. You couldn't hurry this gift of love, you couldn't run to it, it would come to you if you were patient enough, if you wanted it bad enough.

The first shriek of joy, surprise with a slight hint of fear came from up the mountain. The second stronger, happier, more joyful, with no fear only wonder. The chorus that arose was a song of disparate marvel, astonishment, elation, rapture, and bliss.

"Oh, my," came the startled exclamation from Becky as she pointed up the mount and all tuned to see.

The great bear strolled as easy as a mountain stream through the assembled throng of humanity. She was ten-foot long, eight-foot high and moved like the night, yet no one ran frightened or terrified as she wove her way through them.

Though death may take her his heart knows His spirit flies wherever she may go

Love eternal now awoke Can never be put back inside one soul

She is his woman and his home She smiled, and possibilities explodes

A brilliant future true love unfolds Flying higher than both had known

The song followed her like an entourage of admirers, devotees surrounding her with worship. She took no notice.

Everyone was so focused on her—how could you not be, her very presence demanded your rapt attention—they failed to take note of the even larger bear following in her footsteps. Well, those in her wake took note with gasps of awe, exclamations of delight, childish titters of delighted wonder. He was magnificent as he ambled on his hind legs behind her, singing, forepaws directing his performance, his feet attempting dance—the Bear Dance—his attitude focused on her, not his performance. He smiled.

I don't know if you've ever seen a fifteen-hundred-pound bear smile, not smirk nor leer hungrily, but truly smile, but is not something you will soon forget.

There was a time, a long time ago Solitary man wore these travelin' clothes

Wandered this earth lost and alone Searching for something he'd never known

A man of spirit a man of soul She smiles, and life explodes

A brilliant future true love unfolds Flying higher than both had ever known

And the sun shines, honey gold Tired of wearing out both his souls

With one touch she made him whole Time to take off them travelin' clothes

He finished the tune as he stepped into the silence surrounding Alexandra. Without another sound he stepped closer and lay down in front her placing his massive head in her lap.

Her tears fell like summer rain, warm and nurturing, on his head and snout. She engulfed as much of his head and shoulders as she could grasp in her arms and hugged him close and tight with every ounce of love she could muster.

Following his lead, the female tentatively made her way to Alexandra and sat where she could reach out with a freed arm and pull the bear in for a three-way hug. Alexandra was lost in the mountain of bear. She had never been happier, more fulfilled in her life.

"Well, I'll be," exclaimed Suzette hugging Doe and John close to her, who grabbed Becky, who latched onto Sung, Glen, and Jervis. They stood in a muted circle of slobbering, weeping, idiotic and ebullient People of the very First Nations of the earth and the law.

Off to the side stood Coyote, tears rolled down his cheeks as he stood alone and mute. The Great Bear pulled hisself away from his granddaughter and motioned for the wily one to join them. As Coyote sulked his way over bear reached into some hidden pouch beneath his arm and pulled out a long, thin, white stick, "here," he said handing it to Mika, "light this, let's celebrate."

"But Grandpa, how?" Alexandra managed through her tears and amazement.

"The simple answer is, I'm immortal," he shrugged and grinned. It was too easy, she needed more he could read it on her face, "you see, I am a creature of pure spirit." Her scrunched up face made him want to weep. She had been through so much emotional pain, he wanted to take it all away. He couldn't, what he could do was tell her the truth.

"I am not a physical being," he began, "oh, right here I am. When I was with your grandmother I was. When I walk in the world of man—who do not believe, truly believe in such as we," here his great arm and paw took in all The People assembled, "I am physical to them. But to those who were not born but created by the Mother and The Great Spirit which lives in all of us, we are of spirit, energy, we cannot die." The Bear scratched his head in a comical, very human way, "this is almost impossible to explain as I am telling you of something that sounds of magic and mysterioso, wizards, warlocks and witches, yet it is none of that. It is as natural as the sun and the moon, the plants, the air, life, simply different.

"Let me see if this helps, do you remember when I told you I could be hurt, but I had no desire because it could last, literally forever," she nodded in unison with Glen, whom had discussed this very thing the first time he met Evan. "That's kind of what happened here. I was beaten, hurt, damaged, and had no strength left, well, I had enough to hand you off to your grandmother—and that is another story that will take years for you, me, and her to understand—and then collapsed. I was 'killed'. That body died, but I, my soul, the essence of who I am, the creation of the Mother, continued. Though I had to wait for a new body to be reincarnated," he willed understanding, comprehension into her. "Do you understand?"

"Kind of," she admitted, "I will, it is going to take some time."

"The nicest thing about being immortal," he chortled, "is," and here she joined the chorus, "time doesn't matter."

The celebration lasted well into the morning of the sixth day of the year of the Bear. Those who had witnessed carried the story, though few deemed it more than drug induced hallucination. It mattered not, belief is not born of data, science, proof, it, like immortality, just is.

Author's Bio

∞

Mr. Zonneville has spent the last forty-five years as a professional comedian, singer, songwriter and has written five books previous, three novels, American Stories, Carey Come To Me Smiling, and Great Things, A Novel, a biography of his father, Z, and a children's book about one of their rescue dogs, Greta. Harper's is in the works. He has performed throughout the United States, Canada, Ireland, and Holland. He loves his two adult daughters, to travel, write, read, and be married to his most beloved.

www.ingramcontent.com/pod-product-compliance
Lightning Source LLC
Chambersburg PA
CBHW060602310726
48982CB00008B/1210/J

* 9 7 8 1 7 3 4 4 3 3 2 1 0 *